The Stelladaur Series

Book 3

Fraction in Time

The Stelladaur Series

Coming Soon

Stelladaur

Book 3

Fraction in Time

S. L. Whyte

FIREGLASS
PUBLISHING

The Stelladaur Series, Book 3
Fraction in Time by S. L. Whyte
Copyright © 2018 by S. L. Whyte

ISBN: 978-0-9857523-6-1 (paperback)
ISBN: 978-0-9857523-7-8 (hardcover)
ISBN: 978-0-9857523-8-5 (ebook)
Library of Congress Control Number: 2017918458

www.stelladaur.com

Book interior and cover text design by Jill Ronsley, suneditwrite.com
Cover art design by Alicia Lockwood, ALimages
Author photo by Garrett Wesley Gibbons, Aderyn Productions

Summary: When Reilly finally kisses Norah, he experiences bizarre flashbacks of people and places he doesn't remember. Then, after unexpectedly traveling through another portal, he becomes trapped in the Rotunda—a cavernous room hidden far below ancient Stonehenge. There his destiny is revealed, as he trains with the Guardians and Keepers of Stelladaur Light. He must master the secrets of the Stelladaur to keep history from repeating itself, or all he knows and loves will vanish forever—even before it exists..

Printed and bound in the USA.

Guard well your spare moments. They are like uncut diamonds. Discard them and their value will never be known. Improve them and they will become the brightest gems in a useful life.

—Ralph Waldo Emerson

For my dad, a brilliant scientist,
who showed me how to live with passion and
introduced me to time-travel, portals,
and flora and fauna.

For my mom, an exceptional woman,
who embodied compassion, grace, and wit and
lived intelligently with unabashed convictions.

I miss you both.

Contents

Gratitude

My heartfelt thanks to each person who travels with Reilly on his quest to find Tir Na Nog, and to:

My husband who I live the adventure called Life with. Your love and encouragement keeps the journey real. I adore you beyond words.

My children who I find interesting, remarkable, and lovable.

My grandchildren who keep me young and enchanted.

My friend, Regina. Your support, listening ear, and genuine encouragement is priceless.

My graphic designer, Alicia Lockwood, who created the amazing new covers for the series. Thank you!

My editor, Jill Ronsley, whose work is impeccable! Your attention to detail is unparalleled. Your expertise is exceptional. Your heart is like gold.

Finally, to all who have found their Stelladaur—and to those who are still searching—you inspire me!.

Chapter One

Buried Alive

T hree days had passed since Reilly's first kiss. He could still taste her on his lips—warm and delicious. Despite all the bizarre events since his return, the kiss was enchantingly tangible.

He remembered the exact spot in the Suzzallo Library where he and Norah had landed through the portal. Relieved that they were both home safe, he couldn't wait another minute! He took her in his arms, breathed in the sweet scent of her chestnut hair, caressed her smooth neck, and cradled her face in his hands. Their lips touched gently … before the moment gave way to a prolonged kiss—deep, wet and passionate. For three days, he replayed it in his mind, over and over, hoping another perfect moment would come to hold her.

Reilly had been trapped at Black Castle in Wicklow, Ireland, for more than a year in 1896. There, he rescued Norah from an imprinting by Ukobach, the Prince of Hell. Distracted and mesmerized by a powerful force between Reilly and Norah, Ukobach chose to inhabit the body of Travis Jackson, the only person Reilly truly hated.

When Reilly's mom's initial shock of seeing him back home had subsided, sheer exhaustion kicked in and he crawled into bed. He flashed a smile at Tuma, the big, long-haired albino dog, who circled on the bed until she found her spot to settle down for the night, resting her neck on her front paws. For a moment, Reilly felt as if he'd never left Eagle Harbor Drive on Bainbridge Island. Thrilled that his mom had invited Norah to stay at their home all summer, and knowing she was asleep in the guest room down the hall, he drifted off to sleep.

The next afternoon, Reilly woke with his stomach gurgling so loudly that he thought Tuma was growling at something. He reached for her, and she responded with several hearty licks on his face.

"Hey, Grandma Charlotte, let's get something to eat."

Tuma barked, and her tail wagged.

Reilly looked into his dog's silver eyes. It was surreal, knowing she wasn't just a dog. She was *also* his fourth great-grandmother! Tuma understood Reilly better than anyone—except maybe Norah … *Norah!* The empty feeling in his stomach collided with the memory of the kiss, and he bounded out of bed.

This was a welcome relief from the excruciating pain he'd endured in Black Castle. The spell had him doubled over in agony. Every time it happened, he knew that Ukobach was torturing Norah somewhere in the castle and that she was near death. But their unspoken love had saved Reilly and Norah inexplicably from the fatal imprinting at the bonfire. The force was so strong that it halted even Prince Ukobach momentarily.

Pulling on a pair of jeans, Reilly took a deep breath, and wished every bit of it had only been a nightmare. He wished he could turn back the passage of time, change the past—re-arrange history somehow. He just wanted to make his life be as if it never happened—all the horrific stuff—everything in his nightmares about demons that wanted his soul, his body, and the people he loved. But he knew with certainty that nightmares happened when he was completely awake … and alive … when he wished he were dead. Nevertheless, it was in the midst of those haunting realities that he began to recognize pain as an indication that he was still breathing.

More anxious to see Norah with each second that passed, he grabbed a green hoodie and sprinted to the door, with Tuma at his heels. Inside, he ached to kiss her again. He wondered if that was how other people felt after a first kiss and before the second. Or was it because he wasn't like other boys his age—the kind of boys who had their first kiss when they were eleven, claimed half a dozen girlfriends before they were thirteen, and bragged that they'd kissed more girls than they could count by the time they were in high school. Irritated by the unwanted comparison of himself with anyone else, he tried to brush aside the self-scrutiny. Besides, he'd always been different from his peers. It hadn't bothered him before. Why should he care now?

Had kissing Norah changed things that much? Had it changed *him*? Or was it something else?

Suddenly he was tormented by thoughts that he might never kiss her again! As if she were still trapped in Black Castle!

He quickened his pace and followed the hum of conversation into the kitchen where he found Norah, Chantal, James, and his mom seated around the table.

"You're awake!" Norah chimed.

"Still alive!" Chantal added.

"I didn't want to wake you," said Monique. His mom stood up to hug him. "How do you feel?"

"Good, I guess," he said, winking at Norah. "I'm starved."

"I bet you are!" said Monique, releasing her son. "You missed breakfast, but there are plenty of sandwiches and other leftovers on the table." She stepped to the refrigerator and grabbed a gallon of milk.

"It's great to see you, Reilly," said James as he reached across the table to hug him.

As Reilly pulled out the chair beside Norah, he eyed a golden cord around James's neck. "You still have your Stelladaur!"

"Yep! I haven't taken it off since we found it in the library, before you went through the portal."

"Neither have I," said Chantal, tugging the cord around her neck.

Norah reached for her own Stelladaur, bulging under the thin pajamas Chantal had given her.

Reilly looked at Chantal and then at James. "Have you figured out how to use it?"

"We haven't gone through any portals yet," said Chantal, "if that's what you mean."

"That's weird," said Reilly. "I thought you'd go through a portal, too. Maybe to Jolka, where Norah and I went just after we found our Stelladaurs."

"We thought so, too." James sounded annoyed. "I've lost count of how many times we tried to follow you through the paneled door. But the good news is we found my father's key after you used it. It fell to the floor just before you and Tuma disappeared. But," he groaned, "we couldn't get it to work."

"I've learned how to use my Stelladaur … sort of." Chantal tugged at the cord again.

"What do you mean?" said Norah.

"I don't know how to explain it. I'm more confident with my

decisions, even when they don't make sense." She speared a whole dill pickle with her fork.

"What decisions?" Reilly asked.

"Deciding to stay home for a while, for one thing."

"A while?" Reilly gulped half a glass of milk and wiped his mouth with the back of his hand.

"Okay," she said. "A long while."

"Hey! I'm not complaining." James smiled at Chantal.

"I know twenty-seven is a bit old to live at home, but I needed a change. Advertising isn't what I thought it would be, even with the bigwigs in New York. It's a rat race! With Dad gone, and not knowing when—or if—you would return, I decided that helping Mom with the bakery would be the best thing for me."

Reilly reached for Norah's hand under the table. "Yeah, of course."

"Seems everyone in this family has a Stelladaur but me," Monique quipped, as she refilled Reilly's glass with milk.

He thought he detected a hint of sarcasm in her voice. Or was it jealousy?

"Not to worry," she continued. "I believe that several are available, but I don't expect to need one."

Reilly sensed that his mother's assumption was far from the truth, but it hardly seemed the time to be disagreeable. After all, he still had no idea where his own Stelladaur was since it had disappeared.

"James and I have kept things going at Eilam's Kayak Hut," said Chantal, ignoring her mother's comment. "It's been a busy year."

"Eilam!" That got Reilly's full attention. "Any word from him?"

Chantal turned to her mom.

"I'm afraid not," said Monique, shaking her head. "A few days after you left, his kayak was found abandoned just northeast of Suquamish. Rescuers searched for a week. They never found a body."

Reilly squeezed Norah's hand and let it go. He stood up, walked to the window, looked out at Eagle Harbor in the distance and softly said, "That's not far from where Dad drowned."

Silence swept over the room like a fog over the sea on a chilly morning.

"Eilam was like family," said Chantal. "We all miss him."

Reilly stared out the window, blinking back tears. "He didn't die. He was already immortal."

"Perhaps," said Monique.

Annoyed that his mother still had doubts about Eilam and Stelladaurs, and frustrated by his own annoyance with her, Reilly walked back to the table. "I've asked myself numerous times why Eilam left the way he did, without saying good-bye—and just leaving me a note. I still don't know the answer. But I know he's alive! He helped Norah and me come back through the portal."

"What?" James asked. "You saw him?"

"No, but Lottie did. She saw him in Tir Na Nag, and then in Wicklow. It's a long story."

"Who's Lottie?" Chantal asked.

"Charlotte Louise McKinley, our fourth great-grandmother," Reilly replied.

"And mine!" James said before Monique could argue. "Remember? We're like third cousins twice-removed, or something."

"That's right," Reilly said. "Anyway, since I've apparently been gone for more than a year, there's a lot to tell you."

"Obviously!" Chantal pushed her plate away and leaned forward on her elbows.

"The bakery is covered all day," Monique said, settling into her chair. "We have all afternoon."

Encouraged by his mother's response, Reilly nodded. He started at the beginning—the moment he transported through the paneled door of the reading room and landed in the middle of the

Crumble in Wicklow. He told as much of the past year's events as he could remember.

It was especially difficult for Norah to hear the details. A few times Reilly suggested that he finish another day, but she insisted that he continue. She said it was best for them all to hear the whole story together, at the same time. Three hours, four sandwiches, and several glasses of water later, Reilly finished talking.

Too stunned to speak, Monique, Chantal, and James simply stared at Reilly.

"Somebody say something!" said Reilly.

James broke the silence. "I'm perfectly content if I *never* go through a portal!"

"My little brother … an Echtra!" Chantal whispered. "It's all so incredible!"

"It's a miracle you survived!" Monique reached for Reilly's arm across the table. "I don't suppose there's anything I can do to keep you from ever time travelling again, is there?"

"Probably not, Mom." Reilly chuckled. "But I don't plan to go anywhere for a while. Still, I'm bummed about needing to catch up on an entire year of school!"

"Let's get you registered for online classes," Monique suggested enthusiastically. "Considering everything you've been through, I can't imagine that returning to a high school would be the best idea. Homeschool is a much better plan."

"I agree. Thanks, Mom."

"No sense in rushing into any of it, though," she added. "You need to relax, take things easy, and enjoy the rest of the summer."

"So, what day is it?" Reilly asked. "My time-clock is messed up—like I have portal-lag, or something."

"That's funny!" said James, laughing with everyone else. "It's July 31st."

Reilly recalled the date on the online news article he'd read over a student's shoulder at the library. "I hate to ask, but have you heard anything lately about Travis, or seen him since his release?"

Norah flinched. Monique squirmed in her chair.

"There's talk at the bakery that he's back on the island," said Monique. "But we haven't seen him."

"There's other talk, too," James added.

"Like what?" said Reilly.

"An online article today said that Travis claims he was 'redeemed' in prison," said Chantal.

"*Redeemed?*" Reilly shouted. "He was imprinted by the Prince of Hell himself! He cannot be *redeemed!*"

"Absolutely—not that demon!" said Norah.

"Redeemed?" Reilly blurted out again. "What could he possibly mean by such a statement?"

"According to the article, he 'found God' in prison," said James. "He still denies any illegal activity with regard to making fake Stelladaurs and lacing them with drugs. But he did admit that he'd had a drinking problem. He apparently went through a rehab program in prison and said now he's committed to staying clean."

"That's ASININE!" Reilly shouted again and pushed away from the table.

"There's more," Chantal said. "He says he wants to 'settle down and become a family man.' And he pledged fifty million dollars to various organizations for homeless children."

Reilly covered his mouth to keep from spewing the ham and cheese sandwich in his stomach across the table. Then he took a deep breath and stood up.

"The man is a master liar!" Reilly said. "No amount of *redemption* will change his evil soul." Reilly clenched his jaw, remembering the horrific scene he'd witnessed when Prince Ukobach imprinted Travis's body at Black Castle.

As far as Reilly was concerned, the conversation was over. He turned and walked out the front door, with Tuma right behind him.

Reilly sat on the porch steps and pet his dog in slow strokes, from the top of her head along her back. She was shedding, and he dropped her long white hair to the ground in handfuls. A few minutes later, Norah came outside and squeezed in beside Reilly.

"Coming back is going to be more difficult than we expected," she said.

"I never thought Travis would already be out of jail," said Reilly.

Norah nodded.

"I hate him, Norah. I really hate him."

"I know."

"*Redeemed?* He's insane!"

"Ukobach is to blame. He imprinted Travis years ago, after he witnessed the murder of his own family."

"He had a *choice*, Norah!"

"He was just a kid, though—younger than us."

"We've experienced horrific things, too, but we didn't choose Ukobach." Reilly stopped petting Tuma and faced Norah. "It's weird, though, because Wicklow and Black Castle are just memories now."

"*Awful* memories that we'll never be able to forget!" She slipped her hand into his.

"It seems like it all happened a long time ago," he said, caressing her thumb with his. "But I feel like …"

"Like what?"

"Like something inside of me is being buried alive."

Chapter Two

Dust to Ashes

Confusion swept over Reilly. Even Tuma hadn't witnessed the horror of the imprintings at Black Castle.

Sitting beside Norah on the porch, he wanted to kiss her again. But he fought against his desire, because he wanted the second kiss to be as perfect as the first, and it couldn't possibly be perfect if it happened in the middle of a conversation about Travis.

He mustered his energy and changed the subject. "Do you want to go kayaking?"

"Sure!"

"Chantal said my kayak is still docked at Eilam's, just waiting for me. Let's go."

He grabbed the keys, they jumped into the jeep, and he drove Norah and Tuma around Eagle Harbor to town.

At the dock, Reilly slid into his kayak and was filled with the familiar sense of the stillness being on the water always gave him. This time, it was combined with the thrill of adventure. As they paddled out of the harbor, Norah's hair blew in the wind ahead of him. Her sweet aroma blended with the salty spray and made him feel invincible, yet giddy. His own blonde hair blew freely in tangled strands. For a while he forgot about Travis.

As they rounded the point and headed towards Seattle, Tuma plunged into the water and swam near the bow.

"Toss her the rope, Norah," Reilly said, knowing what his dog was about to do. "Not too fast, Tuma. We want to relax."

Tuma opened her mouth, let out her tongue, and grabbed the rope with her teeth. Then, just like the time she propelled Reilly toward his first portal, she moved the kayak forward. Norah squealed and gripped the sides as the white dog increased her speed.

Skimming the water's surface like a powerboat, Tuma steered the kayak for several miles. She slowed considerably to approach the giant petroglyph on the north side of the island. It was high tide, so the rock looked like a small sea stack jutting up from the choppy waves. As they approached, the ancient carvings became more vivid. Intrigued, Norah reached for her paddle and maneuvered around the rock. On the other side, she spotted something.

"Look!" she said, pointing.

"Yeah. I know," Reilly said, dipping into the water with his own paddle. "I didn't get a chance to tell you about that. It's the same design that the Deceptors used for their branding mark." He pressed his right hand over his left chest, wishing the scar from the wound had disappeared.

"Why would that design be engraved here? Didn't you tell me some of the engravings were clues that helped you find the portal in the Suzzallo Library?"

"That's right."

"Then … this is a clue, too."

"This is supposed to be a pleasure ride," Reilly said, starting to paddle away from the rock. "Aren't you tired of finding clues? Let's just relax for now."

Norah paused and looked at him quizzically. Reilly thought she was wondering why he suddenly didn't want to find more clues.

"I'm just saying this is probably important," she said.

"Noted. Now, let's get going, okay?"

He hadn't intended to sound abrupt. The truth was that he'd hoped Tuma would lead them somewhere else. If he was going to discover something about his responsibilities as an Echtra, he wanted it to be something inspiring that would renew his strength—not remind him of the raw pain he and Norah had recently suffered.

"I'm sorry, Norah. I didn't mean to be rude."

"No apology needed," she said, winking.

"Thanks," he said.

Tuma pulled on the rope and steered them out into the Puget Sound. The strong currents between Agate Pass Bridge and Suquamish Point swirled, but Tuma showed no signs of fatigue as she moved them past the point. Herons and ducks flew overhead, and two otters basked in the sun on a private float dock near the shore. Jellyfish dotted the water and bobbed along. Finally, Reilly started to relax.

He closed his eyes for some time and breathed in deeply until the salty air tickled his nostrils. He twitched his nose to keep from sneezing. Tuma slowed her pace and they drifted towards the Suquamish dock.

She jumped aboard the kayak and began to bark.

"Good girl," said Reilly, patting her back. "You want us to get out here?"

"Why here?" said Norah.

"I don't know. I haven't been to Suquamish in a couple of years. There's a great pizza place just up from the dock. Bella Luna's."

"You sure do like pizza."

"They have spicy barbeque wings, too. Are you hungry?"

"Not really. You?"

"Always."

As they eased up to the dock, Tuma jumped off the kayak and vigorously shook the water out of her fur. Reilly slid out and tethered the kayak while Norah teetered onto the dock.

Tuma led the way up the ramp and down the long dock. She trotted past Bella Luna's, turned onto a side street, and raced up the hill.

"Wait up, Tuma!" Reilly shouted. He and Norah sprinted to catch up.

Half a block ahead, Tuma stopped and waited for them at a crosswalk.

"What is she so anxious for us to see?" Norah said.

Pointing to a small sign to their right, Reilly replied, "A cemetery."

They crossed the street, caught their breath, and continued on up the hill until they rounded the crest, and spotted an old church that looked like it belonged on a sympathy card. Tuma stood near the front entrance wagging her tail.

"A church?" Reilly said when he reached Tuma. He peeked in through a small window. "The last time I was in a church was at Dad's funeral. I'm still not keen on them, even if they look cool, like this one."

Tuma barked and led them around the side of the little church to a cemetery.

"I've never been here before," Reilly said.

They walked along a path towards a headstone monument in the center of the cemetery with a towering cross that rose twenty feet above the ground. Tuma stopped to wait for them there.

"It's strange," Reilly said, transfixed by the monument. "There's something about this place. It's different. Like it's ... I don't know ... sacred."

Norah read the inscription below the headstone. "Chief Sealth ... Chief Seattle."

"I studied him a few years ago in school but I've never been here. He was a respected chief and the people loved him," said Reilly.

Norah stepped closer to a three-foot high cement wall that encircled the monument. A conglomerate of items scattered on the ground in front of the wall caught her attention: plastic toys, marbles, dream catchers, candy wrappers, shells, rocks, empty bullet cartridges, sea glass, cigarette butts, soggy origami cranes, coins, strings of colorful beads, cigars that hadn't been smoked, buttons, a small can of breath mints, and feathers.

Reilly moved closer to the wall. Carefully observing the random items, he wondered if some people might mistakenly think it was a disrespectful pile of meaningless junk.

"People honor their dead in interesting ways," he said, gently touching a miniature hand mirror. He absently tugged at the golden cord tied around his wrist, as he often did when he started to think seriously about something. "I wonder what their stories are."

"As diverse as each item, I suppose."

Quietly waiting near Reilly and Norah, Tuma wagged her tail swiftly. Following her cue, they walked towards her and began to circle the wall.

"This is an interesting inscription," Reilly said, letting go of the cord. "It's in a Native American dialect, but it has an English translation."

Norah read it aloud. "*Even the rocks thrill with memories of past events. The very dust beneath your feet responds more lovingly to our footsteps because it is the ashes of our ancestors. The soil is rich with the life of our kindred.*"

After circling the monument, they were back in front of the pile of miscellaneous tokens. They gazed up at the noble chief.

"I want to read the inscription again," said Norah. "Let's walk back to it."

"*Even the rocks thrill with memories of past events ...*" Reilly said.

"*The very dust beneath your feet responds more lovingly to our footsteps ...*" Norah continued.

"*... because it is the ashes of our ancestors,*" they finished in unison. "*The soil is rich with the life of our kindred.*"

Reilly was awestruck, like when he found Charlotte's journal in the library. They walked to a nearby bench and sat down. Tuma sat at Reilly's feet, facing him, as if waiting for a command.

"Okay, girl," Reilly said, patting her. "There's something about my ancestors. Is that it?"

Tuma barked.

"But *you* are my ancestor, Lottie!" He chuckled. "None of our ancestors are buried in this cemetery. This is Native American tribal land."

Tuma perked her ears.

Reilly continued to attempt to decipher the riddle. "What rocks *thrill with memories of past events*?"

Norah put her hand on Reilly's leg. "Where is Lottie buried? Maybe there's a clue on her headstone."

"Probably in Ireland somewhere."

Tuma barked, and Reilly reached to pet her. "We need to return to Ireland?" The dog stood up and wagged her tail.

"We're *not* going back to Black Castle!" Norah declared.

"Of course, not!" Reilly put his arm around Norah and pulled her close to him. "I doubt that's what Tuma is suggesting."

He released Norah slightly and tucked a strand of her hair behind her ear. He wanted to kiss her—again and again—hoping to assure her that she would never return to that dreadful place. He gently gathered her hair in one hand and draped it over her front shoulder.

"Charlotte found Tir Na Nog," Reilly continued. "She went there several times—even when you and I were still in Black Castle. Follow my logic. Eilam said Dad sent Tuma to me. Tuma is Charlotte. Therefore, Tuma knows where to find Tir Na Nog—and I believe my dad is in Tir Na Nog." He looked at her, barely realizing that his eyes were transfixed on her deep, emerald-colored eyes.

Norah threw her arms around his shoulders and moved her hands up to caress the soft blond hair at the back of his neck. She drew her head back slightly and gazed deep into his eyes. "We'll find it together!"

Before either of them knew what was happening, their lips were together, locked in an eternity.

But in the next instant, strange, unidentifiable scenes raced through Reilly's mind.

Stone faces … a ship … waves … rocks …war!

Norah opened her mouth wider, and Reilly's every nerve wanted to drown in the passion.

Weapons … strange writing … dead people … a rose bush.

Desperately trying to get away from the weird scenes, he kissed her harder. But the longer they kissed, the more the images swirled in his head …faster … faster … until they were a distorted blur tormenting his mind.

Reilly pulled away to catch his breath. The moment their lips separated, the blur disappeared.

"That was so strange," he blurted out.

"What does *that* mean?" Norah retorted, as she flipped her hair off her shoulders. "I thought it was going just fine."

"No … not the kiss! The kissing was great!"

"What's wrong then?"

"As soon as you started to kiss me, pictures raced through my mind. Faces I didn't recognize … broken stone … candles … a train … crowds of people."

"What people?"

"I don't know."

"Could it be flashbacks to Wicklow or Black Castle?"

Reilly stood up from the bench and walked towards the statue of Chief Seattle. "I'm not sure. I don't remember any of it from before."

Norah sat forward on the edge of the bench. "So, it wasn't a flashback at all?"

"I wasn't in the images, but I'm sure it was something from my past." He turned towards Norah. "Did you see anything?"

"What are you suggesting?"

"Nothing! It's just so weird."

She reached for his hand. "Should we try it again?"

"Yeah … okay."

Reilly leaned in to kiss her. She reached up to meet him. As soon as their lips touched, the images started to flash in his mind.

Giant-size stones … dead bodies … chariots!

He pulled away abruptly. "Sort of takes the fun out of kissing," he said.

Norah frowned. "Maybe it's some kind of post-traumatic-stress thing."

"Caused by kissing?"

Norah shrugged and started to walk around the wall, clicking photos of the inscription with her smartphone.

"Your ancestors are from Ireland," she said.

"Yes, on my dad's side of the family. My mother's family is French."

"My dad is Italian. Gustalini, as you know. My mother's family came from England." Reaching the end of the inscription, she recited the last phrase again—"*... the soil is rich with the life of our kindred*"—and moved towards the unorganized collection of tokens.

Picking up a small bundle of twigs that someone had tied together, she pulled the string gently, not hard enough to open the bow. "We all come from the same soil ... the same dust ... and return to the same ashes. Our kindred live in each of us," she said.

The exhilarating feeling of knowing something he didn't fully know before suddenly overwhelmed Reilly. It had occurred when he first touched his Stelladaur! And when he first kissed Norah!

At that moment, he realized that his next responsibility as an Echtra had already begun.

He walked around the wall to meet Norah, and she handed him the bundle of twigs. "Yep!" he said. "Somehow, we're each tied together."

Chapter Three

Flash-Forwards

*I*n addition to getting up to speed with schoolwork, Reilly had to catch up on sleep. Time warping had taken its toll, and fatigue settled in. The added pressure of knowing his responsibilities as an Echtra had just begun didn't help.

After the events at the Suquamish cemetery, Reilly was certain he needed to prepare for something. He had the foreshadowing feeling he'd often had—of an impending change. As usual, he didn't know what the change would be or when it would occur. Only that it was lurking.

Lately he was so exhausted that he didn't want to do much of anything, except spend time with Norah. He slept in every day until noon, dreaming. He wished he could kiss her without the strange flashbacks … if that's what they were.

They spent the afternoons relaxing at the beach or hanging out with James and Chantal at the kayak hut and the bakery. They watched movies late at night, but Reilly usually fell asleep on the couch a few minutes into the show. Once, he and Norah went to Seattle, rode the waterfront Ferris wheel, and watched the guys wearing orange fishing waiters at Pike Place Market throw salmon back and forth while onlookers cheered.

Reilly was nervous about the prospect of Travis showing up, but so far, no one in his family had seen him.

In the fourteen days since their trip to the cemetery, he and Norah hadn't kissed. Several times they almost did, but each time, Reilly pulled away or pretended to be distracted by something, which he was. The thought of facing new responsibilities as an Echtra overwhelmed him, and he didn't want to risk finding out what they would be by kissing Norah. The entire situation depressed him.

Monique grew concerned when he was too tired to take out his kayak or even play fetch with Tuma. "Are you okay?" she asked one evening at dinner. "You're not quite yourself."

"Uh … just tired, Mom."

"Maybe you ought to see the doctor and check your iron level. You're looking a little pale."

"He's just recovering," Chantal said. "He hasn't been home even a month."

"I suppose. Still, it wouldn't hurt to make an appointment." Monique reached for the bowl of mashed potatoes. "If you don't have more color in a week, I'm making the appointment. Maybe time travel isn't as safe for a body as you think."

Reilly rolled his eyes, but then forced a smile. "Deal."

He certainly had no intention of going to the doctor and could think of only one remedy: *Norah! She might bring some color back to my face,* he thought, chuckling.

It was a hot August night. Reilly and Norah sat on the front porch talking about nothing in particular. They watched shadows creep under the moonrise. Horses meandered in the pasture that bordered Reilly's yard, and turned to silhouettes against the full moon. Norah snuggled close to Reilly. He took off his baseball cap and fidgeted with it.

"Do you want to talk about it?" Norah asked.

"About what?"

"The fact that you're afraid to kiss me again."

"No, I don't want to talk about it," he said. "I just want to kiss you without seeing bizarre things when I do." He started to pace the front lawn. "This is ridiculous! It's not supposed to be like this."

"Hey, remember the game with the Tah-dah Twig in Jolka?" said Norah. "And Nebo dropping us at the top of Sequoran? And swinging through the trees like monkeys?"

It seemed like another lifetime, but he remembered the imagination game with the magic stick—a version of tag, in which kids of all ages wildly flew around on giant leaves. He could never forget Jolka, where he first saw Norah sketching her dreams on the Drawing Sidewalk. Or Nebo, the wise giant eagle who flew Reilly and Norah on his back to distant places beyond the known galaxies. And, of course, Sequoran, the mighty talking tree (he snored, too), who helped him find his Stelladaur. Reilly slapped his leg with his cap.

"Yeah. But what does that have to do with anything now?"

"Let's just have fun! Be silly!" She grabbed his cap and ran with it towards the pasture.

Caught off guard, Reilly was only halfway across the yard when he saw Norah leap onto the wooden fence that enclosed the neighboring pasture. She perched herself on the top rail, wearing his cap.

She pulled the cap over her eyes. "You-who! Come and find me!" she called, tipping up the brim to watch Reilly.

Adrenaline kicked in and he sprinted towards her. In the shadowy night, he underestimated the distance to the fence, and he toppled clumsily over it, into the pasture. Norah squealed and bounded down into the yard. Seconds later, Reilly jumped to his feet, laughing uproariously. Norah heaved with laughter, holding the hat on her head with one hand. With the other, she reached for the top of the fence and held it until she caught her breath.

Reilly met Norah with just the fence between them. "I believe you have my hat, Miss," he said, reaching over the rail and flipping the hat off her head.

"I believe you have my heart, Mister," she said with a lilt.

"Yes. Yes, I do." He leaned forward and, without thinking, kissed her on the mouth, forgetting everything.

But again ... *Tunnels ... a crack of lightning ... a darkened sky ... a man!*

Reilly kissed her longer, harder, inhaling the warmth of her mouth against his, trying to block out the intrusions.

Ripped parchment ... an eye ... flames ... a demon!

He pulled back and gazed into her eyes, glistening in the moonlight. She drew him in and began to kiss him again.

Massive boulders ... a grassy meadow ... buttresses ... faces of people from centuries past!

The longer they kissed, the more scenes flashed past.

An angel's wings (but not those of the angel in the Wicklow Embassy fountain) ... *a man's muscular torso* (but not a Pucatrow) ... *a bearded man* (but not Eilam) ...

Something about the images seemed terrifyingly familiar. Reilly was tired of trying to figure things out! He just wanted to be a normal teenager for a few minutes!

The taste of Norah drizzled onto his tongue, and he explored her mouth deeply, grasping her hair in his hands.

As the kiss intensified, so did the stream of unidentifiable scenes. Deeper … faster!

Suddenly, Reilly saw *himself* in the flash backs, spinning past his consciousness so fast he could barely breathe.

Kissing … *Running!*

Grasping … *Alone!*

Reilly urged Norah to move up the fence as they continued to kiss. For a few moments, their lips parted and the scenes vanished as abruptly as they began. Holding onto a fence post, Norah climbed up and over, awkwardly trying to kiss Reilly as she moved. She sat on the fence top then leaped into his arms, wrapping her legs around his waist. He swung her around, her hair blowing in the summer breeze. Holding her up with one arm, he reached his other hand behind her neck and pulled her to him, desperate to ignore the images in his mind.

Then he set her to the ground and took her hand. He slowly traced a finger over her lips.

"I love you, Norah," he whispered.

He leaned forward and kissed her gently.

Suddenly, a few of the fragments of time came together, and he realized something.

"They aren't flashbacks," he whispered. "They're flash-forwards, but back in time."

"Excuse me?" Norah leaned closer until Reilly's breath blew over her mouth. "Did you just say you *love* me?"

Reilly threw his head back and laughed. "Yes, I did! I'll shout it out to the whole world, if you want me to!" He climbed to the top of the fence and balanced on a post. "I love you, Norah Gustalini! I-LOVE-YOU!"

"Get down from there! You're going to wake up the neighbors." She laughed. "Or your mom!"

He jumped to the ground in one leap and swung her up in his arms.

"I also said that what I saw when we kissed were not flashbacks. They're flash-*forwards* to somewhere I need to go ... but it's going to happen in the past."

"More time travel!" She sighed. "Did you see me there with you?"

"No, but I won't go without you!" He spun around with her. "Maybe we need to do some serious making-out for me to see that."

"Ha-ha! Very funny!"

Completely invigorated, he said, "I know where we need to go, Norah. Back to the library!"

She squirmed until he released her. "We're not going back to that hellish place!"

"Not *that* library! The Suzzallo Library. There's another portal there."

"How can you be sure it won't take us back to Wicklow in 1896—or worse, to Black Castle?"

"There are three statues guarding the entrance doors. I saw them look directly at me when we were there. And I recognized them just now when we kissed."

"I thought you didn't want to go through another portal. Haven't you seen enough?"

Reilly stepped closer to Norah.

"I haven't seen Tir Na Nog yet," he said.

Norah touched Reilly's face and stroked his cheek. "My Tir Na Nog is right here." She turned abruptly and ran away from him, towards his house.

"Where are you going?" he called out, exasperated.

"I told you we'd find it together!" she hollered. "We're going to need a good night's sleep."

Blackberry Bakers was packed with standing room only when Reilly, Norah and Tuma arrived the next morning. Working the front register, James nodded as they passed behind the long line of customers at the counter. Chantal operated the latte machine, filling mugs while another employee took the orders. Reilly caught a glimpse of his mom through the pass-through window that opened to the kitchen, rolling out a large mound of dough.

In many ways, nothing had changed. Reilly was glad about that. He still half-expected to see Eilam seated at the corner booth sipping herbal tea and nibbling on a lemon scone. He still wished his Dad would come through the front door from a leisurely sail, but he remembered what he'd learned from Eilam: wishing accomplishes nothing unless and until it becomes a greatest desire. A powerful force from within the person who makes the wish transforms it into a greatest desire. This was precisely why he felt compelled to return to the Suzzallo Library—to continue his search for Tir Na Nog and find out what he was supposed to do next as an Echtra.

Reilly scanned the dining room to see if he could grab an empty table.

The bell that rang whenever the front door opened was muffled by the sound of lively chatter in the room, but Reilly was attuned to the ding. He looked up—and nearly fell into the lap of a lady sitting in the booth beside him. Travis was strolling in!

Tuma's ears flattened against her head and she growled. Reilly hushed her.

He had often seen Travis in the bakery over the years, and it usually caused his anxiety to kick into high gear. Fortunately, an unusual effect of surviving Black Castle was that his anxiety faded away considerably. *What could be worse than Hell?* he reasoned.

No doubt, Travis was bound to show up at the bakery sooner or later. Still, any time before the next millennium was too soon for Reilly.

Though he couldn't put his finger on it, he noticed something different about Travis the moment he came through the door. *Is it a new hairstyle? The way he walks? Did he wear glasses before?* Reilly wondered.

The din in the room subsided to a moderate hum. Norah, who had been eyeing the daily specials in the display case, turned around. When she saw Travis, she gasped and covered her mouth.

"It's okay, Norah," Reilly said, grabbing her hand. "He hasn't seen us yet."

They pushed through the crowd towards a booth at the far end of the bakery, and squeezed between it and three customers. They adjusted their positions slightly each time the line shifted, Norah gripping Reilly's hand all the while. Tuma shifted with them, and then sat quietly at attention beside Reilly.

Uncharacteristically, Travis stood in line with the other customers. He didn't push his way to the front or demand that he be served first as he had usually done in the past. *Something is definitely different,* Reilly thought. He could barely make out Travis's words as he chatted with the customers in line.

"… the carrot muffins are an excellent choice, too … best lattes anywhere …" Travis said. He laughed as he chatted with the man beside him, but Reilly didn't recognize the sound—it sounded genuine, like it came from a *nice* person! Reilly had only heard Travis Jackson's laughter reek with arrogance, echoing evil.

People entered the bakery and crowded at the back of the line as it inched forward, with customers at the front making their purchases and leaving. Reilly and Norah slid into a booth as soon as it was empty, keeping out of Travis's view.

"I hope my mom stays in the kitchen," Reilly said. Norah nodded.

Finally, Travis reached the register. James handed him a small sack of baked goods in exchange for cash. Chantal passed him a cup of coffee, continuing to multi-task to cover up her own uneasiness.

Then, without noticing Reilly, Norah, or Tuma, the man who had once hired someone to try to assassinate Reilly in a parade;

who spent a year in prison for manufacturing and selling fake Stelladaurs laced with drugs; who was honored and respected throughout the world for his scientific contributions to humanity; who spent decades searching for a portal to Tir Na Nog, but failed to find one; who stalked Reilly and lusted after Monique; who saw Reilly's Stelladuar and tried to steal it (though he was a billionaire); and who was demonized forever by Prince Ukobach in front of Reilly's own eyes—that individual walked out of the family bakery like any other customer.

Travis appeared to have become a new man.

But Reilly had decided long ago that it was impossible for someone imprinted by the Prince of Hell to be anything but a demon.

Or was it?

Chapter Four

Another First Kiss

A lull at the bakery in the early afternoon meant James and Chantal could leave with Reilly, Norah and Tuma, and take the ferry to Seattle. On the way, they stopped by James's apartment to get the key Reilly had used to access the portal in the library.

Summer enrollment at the University of Washington had declined, and Red Square, the expansive red-brick courtyard in front of the Suzzallo Library, was nearly empty. They walked up the steps to the main door. Norah, James and Chantal wore their Stelladaurs. Reilly's Fireglass was in his pocket.

"Those statues moved the last time I was here," Reilly said, pointing above the entrance. "They shifted on their posts and smiled at me."

"That one is hiding under his hood," said James as he gazed up at the sage.

"The angel is focused on something off in space," said Norah.

"And the buff guy who isn't wearing much is deep in thought," Chantal joked.

"He looks like me!" James laughed, flexing like an ancient Greek Olympian.

Chantal slapped James's butt. "Not the part of him that's deep in thought!"

"I did an internet search on them," Reilly said. "They represent "mastery, inspiration and thought."

"Interesting," Norah added.

Reilly took Norah's hand and they walked into the building. The others followed. Tuma still had the ability to be invisible when needed. Reilly had no intention of going through another portal without Norah and Tuma, and he hoped this time Chantal and James would make it through, too.

They stopped outside the Reading Room to admire the stained-glass window with two crisscrossed keys, which was a powerful clue in Reilly's passage to Wicklow.

"I'm not using your key, James," said Reilly. "It didn't work last time. There was a glitch of some kind, and no one else came with me."

"It worked," James said. "It just didn't take you where you thought it would."

Reilly nodded. "You're right. But *you* need to be the one holding it this time. It's *your* key."

"We've been here so many times, I've lost count," said Chantal. "We tried the key in every door. It doesn't fit any of them. We even tried using it with our Stelladaurs."

They moved into the Reading Room, where only a few students were studying.

"I told you that the key is only a symbol—a symbol of love," said Reilly.

As he gazed up at the massive, intricately painted ceiling, he realized that the key had already served its purpose for him, and that his passage through any other portals would happen in another way. He couldn't say what portals James and Chantal might go through, if any, or what they needed to learn about love, but he was ready to help them.

"If you can get the key to open a door—hopefully one that doesn't go to Wicklow in 1896—we'll go with you," Reilly said.

"I'm not going to Black Castle," James said, shaking his head and stuffing his hands in his front pockets.

"Me neither!" said Chantal, narrowing her eyes. "You meant to find Tir Na Nog—not Hell!"

"That obviously didn't work out," said James.

"Not yet," Reilly said. "Intent is only part of finding what you want." He walked across the room, followed by Tuma. "I wonder if ..."

"If what?" Chantal asked, following her brother, with Norah and James behind her. She caught on when Reilly headed towards a bookshelf on the far wall. "You think you'll find your Stelladaur there? Where James and I found ours?"

Reilly stopped right in front of the ancient astronomy books. "Maybe."

He pulled a few books from the shelf and handed them to Norah. Then he gently reached into the vacant spot and curled his hand behind the other books, where his sister and James had found their hidden treasures, but there were no more Stelladaurs. He moved a few books around. Still he found nothing.

Reilly patted his dog and said, "I guess that would be too simple, huh?" Tuma barked. "Yes, girl, I have you—and I have your journal." He hugged his dog, wishing she could communicate in words. Reilly had intentionally left Charlotte's journal at home, tucked safely under his mattress. It was too big to fit in his pockets. Besides, he could practically recite the entire book. He repeated the last paragraph in his mind: *I found it at last! Please come and see it with me, Reilly! Tir Na Nog is beautiful indeed! Come and find me … through the paneled door of the library. Our family will always need our Echtra.*

Ever since his dad drowned, one of Reilly's greatest desires had been to find Tir Na Nog. But over the past year, that yearning had been overshadowed by other deep desires, especially his overwhelming desire to be with Norah. Even though she stood right there with him, he missed her, as if she wasn't there at all. The anguish he experienced when he nearly lost her forever to the Deceptors in Black Castle flooded him with the fear of losing her.

He and Norah walked along the long row of bookshelves towards the alcove at the south end of the room. They stopped at the exact spot where they'd landed on returning from Wicklow a few weeks earlier and turned to face the same direction. Reilly ran his fingers through Norah's hair. She smiled, knowing his thoughts. They looked intently into each other's eyes, both feeling the excitement of the moment. He pulled her closer and she wrapped her arms around his waist. They closed their eyes and leaned into each other, and their lips met.

Again, flashes of unrecognizable people, places, and events raced through Reilly's brain like a movie on fast-forward. But this time, he heard voices—scrambled and frantic. And this time, he was in every scene! Nowhere did he see Norah! Or Tuma! Or anyone he knew!

He kissed her more passionately, and she responded in kind.

The flashes accelerated until they became a blur.

He kissed her firmly, pressing his mouth hard over hers, as she reached her hands up his back. Then, the scenes became disjointed fragments. It was as if his mind was broken into jagged pieces that were impossible to make sense of because he hadn't experienced any of it yet!

It was as if he'd never kissed Norah—because she didn't actually exist!

When pieces of Prince Ukobach and Travis Jackson appeared in his mind—their demon eyes, evil grins, and grotesque, contorted bodies—Reilly pulled away from Norah.

Before they could catch their breath, they heard Chantal's voice. "Are you serious? This is hardly the place!"

"Wow! You were really getting into it!" James said. "Is this your make-out spot or something?"

"I mean … Now? Here?" Chantal sounded annoyed.

"Uh … sorry … we just …" said Reilly.

Norah tucked her hair behind her ears. "We're just … so happy to be back here. This is the spot where we landed when we came back through the portal."

"I get it," said Chantal, rolling her eyes. "Just keep the P.D.A. in check, okay?"

"Hey, I'm all for a little P.D.A." James chuckled, and then kissed Chantal before she could object.

"Can we please get on with why we're here?" Chantal sighed.

"Exactly why are we here?" James asked. "As Chantal said, we've tried to open every door, every cabinet, and every drawer in this room several times with the key, and using our Stelladaurs, too! No go."

Reilly reached into his pocket and pulled out his Fireglass. "This helped me go through some portals when nothing else worked. C'mon."

They walked into the alcove and Reilly told James to try the key in the keyhole of the first paneled door. As James expected, it didn't work. Reilly extended his Fireglass fully, looked through it, and pointed towards the key while James tried it. Nothing happened. They tried every door—skipping the one through which Reilly had disappeared to Wicklow—using the Fireglass and James and

Chantal's Stelladaurs. When nothing remotely magical happened as it had before—when not a spark of light beamed in through the window, not a single musical note resounded off the chandeliers, not a flame of fire instantly engraved an inscription on the wall, and not a hint of something unexpected occurred—Reilly insisted they try the door that had opened the portal to Wicklow.

He noticed that four students remained in the room, busy working on a laptop or with their nose buried in a book.

"James, try the key with one hand while holding your Stelladaur with the other. I'll focus the Fireglass on both," Reilly said, reaching for Norah's hand. She dug her fingernails into his palm. "Chantal, stand behind Norah and me. Hold your Stelladaur with one hand, and with the other one, hold Norah's free hand. We all need to be touching each other to go through at the same time." Tuma needed no instruction. She wedged herself between Reilly and James, touching both of them.

James took a deep breath as he aimed the key towards the keyhole. "This had better not take us to Black Castle!"

"This is it!" Reilly announced.

James's key touched the keyhole. He inserted it.

Chantal gasped and held her breath.

James pushed the key all the way in. He turned it to the right … until it clicked. He turned it to the left … until it clicked.

Nothing happened.

Chantal exhaled loudly and let go of Norah's hand. "Now what?"

Reilly twisted the barrel of his Fireglass. "The etching of the Stelladaur is supposed to spin. It's not working."

"Why?" James asked. "We've tried everything!"

"I don't understand either," Reilly said as he fidgeted, trying to get his Fireglass to function on its own.

Tuma barked. Startled, Reilly worried that she would attract the attention of the four students, but none of them noticed.

"Invisible and silent, at least to those without a Stelladaur," James said. "That could be handy for people, too."

"Tuma used to be a person," Norah said as she patted the dog's head.

Tuma barked again. "Okay, I'm listening," said Reilly, stroking her back. "What is it?"

The albino bounded out from under their legs and headed to the center aisle of the Reading Room. Still holding his Fireglass in one hand, Reilly darted after his dog. Norah followed. James and Chantal tucked their Stelladaurs into their shirts and ran to catch up.

"Wait up!" Reilly hollered, running past the four students, who looked bewildered by the passing entourage.

Tuma led them out of the Reading Room, down the winding stairs to the main foyer, and out the front doors of the library. Now visible to others, the dog stopped halfway down the steps and turned around, wagging her tail and barking incessantly at the three statues that graced the arched entranceway.

"Something about the statues …" Reilly said, stepping back to get a better view. "I saw glimpses of these in one of the flash-forwards just a few minutes ago."

Norah was already next to him, looking up at the statues. James and Chantal were just exiting the building, running to catch up.

Tuma continued to bark and Norah tried to quiet her.

Reilly lifted his Fireglass and noticed that the Stelladaur was now spinning on the outer surface. He raised his Fireglass to his eye to get a closer look, and at the same time reached for Norah. His fingers barely touched her hand … for a split second … and then slipped away.

In an instant, a burst of sunlight ricocheted off the tip of Reilly's Fireglass.

And he disappeared from Red Square.

Chapter Five

Forgotten Memories

It was too dark for Reilly to see anything. He blinked rapidly, closed his eyes for a few seconds, and opened them again. There was only blackness.

"Norah?" No reply. "*Norah!*" Silence reverberated deep in his core.

He stood still, aware of the solid ground beneath him and a bitter cold wind blowing eerily from behind. Shivering, he squatted and placed his hands on the flat surface to get his bearings. Reaching out along the ground in each direction, he determined that he had landed on rough wooden slats. He sat and listened to his breathing. The air smelled fresh, like an early morning after the rain. He closed his eyes again and inhaled deeply.

A gust of warm air whooshed past him. He rubbed his arms briskly and opened his eyes.

Now able to see, he stood up and found himself on a small wooden platform perched above lush green moss growing across a ravine in a dense rainforest. A square wooden cart, like an old coal miner's cart, balanced directly in front of him on a large, round stone that fit tightly into a ball-and-socket device. He stepped up to the cart and looked inside. It was empty, so he climbed in. Grasping the edge to steady himself, he peered over the edge of the embankment.

"*Noooraaah!*" he called out. "*Tuuummaaa!*"

When he lifted one hand to cup his mouth for another call, he saw the golden-threaded bracelet still tied securely to his wrist. At least *something* was familiar. For that he was grateful.

Without warning, the cart jerked and rolled forward, heading straight for the edge of the embankment. As he reached the top of the ravine, Reilly saw a chute open, and the cart plunged in. Curving right and left, it rolled ahead like a luge, swishing through a massive canopied gully that extended far into the distance.

Whisking past trees draped in hairy moss, dangling vines in tangled webs, and ferns taller than houses, Reilly heard only an eerie silence, while his thick blonde hair streamed behind him.

A faint low-pitched hum emerged in the distance. As he strained to hear it, the volume increased and changed to a deep drone. The cart picked up speed and a gentle whistling joined in … then the steady percussion of a beating drum … and as the cart accelerated, so did the tempo and volume of the music. Faster … louder … faster … louder … until, like an ancient tribal drum ritual, the noise beat so loudly that he wanted to cover his ears! But he held the sides of the cart tightly.

Suddenly, the cart lurched and jolted to a stop, while the drumming pounded incessantly. Reilly steadied himself and climbed out.

In front of him was a clearing at the bottom of a steep hill, edged by a berm covered with grooved stone steps leading up to an ultramarine sky. Covering his ears, he walked towards the steps, breathing steadily, while his heart pounded with the rhythm.

As he climbed up, the tempo of the beat slowed, growing gradually quieter until it gave way to the dull droning and whistling sounds he'd heard first. When he reached the top, he looked out across a gentle grassy meadow and a warm breeze blew past him. Reilly was alone.

Scanning his surroundings, he spotted a massive circle of giant rocks in the distance. There was no mistaking where the portal had taken him. He was at Stonehenge! But how far back in time had he travelled?

Awestruck, he walked towards the outer ring. Sarsens towered in front of him, and he stopped to admire their enormity. Stepping under a lintel, he was astounded by the engineering feat of horizontal stones fitting tightly together in a tongue-and-groove construction. Observing the precision required to place each lintel, he realized they'd been secured by carved knobs and snapped into place to form a circle on top of the sarsens. Knowing that Stonehenge was five thousand years old, he couldn't comprehend how people could have built such a remarkable structure then!

Reilly wove through the rock formations. Warily, he reached out and touched a gigantic stone. Instantly, the ground beneath him rumbled and the sound of pounding drums swirled in the atmosphere! The strange sound resonated in his soul, as if he recognized it.

He moved to a rock about eight feet high, half the height of the sarsens. It stood firmly in a circle of rocks the same size, inside the outer circumference of huge sarsens. He pressed the palms of his hands against it and, above the drumbeats, heard a voice whisper, *"Even the rocks thrill with memories of past events."*

Reilly knew with absolute certainty whose voice it was—Eilam's!

"The cemetery!" Reilly shouted, as if in conversation with his lifelong friend. "That's the first line of the inscription on the Suquamish cemetery wall."

Eilam didn't reply, nor did he repeat the rest of the inscription. Yet Reilly instinctively knew he had come to Stonehenge to learn about the *past events*.

Eager to find signs that Eilam might be nearby, he zigzagged between the massive rocks of the outer circle. Then he moved towards the center, passing the ring of smaller stones. He approached two trilithons: each one had two vertical sarsens joined by a third stone placed horizontally on top of them, so they looked like huge doorframes.

Reilly recalled reading a recent magazine article saying that scientists had identified only five trilithons at Stonehenge.

"What scientists would give to see this place!" he muttered. But he cringed at his own suggestion, knowing a particular scientist—Travis Jackson—would do unimaginable things to witness what Reilly now saw. Reilly strolled between the trilithons. In front of each of them, he counted eighteen smaller stones arranged in groups of three. At Stonehenge, each ring of rocks, every sarsen and trilithon, was precisely positioned. This precision created an unusual sense of perfect order.

In the center of the masterpiece lay a single flat rock that was higher than his waist. Doing a quick calculation, he thought it was roughly ten feet by four. It was the only rock that wasn't too tall to climb. He extended his hands and placed both palms on top of it. Again, the drumming stopped abruptly. He hoisted himself onto the boulder and turned around to take in the view. Emerald grass blanketed the land, blowing like jeweled waves across the field, all the way to the berm, with the rainforest beyond and the ultramarine sky like a dome above.

Light peered through the spaces between the sarsens, as if the sun's rays streamed from somewhere beyond the berm, past the rainforest, and merged on the stone where Reilly stood—right at the center of Stonehenge.

A resounding crack echoed from the rock below his feet. He jumped, half expecting the stone to swallow him into another portal. He circled, looking in every direction, trying to anticipate what might happen next. Thick white clouds appeared in the clear sky, while an intense light streamed between the sarsens and trilithons, converging at Reilly's feet. He tilted his head back and watched the clouds spread into a flat, glossy white ceiling.

Facing forward, Reilly saw three figures approaching in the distance. He couldn't see the figures clearly, but he had the feeling he'd met them before. He squinted as they walked through the ring of smaller stones and under a trilithon, towards him.

Reilly leapt off the large rock and waited for the curious three. When they stopped about twelve feet in front of him, Reilly knew who they were.

"The statues—" he said, as if he'd always known they weren't merely statues, "above the entrance to the Suzzallo Library."

"We are the Guardians of Stelladaur Light," said the woman. She stood between the men, her flowing white gossamer dress folding around her bare feet and her silken ivory wings fanning out behind them.

"We are the Sovereign Protectors," said the bearded man. He reminded Reilly of Eilam, but his voice was lower and his frame, broader.

"We are the Defenders of the Truth of Body, Mind, and Soul," said the other man. He merely wore a loincloth wrapped around his waist, revealing a chiseled torso and muscular legs and arms.

Although Reilly had become accustomed to warping through portals unexpectedly, he usually couldn't anticipate what might happen. Nor did he know quite what to say when greeted by unusual creatures—or, this time, by statues that had come to life! Endless questions raced through his mind, as they always did at times like this, and he didn't know if he should say anything at all. So he waited.

"I defend the truths of the human body," said the Greek god, taking a step forward. "I am called Olektor." He emphasized the first syllable of his name.

"Olektor," Reilly repeated, nodding.

"I protect the truths of the human mind," said the bearded sage, as he lowered the hood of his cape to his shoulders and stepped forward. "I am called Radmund."

"Radmund," said Reilly.

The angel flapped her shimmering wings before she spoke. "I guard the light of the human soul. I am called Afismat."

"Hello, Afismat," said Reilly, tentatively. "Why am I here?"

"You are here to become master over your body," said Olektor.

"… to learn how to discipline your mind," Radmund continued.

"… and to fill your soul with light," said Afismat. "You must use your wisdom for the good of all, as you have done with your Stelladaur."

"Right," said Reilly, trying to sound agreeable. "I figured you might say something like that. It's part of the whole Echtra thing, huh?"

"Yes. Those who inquire after knowledge, as you do, Reilly, will also be required to act on that knowledge, specifically in relation to it," said Radmund.

"Why Stonehenge? Why so far back in time?"

"Understanding the past helps you understand the present and prepare for the future," began Radmund. "But here, under Stonehenge, all time exists in the same moment. It is one of the great mysteries of the mind."

"*Under* Stonehenge?"

Afismat glanced upwards at the glossy clouds. "When the Shield of Forgotten Memories opens, you will better understand that all time is but a fragment of space."

Reilly craned his neck to observe the strange ceiling of clouds.

"There might be a fragment where your voice echoes with the rocks … when you will dance with your ancestors," added Olektor.

Reilly frowned. *They always speak in riddles,* he thought, studying the strange ceiling.

"What about Norah? Tuma? My dad?" He probed the live statues. "Why can't Echtras be with the ones they love?"

"Those you love are with you at the mere thought of them," Radmund replied.

"But they aren't *really* here with me!" Reilly didn't mean to sound annoyed. Learning his responsibilities as an Echtra didn't mean he couldn't vent now and then. "I mean, I understand about having a greatest desire. I do! And I get that a person has to use imagination and affirmation to manifest what they want in their life. I already learned all that! I even learned something about the power of love." Embarrassed by his outburst, he quietly added, "Didn't I?"

"Indeed, you did, Reilly," Afismat said. "You learned a great deal and accomplished more than most Echtras do. Certainly, you were steadfast in shining Stelladaur light, and even in dispelling the darkness that surrounded you. This is what Echtras must do."

"Above all, because you faced Prince Ukobach, you now qualify to become a Stelladaur Ambassador," said Olektor.

"A what?"

"Stelladaur Ambassadors are diplomatic ministers of the highest rank, sent on special missions by the Star King and Star Queen," Olektor explained. "This is why you are here."

Reilly had traveled through numerous portals, and he couldn't instantly recall everything he'd learned, but he knew the Star King and Star Queen lived in Tir Na Nog. Lottie had been there, which meant somehow Tuma had, too. And he still believed his dad was there.

"If I accomplish this mission, will I finally get to stay with those I love?"

"Every greatest desire will be fulfilled," Afismat said. "There will be nothing you cannot have—if you succeed in your assignment."

Reilly paced back and forth in front of the huge flat stone. He looked up at the peculiar sky and took a deep breath. He would do anything, give anything, and become anything if it meant he could be with Norah! That choice had already been made.

Speaking first to Olektor, he made his intention known. "Teach me mastery over my body." It sounded awkward, yet it resonated with him.

Reilly faced Radmund. "Help me understand the truths of the human mind," he implored.

Then Reilly stepped towards Afismat and nearly pleaded for her help: "Light my soul."

Afismat smiled. As she raised her arms and spread her shimmering wings, the rocks began to echo the droning sounds, mingled with the steady beat of drums.

The flat glossy clouds rolled back like a scroll, as the Shield of Forgotten Memories began to open.

Chapter Six

Keepers

A gainst the incessant droning and beating, the glossy sky rolled back, and a strong, cold wind funneled down, surrounding Stonehenge with a great whirlwind. Reilly fell back against the rock, shielding his eyes from the swirling dust. He pulled himself up and spotted the three guides, who now looked like mere statues.

As the sky darkened Reilly watched Stonehenge become rearranged. Great sarsens were sucked into the whirlwind and hurled in every direction. Rocks were snatched by the cyclone and disappeared from his view, up through the glossy clouds, which continued to roll back further. Entire trilithons crumbled into piles of pebbles and were gathered into the violent storm.

Seeing forty-five-ton rocks being ripped from the ground and hurled through the air, Reilly was astonished that he remained on his feet, protected from the chaos. Shivering, he stumbled towards the three unharmed statues, shielding his eyes with his forearms. When he reached Afismat, she lowered her wings and the storm began to recede.

Reilly blinked. He no longer stood on lush grass. The ground was a blanket of fine brown dirt and the landscape was completely different from what he expected to see after the cyclone. There were no mounds of debris or remnants of broken rocks, and the glossy clouds were gone. Instead, he stood in a tremendous rotunda under a domed ceiling. The perimeter of the room was lined with giant sarsens connected with tightly fitting lintels.

Circled around a massive marble slab in the center of the room were eighteen stone chairs, on which vaguely familiar men were seated. At the head of the table were four empty chairs.

Everyone at the table rose and said in unison, "Come, sit with us."

Mystified, Reilly looked at Afismat for clarity.

"Now your apprenticeship begins," she said, leading the way. Reilly followed, with Radmund and Olektor bringing up the rear.

Afismat seated herself in a stone chair adorned with an inlaid Stelladaur, the size of a small platter, on the headrest. Her hand directed Reilly to the chair at her left, decorated with three small Stelladaurs. Radmund and Olektor sat to her right in chairs like Reilly's. When they were seated, the eighteen men also sat down.

Light from the Shield of Forgotten Memories streamed through the room, lighting the table and beaming out towards the mighty sarsens. The Shield, now resembling a two-way mirror, was situated at the center of the domed ceiling, with the familiar twenty-first-century Stonehenge just beyond the Shield.

"Welcome once again, Keepers," said Afismat, initiating the proceedings. "The unscrolling we just witnessed caused extensive damage. By my best calculations, I would say fifty or sixty thousand

Deceptors have infiltrated past the opening and retreated into the Bleak."

Reilly dropped his jaw. *Sixty thousand Deceptors!* He couldn't fathom it.

"Although their power is diminished wherever there is light," she continued, "the Rotunda will only be completely safe when a Stelladaur Ambassador offers the hidden knowledge from Stelladaur Light to the world. As the Guardians of Stelladaur Light, we present a new Echtra, Reilly McNamara." She nodded at Reilly and waved a hand for him to stand.

He stood up and, still bewildered by the eighteen men, muttered a single word: "Hello."

"Only the strongest Echtras come to us, but none have survived the Bleak."

Reilly's eyes widened but he remained silent.

"Centuries of Earth time have passed since an Echtra qualified for an apprenticeship, but this young man faced Prince Ukobach himself. He will have to endure far more if he is chosen as a Stelladaur Ambassador."

"Me?" Reilly's voice cracked as he jerked his head towards Afismat. He coughed to disguise his fear.

Ignoring his outburst, she raised her hands, and said, "Let us begin with our solemn decree."

Everyone but Reilly joined hands around the table, and recited the decree in unison. *"By decree of the Society of Keepers, we solemnly pledge our wisdom, experience, light, and power to writing the Stelladaur Scrolls for the enlightenment of humankind. We will preserve the Stelladaur Scrolls and protect them from the legions of Deceptors until a Stelladaur Ambassador brings their secrets to the world, and thereafter."*

Reilly's eyes widened. Certainly, he was not that ambassador!

The Keepers continued, *"Even the rocks thrill with memories of past events. The very dust beneath your feet responds more lovingly to our footsteps because it is the ashes of our ancestors. The soil is rich with the life of our kindred."* The Keepers released each other's hands and joined their own on the table, sealing the vow. *"We esteem our heritage, revere our ancestry, and respect the family of humankind."*

Hearing the inscription from the cemetery wall reminded Reilly of Norah. She had not come through the portal, and he ached for her company. Yet he was relieved that his chest didn't sear with the pain he'd endured in Black Castle whenever he thought of her. He knew he wouldn't be going home for a long while.

Refocusing his attention on the Guardians and Keepers, he presumed that they used to be human and must now be some sort of extraterrestrial beings. His responsibilities had just increased from an Echtra's to those of a Stelladaur Ambassador in training. From what he could determine, they were still connected to the people he loved. He was also keenly aware that he had not yet faced his greatest darkness.

"Introductions are now in order," Afismat declared. "Reilly, you may be seated. Please listen carefully. You will choose three Keepers to be your tutors. First, choose one of the Keepers who serve under Guardian Olektor."

Olektor bowed and motioned for the man at his right to stand.

"My name is Louis Pasteur."

Of course! Reilly thought.

"As the newest Keeper, I have been here for one hundred and twenty-some years. In childhood, I enjoyed painting. Later, excelling in chemistry and biology, I made important discoveries in science and medicine, including the causes of terrible diseases and how to prevent them. You might, for instance, have heard of the principles of vaccination and pasteurization. Yet, I suffered greatly..." he cleared his throat and straightened his bow tie "... as I could not save three of my five children, who died of typhoid fever." He sat down and folded his hands on the table.

Olektor motioned to the next man. As he stood up to tell his story, Reilly noted his angular jawline and imposing nose, and the strange laurel wreath on his head.

"My name is Dante Alighieri, and I was born in 1265 in Florence. When I was twelve years old, my parents decided whom I was to marry, but my love had been solely for Beatrice since the day I saw her, when she was but nine years of age, and forever shall it be so. Tragically, Beatrice left the world, still a young woman. My world was one of painting, music, and philosophy, but my life became entwined in politics, and I was exiled from my home in Florence due to political rivalries. Propelled by a quest to understand my grief over my lost love, I wrote my greatest work of poetry. You may have heard the title, *The Divine Comedy*. Beatrice inspired me, as did my great-great grandfather, a man of faith, justice and love." Dante smiled and took his seat.

Reilly recognized the next man from the past.

"I am Benjamin Franklin. I have a passion for learning, invention, books and freedom. I treat failures as successes to be embraced, and I have a lot of experience with both. As an international statesman, I helped draft the American Declaration of Independence and the Constitution. I studied astronomy and the weather, and I was a successful businessman, but some people believe the results of my experiments with electricity are among my greatest gift to humanity. Though I believe God created the earth and all of nature, I confess that I do not know if he knows me." Benjamin adjusted his bifocals and sat down.

Reilly listened as three more men stood up and introduced themselves: Justinian I, the sixth-century Roman Emperor who understood the value of engaging administrators and counselors for strong government; Herodotus, the fifth-century Greek writer, who published an account of the Greco-Persian Wars and became known as the first historian; and Johannes Gutenberg, the fifteenth century German publisher who invented the first printing press.

"These men contributed great works to mankind," Olektor said. "As members of the Society of Keepers, they have been under my tutelage to better understand the power of the human body. The Keepers report their progress to the Guardian who oversees them."

It occurred to Reilly just then that the Keepers were each of the other statues he had seen on the exterior walls of the Suzzallo Library. All but one was a statue of men in history. The only woman was the angel, Afismat, who was positioned in the center of them all, over the main entrance door to the library. He wondered if there were other women Keepers in another place.

He shifted, aware of how uncomfortable it was to sit on a chair made of rock.

"We will now hear from the Keepers who serve with Guardian Radmund," said Afismat. "These contributors have learned to master the power of their mind." She signaled to Radmund to introduce the six men assigned to his guardianship.

"We will begin with Keeper William," Radmund announced. A man with a high forehead, dark wavy hair that draped around his shoulders, a narrow mustache, and a well-kept beard stood up at the marble table.

"My name is William Shakespeare. Some say I am a dramatic genius. I prefer to say that I interpret and embrace life from a different point of view, and I have lived enough to write about it. I left the comfort of writing at home and risked vulnerability on the stage. I realized that if I truly wished to transcend human emotion and the conflicts it causes, I must be naked in my expression, whether my poetry is received with sorrow or laughter. Though thirty-eight plays and one hundred fifty-four sonnets bear my name, they are but a drop in the ocean of human expression."

Reilly recalled attending one of Shakespeare's plays, *The Winter's Tale*, and reading another, *Much Ado About Nothing*.

Both were required in his freshman English class. He silently admitted to himself that, although they were entertaining, he didn't understand either one. Shakespeare's sonnets were somewhat easier to follow, but Reilly struggled with the language of the Elizabethan age—everyone seemed to "thinketh," "eateth," "believeth," and "killeth" more that he could "understandeth." Nevertheless, Reilly was honored to be in the same room as the man known to this day as the greatest writer in the history of English literature.

Radmund thanked William and requested another man to stand.

A man with a wrinkled brow, deep-set eyes, a long white beard, and long white hair leaned forward on the table to begin his introduction. "My name is Charles Darwin. Like Louis Pasteur, I have been a Keeper for only a century and a few decades. As a child, I explored nature and the living world around me. While employed on the HMS Beagle, I circumnavigated the world by sea and collected specimens of birds, fossils, and plants. After much study, I determined that species that adapted to changes in their habitat survived, while those that did not evolve ceased to reproduce and died away. I called this my Theory of Evolution. I was ridiculed for my well-researched supposition. In truth, had I remained on earth another century, I probably would have changed my own theory, in keeping with the work of scientists who came after me. Change is a strange phenomenon, one that is greatly misunderstood by those who do not allow themselves to evolve."

The next man wore a robe with a cloth draped over his left shoulder. "My name is Plato. I lived in Athens, where I studied under the great philosopher, Socrates. My passions were the interpretations of virtue and noble character, gaining knowledge of the metaphysical, and understanding whether belief is justified. Why do we believe as we do? How do we know what we know? I wrote extensively on these subjects. I also established the first European

University, called the Academy, where philosophers and educated men could explore these topics and others."

History had not been Reilly's strongest subject in school. Now these revolutionary thinkers from the past, describing their own lives, captivated him!

Reading about history is very different from experiencing it, he thought.

Then he flashed back again to the Suzzallo Library—and he knew for certain why everyone in front of him looked familiar. The eighteen statues on the exterior wall of the library were indeed of the eighteen Keepers. The three statues over the main entrance door were of Radmund, Olektor, and Afismat who was obviously the leader of them all. She had caught his eye and smiled at him before he left the library.

Radmund introduced the other three Keepers under his guardianship: Hugo Grotius, the sixteenth-century Dutch jurist, theologian, and philosopher; Galileo Galilei, sixteenth-century Italian philosopher, scientist, and astronomer, who discovered that the earth is not the center of the universe; and Isaac Newton, the seventeenth-century English scientist whose fascination with planets, orbits, and movement throughout the universe led him to prove his law of gravitation, which brought him the distinction of having one of the greatest scientific minds of all time.

When the first twelve introductions were done, Afismat stood up and motioned to the last group of geniuses that might tutor Reilly. "As Guardian of the Soul, I present to you the remaining six Keepers."

One by one they introduced themselves, fascinating Reilly with their stories. Leonardo da Vinci from Italy was perhaps history's greatest architect and most famous artist. Next was Johann Wolfgang van Goethe, the great German poet. Adam Smith, the Scottish philosopher and economist followed him, and then Homer, the ancient Greek writer of *The Iliad* and *The Odyssey*.

The unparalleled German composer, Ludwig von Beethoven came next, and last was the biblical prophet, Moses.

When they all finished speaking, Afismat raised her wings and told Reilly something about Stonehenge that no one could have imagined.

"The rocks of Stonehenge were carved by wise giants who roamed northern Africa before the great pyramids of Egypt were built. These giants almost became extinct when other civilizations came and destroyed the vegetation they needed to survive. When but two brothers remained, they migrated to Ireland in search of food. There they met another mighty race and established a solid trust in them.

"To mourn the death of a family member, the giants stacked rocks in circles in a sacred ritual, because they believed the dust of their ancestors would live forever within the rocks. In time, they discovered that the rocks contained the power to heal their souls, but there was no guarantee that their race would live on. So, they decided to entrust Stonehenge, with all its secret powers, to their new friends—the Pucatrows."

Reilly gasped! Since his time in Black Castle, he'd known his knowledge of the Pucatrows was limited. He listened intently.

Afismat continued, with her wings held high. "The giants began to tutor them in the healing powers of their sacred circles. At that time, the Pucatrows were beautiful and powerful creatures, not yet cursed by the Deceptors.

"In Ireland, the giant brothers could not find adequate food, so they bestowed the responsibility to care for Stonehenge on the Pucatrows and disappeared to Greenland, where they died in solitude. The Pucatrows had committed to preserving Stonehenge as a reminder for future generations that *even the rocks thrill with memories of past events,* because they held the ancestral secrets of the giants."

Afismat spoke steadily, not pausing long enough for Reilly to ask any questions.

"The Pucatrows believed it was unsafe to keep Stonehenge in Ireland because it was too close to Black Castle, where the Deceptors dwelled. They feared that the evil forces might overpower visitors who came to admire the monument. To honor the giants and preserve their legacy, the Pucatrows transported the trilithons and sarsens to England, where Stonehenge now stands.

"They accomplished this tremendous feat through the Power of Manifestation—one of the great Stelladaur Secrets—which required using the body, mind, and spirit together. The mysterious rocks are a gift to humankind and a reminder of the truth and ancient knowledge hidden in the dust of the earth."

Afismat looked upward, to where the Shield of Forgotten Memories had been rolled back and Stonehenge was visible on a mirage of shimmering glass. She lowered her wings and said, "Not understanding the power of the Pucatrows, the Deceptors cast an evil spell and cursed them with venomous outrage."

She smiled and added, "The Pucatrows are the forgotten heroes of Stonehenge."

Chapter Seven

Three Tutors

It wasn't easy for Reilly to choose the three Keepers that would be his main tutors, because they all fascinated him. Afismat advised him to consider which stories resonated most with him. Finally, he made his selections.

"From Olektor, I choose Keeper Dante."

Dante stood and bowed to Reilly. "It is my honor. Why have you chosen me?"

"Because of Beatrice," said Reilly. "She understands love better than I do."

Dante smiled and moved from his place at the table to Reilly's side.

"From Radmund, I choose Keeper Charles Darwin. He died in the same year that my fourth great-grandmother, Charlotte, was born. Charlotte is also Tuma, my albino dog. Darwin may understand how this happened, and why. I hope this information will help me in my quest to find Tir Na Nog." Darwin took his place beside Dante.

Reilly faced Afismat. "From you, I choose Keeper Moses. Of all the Keepers, I know the least about him, but he's been a Keeper longer than any of the others. He's probably the wisest."

Moses gathered the robes wrapped around his body and walked to the front of the room to join Dante, Darwin, and Reilly.

"You've chosen well." Afismat stated it as a matter of fact rather than assurance. She wasted no time in explaining the procedures of tutoring. "The first thing you must know about Keepers is that they have been Blinked."

Reilly figured it was time to start asking a few questions. "What does 'Blinked' mean?"

"Changed from the state of mortal to immortal," she said. "Mortals who are destined to be Keepers experience the change immediately after their death. In time, it would be measured as a single blink. People who are Blinked enjoy endless energy without the need for food or rest. However, Keepers remember and experience pangs of mortality, which allow them to know how to tutor and guard Echtras, especially those training to be a Stelladaur Ambassador."

"Have you been Blinked?" Reilly asked Afismat.

"As Sovereign Protectors and Defenders of the Kingdom of Stelladaurs—where the noble Star King and Star Queen rule— Olektor, Radmund and I have been Blinked—and Twinkled."

"Twinkled?" Reilly raised both eyebrows.

"We have been renewed with exalted capacities by an infusion of Stelladaur Light."

"Oh," said Reilly, now understanding the white aura that Olektor, Radmund, and Afismat emanated at all times. "I haven't been Blinked … or Twinkled, have I?"

"No. You will be Spliced—bestowed with the ability to travel through time for the purpose of rearranging history," Afismat replied.

Why would I be Spliced? Reilly wondered. *With the ability to rearrange history, would I be able to go back and change what happened to Dad?*

"Is that part of my special mission?"

"It's a gift for Echtras who have mastered the fundamentals of Stelladaur power. Splicing will prepare you for your special mission."

"Which is …?"

"The details of your mission will be revealed later. Becoming a Stelladaur Ambassador requires that you undergo a rigorous, demanding, and dangerous process. First, you will study with all the Keepers, but especially the three Keepers you've chosen for their experience and wisdom. When you've been sufficiently tutored, you will be Spliced. Then you will go with Dante, Charles Darwin, and finally Moses back to their mortal time, before they were Blinked."

"You must perform a remarkable physical feat—one that will challenge your body, your mind, and your soul," said Dante.

Olektor leaned forward at the table and said, "Extreme patience will be required. There will be pain."

Reilly flinched, remembering the pain he experienced before he rescued Norah at Black Castle. Though their separation was different now, he thought about her constantly. He determined to remember the promise that if he became a Stelladaur Ambassador and accomplished his special assignment, his every greatest desire would be fulfilled.

"You must overcome a battle of the mind," said Darwin, pointing a finger at his wrinkled forehead.

"Perhaps a greater torture than any you experienced at Black Castle," said Radmund.

Reilly drew in a deep breath. *What could be worse than witnessing imprintings? Will it have something to do with the tens of thousands of Deceptors in the place Afismat called the Bleak?*

Finally, Moses said, "You must be willing to give everything for the greater good."

Reilly felt that his abilities were weak and inadequate for an Echtra training to become a Stelladuar Ambassador.

Seeing his angst, Afismat turned to him and took his hands in her own. "As I've said before, we are the Guardians of Body, Mind, and Soul. We will assist you in your obligations."

The word "obligations" weighed heavily on Reilly's mind. *Do I no longer have a choice? Wasn't it enough that I faced Prince Ukobach in Hell? Can't I just go home right now to be with Norah? Can't I forget that I went through another portal? I would be happy! Wouldn't I?*

But he knew he wouldn't … and couldn't. Not when he still hadn't found Tir Na Nog! Not when he and Norah were still apart! And not when Prince Ukobach—in Travis Jackson's body—still lurked in Reilly's own world!

He pulled his hands away from Afismat and declared, "I'm ready."

"Very good," said Afismat. "We will begin."

She signaled to Dante, Darwin, and Moses to return to their places at the great marble table.

In unison, each Guardian clasped their hands together over their heart. Reilly watched and wondered if they were going to recite a prayer or chant. They extended their fingers with their palms still pressed together. Then, in a graceful motion, Afismat, Olektor and Radmund reached their hands outward, sweeping them over the table.

The lines and patterns in the marble swirled, creating new designs, as if the stone had changed to liquid. The Keepers kept their forearms on the table as if it were still solid.

Then Moses spoke. "Knowledge begins with inquiry," he said. "It flows like a river when the mind is open and the heart is ready. Reilly, what is your inquiry?"

A million things raced through Reilly's mind. Every time he'd gone through a portal, he ended up with more questions than answers. This situation frustrated him immensely. Even Afismat hadn't given him a straight answer about his mission. Fortunately, in the past he'd learned to trust the noble creatures, knowing they would help him.

Eighteen of the most educated, prolific, creative, and enlightened men who had ever walked the earth were sitting directly in front of him—and there he was, under Stonehenge, just to learn from them! Sensing that he was going to be there a long time, and eager to begin his tutoring, Reilly did his best to open his mind and heart.

"Are there other Keepers?" He directed his question to Afismat, as she was clearly the leader. She did not reply and waited for another Keeper to answer his questions.

"Indeed, there are," Plato declared. He reached through the swirling designs into a magical hole in the table, pulled out a scroll, and opened it. "This is a record of the complete and current list of Keepers." He looked at the scroll and began to read: "Abraham Lincoln, Mother Theresa, Martin Luther King, Pocahontas, George Washington, Buddha, Emily Dickenson, Thomas Edison, Anne Frank, Vincent van Gough, Amelia Earhart, Mark Twain, Julius Caesar, Helen Keller, Catherine the Great, the first Dalai Lama, and Joan of Arc." He rolled up the scroll. "The list is much longer."

"Why are none of the female Keepers here?" Reilly asked.

"All the Keepers come to the Society upon a Blink," said Shakespeare, who sat beside Plato. "Here, they mingle with the Echtra who summoned them. They may be men or women, boys or girls."

"Are you saying I summoned the Keepers?" Reilly asked.

"Yes, when you were on the steps of the cathedral of knowledge, the place of your enlightenment," said Shakespeare. "There, again, you will find your treasures and ease your soul."

"Why are the eighteen statues outside the Suzzallo Library of you?" Reilly asked, as questions started to roll off his tongue. "Why are none of the other Keepers represented? And why is Afismat the only woman here today?"

All eyes turned to Afismat. "In 1923, Henry Suzzallo, the president of the university at which the magnificent library was built, asked his faculty members to submit names of people in history who they believed were great thinkers and contributors to humankind," she said. "The staff nominated two hundred forty-six people, but the eighteen with the highest number of votes were selected. It was simply a matter of vote by the people, a prudent method of decision-making for a community that wants all to benefit. Prominent reminders of other Keepers are found throughout the world. It is my honor to have been made the Guardian of them all and to oversee their transport after they are Blinked."

"Do Keepers know that they're Keepers when they're still mortal?"

Leonardo da Vinci replied, "It came to my attention long ago that accomplished people rarely sit back and let things happen to them. They go out and make things happen. The noblest of Keepers do not consider themselves superior to others. They have a sense of responsibility and feel that others should benefit from their achievements."

Reilly nodded, trying to grasp the Keepers' erudite replies.

Hugo Grotius leaned forward. "Wisdom does not require knowing all things," he said. "But whenever truth is attained, it demands a deeper sense of responsibility. Keepers are great! However, as mortals, some were not always good, and therefore, they progressed more slowly. Mortals are Blinked only when they have become truly accountable for the truth they have gained."

"Where are the others who are listed on the scroll that Plato read?" Reilly asked.

"They are nearby," said Plato. "The walls of the Society of Keepers limit your view. However, the Shield of Forgotten Memories extends across other rooms similar to this one. Each room remains safe under Stonehenge."

A Keeper who hadn't yet spoken added his contribution. "If we blindly attempt to combine the physical with the spiritual, we fail to find the diversity in nature that is suited to different times and places by the command of the greatest One above us."

Reilly scowled at Isaac Newton, trying to comprehend what he'd said. His brain hurt. How would he be able to grasp everything the Keepers told him? How would he retain all the knowledge they expected him to learn as they tutored him? And how long would it take? He had many more questions, but he directed the next one specifically to Afismat. "Where is the Bleak?"

The angel gave Reilly a look of approval. "Far past the berm and beyond the gulley," she said, fluttering her wings. "There is safety in the light of the Rotunda."

He could tell she wouldn't give any further explanation, so he decided to let it go for the time being. Besides, he was too exhausted to continue, and instead asked his hosts if there was somewhere he could sleep.

"Certainly, Reilly," said Afismat. "Mortals require regular rest and nourishment to rejuvenate the body, mind, and spirit. Follow me."

The Keepers stood up in unison with Reilly and remained standing as he and Afismat, with her wings tucked behind her, exited between the two largest sarsens. The Guardian Angel of all Keepers ushered him into a much smaller room, which, to his surprise, was a perfect replica of his own bedroom at home on Eagle Harbor Drive! His bed was there, his dresser and closet, even the dirty socks and jeans he'd left on the floor before he went with Norah,

Tuma, James, and Chantal to the library. The window revealed a night sky blanketing a front yard, which was exactly like his yard back home. The smell of his mom's home cooking wafted past him, and he spotted a plate of food on his nightstand.

Afismat said, "You are welcome to retreat here whenever you need rest and refreshment during your tutoring. The Keepers will wait for you to return to the Rotunda."

"Thank you," Reilly said, relieved to see a door that led to a bathroom, also just like at home. "This is good."

"May I get you anything else?"

He scanned the room, wondering what else he might need. Then, thinking that he should keep notes on what he learned during his tutoring, he asked for a pen and notebook.

"You have your Fireglass, don't you?" she said.

"Yes, right here." he said, quickly retrieving it from his pocket.

"As you know, the Fireglass can accelerate passage through portals, and it can be used as an aide to read auras. It is also a recording device."

"I didn't know that!" He ran a finger across the smooth brass. "How does it work?"

"Extend it, as you usually do. As the etching of the Stelladaur whirs around the surface, tap the crystal knob at the end until the whirring motion stops."

Excited that his Fireglass could do more remarkable things, he did as Afismat instructed. He tapped the crystal knob a few times until the whirring stopped and watched as the intricate carvings on the surface of the device changed into the letters of the alphabet, arranged like a keypad on a smartphone.

"Can I use it to communicate with my family or friends?" he asked, speaking quickly as his fatigue vanished with his excitement.

"No. Although it functions on a frequency much higher than the archaic devices of your time, it can only be used by an Echtra who has been given the responsibility to care for it."

Reilly held his Fireglass as if it were a small musical instrument, and placed his fingers over the miniature keyboard. Using his thumbs, he typed a message: **Day 1: I came through the portal outside the Suzzallo Library on August 16, 2015. Now I'm in a rotunda under Stonehenge.** He looked through the lens and saw both sentences clearly displayed.

"Wow! This is great!"

"Tap the crystal knob once again and the message will be saved forever. Tap it twice and it will be deleted."

He typed another message and peered into the Fireglass. "Cool!" he said. Then he tapped the knob twice and looked through the lens. The sentence had disappeared.

"I'll leave you now to write, eat and rest," Afismat whispered.

As she left Reilly's mock bedroom, he positioned his fingers over the tiny keyboard. He noted the date that he thought it was and proceeded to write everything that had happened from the time he arrived at the Suzzallo Library with Norah, Tuma, Chantal, and James, and since his solo passage through the portal. He felt compelled to record every detail to the best of his ability. When he finished, he tapped the knob once, retracted his Fireglass, and set it on his nightstand.

He ate the still hot food that filled the air with smells of home. He found fresh towels and pajamas in the bathroom, showered, and finally crawled into bed.

Gazing out the window, he watched the stars twinkle in the night sky—more of them than he'd ever seen before!

But two things were missing—Tuma at the foot of his bed and Norah in his arms.

He fell asleep wondering if the starlight reached the Bleak.

Chapter Eight

Spliced

Reilly woke with the sun streaming in through the window. A plate of freshly cooked bacon and eggs and a warm muffin looked delicious on the nightstand. He ate, showered, and put on the clean pair of jeans, blue plaid button-up shirt, socks, and canvas sneakers that he found in the closet. He grabbed his Fireglass, headed out the door, and found himself right under the two large sarsens in the Rotunda.

The Guardians and Keepers sat around the table, engaged in lively conversation, as if they hadn't left their stone chairs since he last saw them. When they noticed him, they turned their attention to him.

"Come, sit down, Reilly," said Afismat.

"Good morning," he said, buttoning a button he'd missed.

"There is no morning or night under Stonehenge," Afismat replied, correcting him. "Keepers don't need rest or food."

"But there were stars ... and this morning, the sun."

"They function here for enjoyment and comfort, not to keep order as they do in your world."

Reilly opened his Fireglass, tapped the end of the knob several times, and began to key in the new information. **There is no morning or night under Stonehenge. Keepers need no rest or food. The stars and sun only function for our enjoyment and comfort.**

Afismat waited until he finished. "You look rested. Are you ready to continue your tutoring?"

"Yes. But may I keep notes as we go?"

"Of course. The Fireglass can also record everything you see and hear."

"Cool! Like a video!"

"It's more highly advanced than any electronic gadget of your time. The Fireglass captures and records information in complete holograms." She asked Galileo to explain.

"Holograms are created to transport through time," said the astronomer. "They are made of energy that's gathered into visible forms through the reflective lens of materialization. They appear improbable to the untrained eye, but they are not new. Like all truths, holograms have always existed while human beings grow and become skilled at unveiling what they could not see due to their misperceptions of reality. Truth exists regardless of what people think."

Reilly loved science, and what Galileo said fascinated him. "Would you repeat that, please? After someone tells me how to record it."

"Select the key with the icon of the human eye," said Darwin. "The Fireglass has an unlimited storage capacity. You can record holographic data and write notes simultaneously. Press the sunburst icon to replay any hologram and the quill icon to review your notes."

Reilly set the device to record mode, and Galileo repeated his words. Knowing that he could record and then replay any tutoring session later, Reilly relaxed and focused on the lessons.

The Keepers had their own advanced technological devices—scrolls stored inside the swirling liquid surface of the marble table. As Plato had done earlier, they simply reached into the table and pulled one out to write, dictate, and record information. One of the responsibilities of a Keeper was to accurately document the knowledge and wisdom they'd learned as mortals, thus making advanced truths available to all.

The scrolls held the very secrets of Stonehenge!

Reilly realized that he wouldn't know how long he'd been there if he didn't number his entries on his Fireglass. For six hundred thirty-nine days, he trained in the Rotunda with the eighteen Keepers. He studied philosophy, complex mathematics, astronomy, geology, advanced sciences, musical composition, theology, literature, art, and diplomacy. It was an intense curriculum of lectures, discussions, inquiry, scroll study, and hologram observation.

As Guardians, Afismat, Olektor, and Radmund taught Reilly to apply what he learned—how to use his body, mind, and soul physically and metaphysically. Then, for another two hundred twenty-five days, he studied strictly under Dante, Darwin, Moses, and the three Guardians in preparation for his upcoming assignments.

During this time, he dreamed of Norah. He woke countless mornings wondering why he couldn't communicate with her using his highly advanced Fireglass. The Keepers never answered this question. Leonardo wrote an answer on one of the scrolls, but it was perplexing: *Why does the eye see a thing more clearly in dreams than the imagination does when awake?*

Reilly reminded himself that if he eventually qualified as a Stelladaur Ambassador by completing his special mission—whatever that was—every greatest desire could be fulfilled and he could be with those he loved forever.

Reilly often wondered about the tens of thousands of Deceptors who had stolen their way through the last unscrolling and retreated to the Bleak. The Guardians and Keepers insisted he wasn't ready to know. Sometimes he'd gaze out the window into the yard and wish he could open the sealed window and step through a portal to his home. Finally, on his nine-hundredth day under Stonehenge—with nearly three years of training—something changed.

"Reilly, your tutoring is complete!" Afismat declared. "You're now ready to be Spliced!"

She raised her wings high, nodding to Reilly to stand up. The Keepers at the marble table cheered and clapped their hands, making him feel ill prepared for what might occur. He'd waited so long for this day! Now, his anticipation melded into a wave of melancholy. He inhaled deeply and stood up, keeping his hands firmly on the table, as the cheers continued.

"Dante," Afismat shouted above the din, "please join Reilly." Dante strode past the other Keepers. He gave Reilly a hug and slapped his back as a father who hadn't seen his son in years might do.

The Keepers sat back in their chairs, waiting for Afismat's next words.

"The Splicing will occur as you travel to Dante's world through the Shield of Forgotten Memories in a Fraction in Time," she continued. "Splicing is a gift for those who train to be a Stelladaur Ambassador. Therefore, Reilly, remember everything you've learned at the Rotunda and in your life before you arrived here. Dante, however, will not remember his time with his fellow Keepers or with you."

"None of it?" Reilly frowned, slightly unnerved.

"Fractions in Time have affected humans throughout history. When they occur, a vague memory—a fraction of knowledge—comes with a deep longing for a place they are certain exists but don't remember. These Fractions are embedded in the soul of every human child forever."

Reilly nodded. It made sense—and he knew he was ready.

"Your task is to decide how you will rearrange history, and for what purpose. The knowledge you've learned from the Keepers will be accessible to you as you listen to your Stelladaur within."

Reilly was confident that he had the Keepers' support, but he also felt completely alone.

"Come this way." Reilly and Dante followed Afismat, with Olektor and Radmund behind them.

Passing between the largest sarsens, they stepped into a vast open space. Reilly had never seen it before, though he was certain he'd explored every sarsen at Stonehenge. An ornate suspended staircase ascended gradually in front of them, up to the Shield of Forgotten Memories. The eighteen Keepers were posed on both sides of the staircase like the statues on the exterior wall of the Suzzallo Library. The surface of the Shield, brighter than usual, cast a golden glow on the stairs. Dante placed a hand on Reilly's shoulder as they gazed up at it.

"It has been my honor to be one of your main mentors. Choose wisely during your assignment to rearrange my history. If you accomplish this feat, you will be one step closer to becoming a Stelladaur Ambassador."

Olektor bowed to Reilly. "As Guardian of the Body, I give you strength," he said.

"As Guardian of the Mind, I give you clarity," said Radmund.

"And as Guardian of the Soul, I give you tranquility," Afismat whispered.

Anxious to start his first assignment, Reilly stepped forward and began to climb the stairs. As he passed the Keepers, he heard them whisper to a melody in unison, *"Even the rocks thrill with memories of past events. The very dust beneath your feet responds more lovingly to our footsteps because it is the ashes of our ancestors. The soil is rich with the life of our kindred."*

Yes, he knew he was ready!

Reilly reached the Shield of Forgotten Memories and bent forward to step through it—first his head, then his shoulders, his torso, his right foot, and then …

Reilly's body was painlessly Spliced and transported to Florence, Italy. It was the year 1275.

"Are you well, baker?" A young boy, about ten years old, waved a hand in front of Reilly's face. "You look unusually pale, Raimondo." The boy snapped his fingers in front of his eyes. "Sir, are you all right?"

The youngster's face was just inches from his own. Reilly blinked, and the child's deep brown eyes and dark eyebrows came into focus.

"I'm not quite myself today," he muttered. Inhaling the smell of oregano, basil and rosemary was rejuvenating.

"Shall I summon a physician?"

"That won't be necessary."

Reilly stepped back to gather his thoughts. He remembered walking up the long stairway and through the Shield of Forgotten Memories. He remembered Stonehenge and the Society of Keepers. In a flash, he remembered it all. Yet nowhere had he learned that being Spliced meant others would recognize him as someone who was already in their life. He had never heard the name Raimondo, but the child in front of him was Dante.

"We've conversed here at the marketplace every day of the academic semester," Dante said. "Yet, I've never seen you so pallid."

A goat bleated and ran past, brushing Reilly's legs. The market teamed with peasants bartering with customers. Reilly stood in front of baskets filled with apples, plums, pears and figs. Behind the fruit he spotted larger baskets with cabbages and turnips. He noticed an open stall a few feet away where he spotted a row of dead chickens hanging on a rope. He heard the squeal of a pig being slaughtered in what must be an alley or courtyard behind him. He inhaled deeply again, now smelling the stench of animals rather than savory herbs, as he tried to regain his composure.

"Please accept my apologies, Dante," Reilly said. His own formal speech sounded awkward.

"Certainly. No apology is required," Dante replied. "Now that I know you are in good health, I must make my purchases and be on my way. When pupils are tardy, the schoolmaster expels them from the learning hall to a small room in the monastery, where there is little light. I've been there once and do not wish to return."

"Then you'd best make your purchases."

Dante eyed the apples. "Have you decided what you will bake for the May Day celebration tomorrow night? Father insists that I join him, and that doing so will lift my spirits." He picked up a pear and tossed it back and forth in his hands. "I don't understand why he believes a festival will distract my mind. It's been over two years now, and I still think it's truly unfair that God took her from me."

Reilly had learned that Dante's mother died when he was seven years old. "It's a cruel circumstance indeed when a young boy has lost his mother," Reilly said, thinking, *I wonder how old I am, now that I'm Raimondo.*

Dante held the pear in one hand and scooped up a handful of figs with the other. He showed them to the merchant and placed them in the leather pouch at his side. Reaching into his pocket for coins to pay the man, he turned to Reilly. "The fig cake my father ordered from you last month for his house guests was delicious. If you bake that for the May Day festival, then I'll go with my father."

"Fig cake it is!" said Reilly. "Now hurry to school so you won't be tardy."

Reilly watched as the boy ran through the market along the cobbled street, dodging barrels, baskets, and hanging pottery, and disappeared out of site.

He tapped his leather slippers on the ground and lifted each foot to see the straps that laced them. He tugged on his green tunic in a failed attempt to cover his thighs and scratched his tights below his knees. Fumbling in the folds of fabric that fell beneath the cord tied around his waist, he hoped to find a pocket with his Fireglass. He found no pockets. No Fireglass. Even his golden thread bracelet was gone. He reached into the large leather bag draped over his shoulder to search the contents. The satchel was empty except for a handful of coins.

Realizing he'd been Spliced as a Florentine baker, Reilly figured that buying ingredients for a fig cake would be a good place to start. He purchased two-dozen figs and meandered through the market looking for other basic ingredients. No milled flour was available, but he found various whole-grains: wheat, oats, barley and rye. He bought some wheat, fresh butter and eggs from a woman at the far end of the market. With his satchel half full, he turned onto a side street that led away from the market.

Reilly admired the intricate craftsmanship of the cobblestone streets and wondered what those rocks might say. What stories could they tell?

He reached a wide road and recognized it as the city's business center from one of the holograms Dante had shown him, with the bank where his father worked in front of him. As he approached the main doors, a well-dressed man exited and stopped in front of Reilly.

"Raimondo Gustalini! What is your business here?" The man chuckled, as if seeing Raimondo at a bank was humorous.

Reilly was stunned by the surname the man had used to greet him. Gustalini was Norah's last name! Her father was in prison for his involvement with the Mafia, and she lived with her uncle,

Martino Gustalini, after her mother died in a car accident—which she believed was not really an accident at all.

Do family names really go back this far? Reilly wondered. Why was Raimondo a *Gustalini*?

Reilly shifted the satchel higher on his shoulder. "I thought I might speak with Alighiero of Bellincione, knowing that he is employed at this establishment. I just spoke with his son, Dante, at the market."

Reilly knew the man was Folco Portinari, the owner of the bank. Folco employed Raimondo as the family chef and baker. "Dante requested that I bake a fig cake for the spring festival, which I understand you've invited his father and him to attend. Perhaps Alighiero has a request, too."

"*Sei un bravo ragazzo!*" Folco said. "You're clever indeed! I will ask Alighiero myself and apprise you of his wishes. I suggest that you also inquire from Cilia and Beatrice when you return to the estate. They will likely prefer a loaf of your fine hazelnut bread."

Reilly nodded, knowing Cilia de Caponsacchi and Folco Portinari were Beatrice's parents. In the Rotunda, Dante had told Reilly about Beatrice—the woman he had loved but did not marry.

"It's already midmorning," said Folco. "You have little time to prepare today's dinner."

"Yes, of course. Everything will be ready, as usual, at midday."

Reilly returned to the market to buy hazelnuts, pork, and fresh fruit for the day's main meal. With his satchel full of food, he walked the streets of Florence towards the home of Dante's beloved Beatrice, knowing the two had not yet met.

There was no mistake about it! Reilly, as Raimondo Gustalini, would indeed rearrange history.

Chapter Nine

Heaven's Rose

hree miles beyond the edge of town, Reilly arrived at a rock
wall nearly four feet high, which surrounded the Portinari
estate. The soaring rectangular building with its terracotta
pantile roof was smaller than a castle, but larger than any house
Reilly had seen on Bainbridge Island. It was a mansion. He walked
towards the back of the property, rather than past the ornate arched
main entrance, passing other hired help at work. The gardener was
pruning a hedge. A stable-hand was brushing a palomino-colored
mare in the stable. He looked up and saw a woman standing on a
small balcony, beating a rug with a straw broom. In a sunny corner at the back of the estate, another woman was hanging clean
laundry on a clothesline. A few chickens scurried about as Reilly
walked towards a side entrance.

A young girl bounded through the doorway into the yard. "What took you so long, Raimondo?" she squealed, gathering her skirts. "My harp lesson was completed an hour ago. You didn't hear my new piece."

"My apologies, Beatrice." Reilly was still amazed that people knew him as Raimondo Gustalini. Being Spliced to rearrange history required that he be incognito. For them, he talked and looked just like the young baker, who Reilly determined was in his early twenties.

"I'm sure the music was as beautiful as you are," he said, winking at Beatrice. He lowered the satchel to the ground and reached into it. "See what I brought you from the market."

"Hazelnuts! My favorite!" said Beatrice, her emerald eyes sparkling in the morning sun.

"Your father suggested that I bake hazelnut bread for the celebration tomorrow night. Would you like that?"

"Yes!" she said, clapping her hands.

Reilly couldn't take his eyes off of the girl. Her slightly unruly, long auburn hair, slender nose, and ivory skin reminded him of Norah, and he wondered if this was what she looked like as a child. Beatrice's vivacious enthusiasm drew Reilly in.

"Very well, I will make a whole loaf just for you."

Beatrice hugged Reilly around his waist. "Thank you!"

"Perhaps you can play your new harp melody at the celebration," he said, patting her on the back. "Today I talked with a boy named Dante, a friend of mine who will be at the celebration with his father."

"A boy?"

"He's nine, just a year older than you. He attends the school at the monastery near your father's bank. His father is a banker, too."

"I might be anxious playing my harp in front of a boy."

"I'll introduce you. Perhaps he'll be a friend." Reilly handed

Beatrice a hazelnut. "I need to prepare dinner promptly. Your father will be home soon."

Reilly was relieved that he could find his way around the medieval kitchen so easily. His training at Blackberry Bakers couldn't have prepared him for the rigors of thirteenth-century cookery and baking. Fortunately, he'd had glimpses of medieval life when Dante's holograms showed him poetic relationships between food and love, and demonstrated how food was cooked over an open fire and in brick ovens.

Like everyone else he'd met, the members of the Portinari household treated him as Raimondo, someone very dear to Cilia. She showed favoritism towards him, though none of the other staff objected. His sleeping quarters were larger and located on the main floor of the home, and on his first night in Florence, he slept well.

A rooster crowed at sunrise and Reilly was glad for the wake-up call. His workday began, making an early breakfast for the family. He spent the remainder of the day in the kitchen, preparing for the May Day celebration. At mid-afternoon, Beatrice arrived carrying a basket of flowers.

"Mother allowed me to take the afternoon away from my studies to gather these flowers for the festival." She put the basket on a side table and sat down. "I'm going to make a wreath for my hair."

"That's a fine idea," Reilly said as he continued to chop figs. "You will be lovely, indeed."

She giggled as she separated the flowers by color and laid them in piles. "Have you seen the ballroom yet? It's decorated so fancily. I do love parties!"

Reilly stopped chopping to look at her, taken with her precociousness. "No, I haven't seen it yet. When the fig cakes are in the oven, I'll have some time. Would you like to show me then?"

"I would."

Reilly cracked five eggs and whipped them in a bowl, while Beatrice chatted about where she'd picked the flowers and added ribbons to her hairpiece. When his work was done, he wiped his hands on a linen towel. "I'm ready for the ballroom tour," he said.

"Me, too," she chimed, lifting the wreath to her head. "It's done! What do you think?"

"I think you are as pretty as a princess."

She laughed and fidgeted with the wreath to make it stay on her head with the ribbons trailing down her back. When she was content that it would stay, she reached for Reilly's hand.

They walked through the main library, passing a stone fireplace that covered half the length of the room, and entered the ballroom through a side door. As the master chef, Raimondo often used secret passageways to deliver food to various rooms on special occasions, or when Folco or Cilia entertained guests.

Decorating the back wall of the ballroom were grand floral arrangements displayed on long tables draped with colorful silks. Dozens of bronze candlesticks with intricate designs, some shaped like animals, sat in wall niches lined with decorative tiles. Seven iron chandeliers with beeswax candles hung from the towering stone ceiling.

After surveying the space on the empty tables where he would lay the food, Reilly lifted Beatrice's hand. "May I dance with the princess?"

"You're silly, Raimondo," Beatrice said. "There is no music."

"Nevertheless, the cook is not permitted to dance among the guests, so I will not be joining in the festivities." He twirled her around in a single dance move.

Beatrice curled her bottom lip. She let go of his hand and skipped around him, humming. With a sudden deep sadness, Reilly watched the ribbons flow around Beatrice.

He hadn't learned all there was to know about time travel yet, nevertheless, he knew he would live as Raimondo for years before he would meet the Society of Keepers in the Rotunda again. It would be even longer before he would see Norah. How would he survive being gone from her for so long? Would Norah be there when he returned home? Or would she have fallen in love with someone else? He pushed the ominous thoughts out of his mind and replaced them with hope: *Of course, she'll be there!*

"That's a lovely tune," he said.

"It's the new melody I learned to play on the harp."

A light flashed in Reilly's mind! Beatrice *must* play the harp that night for Dante! Historically, Dante fell in love with Beatrice the moment he saw her, when she was only seven, but he didn't speak with her until years later. This was the first glitch in Dante's story that Reilly had to adjust.

He reached out to stop Beatrice from twirling. "Beatrice, my little princess," he said, bending down so his eyes met hers, "since I am not permitted to dance at the celebration, would you please me by playing the harp so that I may hear it along with the guests?"

Beatrice playfully pretended to scowl and then threw her arms around Reilly's neck. "Of course, Raimondo."

"Wonderful!" He picked her up and swung her around. "I'll request your mother to add this to her program for the event. I'm sure she'll be delighted by the opportunity to show your talent."

Reilly still wasn't used to the way Raimondo spoke, but so far, he seemed to be the only one who had any idea that Raimondo wasn't quite himself.

After delivering a large basket of hazelnut bread to the ballroom, Reilly met Cilia in the entrance hall and took the opportunity to speak with her.

"What a lovely idea, Raimondo," she said. "You have been like a big brother to Beatrice and have shown her nothing but kindness since she was born. It seems but yesterday that you joined our staff as a young apprentice in the kitchen, yet you have been with us for over eight years!" Cilia examined the ruffles on the sleeves at her wrists. "Indeed, Beatrice shall play her harp as her farewell song to our guests, because she is too young to stay up for the entire night's celebration."

Reilly went to the kitchen to get trays of cheese, butter, and more artisan breads from the pantry. He was glad the butler managed the buttery in the cellar, where beer, ale, and wine were stored. The stench of alcohol churned Reilly's stomach ever since Travis Jackson had breathed drunkenly in his face.

Like this memory, subtle and strange hints of life as Reilly would pop up unexpectedly. They made him keenly aware of the gifts from Afismat, Olektor and Radmund and helped him stay focused on his assignment. Reilly was there to rearrange history and perform a *remarkable physical feat* and a *battle of the mind*. Could he *give everything* he had? What did it mean? Would it be enough?

He made a point of staying busy, arranging fruits and cheeses around the fig cakes, as he watched for Alighiero and Dante to arrive. Beatrice flitted about the room, her hair bouncing behind her, tangled in the long ribbons of her flower wreath. Minstrels wandered through the ballroom entertaining small groups of guests, while a juggler and two jesters captivated larger audiences at one end.

Folco approached Reilly with a pewter wine goblet in his hand. "I haven't seen Alighiero and his son yet. Have you?"

"No. I've been watching for them." Reilly raised himself on his toes. "It's difficult to see over the ladies' headdresses."

"Indeed, it is!" Folco chuckled.

"There they are! Dante and his father have arrived." Reilly signaled their location to Folco.

The host meandered through the crowd to greet Alighiero and some other guests who were arriving late, while Reilly waited at his post near the banquet tables. He scanned the room for Beatrice but didn't see her. Soon Dante and his father noticed Raimondo and wound their way towards him.

"Pleased to see you, sir," Reilly said, bowing slightly. "And you, as well, Dante." The boy nodded, eyeing the fig cakes.

"Thank you, Raimondo," said Alighiero. "Folco has expressed satisfaction with your services. I can see why." He reached for a handful of grapes and admired the display of platters. "I wish my cook were as competent."

Suddenly, Beatrice skipped into view, twirling her ribbons. As she reached for a slice of her favorite hazelnut bread, she lost her balance and fell into Dante's backside, bumping him towards the fig cakes. Startled, she squealed and jumped to hide behind Reilly. Bewildered, Dante lifted his hands out of two ruined cakes and turned around, holding his sticky fingers away from his body. With eyes wide, he exclaimed, "What happened?"

Alighiero laughed heartily. Reilly reached behind his back and gently pulled Beatrice forward until she stood between himself and Dante.

"May I introduce the daughter of Folco and Cilia? The lovely Beatrice."

Beatrice lowered her head.

"Child, you are a sprite!" Alighiero chuckled. "With ribbons and all!"

Reilly's attention was on Dante, whose eyes were fixed on Beatrice. Instantly smitten, as expected, the boy dropped his sticky hands and clasped them behind his back.

"My apologies, sir," Beatrice said, pushing her hair and a few ribbons from her face so she could see who had called her a sprite.

Her eyes met Dante's. Embarrassed, she shifted her attention back to the boy's father, who said, "No harm done. Dante is fond of fig cake."

Chagrined upon hearing his father tell the girl his name, Dante diverted his attention away from her. Reilly intervened. "Come with me to the kitchen, Dante, where you can wash your hands."

Dante nodded. His eyes returned to Beatrice, who nervously twisted a ribbon, trying to ignore him.

"A good suggestion!" said Alighiero. "I must speak with some of the other guests this evening. So many people are here that it may be a challenge to see everyone." He craned his neck. "Raimondo, have you seen Manetto Donati?"

"The statesman?"

"Yes, of course."

"I saw him and his wife speaking with Cilia," Reilly said, pointing to the far end of the room, where a small crowd had gathered around a juggler.

"Very well. Dante, there's plenty of entertainment to enjoy after your visit to the kitchen. Raimondo, I leave my son with you for now," said Alighiero as he turned to join the other guests.

"Come with us," Reilly said to Beatrice as he reached for the platter of the two smashed fig cakes. "You might like to freshen up before your performance."

Realizing that Dante was the boy Raimondo had told her about, but not wanting to appear overly shy, Beatrice smiled.

Reilly held Beatrice's hand behind him as they made their way through the crowd. Dante walked beside him, glancing twice over his shoulder at the young girl. Once they were in the hallway that led to the kitchen, Beatrice stepped to Reilly's other side.

"Dante, how was school today?" Reilly asked, hoping to engage the two children in conversation.

"It was fine enough, though the classes failed to capture my passion for literature and poetry."

Knowing the significant literary and philosophical contribution Dante would give to humanity, Reilly had to stop himself from laughing out loud. "Yes, you're certainly passionate about those subjects. Didn't you recently tell me of your interest in becoming a physician, as well?"

"Yes. Father said that if I do well in my studies, I will be able to attend the University of Bologna. I intend to do just that."

Reilly watched the boy peer at Beatrice, hoping she was impressed by his ambition. The children didn't speak to each other as they walked, but while Dante washed the sticky fig cake from his hands, he tried to catch her eye as she rearranged her hair wreath.

Still hoping Dante and Beatrice might speak directly to each other, Reilly came up with a reason to excuse himself. "I need to prepare another platter of cheeses from the pantry. Beatrice, please assist Dante in finding his way back to the ballroom. I'm sure neither of you wants to miss any of the festivities."

Beatrice jumped, surprised by Reilly's suggestion. "Will you be there in time to hear my performance, Raimondo?"

"Oh, yes. I won't be too long."

Dante and Beatrice returned to the ballroom in an awkward silence. Once there, Beatrice spotted her mother and dashed to meet her, leaving Dante alone.

When Reilly arrived with the platter of cheese, Dante approached him and leaned in to whisper in his ear. "She's the most beautiful girl I've ever seen."

"Beatrice is my little princess," Reilly said softly. "I've known her since the day she was born."

"Someday I'll make her my queen," Dante said.

Reilly sighed. "Sometimes it seems to take forever to get what we want most."

"I'm not yet ten years old, and she's a year younger than I," said Dante. "I may have to wait ten years for her—but I'll wait forever, if I must."

A hush came over the room as Beatrice's father, standing on a raised platform opposite Reilly's tables, clapped his hands loudly to draw the attention of his guests. "Ladies and gentlemen," he said. "Cilia would like to make a special announcement about this evening's program."

Cilia stood next to her husband and curtsied before she spoke. "Our daughter, Beatrice, must soon retire for the evening. However, before she leaves, she will play a musical piece on the harp that she prepared for your enjoyment." Cilia gracefully swept her arm towards Beatrice, who sat nearby with her harp.

Dante pushed through the crowd and stood at the edge of the circle of guests around Beatrice and her parents. Reilly made his way towards Beatrice, too.

"My dear, please introduce the piece to our guests," Celia said, placing her hand on the child's back and nudging her gently.

Beatrice stood up and bobbed twice in a girlish curtsy. "I shall play for you 'Heaven's Rose.'"

Reilly's heart skipped a beat. In his studies, he had learned that Dante, in his most famous poem, *The Divine Comedy: Paradiso*, wrote of a Celestial Rose—a place in the eternal spheres where the blessed and chosen souls could live in peace.

Beatrice began to play.

Reilly watched Dante intently. The boy was transfixed, as if the words to *Paradiso* were coming to him in a vision at that very moment. But he wouldn't write the poem until after Beatrice's untimely death, and he wouldn't finish it until just before his own, over thirty years later.

As Reilly listened to Beatrice play *Heaven's Rose* on her harp—and watched Dante fall in love with her—he grasped the significance of Afismat and Olektor's description of the Stelladaur Ambassador. Accomplishing a remarkable feat to rearrange history and keep it from repeating itself would take an extraordinarily long time. It would require extreme patience. Reilly cringed at the uncertainty and pain it would cause him and others.

As the notes of Beatrice's harp resounded in the room, Reilly knew in his heart that rearranging Dante's history had as much to do with keeping Raimondo Gustalini alive as it did with keeping Dante and Beatrice together.

Chapter Ten

A Secret

The guests burst into applause when Beatrice finished playing. She stood up, curtsied, and lifted her eyes to meet Dante's. The boy stepped forward, but other guests blocked his way, clamoring to shower Beatrice with praise. By the time he could squeeze through them, Cilia had escorted the girl out of the ballroom.

Distraught, Dante approached Reilly near the banquet table.

"I must see her again!" Dante declared with a fervor like that of someone twice his age. "Raimondo, what shall I do?"

To Reilly, there was a fine line between rearranging history and changing it. He decided part of his responsibility was to help Dante discover something he could do to change his own life.

"Sometimes the greatest accomplishment begins with the smallest gesture," Reilly said.

"What do you mean?"

"She smiled at you."

"Yes! She did! It may have appeared as a small gesture, yet to me it was as big as the Tyrrhenian Sea!"

"If you could give her the Tyrrhenian Sea, I expect you would."

Dante patted the belt around his waist, searching for something. He twisted it to bring a small pouch in front of his stomach. Relaxing the leather drawstring, he scanned the room to be sure none of the guests were watching. Most had begun to dance, and no one else stood near the banquet table. He reached into the pouch.

"I will give this treasure to Beatrice," he said, holding a smooth black rock in the palm of his hand. "I found it at the seashore on holiday with my father and mother. I was young, about six years old. Mother told me it had become smooth because the sea had tossed it for centuries, wearing away the rough edges." He closed his fingers over the stone. "She died soon afterwards, and I've kept the rock with me ever since. I am like this rock, tumbling in a dark sea."

Reilly listened intently.

Dante opened his hand and held the stone between two fingers. "Do you see the white lines? They are three intersecting rings. Mother said they represent the past, present, and future, converging at the same moment in time, when the rock was polished. She said rocks keep the secrets of the sea, the earth, and the stars."

Dante handed the stone to Reilly.

"Do you think that's just a silly fable?" the boy asked.

"Not at all. You can't imagine how much sense it makes to me."

"Please give it to Beatrice," Dante whispered. "I will also write a poem for her, to tell of my love for her." Dante froze, fearful that someone in the room had overheard him. "But you must keep my secret!"

Reilly grasped the stone tightly in his fist, knowing it was as precious to Dante as was the ruby that Reilly gave to Norah, which later saved her life.

"That's more than a small gesture, Dante."

A week passed before Reilly saw Dante again. He was at the market, on his way to school.

"I finished the poem for Beatrice," the boy said, clutching a scroll tied with twine. "Will you give it to her today?"

"Certainly." Reilly put his basket on the ground, took the scroll, and tucked it in between the avocados and red peppers.

"Has she spoken of me?"

"She asked me if you heard her play the harp. Afterwards, she couldn't find you in the crowd."

"What did you tell her?"

"I told her that indeed you heard her play, and you tried to reach her after the performance but she'd already left the ballroom."

"Anything else?"

"No. I'll keep your secret, even from her. You must be the one to tell her your feelings for her."

"When will I have the chance? I have no reason to go to Beatrice's home. That was the only celebration my father attended there. Festivals are usually held at *my* father's estate."

It was strange for Reilly to glimpse himself through Dante's eyes. Even though others saw and heard Raimondo as he'd always been, Reilly felt like Reilly. Being Spliced gave rise to new questions about time travel. *Has Raimondo gone somewhere else? Or are we coexisting in this body, without Raimondo knowing anything has changed?*

"You'll have other chances, Dante. But chance is not luck or happenstance, as some might think. Chance is the moment between waiting to do something because you're not sure it's what you want—or even whether it's the best thing to do—and jumping in and just doing it. Chance can also be *not* taking an action, and trusting that decision. Chance is decision perfectly aligned with destiny."

Dumbfounded, Dante stared at the baker.

"I'll give Beatrice the stone and the poem today," Reilly said, picking up his basket.

"Thank you, Raimondo. I hope my gifts will thrill her."

Reilly hadn't heard the word "thrill" since the Keepers recited their oath as he climbed the stairs to the Shield of Forgotten Memories. "They will, Dante," he said. "Your mother was right—rocks hold secrets."

That afternoon, Beatrice waltzed into the kitchen and found Reilly on his hands and knees.

"Hello," she said cheerfully. "What are you doing?"

"Today, the kitchen staff have the afternoon off, and they went to a country fair, leaving me to do all the work. I'm picking up scraps for the pigs. Would you like to help?"

Beatrice plugged her nose. "No thank you. Pigs are stinky!"

Reilly threw his head back, laughing. "This certainly is not a job for my princess." He winked at her. "But I do have something perfect for a princess—or at least a little girl who may have stolen a boy's heart."

"Dante? Something from Dante?" She jumped up and down, holding her skirt in one hand. Then catching herself, she stopped to confide in Reilly. "I think about him all the time," she whispered.

Reilly walked to the pantry. He had folded a flaxen cloth around Dante's gifts and hidden the parcel behind jars of nuts and dried fruit. He returned with it to the worktable in the center of the kitchen, where Beatrice waited eagerly.

"Dante asked me to give these to you." Reilly unfolded the cloth and handed her the stone. She turned it over, admiring the smooth surface, and tracing the white lines with her finger. "And this." He handed her the scroll.

She clutched the gifts to her chest.

"I'll let you read it alone, as I have an appointment with the pigs," he said, picking up the bucket of scraps.

When Reilly returned to the kitchen, Beatrice was gone. He took a ball of lye to go about his work. While he was scrubbing the worktable, Beatrice walked back in carrying something in her hands.

"I have a gift for Dante," she said timidly. "I hope he'll like it as much I as like the stone … and the poem."

She opened her hands and showed Reilly a pile of pressed tiny blue flowers.

"I saved them from my wreath the night I met Dante," she explained, "so that I wouldn't forget that night. They're forget-me-nots. Will you give them to him?"

"Certainly."

Reilly was struck by the innocence of the young girl and her affection for a boy she hadn't even spoken with. He was reminded that pure love transcends time and age—it has no limits. He hoped his love for Norah, and her love for him, would remain transcendent.

"Perhaps they'll inspire him to write more poems," Beatrice said eagerly.

"Inspiration comes from simplicity," he said. "It's the perfect gift."

Beatrice carefully spilled the flowers into his hand.

"They're very delicate," she said, not knowing this was a reflection of herself.

"I have just the thing to keep them safe." Reilly walked towards the pantry to retrieve a small wooden box on the shelf. He lifted the lid and turned the box upside down to empty it. "This herb box will do the trick. There was just a bit of thyme left inside." He laughed at the irony of what he'd said. "Don't worry, Princess, another time will come for you and Dante to meet again."

Beatrice pulled a blue silk ribbon from her hair. "Tie this around the box … to keep the lid secure."

Reilly did as she requested, wondering if this might be a thread of time itself that would bind Dante and Beatrice together. He glanced at his wrist, as if his own golden thread were still tied to it, and was silently grateful for being allowed to know Beatrice.

The following morning Reilly met Dante at the market.

"Raimondo, you're a true friend!" Dante exclaimed, looking at the box tied with the gold ribbon. "I can't tell another soul of my feelings for Beatrice. My classmates would tease me relentlessly, and my father is too old to understand. He still believes in the old-fashioned custom of arranged marriages. It's a tradition I don't wish to endure."

"Nor would I like it," said Reilly.

Raimondo was more than twice Dante's age, but the boy seemed so much older than nine.

"Do you love someone?" Dante asked, leaning forward as if Reilly was going to tell him a secret.

Reilly hesitated before he nodded and replied, "Yes."

"What's her name?"

"Norah."

"Does she live in Florence? Where did you meet her? May I meet her? When will you marry her?"

"So many questions!" Reilly laughed out loud. "Sometimes you are a lot like me."

"Tell me about Norah."

"Norah doesn't live in Florence. I met her in a city far from here, when I was … employed as a baker … in another household. She lives there now. I don't know when I'll see her again, but I miss her fiercely. Does that answer all your questions?"

"Almost all. When will you marry her?"

Reilly turned abruptly to select some apples from a barrel next to him. Marriage was a big decision. He was only seventeen!

Wasn't he? Of course, he wanted to be with Norah every minute of his life—and forever. He decided the word 'fiercely' accurately described how much he missed her.

The more he thought about it, the more he thought marriage was a great idea. If a boy who wasn't yet ten years old could be truly in love and know whom he intended to marry, then so could he. Besides, by the time Reilly returned home, he might actually be much older than he was when he left.

On the other hand, sometimes he was afraid that Norah would move on without him. He might already have been gone for years without her hearing a word from him. The grim thought began to haunt him.

The amount of present time that passed when a person was Spliced to the thirteenth century was a topic Reilly had never been allowed to discuss with the Keepers. He bit into an apple and made a firm decision.

"I'll ask her to marry me as soon as I see her."

Dante placed the herb box in his school satchel. "We're both in the same predicament," he said with a sigh.

"Predicament? What a large vocabulary you have for a youngster."

Ignoring the teasing, Dante continued. "I have no idea when I'll next see Beatrice, and you don't know when you'll see Norah."

"No," said Reilly. "No, I don't."

Chapter Eleven

Betrothal

Weeks turned to months, and the months never seemed to end. For almost three years, Reilly worked in the kitchen at the Portinari estate. Occasionally he hiked on nearby trails or wandered through the estate gardens. He took up horseback riding, which allowed him to explore the lush Tuscan countryside. Riding horses didn't have the same calming effect on him as kayaking near Bainbridge Island had, but it was a diversion from the monotony of life in a medieval kitchen.

He did his best to consciously notice the good in his situation, but on some days he missed Norah terribly and depression overwhelmed him, so that finding anything positive about his circumstances required a huge mental effort. Without his Stelladaur,

Fireglass, or any other device or token that he'd had before, he could rely solely on his instincts and previous experiences to cope. Even the gifts of strength, clarity, and tranquility had faded.

Strangely, there were times when he missed the pain that had seared through him in Black Castle with the mere thought of Norah. The pain had given him something to fight against. Now, mustering the energy to face his loneliness without her was grueling. When he was alone, he'd hum their song, which had given him strength to face the Deceptors and rescue her. Now, it brought hardly a modicum of hope.

Reilly desperately wished he had some way to communicate with her. He spent countless hours trying to think of a solution, but despite his intense tutoring, nothing came to mind. His imagination wasn't as fluid as it had been before. It took a tremendous effort even to imagine that she was there with him, and then, the images were vague. He assumed that passing through the Shield of Forgotten Memories had actually blocked his memory.

It was at night, in his dreams, that he could see her clearly, and relive moments when they were together. When that happened, he would wake up with the fleeting feeling that she would always be with him.

The days became a nightmare of uncertainty. Stuck eight hundred years in the past, Reilly had to endure time passing at an insufferably slow speed.

Reilly also thought it was peculiar that in all the years he'd been in Florence, no Deceptors had confronted him. Perhaps their influence on an Echtra who had been Spliced was limited. Or maybe the demons simply mistook him for Raimondo and had no interest in an unassuming baker. However, based on his travel through other portals, he knew the status quo could change. Change—he had learned in a different time and place—was inevitable and impending.

Lately the demons he fought were in his mind.

Reilly would see Dante passing through the market on his way to school. The boy gave him new poems for Beatrice, which made her love him all the more, even though they hadn't seen each other since the night they met. Reilly kept their secret.

It became clear to Reilly that the reason he'd been Spliced was to ensure that Dante married Beatrice, but they were still preteens in their present time. Soon after Dante's twelfth birthday, he brought the news that Reilly had been expecting.

"Raimondo!" Dante shouted. Reilly was buying bacon from the butcher. "My father has announced a betrothal party for me—but I'm *not* to marry Beatrice!" The butcher raised his brow but pretended to ignore their conversation.

In the Rotunda, Reilly had learned that Dante's destiny was to marry Gemma. He hadn't anticipated the utter despair on the boy's face at the thought of being betrothed to a girl he didn't love.

"Be calm, Dante," Reilly said.

"Calm? My heart is shattered. It lies in fragments!" he cried. "Without Beatrice, I cannot live!"

Reilly put a hand on Dante's shoulder. "Does your father know of your love for Beatrice?"

"No, you are the only one who knows. She hasn't told anyone of our secret letters, either."

Reilly caught the butcher cocking his ear towards them as he wrapped the bacon. He paid and led Dante to a quiet alley where they could speak privately.

"Tell me the details of the coming event," he said to the boy.

"The papers will be signed before a notary at an engagement party in two weeks, on the ninth of February. I have no say in the matter. My father first discussed the arrangement with Manetto Donati at the May Day celebration three years ago. Manetto's daughter, Gemma, didn't attend Folco's party because she and her mother were taking care of a cousin who was ill. I've never met

Gemma, and now I must marry her! Father has already spoken to Folco about hiring you to cater the banquet. Did you know this?"

"He hasn't mentioned anything about it."

"My father and Manetto planned my marriage with Gemma to solidify their political agendas. How can he care merely about money and his political reputation?"

"The news must be excruciating," Reilly said, truly understanding the boy's anxiety. "I know you love Beatrice with all your heart. You've trusted me with your secret and I've honored it. Now I ask that you honor me with your trust."

"What do you mean?" said Dante.

"I'll help you, Dante. You will *not* marry Gemma, but you'll need to submit to the betrothal."

"That doesn't make sense!"

"You must trust me," said Reilly.

"Gemma's dowry deed has already been drawn up. Once the papers are signed, the betrothal will be legally binding. I'll have to marry Gemma in six years, when I am eighteen."

"Much can happen in six years' time. I'll bring Beatrice with me to the betrothal ceremony on the ninth as my assistant. She's been depressed lately, and her parents don't know why. Of course, it's because she wishes she could see you. You've become close friends through the letters you've shared."

"*Dear* friends," Dante corrected.

"Folco and Cilia will surely attend the event to offer their congratulations, and since Beatrice loves parties, bringing her along would be a logical solution to lighten her sadness. Furthermore, I'll suggest that she be permitted to be my assistant for the day."

Dante beamed with hope. "That's a wonderful idea, Raimondo! Finally, I'll see her. But this time, I must speak with her."

For the next two weeks Reilly ruminated over what he could do to ensure that Dante and Beatrice had a few private minutes together at the betrothal party. He had to trust that some feasible idea would come to mind.

Beatrice's melancholy mood changed dramatically when he told her of his conversation with Dante. After hearing that she would attend the event, she nearly floated around the Portinari estate.

On the day of the betrothal, Reilly and Beatrice arrived at the Donati mansion at mid-morning and spent all day with the staff, preparing food for the engagement festival. While cutting spinach in the garden, they caught a glimpse of Gemma sitting on the veranda.

"She's pretty," Beatrice said, "but she looks unhappy."

"Maybe she doesn't like this arrangement either," Reilly said.

"Maybe she's in love with someone else, too. It's a wretched thing for parents to decide whom their children will marry! Why is marriage used for political bargaining, as if a country is at war with itself?"

That was the answer! What if Dante and Beatrice went to another country? Reilly could devise a plan for their escape from Italy to a place of voluntary exile—a place where neither the Portinaris nor the Donatis would ever find the devoted couple. The plan was brilliant.

Reilly was filled with hope. Then a myriad of questions peppered his mind: *What country? How would they escape? When would they leave? Did they love each other enough to leave their homes and families, just to be together? How will I assure their safe passage?*

Was this the *remarkable physical feat* he must perform?

It wasn't unusual for Reilly to be tormented by difficult questions. But if he'd learned anything about finding answers, it was that they came at precisely the right time, in just the right way, when he was perfectly prepared for them.

"Countries don't engage in war. People do," he said. "Competition breeds discontent, selfishness, greed, and even hatred—like a plague. Marriage can be an ally or a decoy that strips the sanctity of the vow between a man and a woman."

They were serious words. He determined, once again, that he would ask Norah to marry him.

The Donati estate was much larger than the Portinari property. Manetto Donati employed dozens of servants, but he was never completely satisfied with any of his cooks. Reilly was glad he'd had bakery experience at home. It gave him the confidence he needed to prepare pastries, cakes, and cookies for the betrothal. He and Beatrice were setting up a display of strawberry-glazed lemon tarts and raisin-spice cookies when Manetto approached them.

He took a tart and ate it in one bite. With his mouth still full, he moaned his approval. "Raimondo, this is delightful! I've never tasted such delectable confections! I will double your pay and give you two days off each week if you leave Folco to work at my estate."

Beatrice gasped. Reilly laughed. "That's a generous offer, sir," Reilly said. "Nevertheless, I've been with my princess, Beatrice, since she was born. She would miss me far too much." Reilly winked at her.

"Ah, yes," Manetto replied, picking at a strawberry seed that had lodged between his teeth. He peered down at Beatrice. "You are your father's *passerotto*. As a matter of fact, at the May Day celebration he hosted a few years ago, we had a brief discussion about the possibility of *your* betrothal to Dante. However, after some negotiations, it was determined that the dowry he could provide didn't include sufficient property and valuables to meet Alighiero's demands. It's a pity. Gemma does not have your radiant beauty."

Beatrice's face turned pale as she looked up at Reilly, and her eyes filled with tears. Before he could say a word, she turned and ran to the door.

"I didn't mean to offend her father," Manetto sneered. "Did my compliment on her beauty upset her?"

"She's fatigued from helping me in the kitchen all day," Reilly lied. "Besides, she is rather shy."

Manetto shrugged. "I must find my wife. She's likely dividing part of Gemma's dowry between various charities, even before the papers are notarized."

Reilly finished the display and weaved through the cathedral room, looking for Dante. Unsuccessful, he exited through a side door into a small courtyard on his way back to the kitchen, where he presumed he'd find Beatrice. As he passed the olive tree in the middle of the courtyard, he heard people talking behind it in low whispers.

"He said Gemma and I must be betrothed, but we will not marry. We can trust Raimondo. Do you agree?" It was Dante.

"Yes, certainly." Beatrice sniffed. "Yet, I don't see how this could be possible."

"Nor do I." Dante dabbed a cloth on her cheek. "We must agree here and now—with vows—that we will be together."

Beatrice threw her arms around Dante and cried.

"These three years since we met have been bittersweet," said Beatrice. "Without your letters to read over and over, there would have been times I'd rather have died."

"I've kept the box tied with your blue ribbon and forget-me-nots hidden under my bed. I pull it out every night before I write. You are my inspiration, Beatrice. Without you, words are mere scratches on parchment. Without you, the poetry of my soul turns to ashes."

For a moment, there was silence, and Reilly peeked around the tree again to see the young couple locked in a sweet embrace. Then Dante pulled away to gaze into Beatrice's emerald eyes.

"The betrothal means nothing to me. It's simply a legal document for the exchange of goods," Dante said. "It says nothing of love."

"It's a ridiculous tradition," Beatrice said, wiping her nose with her sleeve. "I don't know if I can go through this if it will be three more years before I see you again."

"You're twelve now, old enough to be allowed the privilege of going to the city without your parents. Ask your mother if you may join Raimondo on his visits to the market. Tell her you've discovered that you have a great interest in culinary arts and you'd like him to be your tutor, as part of your education."

"That's a grand idea!" said Beatrice. "I could see you every week!"

"Yes, but we must be cautious whenever we're in public. We must not show even the slightest affection for each other. Quite the opposite! You must be coy with me … aloof. I will feign my devotion to Gemma but my affection will be forever for you alone, and revealed secretly through my poetry. You must always know this, Beatrice!"

"I will, Dante."

Dante reached into a fold of his tunic.

"Another poem for me?" Beatrice asked eagerly, admiring the small parchment scroll.

"My vow to you—my Beatrice." He let go of her hand, unrolled the scroll, and began to read:

When time weaves breath into the budding flower,
Painting fuchsia lips that speak to your sacred heart,
The seasons will pass with sparkling rain and starlit nights
Until they unite us in heavenly delights
And nature whispers, "You ne'er will be apart."
My love for thee cannot be written on devil's parchment,
Nor comprehended through mere drops from my quill,
Yet God will atone for each petal that drifts
To the depths of the Tyrrhenian Sea; then lifts
Us to dream of our divine love blooming, still—
Our love is but a winter rose—fresh, yet melts the ice

That binds unfeeling traditions of conformity
With attempts to plant seeds of doubt and fear;
But lo! Deliverance from such anguish is near—
Alas! Spring will yet come with promise of our eternal unity.

It wasn't until Reilly heard Dante read the poem to Beatrice that he knew why the man had been so misunderstood in his time. The poem was transcendent, born of the innocence of youth, yet it expressed a deeper love than most people would ever know. The poem didn't exist in Reilly's time.

He peeked around the tree. Dante shifted, as if he had heard a noise. He rolled up the scroll and gave it to Beatrice. "I hear someone coming," he whispered. "I must get to the ballroom before the announcement is made and the papers are signed."

Reilly heard the voices of two people coming from the other side of the courtyard.

"You must go!" Beatrice whispered. "I will trust that Raimondo is right about the betrothal. I'll always love only you, Dante."

She reached up, kissed Dante quickly on the lips, and ran out of the courtyard, never knowing that Reilly had been behind the tree.

Chapter Twelve

Addio

Reilly had stopped counting the months since the betrothal ceremony. He'd resorted to counting years instead. This made it easier to deal with the fact that he didn't know when the Splicing would end and when he would return to the Rotunda. Or when he could go home.

Neither would happen until after he rearranged Dante's marriage, but the details of how to accomplish the task still hadn't come to him.

He relied on the gifts he'd received from the Guardians: strength of body from Olektor, clarity of mind from Radmund, and tranquility of soul from Afismat. Somehow these invisible gifts sustained him through bouts of deep depression and utter loneliness for Norah.

For six years, he continued in his role as cook and baker for the Portinari estate.

Splicing caused another interesting phenomenon in Reilly: he believed and felt as if he was still seventeen, though he estimated Raimondo to be in his early thirties. Time ticked by slowly in Florence. He hoped it had been put on a long pause back home, and that Norah was still the same age that she was when he last saw her. To keep his sanity and cope with the monotony of medieval life, he daydreamed about proposing to her and the life he hoped they'd share.

It was strange to Reilly that the Deceptors still showed no interest in him as Raimondo. Forms of degradation and depravity lurked everywhere. Sometimes he hoped the remarkable physical feat he'd been assigned was simply to live in the Middle Ages, waiting for Beatrice to grow up so he could rearrange history. But reason and experience made him think otherwise.

Reilly spent countless hours devising Beatrice and Dante's escape. Finally, two months before the marriage of Dante and Gemma, Reilly decided the time had come to share his plan with Beatrice.

As they carried their empty vegetable baskets from the kitchen and through the garden, he said, "Today, when we're finished at the market, we'll meet Dante upstream on the Arno. He crosses the stone bridge there late each morning, after visiting his father's burial place."

An hour later they turned onto the road that led to the city.

"It's been five weeks," Beatrice said, "and a great torture for me, not being able to comfort him in his grief. My letters are hollow when I cannot give him strength through my embrace."

"Your letters always give him strength, just as his poems give you hope. Soon you'll hold him in your arms, Beatrice. The bridge is at a busy intersection, where we can discuss something of great importance without being overheard or noticed as we would be in the market."

"The wedding date is approaching, yet you've said little about it all these years. Why?"

"It was better that you lived without the burden of knowing how your life would change."

"Dante and I have imagined our lives together, trusting that you'd honor your promise to help us. We've also thought of a solution that will meet the demands of tradition and the legal documents of the betrothal."

Reilly wondered if Beatrice and Dante had also thought of escaping.

"What solution is that?"

"Raimondo, Dante and I are no longer children," she said, as they walked along the cobblestones. "We may need to conceal our love even after he marries Gemma."

Reilly stopped abruptly and faced her. "Are you suggesting you'd be his *mistress*? This is your *solution*?"

"What else can we do, Raimondo?"

"Dante and Gemma will *not* marry each other! I've remained in Florence all these years—away from *my* love—to help you and Dante. My efforts will *not* be in vain, nor will your devotion to each other be stained by infidelity! Do you know the punishment for adultery?"

Beatrice lowered her head. Reilly paced a few feet away from her, allowing her to reconsider and regain her composure. Then he stopped and reached out to lift her chin. She raised her eyes to meet his.

"Why, Raimondo? Why did you do this?"

It was a question he never allowed himself to think about. He'd simply gone through the portal ... arrived under Stonehenge ... spent over two years in the Rotunda being tutored by the Guardians and Keepers ... lived in thirteenth-century Italy incognito for nine years ... and dreamed of Norah countless nights.

"Sometimes love requires sacrifice," he said. He could see that she didn't understand what he meant.

"Must I sacrifice my love for Dante by withholding my love from him forever?"

Reilly lowered his hand and turned her around so she could see her home in the distance. "No. However, you must leave behind something you love dearly."

"My *home*?"

"Not only your home."

"My *family*?"

"Everything."

"What are you saying, Raimondo?"

"I've arranged for your escape to another country, where you and Dante can be married."

"Another *country*?" She started to cry. "Do you mean to say that I'll have to leave Italy?"

Beatrice had never considered this. Tears trickled down her face.

At that moment, Reilly looked at the stones beneath his feet and heard a sound. It was Eilam! He was repeating the message he'd given years earlier, when Reilly walked among the sarsens under Stonehenge.

"Even the rocks thrill with memories of past events."

It was a welcome and rare reminder that he was indeed recreating events in the past, and moreover, that his responsibilities as a Stelladaur Ambassador in training were on track.

"Florence is the only home I've known," Beatrice said, wiping her tears as she came to terms with the inevitable. "Yet Dante is my heaven. Italy would be the depths of hell without him."

Her resolve infused Reilly with renewed energy, strengthening his commitment to do whatever was necessary to be with

Norah—and ultimately to have every greatest desire fulfilled, as promised.

It had been years since Reilly felt such a surge of confidence.

"I'll explain when we meet Dante," he said.

The market was bustling and it took longer than usual to purchase their items.

"If we don't hurry we'll miss Dante at the bridge," Beatrice implored.

"Don't fret, Beatrice. He'll wait for us." Reilly took a ham hock from the butcher and placed it in his basket. "I also need some sausage."

"Certainly, Raimondo," said the butcher. He wrapped another small package and gave it to Reilly. "This is all I have. The shop will be closed for the next ten days, as we leave for Venice at noon for the annual family gathering."

"Thank you," Reilly said, placing the packages in his basket. "Enjoy your time in Venice."

The stone bridge arched gracefully over the Arno River. Carts, wagons, horses, and crowds of people crossed the bridge in both directions. Reilly spotted Dante first.

"There he is!" Reilly waved his hand high above his head.

Beatrice drew in a deep breath and swept her hair over her shoulder. Dante nodded, following Beatrice's gaze as she and Reilly approached him on the bridge.

"Thank you for waiting," Reilly said, as he set his basket on the ground. He clutched Dante's shoulders affectionately.

"Of course," said Dante.

Beatrice nodded but said nothing. Facing the river, Reilly stood between them and leaned over the bridge, resting his arms on the ledge. The noise from the pedestrians and animals behind them provided an ample sound barrier for their private conversation.

"The wedding is scheduled to take place in two months," Reilly began. "I promised you both that Dante would not marry Gemma. At the time, I didn't know how the betrothal agreement could be nullified—simply that I must rearrange these plans. You've both been blessed, living in comfortable circumstances with families of prominence and influence. However, the time has come for you to make your own home together ... to start a new life ... in another country." He paused, staring out across the river. "I've made arrangements for your safe passage to Barcelona. You must leave tomorrow."

"Tomorrow?" Dante said, louder than he intended. "Barcelona—in Spain?"

"Like Florence, Barcelona has become a wealthy city. The demand for luxury goods has increased trade between the countries. Look there!" Reilly pointed to a small ship docked upstream. "That vessel will set sail tomorrow along the Arno and south to Livorno after it reaches the sea. There, its shipment of olive oil and wine will be transferred to the great ship *Ezequiél*, which will sail across the Ligurian Sea to Barcelona."

Reilly checked to be sure Dante and Beatrice were following everything he said. Wide-eyed, they waited for him to continue.

"Over the past few years, I've become acquainted with the cook on that vessel. Whenever it's in port, he frequents the market. His uncle is the captain of the *Ezequiél*, and when the ship is docked at Livorno, he allows his nephew to visit Florence, while he awaits goods to be traded at different Mediterranean ports. Both men can be trusted. There is little room on the small vessel for two extra passengers, so you won't be allowed any baggage—just what you can carry and keep at your side during the voyage. I could send a few of your belongings on another sailing."

Reilly stepped away from the edge of the bridge. Dante reached for Beatrice's hand as they stared out across the river.

"Exile is the only way," Reilly said.

Dante squared his shoulders as he gripped Beatrice's hand tightly. "Even devotion to one's country fails to compare with the capacity for a man and woman to love each other as we do. Our love extends further than a thousand times the distance between Barcelona and Florence." Dante and Beatrice faced Reilly.

"I will miss you, Raimondo," Beatrice said, her lip trembling. "You are my family, too."

"You'll always be my little princess, Beatrice," Reilly whispered, pulling back a strand of hair that had blown across her face. "I'll escort you to the docks tomorrow at this same time. You should both wear something to conceal your identity until you've safely boarded the boat and sailed some distance along the river. There isn't much time. You must go home now … to bid your silent farewells."

The next morning, Reilly gathered eggs from the chicken coop and prepared breakfast for the Portinari family, as usual. Soon after she had eaten with her parents for the last time, Beatrice entered the kitchen carrying a wooden box. There she found Reilly putting scraps into a bucket for the pigs.

"This is the single treasure I want you to keep safe for me," she said. "All my other belongings can be replaced in Barcelona. Dante is a brilliant man and he'll make a fine life for us in our new home. If I should ever be without him—may God never be so cruel—these would be my only comfort. Dante's poems." She handed the box to Reilly.

"Yes, of course, Beatrice," he said. "I'll keep them safe."

In that moment, he understood that he, too, was a Keeper—a protector and guardian of something infinitely valuable.

"I've saved but one scroll to bring with me," Beatrice continued. "His sacred vow, which he declared to me the night of our only kiss."

Reilly was certain a kiss could transcend time. Remembering his perfect kiss now told him he, too, would soon leave Florence.

"Are you ready?" he asked.

"I did my best not to be glum during breakfast, but Mother asked me if I was ill."

"What did you tell her?"

"I admitted that mornings filled with grey clouds sometimes make me melancholy but insisted that my usual walk with you to the market will lift my spirits. She believed the lie." She fingered the delicate pearls adorning her neck.

"Not a lie at all, Beatrice." He placed one hand firmly on the box of letters. "Give me a moment to hide these."

He walked to the opposite end of the kitchen, entered the pantry and lifted the lid of a barrel half-filled with barley. He dug into the grain, put the box inside the barrel, and swept the barley over it to hide it. Then he went to meet Beatrice at the far side of the yard, passing the servants, who attended to their daily tasks as usual.

"Are you sure you put everything you want in your basket?" he asked.

She lifted a light blue tunic draped over the top of the basket. "I'm wearing the necklace that Father gave me for my twelfth birthday. I have a comb from Mother and this spare cotte." She moved the blue, long-sleeved tunic to lift each item as she spoke. "Also, a barbet complete with a coif and couverchef that mother gave me on my eighteenth birthday. I haven't worn them yet, as I still prefer to wear my hair in braids, but the headdress will be my disguise. I'll put it on when we're out of sight."

"Do you have any money?"

"I have enough silver coins and florins for the journey. I pray that my father will forgive me—I've taken them from my dowry."

"You have what you'll need."

Beatrice gripped her basket in front of her.

"Raimondo, when we leave this place, I will not look back." She inhaled deeply and her eyes filled with tears. "Not ever."

She turned to gaze at her home—the only home she'd ever known—and let the tears fall silently. Then she swallowed hard, clenched her jaw and raised a hand to her forehead to shade her eyes from the sun as she scanned the estate. Tilting her head, she heard a few chickens clucking and a servant laughing in the yard. She stood on her tiptoes, compelled, searching in vain for one last glimpse of her parents.

"Addio, Mamma," she whispered. *"Mi mancherai, Papà."* She clasped her hand over her mouth to keep from heaving. As the morning sun glistened on her wet cheeks, Beatrice spoke her final goodbye. *"Ti amerò per sempre."*

Chapter Thirteen

Betrayal

eilly and Beatrice pushed through the crowd at the waterfront and met Dante on the dock. Beatrice pulled at the awkward headdress now fastened securely at her chin. Dante wrapped his brown cloak tighter around his shoulders, shifting nervously.

"Did anyone recognize you?" Reilly asked.

"I don't think so," he replied.

"Once you've boarded the boat, your concerns will be over. The other passengers are crewmembers who do not know your families or their political loyalties. For an added measure of safety, you will travel under the names *Antonio* and *Nicola*. You both must stay in the cargo area, as there is no other space available. When you reach Livorno, the *Ezequiél* will provide you with comfortable accommodations."

"Thank you, Raimondo," Dante said. "You've taken a great risk. We are indebted to you."

"Rearranging history comes with the price of uncertainty," Reilly said. "But love promises the richness of life."

"What do you mean?" Beatrice asked.

He reached for Beatrice's hands and took them in his. "I mean that you've given me hope that I, too, will someday be with the one I love. I've never told you how much you are like her." Reilly leaned forward and kissed Beatrice on her forehead. "If you are ever asked who arranged your escape, tell them it was a boy, about your age. A boy named Reilly."

Beatrice scowled. "Who?"

"There's no time to tell you that story, my little princess. Just don't forget that name."

Beatrice nodded and blinked back tears.

Reilly turned to Dante. "Perhaps we'll meet again, Dante, in another time and place."

They held each other's forearms in a grip of brotherhood that meant something different to each of them.

"Yes, perhaps you'll come to Barcelona," Dante said.

"Or perhaps to another distant place," Reilly said.

Reilly saw something in Dante's eyes that he hadn't seen before. "Is *she* in that place?" Dante asked. "The woman you love?"

"Sort of."

It was the first time since he'd been Spliced that he sounded like himself—not like Raimondo—even to Beatrice and Dante.

"Do you know of *Stonehenge*?" Reilly continued, in his own voice.

"The ancient rocks of England? I heard about them during my studies."

"Someday we'll meet there." He hugged Dante tightly. "You must go now."

Then, as if he had always known that history could be rearranged, Reilly watched Beatrice and Dante step over the short gangplank and disappear into the hull of the boat.

As soon as Reilly returned to the Portinari estate, he checked to make sure the box of poems was still in the barrel of barley. Before long, Folco and Celia would notice that their daughter hadn't come home with him and would expect him to have answers. He chopped carrots and onions, waiting for the inevitable. While he was stirring a pot of soup, Celia entered the kitchen and scanned the room.

"Raimondo, I've not seen Beatrice since breakfast. I assumed she'd gone with you to the market and that she'd be here with you, as usual. Have you seen her?"

"She did go with me to the market this morning." Reilly was aware that the intonation in his voice sounded more like Reilly's than Raimondo's.

"I've searched the premises and can't find her. When you see her, please tell her she has a fitting with the tailor early this afternoon." She hadn't noticed the change in Reilly's voice. "We will all be attending the wedding of Dante and Gemma. Beatrice must have an appropriate dress for the occasion." She twirled around to leave the room, adding, "Folco will not be joining Beatrice and me for dinner. He's meeting with Alighiero to discuss financial matters. Now, where is that dear child?"

Reilly gripped the knife firmly as he continued to chop. He wanted to blame Raimondo for the half-truth he'd just told Celia, and for the pain the entire Portinari household would soon experience because of him. He'd practically raised Beatrice! But it wasn't Raimondo who had done the deed. It was Reilly himself!

He felt naked and vulnerable, as if something terrible had gone wrong with the Splicing—as if the faux identity he'd been trapped in for nine years was being stripped away. Since his arrival in Florence his voice had sounded like Raimondo's, and he used words and phrases that were foreign to him. But now his voice sounded like his own. He worried that he might also start to *look* like himself! What then?

Change was imminent, and knowing he needed only to allow it to happen, Reilly stayed in the kitchen, baking bread for the evening meal as usual. By mid-afternoon, he'd yielded to the fact that it would be one of the last loaves he would bake at the Portinari estate.

"She is nowhere to be found, Raimondo!" Celia blared as she rushed through the kitchen door. "I'm becoming anxious about my daughter's whereabouts. The staff has scoured the estate. I've sent for Folco. He should arrive shortly."

Reilly set a loaf of bread on the table, hesitant to say anything as Beatrice's mother approached him.

"She's always returned with you from the market unless she notified us in advance of a change in her plans," Celia said, in an increasingly strident pitch. "She must get our permission!"

"Yes, that's true." Reilly said, straining to sound like Raimondo. "When did you last see her?"

"We parted late in the morning, after I talked with the butcher."

"Did she say where she was going for the day?"

"No." He could justify his reply, because Beatrice hadn't actually mentioned where she was going—it was Reilly who had told *her* and Dante that their new home would be in Barcelona.

Celia paced around the table, wringing her hands.

Reilly calculated that Dante and Beatrice would need almost a week's head start to ensure their escape, so he tried to calm Celia with partial truths.

"Since her birthday, she has focused on establishing her independence," he began. "She mentioned to me on a few occasions that she'd like to spend time with a friend. I assumed that she had apprised you of her plans for the day." He tried to choose words that Raimondo would use.

Celia stopped pacing and addressed Reilly directly. "What is wrong with your voice? Are you ill?"

"Uh … no … I … it's …"

"Raimondo! Would you lie to me?" she demanded.

"I'm merely anxious for Beatrice's well-being," he said, now completely truthful.

"You must know *something*!"

"I know Beatrice loves you and her papa dearly. She would not wish to cause you any sorrow or grief."

Celia sat on the bench at the table and buried her head in her hands. "I'm sorry, Raimondo. I know you care for her as if she were your own. I suppose my mind is playing tricks on me. Yet I fear for her safety! Florence is a big city … and there are dishonorable men who would …"

Reilly sat across from her, knowing her pain and wishing he didn't have to be the cause of it. "I'm sure she's safe, Celia."

"I hope you are correct in your assumption. Perhaps Folco will have some answers."

Hoping to do something to comfort Celia while futilely attempting to justify what he'd done to rearrange history, Reilly cut two thick slices of bread and sat to eat with her. He took a few bites and watched her as she poked at a slice of crusty bread. A few minutes later, Folco burst through the door.

"My dear, Celia!" Folco began. "I received an urgent message that I was needed at home. Are you all right?" Celia stood up and thrust herself into her husband's arms.

"Beatrice is missing!" she sobbed. "She is nowhere to be found!"

Folco allowed his wife to cry a few moments. Then he said, "Calm yourself. She must not be far. Where was she last seen?"

"In the market with Raimondo, as usual."

Folco turned to Reilly. "What can you tell me?"

"She talked of spending time with a dear friend, though she didn't say who." Reilly cleared his throat and again tried to sound like Raimondo. He struggled to be as honest as possible but cringed inside at the thought of the web of lies he'd begun to weave. "She departed from me after we finished at the market this morning."

"I don't keep up with her social engagements, Celia, but surely you know the names of her acquaintances," Folco said.

"I've sent for word from Gigi and Francesca, her two closest friends, but have not heard anything yet."

"Very well. In the meantime, I'll call for a search of the city by our Guelph affiliates, including Alighiero. However, Dante will not be available to assist, as he left today for a symposium in Rome. His father said the young man has been anxious with all the discussions about his approaching wedding, and he insisted on leaving town to refresh his mind."

Folco left the kitchen sounding confident that Beatrice would be found soon.

Reilly was relieved that Dante had so cleverly prepared his father to believe he would be out of town.

By late evening, when there was still no sign of Beatrice, the entire Portinari household was worried. Celia's hysteria made Reilly momentarily doubt his plan to help her daughter escape with Dante. Every servant on the estate was thoroughly interrogated but exonerated of withholding any knowledge of Beatrice's whereabouts.

Though the law stated that a man or woman could be put to death for refusal to abide by the legal decree of an arranged marriage, Reilly, Dante, and Beatrice had taken the risk, hoping they would remain safe in exile in Barcelona. Three days later, when the Portinaris still had no answers, Folco confronted Reilly a second time. He maintained his story that Beatrice had left his side at the market, shortly after he purchased a ham hock and sausage.

Meanwhile, Reilly spoke as little as possible, made up excuses for the change in the sound of his voice, and feigned a terrible cough. In quiet moments by himself, he read Dante's poems, which he'd transferred from the barrel to his satchel, which was always in view. He hoped to give them to Beatrice someday ... somehow.

With each day that passed without Beatrice at home, Celia grew more upset, and she fell into a deep depression. Reilly desperately battled against his own guilt. Folco remained hopeful that his daughter would return. He gave no indication that he suspected any connection between Beatrice's disappearance and Dante's extended stay in Rome.

Every evening, Reilly calculated the distance Beatrice and Dante would have traveled that day. After a week, he suspected that they had crossed the Ligurian Sea, turned south, sailed past the border of France and Spain, and nearly reached Barcelona.

He woke one morning with a powerful sense that Raimondo Gustalini's life was about to change forever. He dressed, carried his satchel to the kitchen, and set it on the chair closest to where he worked. As he scraped cooked eggs from the side of a pot, he heard horses in the distance. He eyed the satchel and continued to stir the eggs.

The chickens clucked loudly as men's harsh voices shooed them away. As Reilly lifted the pot from the open flame and set it on the table, four men entered the kitchen from the yard. Reilly swept his satchel over his head and shifted it towards his back.

Folco and Celia rushed in through the inside door. "What is happening?" Folco demanded. "The servants alerted us that some grave matter must be dealt with immediately in the kitchen. We came at once."

"Raimondo Gustalini?" One man stepped forward while the others stood in a semicircle around Reilly, trapping him between the table and the wall.

"Yes, I am Raimondo." Reilly replied.

"You are hereby under arrest for the abduction of Beatrice Portinari, for concealing evidence, and for facilitating the abnegation of the legal duty of Dante Alighieri to marry Gemma Donati under a signed contract of betrothal."

Celia gasped and her knees buckled.

"Is this true?" Folco demanded, holding up his wife so she wouldn't fall to the ground.

Reilly opened his mouth to answer, but the constable replied for him. "We have evidence that Raimondo arranged for the departure of Beatrice from Florence. She left with Dante."

"Dante?" Celia gasped.

"So the butcher knew after all," Folco said, glaring at Reilly. "I questioned him myself last evening, upon his return from Venice. When he indicated he'd overhead Beatrice say you, Raimondo, and she would be meeting Dante at the bridge the day we last saw her, I involved the Office of the Magistrate to investigate further. I didn't want to believe that it was true!"

"The couple escaped by boat to Livorno," the constable stated forcefully. "There they boarded the *Marcella* for Athens."

Reilly concealed his surprise as he realized that the captain of the *Ezequiél* had followed his meticulous plan. He was to divert anyone who asked questions or showed any sign of suspicion, and had clearly directed inquirers east to Greece instead of west to Barcelona.

The man grabbed Reilly by his arm and jerked him to stand directly in front of Folco and Celia.

"You were like family!" Folco's bitter tone was unlike any that Reilly had heard him use before. "Now, with this unforgivable crime, the name Raimondo Gustalini shall never be uttered in this household again. You are banished to Gorgona! May that tiny, lonely island be your dwelling place until your demise!"

Celia wailed and fell to the ground, unconscious.

"Betrayal demands the highest punishment!" Folco shouted, shaking a fist at Reilly, as the men escorted him out of the kitchen, never to return to the Portinari estate.

Chapter Fourteen

Bloodlines

Reilly was no stranger to pain.

The agony of losing his father still plagued him, and he often battled with the heavy guilt he felt about his drowning. Pain had tormented him so deeply in Black Castle that he thought his heart would slowly bleed to death before he could free Norah. Harrowing fear had accompanied him through portals to different times, in the forms of the haunting shadows of Travis Jackson and Prince Ukobach.

He had known excruciating physical pain, too. There was the time when he travelled through the portal and landed in the chaotic forest of Wicklow, with trees falling all around him, and a huge trunk pinned his leg to the ground, injuring it badly; when the

Deceptors branded the front of his shoulder with a hot iron; and when his Fireglass malfunctioned, making his eye burn and ooze black tar-like pus.

But now agony filled his body and tormented his mind and soul. Death could not come fast enough. He guessed he'd laid on the stone floor beneath him, with his eyes closed, for a couple of days. His breathing was shallow, but in his head, it sounded like a tornado devouring him. He was terrified to open his eyes, fearing he would see the physical effects of the torture he'd endured.

Then his toes twitched. He didn't know if it happened involuntarily or not. The twitching was new information for his brain to process—he still had toes! He waited for them to twitch again. They didn't. Somehow, despite the incessant noise in his ears, he heard himself whisper, "Move your toes!" and he realized that his toes didn't hurt when they moved. So, with another semi-conscious thought, he made his toes move again … stretched the arches of his feet … and turned each foot slightly at the ankles. That victory was enough!

He took a deeper breath through the pain, and opened his heavy eyelids, which took a greater effort than wiggling his toes did. The deafening sound of the tornado faded to an ambient hushing noise. He stared blankly, waiting for the room to come into focus. His eyes burned from a light streaming in from above.

His eyes fluttered and closed. Then, there was only silence— penetrating silence.

Reilly wasn't alone in the room. He sensed someone nearby—a warm and gentle touch on his cheek. He wanted to open his eyes to see who was there, but he couldn't. He just lay there, imagining it was Norah who'd come to rescue *him*. His daydream ended when someone spoke.

"She will only exist if you live," a man's voice reverberated.

Reilly knew the voice … but whose was it?

A breeze blew across his neck, and another man's voice interrupted his semi-consciousness. "She, too, is a Gustalini."

Reilly strained to move his toes again. *Norah!* he shouted in his mind.

"She comes from you—Raimondo—a man of the past." This time it was a woman's voice that lilted past Reilly's ears and through his soul. "She lives now, to be in your future."

Splicing … rearranging … Stonehenge …

Think! Move! He commanded his body to respond. *Live!*

As if startled awake from a nightmare, Reilly opened his eyes wide. The stone floor stared at him inches from his face.

Strangely, the severe pain subsided almost instantly. He pushed his hands against the ground to turn from his stomach to his side. Except for the sound of his own groans when he moved, he heard nothing.

Slowly, he pushed himself up to a sitting position. He lifted his hand to see some dry dirt sticking to the palm and brushed it away. He studied the crease lines on his wrist, his knuckles, his grimy fingernails, and the blood vessels under his skin.

He moved both hands up and put his palms over his cheeks. Then he closed his eyes and traced his fingers over his eyebrows, across his temples, over his cheeks, under his eyes, down his nose, and around his lips. He reached for his hair, falling across his shoulders, and held it out to observe it as if under a microscope.

"It's me!" he whispered, twisting his blonde hair around a finger.

He stood up and frowned at his clothes. "But still Raimondo, too."

The circular stone cell was about eight feet in diameter. There was no door. Light filtered in through a large window about twenty feet up. He had been told that he would be taken to Gorgona, a small island twenty-three miles from Livorno, where the most heinous criminals of Tuscany were imprisoned. The lingering sting on his back and the puncture wounds dotting his arms and legs—now crusted with dried blood—told him that he'd survived the torture chambers of the newly constructed castle. He was relieved that he had no recollection of the methods of torture he'd endured.

"This could be tougher than Black Castle," he thought, as he walked the perimeter of his cell. "These walls are solid stone, with no little crevices or grooves to find a secret passageway."

Contented by the sound of his own voice, and the fact that he retained a hint of humor, he continued. "What are our assets, Raimondo?" He waited, half expecting someone else to appear in the room. "Right. Just me and you ... and a window too high to reach."

He paced around the room, grateful to be able to stretch his legs.

"There must be more! What *else* do we have?" He considered his tunic but it was in shreds. "There's certainly not enough here to make any sort of rope."

The cold stone under his feet brought his attention to the fact that his discomfort now consisted of a dull sting on his back and gritty dirt chafing the skin between his toes.

Touching a spot on his shin where blood trickled slightly, he wondered how he'd so quickly regained his strength, and why only discomfort was the extent of his present pain.

Then some of the pieces came together.

"*Strength* ... Olektor gave me strength. Clarity from Radmund. Afismat ... tranquility. *They're* the ones who just spoke to me!"

He stared up at the light streaming in through the window and watched thousands of dust particles vacillating directly in front of him. He noticed that the window was cracked higher up.

"That's the only way out, Raimondo!" Reilly said, staring at the beam. "Through the light in that crack there is another Fraction!"

He stepped beside the light stream and watched the dust particles converge in a sparkling path to the floor on one side of the towering room.

"*Strength … clarity … tranquility*," he whispered. He reached out to block the dust particles with his hand and observed the break in the light beam. "The dust is always here … even if I can't see it," he mused as he lowered his hand and watched the particles converge.

Reilly stepped closer to the glittering dust floating in a thick and steady beam to the floor.

Though he'd been in Florence almost ten years and accomplished his assignment there, he had to do one more thing for his own posterity! Now he needed to use his higher power of intelligence—which the Guardians and Keepers had taught him to access—to rearrange not just history. If he hoped to get through the Fraction, he had to rearrange the dust itself!

He circled the room, observing the dust and searching for answers with each step. His feet tingled as they brushed the ground. Exhilarated—as if his Stelladaur was still hanging around his neck—he felt more like himself than he had in a decade.

Moments later, a heavy darkness oozed into the room and permeated the air. Thick blackness swirled around, as if trying to engulf him and swallow the beam of light.

Uncertainty crept over Reilly like an alien disease attacking his body and mind. He was overcome with fear that he might be trapped in the tower forever! Panicking, he gasped for breath. He pulled his hair, fighting insanity. He couldn't tell if he was Reilly or Raimondo … or an evil spirit—a Deceptor—that had suddenly possessed his body.

For ten years Reilly had been free from any personal encounters with Deceptors. Being Spliced had its benefits. Still, throughout those ten years, he wondered when he'd have to face the demons next.

He brushed his hand across his head and face. He violently slapped his arms and legs, as if deadly bees had landed on his body, hungry to taste his blood and leave red sores after their fatal stings.

He twirled around the room swatting at the invisible demons. An eerie wailing echoed off the walls.

Had the guards poisoned him with a hallucinogenic? He struggled to think clearly. Why had the exhilarating feeling vanished so abruptly and changed to delusion?

Searching for strength, he noticed that the beam of light had moved higher up, illuminating the dust particles at a steeper angle. Soon the direct sunlight would move past the window and no longer shine into the room or onto the dust. There was something about the dust! What was it?

With enough clarity to realize he couldn't survive the choking darkness much longer, Reilly staggered to the spot on the stone floor where the dust particles collided in a swirling motion. Despairing, he fell to the ground in a crumpled heap. Then, straining to lift his head, he focused on the rays of light ascending from the window.

He grabbed at the dust wildly, watching it disappear from his fists.

The demons pressed in on him!

Madness crept over him—more excruciating than anything he'd experienced in Black Castle. He screamed out in agony!

Beads of perspiration covered his face and his entire body. His head dropped back and his neck tightened. He felt his blood vessels thicken, engorged, as if they would explode. He staggered towards the light, clawing at the blackness that engulfed him. He shook his head as he screamed, but still forced himself to concentrate.

Then a collection of far distant memories flooded his mind. Fragmented thoughts: a box carved of yew wood … his dad's sailboat … the Sea of Stelladaurs off the coast of Ireland … millions of unclaimed and discarded jewels dancing on the water ... some of the Stelladaurs transforming to rubies, as if by magic … prisoners of Black Castle … saving Norah's life.

The light shimmering off the dust particles in front of him reminded him of his own Stelladaur. It was enough!

"My Stelladaur was never discarded!" Reilly cried.

Strengthened with renewed hope and determination, he reached upward and grasped at the sunlight. Knowing his survival depended on his ability to move his *entire* body into the beam of light, he pressed forward, dragging himself by his elbows. Still battling the demonic force, he painstakingly rose onto his knees and inched along.

Finally, with his whole body illuminated in the light, he reached up as high as he could, splaying his hands and ignoring the hellish cries that assaulted his ears and mind.

Then, he heard a voice. It was Eilam!

"Even the rocks thrill with memories of past events. The very dust beneath your feet responds more lovingly to our footsteps because it is the ashes of our ancestors. The soil is rich with the life of our kindred."

As if on cue, the swirling dust transformed into a glittering staircase, similar to the one he'd climbed up to go through the Shield of Forgotten Memories a decade earlier.

Taking a final step out of the dungeon shadows, he moved fully into the light of the mystical staircase and began his ascent.

When he reached the top step, he did not look back. He simply walked through the Fraction in Time and found himself standing in the Rotunda under Stonehenge, where the Guardians and Keepers sat at the marble table, awaiting his arrival.

"Come in, Reilly," Afismat said, motioning to the chair beside her.

Reilly examined his smooth arms, no longer pocked with torture wounds. Scanning his surroundings to be sure he was safe and out of reach of any Deceptor, he made his way to the chair.

The Guardians and Keepers were exactly as they were when he'd last seen them. They all sat in the same positions around the table. He wondered if they'd been changed to stone when he left and remained statues until the moment he returned through the portal.

The Guardians and Keepers watched Reilly expectantly.

"The reporting will now begin." Afismat nodded to Dante, who sat at the opposite end of the table. "You may begin."

"The Splicing was seamless and the rearranging a success," said Dante. "Beatrice and I had six years together, basking in our union in Barcelona. Truly, I thank you, Reilly."

All eyes were on Reilly. He paused, wondering if he was supposed to say something during a reporting.

"Only six?" Reilly asked.

"Rearranging doesn't change all of history," Dante said. "An illness attacked Beatrice and rapidly overtook her body. She died at the age of twenty-four, as history claims, but she died in my arms. I returned to Florence to make amends with my family and to attend to my political responsibilities. Recognizing my grief, both my father and Folco exonerated me. Nevertheless, my father insisted that I marry Gemma, who was still without a husband. Knowing my heart would always be with Beatrice, I consented to marry Gemma with the understanding that it was, and would always be, nothing more than an arranged marriage."

"Beatrice asked me to keep your poems safe, which I did for some time," Reilly said. "But the satchel where I kept them was ripped from my shoulder when I was taken from the Portinari estate. It was thrown off the carriage just outside Florence. I'm so sorry."

Dante reached behind his stone chair and lifted a satchel onto the table.

"Where did you get that?" Reilly asked, jumping up for a better look.

"When Beatrice was ill, a beautiful dog appeared at our doorstep, holding the satchel in her mouth."

"A *dog*?"

"A dog as white as snow."

"Tuma!" Reilly whispered.

"The dog left the next day and we never saw her again. We read the poems over and over together. It was a great comfort to Beatrice. When she died, I buried the poems with her."

"Do you have them now?"

"Yes. The ashes of our ancestors rest in the rocks and dust of Earth. Thus, our family members from the past assist us in ways we rarely see or understand." Dante glanced around the table and faced Reilly. "We're seldom aware of their continuing influence in our lives."

"Whose ancestors?"

"Yours. Mine. We all come from the same dust."

Reilly sat down, amazed that he still had so much to learn. This place hidden under Stonehenge wasn't just a warp in time, or a university where Echtras trained to become Stelladaur Ambassadors. It was a place where dust and stardust intertwined!

"What happened to Raimondo?" Reilly asked.

"When your Splicing ended, he was transported instantly through the tower window to the village of Augusta, in Sicily, where he married a peasant woman. They were poor farmers but very happy. Years passed, and Raimondo and his wife died. The Gustalini family remained in Sicily, developing land throughout the region. By the seventeenth century, they'd become the wealthiest family in southern Italy. Later, a dispute between two of the brothers over land ownership divided the family. In his greed, the brother who owned less land became involved with a band of sophisticated thieves, who stole art, antiquities and books to sell in the foreign markets. One of the first printings of my own *Divine Comedy* was among the stolen works, as well as writings of Thomas Moore, Kepler and Galileo."

Reilly listened intently, trying to connect the dots in history. "As Raimondo Gustalini, I helped save your work. Later, a descendent of Raimondo tried to destroy the greatest of your works ever known to the world!" Reilly paused to consider the meaning of what he'd just said. "That's when the Gustalini family became corrupt."

"Indeed."

Struck with new understanding, he looked at Olektor. "And that's what you meant when you said Norah would exist only if Raimondo lived. Her ancestors were those thieves! Now, in my time, her father remains in prison because of a way of life that was handed down from generation to generation, and which he was born into. The Mafia—another kind of *imprinting*!"

"A person must be responsible for his or her own decisions, despite blood lines," Olektor replied.

"Have you forgotten, Reilly, that a Star Door is created for every person," said Radmund, "to launch their own Stelladaur? It guides their way, regardless of circumstances, imprinting, or even birthright. As you know after witnessing the Sea of Stelladaurs and the Stelladaur Sky, those who have not claimed their own Stelladaur or who have discarded it, need our help."

"The ancestors make a secret known through the stardust found in every Stelladaur. This knowledge lights the body, mind and soul with greater truth and understanding," Afismat declared as she raised her wings high.

"What is that secret?" Reilly asked.

"The blood of royalty runs through the entire human race," she said.

Chapter Fifteen

Triviality

It wasn't clear to Reilly whether he'd actually been away from the Rotunda for ten years or if time had halted during the Splicing. He still felt like he was seventeen, but considering everything that had happened to him in Florence, he also felt like a full-grown man.

Something about his feelings for Norah told him he was older than when he last saw her—at least in some ways.

Ironically, the long separation from Norah increased his love for her. There was no magical device or mystical token to reassure him. No red flower. No ruby. No voice echoing her love-song through a dark castle filled with demons. But memories of her gave him hope. His body ached to hold her. In his mind, he had to assume she was safe. In his heart, he hoped she hadn't forgotten him.

During his continued tutoring, he was allowed to ask the Guardians and Keepers anything, and they provided detailed answers to all his inquiries except two: How old am I now? and, Will Norah be waiting for me when I return? Nor was he allowed to ask why he couldn't ask those questions.

Since the Guardians and Keepers didn't need sleep, Reilly paced the lessons and excused himself when he was tired. He recorded data, holograms, and information in his Fireglass, and often retreated to his bedroom to review his notes on the device.

He'd been cosmically chosen to train with eighteen of the greatest scholars, scientists, philosophers, and artists in history in preparation to become a Stelladaur Ambassador. He still didn't know exactly what that meant, how it would happen, or what his special mission would be. Although he'd escaped Black Castle and faced Prince Ukobach, which apparently no other Echtra had done, he still often asked himself why *he* had been chosen.

Often pressing on his mind was the inevitable possibility that he might be sent to the Bleak, where an untold number of Deceptors lurked. To ease his fears, he told himself there were things he'd know when he needed to know, and not before.

He spent most of his time studying with Charles Darwin. He soon realized that what he'd learned in ninth-grade history class barely touched the details of Darwin's impressive mind, vast expertise, and depth of scientific theories. However, the history books were correct regarding some aspects of his life: he wrote hundreds of books; compiled thousands of pages of notes, diagrams, and drawings; kept personal letters, journals, and diaries; and, for the most part, documented his research. Reilly wished the internet was available in the Rotunda, so he could get more information about Darwin: collections of his scholarly articles; names of organizations, songs, theories, blogs, websites, and movies that targeted believers and nonbelievers in evolution; and endless trivia. Yet, Darwin told Reilly that nowhere—not even in his private journals—had he accurately documented his greatest challenge.

One day as they wandered between the sarsens, Darwin revealed to Reilly something about it.

"I studied the works of a geologist named John MacCulloch," Darwin began. "For twenty years I disagreed with one of his theories, but later admitted that my own theory on the matter was indeed a great blunder, which caused me decades of gloom and depression. My dear Emma tried desperately to lift my spirits, reading to me each morning and afternoon in the drawing room and playing backgammon with me daily. I kept a tally of who won each game—what madness!—and feigned anger at my losing. She was a gifted musician, taught by Chopin, and she soothed my troubled mind with private concerts in our conservatory."

Reilly had learned to simply listen when a Keeper reverted to reminiscing about life before being Blinked. It was during those times that he wondered if the Rotunda wasn't the Keepers' final destination at all, but rather a holding place until a Stelladaur Ambassador freed them from some unseen prison of their own. Perhaps the Rotunda was a place where some of the greatest scholars went to find their unclaimed or discarded Stelladaurs.

He was convinced that it all had something to do with his responsibility to rearrange history, specifically for the three Keepers he'd chosen to tutor him.

Darwin rubbed the crease lines of his forehead as they walked, and continued to explain. "Mr. MacColluch said this: *It is by an attention to circumstances, which at first glance appear trivial, that abstruse truths are often discovered.* My greatest failure has little to do with what the eye can see, what science can prove, or what theories of mine were disproved. It is the brutal realization that I neglected to write about the most profound discovery of my life."

Darwin stopped walking and stood under a lintel, looking far into the distance past the berm and gully, towards the Bleak. Reilly checked to be sure his Fireglass was on record mode and waited for the nugget of truth.

"Triviality is a product of the human mind, and it causes madness. The fact that no human experience is wasted, and that laws of nature exist beyond the capacity of the human mind to comprehend, but which we are subject to, is the antithesis of triviality. These laws existed long before the universe and all the planets were formed. They are eternal."

Until then, Reilly hadn't known that history had been unkind to Darwin—that as a scientist, he was misunderstood, and as a philosopher, he was misjudged.

"Why didn't you ever write about this discovery?" Reilly asked.

"I refused to acknowledge the laws, or that I was bound by them."

"But you didn't know then what you know now."

"I knew enough."

"What do you mean?"

"I was subject to change, like all creatures. Only on my deathbed did I see myself as a creature of beauty. That was when I saw that I possessed the power to change infinitely."

Reilly assumed that he knew what Darwin meant. "The power of love."

Darwin took a deep breath. "More," he whispered before exhaling. "The power to become a *master creator* of love."

Stunned by Darwin's presumption, Reilly waited for him to explain.

"What is love, if it is not God? What is God, if he is not perfect love? As humans, we undergo change from the moment of conception. We evolve throughout our life to adapt to our circumstances, environment, and experiences. As a species, we are resilient to change yet as individuals, we resist it. Resistance cripples the mind, the body, and most importantly, the soul. In our weakened state, we fail to comprehend that the potential from which life originates is within us."

Reilly tried to process what he'd just heard. The juxtaposition of the origin and potential of humankind—coming from the Father of Evolution himself—filled his mind with a steady stream of questions. He doubted that most of the questions could be answered. Not even by the Guardians and Keepers.

"This isn't trivial at all," Reilly said, gazing into the vast open space past the berm and the gulley, towards the Bleak. "If you hadn't *resisted*, as you say, before your death, would you have done something differently?"

"Indeed," Darwin said. "I would have lived life defined by what I did *not* know, rather than by what I did know."

"How would you have done that?"

"I would have been a man of faith."

"Faith?"

"A human being knows nothing until he dares to see further than the eye can see. That is faith. There the view is endless."

A sudden bitter chill swept in and Reilly caught his breath. He shivered and wrapped his arms around himself. Moments later, a warm breeze blew from behind.

He turned to face the warm wind and said, "It's time."

The suspended staircase reached in front of him, up to the Shield of Forgotten Memories. The Keepers stood like statues on both sides of it, waiting for Reilly to begin his ascent. The Guardians stood next to him, focused on the shimmering shield.

Olektor spoke encouraging words. "Strength will be with you."

"Clarity will give you assurance," said Radmund.

"Tranquility follows faith," said Afismat, spreading her wings. "Use knowledge wisely."

Reilly climbed the stairs and nodded at all the Keepers as they repeated the mantra in unison.

"Even the rocks thrill with memories of past events. The very dust beneath your feet responds more lovingly to our footsteps because

it is the ashes of our ancestors. The soil is rich with the life of our kindred."

As they spoke, Reilly understood that each of the Keepers counted on him to complete his assignments and to become a Stelladaur Ambassador—to do what they couldn't do! Nor could *he*, unless he rearranged history.

The Keepers were the dust, and somehow, he was their kindred.

Reilly passed Darwin near the top of the golden staircase. Eager to be Spliced, he took the steps two at a time, until once again, he left the Rotunda and stepped through to another Fraction in Time.

Chapter Sixteen

Announcement

"This is conceivably the most vibrant display of orchids we have ever grown," said Darwin, gesturing with his hands, as he often did when he spoke, to emphasize his words. "Truman, without your assistance, my work would be cumbersome indeed."

Quickly surveying his surroundings, Reilly picked up a watering can from a stool in front of him. "They are beautiful, Mr. Darwin," Reilly replied, as he viewed dozens of orchids dotting the greenhouse. "Magnificent."

"The findings are not yet conclusive; however, it appears that the exposed plants are the ones that produce fertile seeds." He coughed heavily and reached for a bell-shaped glass cup on a nearby table.

"None of the plants covered with these bells have shown the same effect. I find that fascinating! Don't you?"

"Yes, Mr. Darwin. Quite."

"Truman Hadley!" Darwin boomed. He coughed again, as he often did from years of ill health, before he replaced the glass bell. "You've been under my employ since I moved my family here to Down House fifteen years ago. When did you decide to address me with such formality?"

"I ... uh," Reilly stammered, looking up into Darwin's piercing blue-grey eyes—and trying not to stare at his overhanging bushy eyebrows.

"Are you well?"

"Yes, of course, Charles! My apologies." Reilly lifted the watering can to water one of the orchids.

Darwin laughed heartily and slapped his hands on his thighs. "Accepted, my dear Truman. Now come with me. I have an announcement to make to my family, and you must hear it, as well."

Reilly followed Darwin out of the large greenhouse. The scientist swung his cane as they wandered through the English garden, occasionally tapping it on the ground beside him. Before they reached the side yard, a girl about fourteen years old skipped towards them.

"Hello, Father, I was just coming to find you!" She stopped skipping and walked beside Darwin as he made his way past three blooming rhododendrons. "May we play lawn tennis this afternoon? Mother said I am free for leisure enjoyment."

Darwin smiled at his daughter but kept walking. "Not today, Henrietta. I have an exciting announcement to share. Fetch your siblings and meet us under the lime tree."

"Oh! A story about your adventures sailing around the world on the *Beagle*?" Henrietta squealed. "Or about your discoveries on the Galapagos Islands?"

"Today, not a story, but certainly an adventure! Now run along." He waved his daughter down the path.

"There's George and Francis," Reilly said, pointing towards the orchard.

Reilly was relieved that, except for the mistake of addressing Darwin as "Mr. Darwin," he'd stepped into his new persona effortlessly. In the Rotunda, Darwin had briefly mentioned his gardener, but Reilly hadn't thought to ask the man's name. After all, neither Reilly, nor the Keepers had the advantage of knowing *who* he was going to be after a Splicing.

"Collecting worms, no doubt," Darwin said, waving at George and Francis. "My supply has run low in the observatory and I insisted they replenish it with some healthy samples. They are much better at finding the critters than Leonard or Horace. And Elizabeth won't touch the wiggly gems."

Reilly did some fast calculations in his mind to determine the ages of Darwin's children. If Henrietta was fourteen, then it would follow that George was twelve, Elizabeth was ten, Francis was nine, Leonard was seven, and Horace was six. The eldest, William, was eighteen, and the youngest, Charles, was barely a year old. Darwin's beloved daughter, Anne, had died six years earlier, when she was ten. The following year, his wife, Emma, had given birth to another girl, Mary, who died in infancy.

For Darwin, the tragedy of Anne's death seemed to have happened yesterday. He remained consumed by grief, which often made him physically ill and depressed. Nevertheless, he tried to engage his other eight children in his work and daily routine.

Darwin motioned to George and Francis to join him, as he and Reilly meandered towards the orchard beside a short rock wall. Just past the gate, they stood in the shade of the lime tree and watched the boys approach with a bucket in each hand.

"See how many we dug up this time, Father!" George said, digging his hands into the worms. "Big fat ones, too!"

Darwin surveyed the buckets and reached in for a handful of worms. "You've worked hard. I didn't suppose you would find this many in one afternoon."

"I started to count mine," said Francis, lifting up his buckets. "But some wiggled out faster than I could put them back in. I lost count at one hundred twenty-something."

"Fabulous specimens!" Darwin scratched his thick, curly sideburns with his free hand.

"How many worms do you think there are on our entire property, Father?" Francis asked.

"That's an excellent question," Darwin replied, dropping the worms back into the bucket. "There are approximately fifty-three thousand worms on each acre of damp land if it's not too sandy or rocky. Down House includes twenty acres. Can you calculate the number of worms there might be?" Darwin made a habit of answering his children openly but refused to rob them of the opportunity to find solutions to problems.

Francis shook his head. "I can't."

"Over one million?" George asked.

"You're correct. Over one million."

"I don't think I can find that many," said Francis.

Darwin laughed and tousled the boy's hair. "Well, we need to leave most of them in the earth to do their job."

"What's their job?" Francis asked, poking his hand into the bucket.

"Worms are nature's ploughs. They are deaf and blind, but incredibly intelligent. Their job is to change the structure of the environment."

Henrietta and Elizabeth approached from the house. They ran up to their father and peered into their brothers' buckets.

"How do worms change the structure of the environment?" Francis asked, intrigued by his father's knowledge.

"By ingesting the soil, allowing it to pass through their bodies, and then regurgitating it back to the surface."

"Regurgitate? That's repulsive!" said Henrietta, turning her nose away.

"I prefer the task of catching beetles," said Elizabeth. "I can capture them quite easily without having to touch them. Thank you for not asking Henrietta and me to dig for worms, Father."

Darwin chuckled. "My current research on the study of earthworms revolves around a single concept. Someday I will write an entire book about my findings." He coughed heavily and leaned on his cane.

"Charles?" said Reilly, reaching a hand to steady Darwin.

"I'm fine, thank you." He sat down on the grass and leaned against the trunk of the lime tree. "Ah, and here come Leonard and young Horace."

The two boys bounded through the gate with their hands in their pockets.

"We found pebbles for your collection, Father. See?" Leonard said emptying his pockets and letting the small rocks fall to the ground.

"Every rock is so interesting and unique," said Horace. Frowning, he held out a handful of small stones and added, "You have boxes and boxes of rocks, Father. May I keep these?"

Reilly watched, amused by Darwin's children.

"Certainly, you may keep them," Darwin said. "I know precisely how you feel. When I was a young boy, not much older than you, I enjoyed collecting stones. I distinctly recall my desire to know something about all the pebbles in front of the hall door. What was their composition? When and how were they formed? What was the story of their existence? Were they as old as the earth—and how old was that? It was the first time I thought about the study of geology. Horace, rocks provide untold information. They know the secrets of the earth."

As Reilly watched Darwin interact with his children, he thought of his own dad—something he hadn't done in days, or even weeks. Maybe it had been years. Time had become elusive. Life had gone by.

Now, listening to Darwin, Reilly thought about how his dad had always spent time exploring with him, playing games, listening to his concerns, and sailing with him in his boat, *The Ark*. Reilly silently knew that he still desperately missed his dad. But some time after his death, despair and grief turned to emptiness. Then the emptiness turned to a passion to find Tir Na Nog—to go where he believed his dad was now. Grateful, but not fully knowing why, Reilly became keenly aware that his unjustified guilt for not saving his dad from drowning was gone.

Somewhere in the middle of time travel and portals, demons and Deceptors, Stonehenge and lost Stelladaurs, Reilly's greatest desires had changed. Again!

There grew inside of him a resolute stillness with regard to his increasing responsibilities. He wanted to become a Stelladaur Ambassador! If he wanted anything at all, if his ultimate greatest desire was within his reach, and most importantly, if he hoped to ever be with Norah, it would come through his complete willingness of body, mind, and soul to survive the training. No matter what!

"Did you say *secrets*?" Emma smiled at her husband as she closed the gate behind her. "Children, your father can do wonderful things and is remarkably intelligent, but he can *not* keep secrets. If he has a surprise, his delight in telling us what it is will be almost as great as the having of it."

Darwin stood up and stepped beside his wife, linking her arm through his. "My dear, Emma," he said, patting her hand. "I dare say that you know me too well."

"Perhaps. Yet I am not privy to the surprise for which you've gathered us here."

"Where is William?" Darwin asked. "I sent him to the lake hours ago to gather cattails."

"He has not yet returned," Emma said.

Darwin grinned as he released Emma's arm and faced his children. "Well, then, we shall carry on without your eldest brother. Mother is quite right. I do have a great surprise! I cannot wait another minute to tell you."

The children giggled and Reilly leaned forward.

"In two weeks, we shall all venture on a great excursion!" He clapped his hands. "Can you guess to where?"

"The seashore?" Elizabeth guessed.

Darwin shook his head.

"London?" Francis said.

"It does involve first going to London," Darwin teased.

"First?" Leonard asked. "Then where?"

"Charles, don't keep us in suspense any longer!" Emma demanded.

"Very well," Darwin said, tugging at his right sideburn. "We will take the carriage to London and then go by train directly to Salisbury Plain for the Summer Solstice Fair at Stonehenge!"

"The entire family?" Emma blurted out. "That will most certainly be an adventure! Of course, Josephine must accompany us. Little Charles cannot be left too long without me." Reilly assumed that Josephine was the family governess.

"Yes," Darwin agreed. "Truman will come, too. The outing is certainly intended for play and entertainment. However, when the fair is over, we will remain there a few days longer so that I can conduct research near the stones. You will busy yourselves with picnics and games while Truman and I dig for earthworms. If there are secrets to be unfolded, I propose that they lie near Stonehenge, likely buried there by earthworms."

It wasn't until Reilly studied with Darwin in the Rotunda that he learned of his work with earthworms, and that Darwin had actually visited Stonehenge to conduct some of his research. In fact, Darwin's last published book was about earthworms, how they affected the environment, and what effect they had on archeology.

Reilly also knew some things that Darwin did not. The scientist had no idea about what deeper secrets lay beneath Stonehenge.

"We will dig, too!" Francis said.

"Perhaps." Darwin nodded. "However, Truman is like an artist with plantings and soils. He is careful and will be a great help to me." He tapped his cane on the ground and began to walk away. "The day is getting late, and I should like to stroll along The Sandwalk so that I can think. Children, when I return, your mother and I will be in the drawing room, enjoying our game of backgammon and reading *Dickens*. Please do not disturb us. I will see you this evening."

With that, Darwin walked into the orchard, towards the path where he wandered most afternoons to meditate before retiring inside Down House. Emma and the children dispersed. Reilly was left alone on a hill under the lime tree. Viewing the entire estate, he absorbed the landscape as if he'd never seen it before, yet he instantly knew the location of every pathway, shrub, tree, bush, flower, garden vegetable, herb, and mound of loose soil.

Reilly was intrigued by the fact that though he had never seen any lime trees before, Truman knew all about them and was well educated in horticulture. He scanned the orchard and mindfully identified every variety of plum, peach, apple, pear and cherry. Splicing gave him the advantage of remembering what he'd learned during his apprenticeship in the Rotunda, but it also revealed to him all of Truman's knowledge. Truman, and thus, Reilly, was an expert gardener.

He was satisfied with his new responsibilities and didn't shirk his duties as the Down House gardener. There was, however, a difference between being Spliced as Truman and as Raimondo.

A certain *knowing* resonated inside him. He didn't merely have information *about* plants, but he truly knew them!

It was a strange phenomenon. It was like the time when he passed through portals and saw the molecular and cellular structure of sea creatures; and the intergalactic stars and planets, extending forever. And when he found his dad's wool sweater in *The Ark* a moment before discovering his Stelladaur in the yew wood box—and then, in a flash, he saw everything about the sweater: the bleating sheep, the dyeing process, the woman hand-knitting it, buying it at Pike Place Market, giving it to his dad for Christmas, and watching his dad unwrap the gift.

It was as if something on Darwin's estate beckoned Reilly. A *living* thing!

No trees spoke to him, as Sequoran had done near his home and Grania did in Wicklow. An unseen force drew him away from the lime tree, past the gate, along the rock wall, and into the rose garden in the center of the manicured estate. Admiring the display of color, he weaved his way through the rosebushes. A small signpost beside each one indicated the species and the year Darwin had planted it.

He spotted a stunning rosebush ahead and moved towards it. It was covered with small, white, delicate buds, except for one large flower in full bloom in the middle of the plant, unlike any he had ever seen. He peered into the center of the petals and beheld a constantly changing spectrum of iridescent swirling colors.

Darwin had dozens of hybrid roses and other unusual plants, but Reilly suspected that the scientist had not seen this flower.

He watched the colors forming patterns and designs on the petals, like a rotating kaleidoscope. The high afternoon sun cast a low shadow on the earth, snuggled beside the bush. In the shadow he noticed a small mound of dirt.

Reilly knelt and scooped the dirt away with his hands. Buried in the shadow of the Damask Rose bush, which Darwin had created through cross-pollination and named *Anne Elizabeth*, was a small box on a post, inscribed with his daughter's name and death date. The box was made of yew wood.

Chapter Seventeen

Annie's Gift

Ignoring his pounding heart, Reilly dug deeper. When the entire box was exposed, he brushed away the earth and gently lifted the box out of the hole. He blew off a residual film of dirt, and his heart beat faster. He was gazing at a Stelladaur carved on the lid!

Reilly had no idea how long it had been since he'd found the yew wood box on *The Ark*, which had revealed his own Stelladaur. Time had become elusive and was now irrelevant. Everything he'd experienced before seemed to have occurred in moments. In that precise fraction in time, he lifted the lid.

Reilly gasped, having forgotten how brilliant a Stelladaur truly was! He picked it up by its golden cord, let the jewel hang down, and watched it twirl in the afternoon sun. Brilliant beams of light streamed in all directions, dancing gleefully, as if alive. Then he held the stone in his hands. Turning it over and over, he traced the facets with his finger.

Awestruck that he now held another Stelladaur, it was, nevertheless, obvious that this gem wasn't his. The same unspeakable sensation he experienced when he first touched his Stelladaur wasn't there. Besides, the facets were cut slightly differently.

Reilly reached for a folded piece of paper that had been tucked under the stone. He laid the Stelladaur in the box and carefully unfolded the paper. After glancing around to be certain he was alone, he read the note aloud.

> *If you find my treasure when I am afar, you must know this: it is a Stelladaur. I found it in this box, in this very spot. I have not told anyone my secret, and at times I feel a twinge of guilt for not having done so. Soon, I wish to tell Papa, because he knows a great deal about rocks and stones and science, and he would be pleased to see it. But even a scientist would not be able to explain what it truly is, so I will tell you part of the secret. Stelladaurs do not come from our planet. They are created from Stardust—near a place called Tir Na Nog—one jewel for each person ever born. I use my stone to transport to Tir Na Nog, where I play with my sister, Mary Eleanor. We have terrific adventures there. If Papa does not find his own Stelladaur, please give him mine.*
>
> *Annie Darwin*

Reilly was stunned by a déjà vu! The letter brought to his mind a similar letter that Charlotte had written about her own great-grandmother's adventures in Tir Na Nog. For a moment, Reilly thought he'd been transported to the Suzzallo Library, where he first found Charlotte's letter; and then to Wicklow, where Charlotte told him that she'd actually been to Tir Na Nog. He reread Annie's note, to be sure of the girl's intentions.

Anne Elizabeth had died of tuberculosis six years earlier, yet Darwin still suffered from the loss, often becoming physically ill or mentally tormented by unanswered questions about life and death. As a fearlessly pragmatic scientist, he made a habit of analyzing everything thoroughly. However, he reserved sharing his deepest thoughts, discoveries, and theories with anyone until he was absolutely certain of them. Even so, there were times when he'd had to admit great errors. His misconceptions about what a person could *absolutely* know nearly drove him mad.

Emma, on the other hand, had chosen faith, not reason, to make sense of life and provide a way to endure her pain and sorrow. It was a quality Darwin admired but didn't understand. Fortunately, their different philosophical views didn't put a wedge between them. Emma often referred to her husband as her *greatest treasure* and addressed him as such in letters she wrote to him.

With these things in mind, Reilly folded Annie's note, tucked it under her Stelladaur, and shut the lid of the box. He scooped the dirt back into the hole and leveled it with his hand.

Holding the box with both hands, he stood up and watched the magnificent rose swirling in a kaleidoscope of colors slowly close and turn into a white bud, like the others on the bush.

Reilly ran out of the garden and through the pristine yard to the far entrance of the Sandwalk, hoping to see Darwin coming his direction. The pathway was empty. He bolted ahead towards a bend in the distance, turned the corner, and checked once more for Darwin. He stopped to catch his breath. Then he ran as fast as he could to Down House.

He entered the hallway and stopped outside the drawing room door to listen to Emma play Chopin's *Spring Waltz* on the piano, a favorite piece of Annie's. He waited until the song ended before he knocked on the door.

"Truman!" Darwin said, swinging the door open wide.

"I apologize for the intrusion," Reilly said, holding the box to his side.

"Surely it must be important," Darwin continued, motioning for him to enter. "I recall but a few occasions when you deemed it necessary to interrupt our afternoon relaxation and meditation time."

"Yes," Reilly agreed. "It's most important."

Emma stood up and left the piano to meet Reilly. "Is there a concern about one of the children?" she asked, clasping her hands and then holding them above her waist.

"The children are well, but there is something of great significance that I must tell you."

"Certainly," Emma said, sitting down on a blue tufted chair near the fireplace.

The intricately carved grand piano was the focal point of the room, with a music stand and bassoon resting nearby. Reilly stood in front of a round, three-legged table on which books by Shakespeare, Dickens, and Sir Walter Scott lay. Darwin stood near the fireplace, resting a hand on the white mantel.

"What is troubling you, Truman?" he asked, glancing at the box in Reilly's hands.

Reilly's mind raced. He took a deep breath and hoped the words would come naturally. "I found this in the rose garden." He lifted the box in his hands. "It was buried beside Annie's rose bush, about seven inches under the surface."

Emma drew in a short breath and leaned forward. Darwin dropped his hand from the mantel and stepped close to Reilly.

"A box?" said Darwin, reaching for the object. "How exquisite!"

He held it, as if spellbound, tracing his fingers over the carved designs on the lid. "Whatever inspired you to dig in the rose garden—beside Annie Elizabeth's Rose, no less?" He hugged the box to his chest and coughed loudly.

"I'm not entirely certain," said Reilly. "Just yesterday I weeded the entire garden, so it was strange to feel inclined to go there today. However, something compelled me."

Emma stood up and moved towards her husband. "Compelled?" she asked with a lilting sound of hope in her voice. "Something beckoned you?"

"Yes. The rosebush itself. From a distance, I spotted a large blossoming white rose in the center of all the small buds and was drawn towards it. When I looked into the flower, I saw a myriad of colors swirling inside the petals. I've never seen a flower like it before."

Darwin coughed harder trying to clear phlegm from his throat while Emma patted his back. "Shall I call for some tea?" she said.

"No, my dearest Emma," he said, addressing her with his usual term of endearment. He turned to Reilly. "I visit Annie's rosebush almost daily, yet I've never seen such a rose."

"I know it's strange," said Reilly. "It happened just as I said it did. There was a mound of dirt that I'd never noticed before. I was compelled to dig into it … and I found the box."

Darwin looked at his wife and held her gaze for a moment.

"Perhaps we should see if there is something inside?" Emma suggested, placing her hand over Darwin's.

He nodded and together they lifted the lid.

The bright light that escaped startled Darwin. He threw his hands in the air and the lid closed as the box fell into Emma's hands. She held it tightly, waiting for her husband to regain his composure.

"What in tarnation did you find, Truman?" Darwin demanded, pulling his sideburn.

"It's nothing to be feared," Reilly said. "It's extraordinary!"

While his wife held the box, Darwin reached out and, once again, slowly lifted the lid.

Awestruck, husband and wife stared at the jewel. Darwin reached in, lifted the Stelladaur by the cord, and watched the light from the window reflect off the jewel, ricocheting in every direction. Emma squealed.

"It's a diamond!" she said, watching the jewel twirl.

"No," Reilly whispered. "It's value is far greater than that of a diamond."

"Indeed this is *not* a diamond!" Darwin declared, with a tone of certainty that surprised Emma. "I've been fascinated by rocks since I was a young child. Yet, in all my travels across the great oceans to distant lands, and with all the research, hypotheses, findings, and recordings of my theory of evolution and natural selection, I always believed there was something greater—something of which I've not yet spoken to anyone, nor written anywhere."

"This rock inspires you to tell us now?" Emma asked earnestly.

"It does."

He took the jewel and rested it in his open palm. Mesmerized, he paused before continuing. "Rocks can speak! I always believed it, yet now I have proof. They know all the events of history. The secrets of life lie within the rocks of the earth. Equally profound is … I hear Annie speaking to me through this rock."

Emma lowered the box to her side and grabbed Darwin's forearm, nearly sending the stone to the ground. "You can *hear* Annie?" she cried. "She's *speaking* to you *now*?"

"Not with my ears, dearest." He closed his fingers tightly over the stone. "Surely you understand that there are things we can only hear with our heart." She nodded, blinking away her tears.

"In the six years since little Annie's passing," Darwin said, "I've not felt her presence the way I do at this moment. I don't know what this means, but I know she is near. This stone is a thrilling discovery, and it entreats me to know its origin and elemental composition. Yet … so much more!"

Reilly didn't want to interrupt Darwin's epiphany, but he determined that he must read Annie's note immediately. "There's another treasure in the box," he said quietly.

Emma held the box open for Darwin. Still holding the glistening stone, he peered inside and saw the piece of paper. He cleared his throat to read aloud, but when he came to the word "Papa," he choked and blinked away the tears. The shadow of loss made him almost unable to speak the name of his infant daughter, Mary Eleanor.

Emma covered her mouth to keep her emotions from spilling over, and whispered, "It's a Stelladaur."

Darwin juggled to hold the stone and the note in one hand as he rubbed the crease lines on his forehead with the other.

"At ten years of age, Annie knew more than I will know in a lifetime," he said. "This jewel was the source of her knowledge and grand adventures, and it is the channel to her convictions."

Reilly stood behind Darwin, not wanting to impose on the man's discovery. It was an ethereal moment—pure revelation.

Emma closed the lid of the empty box and placed it on top of a small pile of books on the table next to her. She moved towards her husband and cradled her hands under his hand, holding the Stelladaur with him.

"She knew," Emma whispered, acknowledging her own epiphany.

Darwin held his wife's gaze and nodded several times, as if each bob of his head confirmed their expanding knowledge. "She had other places to go to."

"A path to this place called Tir Na Nog," Emma said, stroking the stone with one finger, as if it was the delicate body of a newborn child.

Suddenly everything Reilly had learned about Stelladaurs raced through his mind and coursed through his soul. He wanted to interject, to tell them all about Stelladaurs and portals and Deceptors and Splicing and Fractions. He opened his mouth to speak. Nothing came out. In another time and place—in years past—he'd been able to tell a few people whom he trusted about his own Stelladaur. Now, Darwin and Emma were oblivious to Reilly's attempt.

For a split second, Reilly thought his assignment was over and that he might be zapped through a Fraction to the Rotunda. He had, after all, uncovered the jewel and delivered it to its rightful owner. Maybe that was enough.

Reilly's split-second wish passed. Being Spliced included limitations and conditions.

"Duh," he whispered to himself, rolling his eyes. He silently admitted that when a person, particularly one in training to become a Stelladaur Ambassador, attempts to rearrange history and keep it from detrimentally repeating, anything can change in a mere moment.

This was one of those moments.

Since a moment is longer than a split second, he stepped back to let the great scientist and his dearest Emma begin the remarkable discovery of their true nature ... and to enable the brilliant Charles Darwin to rewrite his as yet unwritten book of historical fame and magnitude, *On the Origin of Species.*

Chapter Eighteen

Journey

L ogical thinking told Reilly his assignment with Darwin was complete, but when it came to matters of a Stelladaur, he knew that logic did not take precedence over intuition. He reminded himself that if he hadn't learned to submit to his own heart, he would have been trapped in Hell long ago. How long, he didn't know anymore.

So it was no surprise to Reilly when, on the following day, as he and Darwin walked through the gate into the rose garden, he said, "If Annie found Tir Na Nog, why couldn't you?"

The question left Reilly's mouth and crushed his chest like a lead weight. The fact that he still hadn't found Tir Na Nog was a brutal paradox that momentarily froze his heart in a vaguely familiar desolate place. He shivered, glancing around to see if the wind had picked up, drew in a deep breath, and half expected to see it to circle in front of him as he exhaled. For perhaps the ten-thousandth time, he chose hope over despair. Shutting the gate behind him, Reilly still trusted that the time for his greatest desire would come.

"She must have accessed a portal somewhere," Reilly said, relieved that he could voice the thought without divulging information that the Guardians and Splicing didn't allow. "Maybe it's here in the garden."

"A portal?" Darwin asked, stopping abruptly. "Are you suggesting a doorway of some kind? To another world?"

"Yes."

"That is a remarkable concept indeed!" Darwin said, his bushy eyebrows thinning as his eyes widened. He walked to the spot where Anne Elizabeth's Rose bush grew. "I was awake most of the night contemplating her message. I concluded that the effects of her illness and declining health must have carried her mind to a place of elaborate fancy. Nothing more."

"You don't believe there is a place called Tir Na Nog, as she said?" Reilly asked.

"Annie often used exaggerated language, and thought it a pity when I confronted her on it." Darwin stroked the white petals of a large flower. "Her manner was frank and straightforward, unsuspicious. Yet … she exuded a joyousness and transparency of her soul, which all who met her noticed. She enjoyed reading and had a fine habit of checking the meanings of words in dictionaries and gazetteers; and she would compare two editions of a book to determine if every word was precisely the same in both. She also spent endless hours verifying whether the colors of things in nature were correctly replicated in my books, because I organized my botanical findings by color and name. It was a strange pastime."

Reilly watched Darwin tenderly pry open the rose petals, as if doing so would soothe his grieving soul.

"She was delicate and lovely," he continued, "with a rare sensitivity to people and their plight. When she was but four years of age she contemplated her own existence and earnestly implored her mama to explain what happens upon a person's death."

Reilly remained still and waited for Darwin to set logic aside—to allow his heart to take charge—so that the supernatural melding that occurs when a person finds their own Stelladaur would happen to him.

Darwin hadn't found the gem himself, but Reilly figured he couldn't be the only one whose Stelladaur came as a gift. If Darwin, or any other person, was a genuine seeker of truth, and was prepared to uphold the responsibilities of ownership, their Stelladaur could indeed be gifted.

Reilly concluded that the current series of events was essential to rearranging history and was a result of his being Spliced. He remembered that his own Stelladaur had first belonged to his grandfather and then his father, and suddenly a new possibility sprouted in his mind: Had *they* been Spliced, too?

Darwin interrupted Reilly's thoughts. "Since Annie's passing, I have often pondered the subject of death. Our precious Mary Eleanor ... an infant ... such heartache. And the agony with the loss of Annie ... Six years of sorrow."

Over the years, Truman had assisted Darwin through various states of depression, and the current tone of the scientist's voice indicated that receiving the Stelladaur had triggered deep new emotions.

"What little time we have here in this desolate place!" he declared.

Attempting to bring Darwin back to the present moment and the idea that there might be a portal nearby, Reilly said, "Perhaps time is measured differently in places like Tir Na Nog."

Darwin frowned as he closed the rose petals he'd opened. He stared out, past the garden, as if beyond his property's borders. He reached inside his vest pocket and fumbled for his Stelladaur. He rested the jewel in his palm, and its light mesmerized him.

"As a naturalist, a botanist, and a geologist, I have not truly considered studying the relationship between body and spirit. Heretofore, my research and efforts have led me to believe that only a mere connection could exist between us, and a vast time-and-space continuum. Soon after Annie's death, I declared that I was a theist-turned-agnostic. This philosophy has brought me false understanding. Truman, from this day forward, I shall set my other professional endeavors aside, and begin a new quest." Tapping his cane to the ground, he declared, "I shall find this Tir Na Nog! I will live to write about it!" He lifted the cane above his head and waved it in the air, while the Stelladaur, suspended at the end of its cord in his other hand, dangled in front of his eyes. "It will be my greatest work!"

Surprised that the shift had come so easily for Darwin, Reilly tried to prepare him for inevitable setbacks.

"No doubt, Charles, you will find it!" Reilly confirmed his own conviction to himself. "However, sir, it could prove to be a lonely journey. What if you stand alone in your beliefs?"

"That would not be the first time—nor do I expect it would be the last!" He laughed, steadying himself with his cane, and closed his fist over his Stelladaur. "Are you with me, Truman?"

"Of course!"

"As Emma will be. How supreme the future will be if my family surrounds me!"

Emotions were triggered inside Reilly. He could only guess how long it had been since he had last seen Norah. At that moment, it was as if eternity had jumped into his heart.

For the next two weeks, Darwin spent his waking hours searching the rose garden, scouring his property, or pacing the Sandwalk, contemplating how Annie might have used her Stelladaur to access a gateway to the magical places she'd been. He found nothing.

Emma often stood at the drawing room window, praying that her husband's quest wouldn't drive him to madness.

Reilly did his best to encourage Darwin without disclosing his own knowledge of Stelladaurs. It was strange to be so sure of the fact that restraint was essential, especially when he was certain that Darwin would believe him if he told him about his own Stelladaur. Splicing had its boundaries.

Early one morning, after he had combed the grounds around Ann Elizabeth's Rose yet another time with a fine-bristled brush and an awl, Darwin pulled the Stelladaur from his pocket. He sat on the earth, watching the sunlight stream through the jewel for perhaps the hundredth time, unaware that Reilly had just walked through the garden gate.

"Any luck today?" Reilly asked.

"I don't understand," Darwin droned. "I thought it would be right here."

Reilly watched the light bounce off the Stelladaur and glisten on the dew, taken in by its beauty.

Shaking his head to bring himself back to his current responsibilities, he tried to say something that would let Darwin know he empathized with him in his disappointment. "Some journeys take longer than we'd like."

If Eilam had said it, or Fiala or Sequoran, it wouldn't have sounded so final, as if the journey would never end. But coupled with the awkwardness he felt in becoming a Stelladaur Ambassador, Reilly held to the hope that he was still seventeen years old. He couldn't wrap his mind around being ageless like Eilam, but he presumed that a time would come when he'd have to face that possibility.

Darwin put the jewel in his pocket and stood up. Leaning on his cane, he looked past the garden towards Down House. "Journeys.

Journeys, indeed! ... Thank you, Truman. I promised the children we would journey to Stonehenge. I've been so consumed with finding Annie's portal that I nearly forgot. We must go there for *her*, as well."

Without waiting for a response, Darwin tapped his cane on the ground and hurried past Reilly. "The Summer Solstice begins the day after tomorrow," he shouted, as he rushed out of the garden, towards the house. "Come along, Truman, there's much to get ready!"

Reilly caught up with Darwin and followed him into the children's parlor. There they met Emma, who was playing with the two youngest, assisted by Josephine.

"My dearest Emma," Darwin began, leaning his cane against a toy chest before he swept up young Charles in his arms. "I have been so preoccupied that I've left you wondering about our family adventure to Stonehenge. Truly, I apologize. Little Charles will come, as well. We must all be there together. Even Annie ... and Mary, too."

"Annie and Mary!" Emma scowled. "What do you mean?"

"I'm not entirely sure." He laughed, sounding more jovial than he had in years.

"She spoke with you? ... In your heart?"

"That she did!" He gently lifted Charles up and kissed his rosy cheeks.

He turned to Josephine and said, "Kindly gather the children and see to it that their belongings are packed in the travel trunks. We shall have to limit ourselves to four trunks in all, including one for my specimens and apparatus."

"Yes, sir," Josephine replied. "Come along, Charles." She took the baby from Darwin and left the room.

Emma pressed her husband for information. "What else did Annie tell you?"

"That we must go to the Summer Solstice before she will help me find her magical portal. After the festivities, I'll continue my work with earthworms," he replied, taking his wife's hands in his. "If I am to find Tir Na Nog, first there are truths to discover in the rocks of Stonehenge, and in the soil where they rest."

Reilly smiled inside, knowing that Darwin had indeed received a message from Annie through his Stelladaur.

Seconds later, a sharp shiver coursed through his body. It was hauntingly clear that what Darwin might discover at Stonehenge would be completely different from what lurked there waiting for Reilly.

Chapter Nineteen

Secrets

Two large stagecoaches were needed to fit everyone comfortably along with the four trunks. Josephine rode in one coach with William, Henrietta, George, and young Elizabeth, who sat up tall, trying to appear grown up like her older siblings. Darwin and Emma kept with them the four youngest, Francis, Leonard, Horace, and baby Charles.

Reilly rode outside with the driver, who didn't engage in conversation, which suited him just fine. He wondered why he was so chilled on this unseasonably warm June day, with the sun beating down on them. Arriving at London's Euston Station in less than two hours had hardly given him enough time to sort through his thoughts. For some reason, he dreaded the train ride.

The driver unloaded the trunks, stacking them two-high on the arrival platform opposite a northbound train waiting to depart. The younger Darwin children chased each other around the trunks in a figure eight, while the teenagers craned their necks to study the intricate wrought-iron filigree roof that towered seventy-two feet above them. Little Charles slept against his father's shoulder while Emma and Josephine rummaged through their carpetbags to distribute the apples and nuts they'd packed for snacking.

"Truman, when our train pulls up, please ask William and George to help you load the trunks," Darwin said, shifting the baby slightly in his arms. "It would be a pity to wake this little one, since our journey will take another two and a half hours once we board."

"Uh … of course," Reilly replied, distracted by the word *journey*.

Just then he remembered learning in the Rotunda that the Darwin family had traveled by train throughout England on numerous occasions, and that the direct service from London to Stonehenge had started earlier that year, in 1857. Although he'd recorded all of his tutoring sessions on his Fireglass, this was a fact he had forgotten.

The thought that he was living in 1857 made him feel out of place, as if he didn't belong in that time. He touched his face and hair, hoping nothing bizarre had happened to change his disguise as Truman, or that an *un*Splicing, if there was such a thing, wasn't occurring right then and there on the platform in front of the children.

He turned his gaze towards the tracks. "I think I'll stretch my legs a bit," he said. "I'll walk the length of the platform to see if the train is approaching."

He made his way through the crowds of people who shuffled luggage, organized belongings, and chatted about the thrill of visiting Stonehenge. Near the end of the platform a space opened up, where he noticed a man standing alone, peering down the tracks.

From behind, he noted that the man wore a loose-fitting black trench coat and an unusual hat—not the top hat or bowler worn by the other men at the station. Reilly pulled his own bowler down, slightly covering his forehead. As he approached the stranger, he could see that his head covering resembled a Scottish tartan hat, but it was made of smooth black leather, rather than the typical plaid wool.

Not wanting to stare at the man or his hat, Reilly stopped about fifteen feet away, closer to the edge of the platform than the man stood. He waited anxiously for signs of the train to Stonehenge. A gust of wind blew through the corridor between the arrival and departure platforms. Reilly pulled his tailored overcoat tightly around him, buttoned it, and adjusted his bowler.

A shrill whistle blast signaled that the train was approaching, and he hurried back through the crowd. He found Darwin already holding the handles of two of the trunks, one in each hand, with his two oldest sons each holding the handle at the other end of one of the cumbersome pieces of luggage. Emma was bouncing the baby, and Josephine had corralled the other children into a tight line.

"Truman, put one of those trunks on top of this one," Darwin said, nodding to the trunk on his left, which William was holding. The boy was taller than his father and anxious to show some muscle. "Grab the smaller one yourself. We shall make our way up to the other side of the platform."

Reilly placed a trunk as instructed and hoisted the last and smallest one onto his shoulder. The group made their way from the far side of the platform to the third passenger car, where a steward was assisting a passenger ahead of them. Darwin and his boys set the trunks on the platform and the family waited until it was their turn.

"Tickets?" said the steward, holding out his hand.

Darwin retrieved the tickets from his vest pocket and handed them to the man. "Twelve of us are traveling together."

The man counted the tickets and then did a quick headcount. "Very well." He turned to Horace and chuckled. "You'll have a jolly good time visiting Stonehenge. I expect this will be your first time there?" Horace nodded shyly. The steward tore the corner of the tickets and handed them back to Darwin. "The porter will handle your trunks. All aboard!" he shouted.

Reilly held back, waiting for the family and Josephine to board. As he stepped up onto the train, he saw the man with the strange leather hat boarding at the far end of the car. Their eyes met briefly and Reilly had a peculiar sense that he had met the man before. He shivered again and entered the train.

He settled in a window seat beside William, who yawned with boredom, facing Emma and Darwin. The other children bounced noisily in their seats.

Soon, the short whistle blast and hiss of the steam engine interrupted the children's chatter. The younger children jumped and covered their ears.

Darwin smiled at each of his family members. "Children, the adventure begins!" he said. "We're off to Stonehenge!"

Reilly placed his hat on his lap and ran his hands through his hair. He wondered what the message from Annie had said about Tir Na Nog, which had kindled Darwin's zeal to visit Stonehenge. There had been no opportunity to discuss it before they left Down House, and now was not the time. He tried to relax, but strangely, his dread and anxiety increased as the train pulled out of the station.

The train accelerated until it reached full speed at about thirty-five miles an hour.

Reilly daydreamed of a time when he'd taken an Amtrak train from Seattle to Portland with his parents. The trees of the Pacific Northwest whipped past the window in vibrant streaks of blended shades of green. But now, on the train to Stonehenge, the colors appeared separate and dull. His life as Truman felt distant. He missed his parents terribly!

Reilly's melancholy emotions confused him. He reasoned that the most logical place for a Fraction back to the Rotunda would be somewhere at Stonehenge, so he ought to be more elated about where they were headed than anyone else on the train.

But he wasn't elated. He wasn't thrilled at all. He felt only anxious dread.

He took a few deep breaths and put his hat on his head.

"Are you all right, Truman?" Darwin asked.

Reilly watched the countryside go past knowing it was lush but seeing only dreariness.

"Truman?" Darwin repeated, leaning forward. This time Reilly jumped, hearing his alias. "Do you not feel well?"

Reilly shook his head and blinked, as if he was coming out of a trance. "I'm fine. I'm just not quite myself today."

"The wonder of seeing the ancient Stonehenge has probably overwhelmed you," Darwin said. "And the secrets it holds!"

Darwin meant to be encouraging, but Reilly was already privy to secrets about Stonehenge that no one else knew. It was at times like this that the responsibility of keeping those secrets *secret* was utterly lonely.

"What kind of secrets?" William asked his father, loudly enough for the other children to hear.

Emma shook her head meaningfully at her husband to let him know she didn't think he ought to say much. To Reilly's knowledge, only Darwin, his wife, and he were aware of the Stelladaur and Annie's message to her father. The children leaned forward in their seats, eager to hear what Darwin would say.

"The earth has countless hidden secrets awaiting discovery," Darwin began. "I suppose that in all my years of travel and countless hours of laboratory research, I've uncovered but a mere pebble's worth of information."

"But those aren't secrets," Henrietta insisted. "You've written books about all that!"

"People all over England know about your work, Father," Francis piped up.

"Francis! Much further than England!" William said, annoyed by his younger brother. "Father is known throughout Europe for his research."

"I suppose you're correct." Darwin chuckled. Considering it irrelevant for his children to know he was famous throughout the world, he diverted their attention. "The Summer Solstice Fair will be magical. Part of that magic will happen because every person who attends will experience it a little differently. There are many ways to look at something—certainly, at the rocks of Stonehenge. Children, I promise that whenever you witness something magical, it will be unique and personal. You alone must determine whether to keep it secret or share it with another person."

Darwin held his hand over his bulging right vest pocket, where he kept the Stelladaur, while his pocket watch dangled from a silver chain in the left pocket. He looked at Reilly and furrowed his brow slightly, as if he suspected that his assistant knew a secret he was not privy to.

Reilly faced the window, frustrated by his own mounting uncertainties as they drew closer to Stonehenge. He tapped his fingers on his knees, and then sat on both hands to hide his nervousness. Annoyed with himself, he stood up.

"I'm hungry." He lied as nonchalantly as possible. "I think I'll see what the dining coach has to offer."

He scooted into the main aisle and headed towards the back of the coach. Most passengers were content and comfortable, but he was increasingly unsettled. He opened the door to the gangway, which led to the next passenger coach, and stepped into the open air.

The floor rumbled beneath his feet. Dizzy, he steadied himself on a side rail and watched as they passed along the River Thames, meandering west towards Amesbury. He lowered his eyes and watched the ground blur to speckled grey, as if in slow motion.

A wave of nausea assaulted him. He gasped and held his breath, trying not to retch. His clammy hands slipped on the handrail. He lurched forward and fell down, grabbing at a side handle just in time to save himself from falling off the gangway. His eyes widened as the whistle blew and the train sped past a lush field dotted with black cattle. He wiped his left palm on his pants and reached up for the railing, steadying himself with his right hand on the floor. Still breathing deeply to control the nausea, he slowly stood up and gripped the rail with both hands. When he turned to face the door of the adjoining coach, the man with the strange leather hat was standing in the shadows of the gangway.

"Good day," the man said, with a strong Scottish accent. "May I be of assistance to you?" He reached out in an attempt to help Reilly steady himself.

"No … I'm fine, thank you," Reilly said, instinctively pulling away.

"My name is Thomas Jamieson," he said, ignoring Reilly's resistance. "You must be Truman Hadley."

"How would you know my name?" Reilly tried to focus on the man's eyes, but they were hidden beneath the rim of his hat. "Have we met before?"

The man chuckled and tipped his hat slightly. "No, we have not. However, I have met your employer, Charles Darwin."

"I don't recall him mentioning your name."

"Perhaps not. However, we met in London four years ago at a lecture he presented to the Geological Society. Thereafter, he was kind enough to spend the afternoon with me, as I implored him to give me some guidance in my graduate studies in petrology, at which time he mentioned your name. Since then, we have corresponded by letter, on occasion."

Reilly leaned forward and tentatively extended a hand. "Mr. Jamieson, is it?"

"Please, call me Thomas. I noticed you earlier on the station platform. You looked familiar. I thought perhaps you were a school chum from Aberdeen. When I saw you board the train, I inquired about your name from the ticket master. It was then that I recalled Mr. Darwin telling me about his fine gardener, Truman Hadley. I can see now that I am a fair bit younger than you—no disrespect intended, mind you." He tipped his hat.

Thomas stepped out of the shadows. When their eyes met, Reilly, not meaning to be impolite, scowled. Something about Thomas made him feel uncomfortable. If Truman was older than Thomas—who appeared to be in his late twenties—how old was Reilly now?

"Forgive me," Reilly said, shaking his head. "The motion of the train has left me quite unsettled."

"Of course." Thomas opened the door to the coach Reilly had exited and held it for him. "Are you traveling with Mr. Darwin, by chance?"

"With his whole family."

"Heavenly providence!"

Reilly led the way down the aisle to the end of the coach, all the while thinking that meeting the man was a vicissitude, rather than a bout of divine intervention, or even luck, though he couldn't say why.

When they reached the Darwin family, Reilly hesitated, hoping that Darwin would recognize Thomas Jamieson and confirm his identity.

"Mr. Darwin!" Thomas exclaimed, tipping his hat as he reached out to shake Darwin's hand. "Indeed, it's a pleasure to see you here!"

Darwin stood up. "Mr. Jamieson! I might have presumed that our paths would cross, as you mentioned in your last letter that you planned to attend the Summer Solstice. I'm afraid I've been quite preoccupied and failed to find time to reply."

So, Thomas Jamieson was telling the truth. Why did I feel that he wasn't? Reilly wondered, as he settled back into his window seat.

Darwin introduced his family to Thomas and invited him to sit beside Reilly.

"How is your research coming along?" he inquired.

"Well enough," said Thomas, "although I do hope for a break-through during my visit to Stonehenge."

"Are you a geologist, Mr. Jamieson?" Emma asked.

"My expertise is petrology," Thomas replied. "Your husband's experiments and research with rocks is generally in relation to how rocks react to the forces of nature. I, on the other hand, study the origin of rocks, as well as their structure, unique properties, and composition."

"I see," said Emma.

"Thomas is passionate about a variety of subjects," Darwin said, chuckling, "rather like me."

"You obviously started your research at a young age," said Emma.

"Yes, ma'am," Thomas replied. "I began my studies earlier than some, and was recently fortunate to have received my undergraduate degree from the University of Aberdeen."

Interrupting an adult conversation was not acceptable, so the Darwin children listened intently, as they did when their father told adventure stories.

Reilly shifted, wanting more space between Thomas and himself. "What breakthrough do you hope for in your research at Stonehenge?" Reilly asked.

"I contend that the properties of some rocks are so unusual that their origin must be another planet," Thomas replied. "Perhaps even another galaxy."

"Asteroids … found on Earth?" Reilly didn't doubt Thomas's

supposition, but he was afraid he sounded skeptical due to his uneasiness with the man.

"Well, yes. As a matter of fact, one of the reasons for this visit to Stonehenge is to pursue my hypothesis of its origin. My doctoral studies focus on the theory that Stonehenge is a collection of remnants from an asteroid."

"Some might call that preposterous," Darwin said. "However, although I'm still coming to terms with my own absurd theories and erroneous beliefs—some of which caused me tremendous grief because I clung to them for so long—I would not dissuade anyone from pursuing a proposition such as yours." Darwin coughed into his fist; then he rested his hand over his bulging vest pocket. "It's a human right to use all one's faculties to discover truth."

"Do you have an explanation for the precise placement of the sarsens and trilithons?" Reilly asked, trying to appear interested in Thomas's theory only because he wanted to know more about Thomas.

"That's one of the great secrets of Stonehenge." Thomas directed his answer to Darwin. "Nevertheless, a recent discovery has led me to believe that there are two major factors. The first is related to the microscopic particles in the composition of the rocks. The second is associated with glacial formations."

Reilly saw Darwin's eyes widen. He frowned, though not intentionally.

"Might we be privy to your recent discovery?" Darwin asked.

Thomas tugged nervously on the brim of his black leather cap and pulled it tightly over his brow.

"It would be my honor to tell you, Mr. Darwin," Thomas replied. "Midway through my studies, a student of veterinary medicine lived in the flat adjoining mine. He was from West Amesbury, so Stonehenge was his childhood playground, and he often rode his horse there, exploring, as young boys do."

Reilly saw Thomas eye William to make sure he was listening.

"When I told him about my interest in rocks, he showed me several small rock specimens that he'd chipped away from Stonehenge to keep as souvenirs. He gave me one of them." Thomas reached into the pocket of his overcoat and held it out for Darwin and the others to see.

"I do not consider it prudent to destroy any of what remains of Stonehenge. Nevertheless, I can tell you that I've studied this small rock, and some of its properties are most unusual. I have not been able to identify them anywhere else, though I've studied the composition of thousands of rocks." He extended his hand towards the children so that they could see the treasure.

"I believe the rocks of Stonehenge are fragments of an asteroid that fell through the atmosphere billions of years ago, triggering a glacial era that contributed significantly to its preservation."

The children gaped at the rock as if it was really from another planet and epoch. Reilly's chest tightened. He, of all people on that train, ought to be open to the suggestion that some things exist beyond what the eyes can see—and eons before any creature with eyes roamed the planet.

"That sounds like the basis of a geologist's doctoral thesis," Darwin said.

"That is true, sir. However, the student who gave me this rock also gave me another unusual stone. It was nothing like this one." He leaned closer to the children and spoke slowly to emphasize his words. "It was crystal clear ... and stunningly brilliant. It looked like a diamond, though he insisted that it wasn't."

Reilly drew in a quick breath. Darwin pressed his hand against his pocket, and Emma stared at her husband. The children were captivated, eager to hear more.

"What kind of rock was it?" Reilly asked, trying to sound as if he'd never heard of such a thing—and hoping Thomas didn't suspect that he had.

"He didn't know." Thomas closed his fingers around the rock and put it back into his pocket. "I only saw the gem once. Soon thereafter, the fellow returned home for the summer, but on the way, he was thrown from his horse when something spooked the animal. He suffered a broken neck and died."

"How tragic!" Emma cried, cradling the baby.

The children sat back, entranced with the story. The younger ones clung to each other.

"I attended the funeral, and I'm ashamed to say that I inquired about the gem. I didn't mean any disrespect to the family. I simply wondered if he had told anyone else about his treasure. My father is a gemologist, and I hoped to offer his assistance in determining the jewel's value—for the family, of course. However, they knew nothing about it."

Reilly silently caught Darwin's attention and narrowed his eyes, signaling to him to use restraint as the conversation continued.

"Did he say where he found the jewel?" Reilly asked.

"At Stonehenge."

Chapter Twenty

Summer Solstice

"Oh, Papa!" Francis said, bouncing on his seat. "Do you think I could find a treasure like that at Stonehenge?"

"Me, too!" Leonard and Horace chimed in.

"Could it have been a queen's jewel?" Elizabeth asked.

"Perhaps from her crown!" Henrietta added.

"Not if it came from an asteroid," William said decidedly.

Darwin tapped his cane to the floor. "Now, now, children! I assure you that there are indeed secrets at Stonehenge, as Mr. Jamieson has indicated. However, you must be polite and allow him to tell his story."

Thomas smiled at the children. He nodded to Darwin and Emma, but avoided Reilly's gaze.

"Thank you, Mr. Darwin. However, with all due respect, this is not merely a fantastic story. I actually saw the brilliant treasure!"

"No doubt!" Darwin agreed. "Did the student offer any other information about the stone?"

"Only that when he first held it, he knew that it belonged to him—as if it had deliberately come to him."

"What do you suppose he meant?" Reilly interjected.

Thomas continued, as if he was speaking to everyone except Reilly. "It's perplexing. This will be my tenth visit to Stonehenge, yet I've not found any such brilliant stone. Nevertheless, I'm certain that, in time, my efforts will unveil other secrets within Stonehenge."

"Within?" Darwin asked. "Do you mean *inside* the rocks?"

Reilly squirmed, uncomfortable because the conversation was suddenly a déjà vu, and what Thomas said next was what he expected to hear.

"Yes … but perhaps *beneath* Stonehenge, as well," Thomas replied.

The way Thomas emphasized the word *beneath* suggested to Reilly that the man was privy to some knowledge about him that neither Darwin nor anyone else had.

Reilly scooted right up against the window, trying to make sense of his increasingly unsettled feelings about Thomas. He had a suspicion that Thomas knew more about Stelladaurs than he was saying.

Am I jealous? Why do I care that Thomas has seen a Stelladaur? Darwin is holding one himself this very moment! Reilly reasoned.

Although a Stelladaur had been made for every person ever born, something in his gut told him Thomas wasn't speaking the whole truth.

He closed his eyes to concentrate. Then it came to him!

He and Norah had been to Jolkavatar—near Tir Na Nog—at the Pool of Manifestation, where they watched the Star Fairies gather nuggets of truth for Stelladaurs. Now, he remembered the exact words spoken by Sitara, the small winged creature who was their guide:

"Truth is the first ingredient of a Stelladaur. It is what makes the jewel shine so brightly. Every truth is manifested as its own grain of light. When truth is disregarded, ignored, or in any way shunned, the grain of light will fade."

The truth in that moment was that although the entire Darwin family was enthralled with Thomas, Reilly didn't trust him.

He heard someone open the door to the corridor gangway. He tugged at the cuffs of his sleeves, pulling them over his wrists, and folded his arms to warm himself. With enough space now between himself and Thomas, Reilly watched the man as he spoke, noting his rugged profile under the brim of his cap.

"I'd be delighted to collaborate," Thomas said, as his mouth curved upward in an awkward grin.

Collaborate? Reilly panicked. Had he just missed something in the conversation because his mind wandered? He tried to focus.

"Where will you be lodging?" Darwin asked.

"At the Druid's Head Inn," Thomas replied, nervously adjusting his hat again. "It's a small establishment close to Stonehenge, but it draws a raucous crowd during the Solstice Festival."

"Indeed, not a suitable place for children!" Emma said. "We have reserved accommodations near Amesbury Station at The Rosemary Hotel."

"I've secured a large carriage for our use during the week," Darwin said. "This will ensure that the littlest ones don't become cross due to unnecessary fatigue from travelling to and from Stonehenge, and that they will be able to enjoy the festivities."

"Shall we meet the day following the Summer Solstice?" Thomas said. "Just north of the sarsens?"

Darwin and Thomas stood simultaneously.

"Midmorning, the day after tomorrow," Darwin said, reaching to shake Thomas's hand.

"Of course, there is the possibility that we'll happen upon one another at the gathering or sometime during the festival, though the crowds are larger every year." Thomas tipped his hat at Emma. "Ma'am." Nodding to Reilly, he added, "Until then."

At that moment, Reilly caught a glimpse of something attached to the far side of the man's cap—a crest or tartan pin—but he couldn't get a detailed look at it. Thomas walked down the aisle, and as he opened the door to the gangway, another chill wind blew through the carriage. Reilly rubbed his arms vigorously, trying to warm himself.

Reilly sat at a small desk in his room at The Rosemary Hotel, gazing out the window at the sunset. With Stonehenge less than two miles away, he was homesick for the Rotunda, and the room designed to look like his own bedroom, though of course, it wasn't. Staying with the Guardians and Keepers hadn't been so bad, he thought.

It had, however, been so long since he'd been to his home on Bainbridge Island, that there were times when the details were a blur. Unfortunately, that kind of homesickness couldn't be a true longing. Instead, it gave him determination and hope that someday it would all be worth it. He'd learned not to be surprised by what *all* or *it* might be. In his heart, finding Tir Na Nog and being with Norah was the *worth*.

Deciding that time had become like the melding reds and oranges in the sunset, he allowed the beauty of the scene to ease the pain of separation from those he loved.

The colors faded and darkness crept into the room, casting shadows on the walls. Reilly crawled into bed and pulled the covers over his bare chest. He lay awake for hours, trying to make sense of his negative feelings about Thomas. He repeatedly asked himself why Darwin, who had found his own Stelladaur, hadn't noticed anything disturbing about Thomas?

Finally, knowing the Summer Solstice sun would rise over Stonehenge in a few hours, he wrestled with the squeaky mattress in a final attempt to fall asleep.

A horse whinnied and woke Reilly. Footsteps pattering past his door and the chatter of children's voices told him the Darwin family was already dressed and ready to leave for Stonehenge. He threw off the covers, dressed quickly, and bounded down the stairs to the crowded lobby.

There he found Emma and Josephine rallying the children, their arms filled with blankets, picnic baskets, umbrellas, writing pads, and a few small toys. Reilly followed them out the front door into the still dark morning. Colder than usual for late June, he lifted the collar of his overcoat around his neck.

He found Darwin adjusting the bridle on one of the carriage horses.

"Did you sleep well, Truman?" Darwin asked exuberantly, as he cinched the noseband.

"I was restless."

"Filled with excitement for today's events, no doubt!" Darwin stroked the horse's jowls. "Count yourself lucky that eight children weren't sprawled about your room! I thought the two sleeping chambers of the main suite would be large enough, but now I'm hopeful that there will be a vacancy for Josephine and some of the children after the festival, when the crowds check out of the hotel."

"It's generous of you to provide me a private room," Reilly said, rubbing his hands together and blowing into them.

"It's quite brisk, indeed." Darwin coughed into his hands. "The morning air clears my lungs."

"If you can manage the coach without me, I would enjoy a walk," Reilly said. "The exercise will warm me."

"Certainly. William and George can ride up front with me. We'll meet you on the west end of the circle, perhaps twenty meters back."

The stars were no longer visible as dawn lit the path from town to Stonehenge. With a couple of hours before sunrise, Reilly had enough time to make the three-mile trek. He let several people pass him on the trail, preferring to be alone with his thoughts before the crowds and activities of the solstice fair began.

The air was damp and dew rested on the tall grass. The countryside smelled fresh and crisp, with the scent of late-blooming honeysuckle and the last purple orchids. For the moment, Reilly was glad that, as Truman, he was an expert at identifying hundreds of plant varieties. The fragrances were welcome and soothing.

His thoughts reverted to where they had left off in the middle of the night, when his attempt to figure Thomas out kept him from sleeping. He picked up his pace as he reviewed things in his mind about the man.

First, it was clear that Darwin knew Thomas. He had considerable confidence in the budding scientist and had conversed with him several times by letter, discussing various perspectives and theories of petrology. Second, Darwin had asked Thomas to join him in his work at Stonehenge—not an insignificant invitation! Last, Darwin was thrilled, and not the least bit skeptical, when Thomas told the family about his friend's unusual, remarkable stone.

It wasn't logical to Reilly why he should have reservations about Thomas. Did the fact that the man wore a peculiar hat and didn't want to make eye contact with him when he spoke justify his mistrust? Reilly thought it did. After all, relying on logic at the expense of his gut feelings had never proved to be a smart choice.

He saw dozens of people ahead on the path as it narrowed in the distance. He heard a soft drumming, like the drumming he'd heard from the miner's cart when he first rode towards Stonehenge. Reaching a narrow point in the path, he stepped into a vast grassy field, and the silhouette of the ancient towering stones came into view.

Like before, the drumming sound gradually increased as he continued towards Stonehenge. A shrill whistle began, sounding like an alarm; it was not the tone of the whistle he heard on his way to the Rotunda. The beating accelerated, rising to a piercing crescendo that made him shiver, and he covered his ears for a moment. Then his walk turned into a run, as he headed through the field towards the towering circle of stones.

The sunlight filtered in below the horizon, creating a delicate halo over the field. The whistling sound increased in volume and pitch, and a strange black ring began to form around the edge of the halo. Reilly's head throbbed from the noise, with the beating drums rebounding between the great sarsens and trilithons.

He could see his breath, like a fog in front of him. He ran faster, searching for Darwin's carriage. Spotting it in the crowd, he bolted forward.

Something caught his foot and he tripped, falling hard to the ground. His hat toppled off, and the bristly grass against his cheek made him grimace. He stretched out his arm to reach for his hat— but someone grabbed his hand.

"Let me help you."

It was Thomas. The man's hand was as cold as ice, and Reilly unintentionally jerked his own hand away. He took a deep breath and jumped to his feet.

"You must be careful," Thomas said, holding out Reilly's hat. "The shadows in the path to Stonehenge can make it difficult to see."

Reilly brushed off his overcoat. Thomas's hat shaded his forehead, eyes and nose, as before.

"Thank you," Reilly said, placing his bowler firmly on his head. "I think the intense noise disoriented me in the obscure light."

"Intense noise?" Thomas grinned crookedly. "It's merely the folk musicians tuning their instruments for the moment of sunrise. Nothing more."

Reilly scowled.

"We'd best hurry now," said Thomas. "We'll want to be in the perfect spot when the sun rises. I see Mr. Darwin now." The man pointed towards the east.

As Reilly turned, he caught a glimpse of the tartan pin on Thomas's hat. There still wasn't enough light to see details, but he could tell it was shaped like a dagger with a strange crest in the center. Was it a gargoyle?

Reilly and Thomas hurried to meet Darwin.

"You made it!" said Darwin, greeting them. "I was beginning to doubt that either of you would find us in this crowd."

"The numbers increase each year." Thomas repeated what he'd said on the train.

"I wonder how many visitors are earnest in their purpose for being here," said Darwin. "The Summer Solstice may just be an excuse for them to socialize in the name of astronomy."

"Perhaps," said Thomas. "I suppose there are a variety of reasons why there would be interest at this particular time of year."

"I've heard that some attempt to disfigure the stones," said Reilly. "They chip away at the rocks with hammers." He shuddered, thinking of the Deceptors who chipped away at the tree-homes in Wicklow.

"Emma and Josephine have decided to stay near the carriage with the children," Darwin said. "It's too crowded for all of us to make it to the center of the circle together. I believe the three of us will manage to weave our way up." He turned to his children and tapped his cane on the ground. "Stay close to your mother and enjoy the splendid sunrise! I shall return soon."

Darwin, Thomas, and Reilly set out into the crowd, making their way towards the circle.

Reilly zigzagged ahead, keeping his eye on the Heel Stone—the spot above which the sun would rise, between the giant trilithons, precisely in the center of the circle of stones. The high-pitched whistling increased as the sky gradually turned pink.

When he reached the circle's opening, he squeezed his way past dozens of people and found a spot on the large flat stone that lay on its side, right in the center of Stonehenge.

Reilly waved to Darwin, but he couldn't see Thomas anywhere. When Darwin reached the flat stone, he handed Reilly his cane and tried to hoist himself up. Reilly reached out and grabbed Darwin's hand. At that moment, Thomas appeared and gave Darwin a boost so that he landed successfully on top. Thomas jumped up and stood on the other side of Darwin.

The three men silently watched the pink sky change to fuchsia, and waited eagerly for the yellow ball of the sun to appear.

Darwin spoke first. "It reminds me of the colors inside Annie's Rose … swirling and changing …"

Reilly watched Darwin carefully as he spoke, practically needing to read his lips because of the loud drumming and whistling, which only he seemed to be affected by.

"… such mysteries." Darwin said, resting his hand over his vest pocket, entranced as he stared out towards the Heel Stone.

Reilly saw Thomas eye Darwin's hand.

"I've come to Stonehenge frequently over the past decade, hoping to find someone who I might entice to linger longer and dig deeper …" said Thomas.

Reilly felt uncomfortable, once again. He thought Thomas's tone had a sinister ring and strained to hear the man over the noise of the crowd and the whistling alarm.

"… to go beneath, where the greatest ancient secrets lie." Thomas's mouth curled up in an odd smile.

"Tomorrow, let us continue that search together," Darwin replied, still staring at the horizon, "after the children have enjoyed a day of adventure, picnicking, and frolicking about the rocks." He steadied himself on his cane with one hand and reached into his pocket with the other. "Annie would have found such delight in this occasion."

Reilly wondered what Darwin was doing! He needed to speak privately with Darwin, or to at least whisper in his ear and tell him not to pull his Stelladaur from his pocket! But a whisper never would have been heard, and the minute passed in what seemed to be a mere fraction of a second

"Certainly, great adventures await us!" Thomas nearly shouted. He removed his hat and held it at his heart.

Shifting his attention back and forth between Darwin and Thomas, Reilly was certain something more extraordinary than the Summer Solstice of 1857 was occurring.

Then, as if signaled by an invisible maestro, the noisy crowd quieted to a hush, and on the horizon, the sun rose with its brilliant radiance.

An eerie silence overwhelmed Reilly—his body, his mind, and his soul. He shivered, and his breath blew in front of him in a cold cloud. He felt completely alone.

Then, slowly but perceptively, the sun's rays merged into the blue sky and the yellow fireball rose majestically above the Heel Stone.

At that moment, and before Reilly could do anything about it, Darwin took the Stelladaur out of his pocket and held it in front of him, mesmerized. Startling, bright beams of light shot through the stone, casting rays inches in front of Reilly's feet.

In the same instant, Reilly noticed a black cloud beginning to strangle the haloed sky high above Stonehenge. Even the bright rays of the new day's light could not penetrate the looming darkness.

Thomas shot an icy glare at Reilly.

Reilly had seen those eyes before! Cold! Dark! Evil!

The hostile stare held Reilly's gaze, as if it had frozen his feet to the ground and his eyeballs in their sockets. He tried to step back so he could jump down from the rock, but he couldn't move. He couldn't blink.

A long, thunderous crack ripped through the silence and reverberated between the sarsens, as if the Devil himself was cackling in Reilly's ears, deafening him. The rock he stood on split open and morphed into a grotesque stone gargoyle. The monster opened its mouth wide, gaped at Reilly, lunged forward—and swallowed him. Reilly plummeted down a black hole, far beyond the depths of Stonehenge.

Chapter Twenty-One

Craters

Reilly fell helplessly into the agonizing abyss.

This was no ordinary portal! It wasn't the arch of a rainbow leading to an intergalactic space. It wasn't a brilliant firework display taking him to a place of enlightenment. It wasn't a seamless step into a magical world, or an intriguing doorway in a library that led to a forested town, where Pucatrows lived in Undertunnels and people lived in treehouses. And this certainly was not a painless Splicing from the Rotunda through the Shield of Forgotten Memories.

Powerless as he spiraled downward, Reilly screamed into the darkness. Shards of razor-sharp icicles sliced through his clothes and tore at his flesh. His eyes burned and his head throbbed, and he felt as if an excruciating brain freeze had attacked his entire body. He couldn't tell if he was subconsciously holding his breath to mitigate the pain, or whether breath was there at all.

There were worse things than death and Reilly had seen plenty of them. Until now, he hadn't wished that he would actually die in any given instant. Unfortunately, he could still hear himself screaming. His eyes stung with a deep and bitter chill when he blinked in a vain attempt to focus and see what was happening.

After what seemed like an eternity, Reilly stopped spinning in the savage vortex. He landed flat on his back.

An invisible weight pressed on his chest, forcing his breath to be shallow. A thick fog, as black as tar, swirled around him allowing barely enough light to filter in. From deep in his subconscious came a whisper, telling him who he was: Reilly McNamara, an Echtra and a Stelladaur Ambassador in training. He was still alive!

Reilly summoned just enough strength to move his fingers. He wriggled his nearly frozen bare toes, and then his feet. His hat had fallen off his head and his tattered overcoat covered his body in shreds. His pants and shirt were ripped and frayed, and blood oozed beneath the fabric from dozens of open cuts.

He closed his eyes and painfully moved his hands to his head. With numb fingers, he rubbed his temples gently.

Stand up! Keep moving! he told himself.

He was in too much pain to consider where he was or why he was there. He rolled onto his side and curled his stiff legs up against his body, groping for his shredded coat to pull around him.

Get up! Start walking!

He took a few deeper breaths, pushing through the stabbing pain. *Now!*

Leaning on one elbow, he steadied himself with his other hand on the frozen ground and gazed into the murky air. The movement revived him enough to spark an unadulterated determination. He continued to rise to his feet.

It was too foggy to see more than a few feet ahead. He struggled and took a step forward. Though his heels were almost numb, he could feel the ground enough to know it was hard and rough. His toes had turned bluish-white, and they burned with pins and needles.

Reilly pulled a few strands of icy hair from his face. He could blink now, without his eyelids scratching like sandpaper. For that he was grateful.

As his senses began to work, a putrid stench assaulted his nostrils and invaded his lungs. He coughed to keep from gagging. The cough echoed, as if from far away—and then, the sound of beating drums began. Or was it his heart, pounding as if it were outside his own body, determined to keep him alive?

As he walked on, the fog dissipated into a dismal haze. The frigid air finally cleared, and his surroundings came into focus. Craters small enough to jump across dotted the ground, and he wondered if he had landed on a strange moon. The pits bubbled with grey muck erupting and spewing like chilly mini-geysers.

Behind him there was nothing else, so he moved ahead, dodging the craters. The barren, frigid tundra stretched as far as he could see.

After a considerable time, his legs ached from walking, though his feet and toes were still numb. The blood from the open wounds had stained his shabby clothes, freezing them against his body with dark red streaks.

Something appeared on the horizon. Was it buildings? He pressed forward jumping over smaller pits and avoiding the larger craters. Soon an unmistakable scene marked the wasteland. In the distance, a dreary, desolate Seattle skyline came into view.

With renewed strength, Reilly picked up his pace. When he reached the outskirts of the city, he noticed the first signs of life. Ghastly children and teenagers dressed in ragged tunics, who looked hollow, pale, and terrified, retreated down side streets, into alleys, and behind stone buildings. The creatures blurted out sounds like shrill whistles when Reilly approached. He tried to open the doors of a few buildings but they were locked. Or frozen shut.

There were no cars. No signs of technology. No noise, other than the haunting, steady drumming and the *eeking* sounds from the ghostlike creatures he passed by.

Icicles hung from the tops of the buildings like massive stalactites, and windows were frosted over. A frosty mist swirled around the city, as if the craters surrounding it were breathing, causing a freakish sublimation.

The strange annihilated city was merely the skeleton of the place near his home. The city was once called the Emerald City because of its luxuriant green forests. Now it was black and grey and haunting.

Compelled to find a broader view of the landscape, Reilly worked his way towards the building that resembled the Space Needle, hoping he could figure out a way to get inside. It towered above the other buildings like a dreary excuse for a city icon.

Dozens of translucent frightened young people hovered on the ground around the bottom of the Space Needle, clinging to each other. Most of them scattered out of sight when he approached. He noticed a teenage boy hiding behind a wide cement post when he tried to open the main entrance door.

The handle wouldn't budge. He couldn't tell if it was locked or frozen shut. He scraped frost from the window with his thumbnail and pressed his nose to the glass. The gift shop, once filled with memorabilia and gadgets, was empty except for a few small souvenirs frozen to the shelves in blocks of ice. The elevator shaft was a pillar of dirty ice that extended as far up as he could see.

On the opposite side of the lobby, the stairway was encased in its own frosted glass, but for some reason, the steps themselves were not ice-covered.

Reilly walked around the building, trying every door handle, but to no avail. Back at the main door, he found the ghostly boy still hiding behind the post, waiting for him.

"There's only one way to get into the Tower," the boy whispered, glancing from side to side. "We're not sure why they haven't figured it out. It doesn't really matter, but we pretend it does. How did you get here?" he asked. "You obviously weren't deposited like the rest of us."

He adjusted his tattered, yellowed tunic to cover his broad shoulders.

"Deposited?" Reilly asked, noticing that the boy's arms and legs were extremely muscular, despite his unhealthy pallor.

"C'mon. You need to get off the streets." The boy motioned for Reilly to follow him. They circled halfway around the base of the Tower and stopped at a door Reilly had missed. "This way." The boy held the door open, and as soon as they were inside, he bolted the door behind them.

"I'm Alex." He reached out to shake hands.

"Reilly." He held the boy's hand firmly. It was warmer than he expected it to be.

"No one has ever arrived here without being deposited," Alex said. "What are you doing here?"

"Good question," Reilly began. "I was at the Summer Solstice at Stonehenge. A strange series of events happened just as the sun rose above the Heel Stone. A giant crack opened in the stone I was standing on, and I was swallowed into a violent vortex. I thought I was going to die."

"I've never been to Stonehenge," Alex said. He looked Reilly over from head to toe. "You're not dead, that's for sure. And you certainly weren't deposited!"

"What does that mean?"

"Deceptors can decide to leave a body they've imprinted, deposit the person here, and go into hibernation. While they're in hibernation, they can't take over another body and they forfeit attendance at a Festival of Fire."

"You know about Deceptors? And Festivals of Fire?" Reilly's voice rose in pitch.

"Of course," Alex said. "Everyone here imprinted at a Festival."

Reilly's eyes widened and his mind raced.

"At least we didn't get ripped to shreds—like you!"

He led Reilly through another door, and they meandered a short distance through a winding tunnel.

"There used to be an entire underground city and rails to take people wherever they wanted to go."

Of course! The Seattle underground, Reilly thought.

"This used to be prime real estate, but it all caved in and then froze solid. We dug this tunnel ourselves when we figured out that the Tower was the place to get a decent view ... and to stay warm. It has survived numerous sizeable earthquakes, among other disasters. Most of the city has been destroyed. It's desolate, and what once were buildings have either been reduced to piles of rubble or one- or two-story ruins."

The tunnel ended abruptly. Alex climbed a short ladder and opened a trapdoor.

"The other Watchers saw you coming. They'll be glad to meet you."

They stepped into a glass-encased stairwell that overlooked the frozen gift shop.

"The elevators were inoperable when electricity became obsolete—a long time before I was deposited." Alex craned his neck to observe the towering staircase. "The hike will warm you up."

Reilly chuckled and ascended the stairs behind Alex. As they climbed the first few floors, he regained some feeling in his toes.

"So, you're a Watcher?" Reilly asked.

"Yeah. There are nine of us. The Dwellers would rather just come on their scheduled Warming Day. They don't want the responsibility that comes with being a Watcher. Do you have any experience Watching?"

Reilly thought for a moment. "Some," he said, assuming that reading auras from the Vantage Post at the Embassy in Wicklow counted. "How many have been deposited?"

"We stopped counting the ones who die right away. Thousands."

"That many?" Reilly gasped.

"Newcomers arrive every day, but most don't survive the cold longer than a week. Twice a year we conduct a census. At last count, there were two-hundred sixty-nine Dwellers, plus the nine of us."

"Where do you put the ones who die? And where do the Dwellers live?"

"They live here in the city, as close to the Tower as possible. There's nothing further out, not for hundreds of miles. Anyone who leaves, thinking they might find a safer city ... well, no one has ever gotten past all the craters. I'd sure like to know how you just waltzed into town past them."

Reilly shrugged his shoulders, deciding not to inquire further about what was done with the people who died, at least for now.

They climbed another hundred feet and Reilly stopped to catch his breath. He was nauseous from the stench of dead fish, seaweed, and a nasty odor he couldn't identify.

"We're almost there." Alex laughed. "You'll get used to it."

"To that awful smell?"

"No, the hike."

When they reached the top of the Tower, the other Watchers were eager to greet them.

"This is Reilly," said Alex. "Obviously, he wasn't deposited. He hasn't told me the whole story yet."

"I'm Thaddeus," said a tall, muscular boy with perfect teeth. He shook Reilly's hand. "Call me Thad."

"Okay," Reilly said.

"I'm Zeke," said a boy with red hair. "Short for Ezekiel. Not sure what my parents were thinking on that one." Zeke's copper freckles stood out against his white skin.

"It's a cool name," Reilly said. "What I mean is … uh … do you know what the name means?"

Ezekiel laughed. "It means 'God strengthens.' Not sure about that, either."

A tall girl with curly brown hair pushed in front of Ezekiel. A belt was tightly fastened around her waist, keeping her baggy pants from falling down. "Mila. It's a Slavic name that means industrious. I suppose it fits me, because I'm usually the one who figures out how to use our resources optimally."

"We wouldn't survive without Mila," said another girl, stepping forward. "I'm Abigail. I do my best to welcome the Dwellers when they come up on their Warming Days. I visit with them and give them hope."

"Hope is useless if you're powerless," said another boy.

"Don't mind Emmett. He's fairly new here and has a lot to learn," said a girl with jet-black hair, who looked about fifteen. She threw her arms around Reilly. "I'm Tessa. I totally understand that it takes a while to get a good grasp on things."

"Don't grasp too tightly!" said an older girl, pulling Tessa away. "Let the young man breathe." She had long blonde hair woven into a thick French braid, draped over one shoulder. "I'm Shay—short for Shayla. Mila and I were the first ones deposited here."

The last Watcher, a slender boy with blue eyes and a broad smile, stepped forward.

"Last, but not least," said Alex, tousling the boy's already disheveled hair, "my little brother."

"I'm Wyatt." He brushed Alex's hand away.

Reilly looked at the nine Watchers. All except Wyatt were around his age—teenagers—the age Reilly hoped he still was. Wyatt looked the youngest, and he guessed that Thad or Mila was the eldest. Then he assumed that it didn't matter one way or the other, because they'd likely been there longer than they cared to admit. "Glad to meet you all," he said.

"Does it hurt?" Tessa asked, pointing to the cuts on Reilly's body. She stepped close to him and reached to touch a wound on his chest.

"It did. Worse than anything," Reilly said, looking at the streaks of dried blood on his arms and chest. "I probably look like a freak from some horror movie."

"*I* don't think so," Tessa nearly sang.

Shay rolled her eyes. "You wouldn't."

"I guess I'm too cold to care," said Reilly.

"If you become a Watcher, you'll warm up," said Alex. "It's not exactly a penthouse suite, but the Tower has its perks."

"We'll give you the grand tour," said Tessa, jumping forward. "Right this way." She swept her hands forward to show Reilly where to go.

Everyone followed her from the stairwell to the south-facing windows.

Reilly had visited the Space Needle numerous times, but he wasn't sure whether the Tower was the same place. Although there were similarities, the Tower floor wasn't rotating and, due to the heavy black clouds outside, not much light filtered in through the glass wall of windows.

"The observation windows extend all the way around the Tower," said Tessa, stopping at a window and waiting for everyone to gather around.

"We brought the telescopes inside. We *always* leave the doors to the outer balcony closed," said Mila, as if she was giving instructions.

Reilly stared out at the desolation. He moved to a nearby telescope and looked through it, aiming south, past the rubble of the city. He adjusted the focus to scan the entire landscape and saw a sea of oozing craters.

"What *is* this place?" he asked, squinting as he stepped back from the scope.

The others exchanged glances as if no one wanted to answer.

Finally, Shay replied. "The Bleak," she said.

Even before she said it, Reilly knew! When Afismat first told him about the Bleak—and that no Echtra had survived it—he could tell that the day would come when he'd be sent there. To do what, he didn't know.

"It's way past the berm and beyond the gulley, right?" said Reilly, remembering what Afismat had said about the outskirts of the Rotunda.

"Can't say if any of us have been there," said Emmett. "But this place is as messed up as it gets."

"He's right about that," said Thad, glaring at Emmett. "But Emmett would adjust more easily if he pulled his share of the work."

"Hey, I just don't like bathroom duty," Emmett whined.

"Likin' it has nothin' to do with it!" Thad retorted. "I'm sick of hearin' you moan and complain. There are worse jobs, and you know it. Get a better attitude or you're out in the streets!"

"Who put *you* in charge?" said Emmett.

"Stop it!" Shay commanded, folding her arms. "You're both so annoying!"

"Getting back to your question," said Alex, "the Bleak is where the Deceptors hibernate … inside the craters."

"They *live* in the craters?" Reilly asked.

"They aren't exactly living there," Alex explained. "They're frozen solid, cold as dry ice, but they bubble like geysers. The bubbling sounds like beating drums. You won't notice it after awhile."

"It's louder today," said Wyatt. "Weird."

Reilly peered through the telescope. "The craters are every-where—as far as you can see!"

"There are more every day," said Alex. "A new one appears each time a person is deposited. We can't get out there to help them all as they make their way to the city. Most of the Dwellers are too frightened to go near the craters."

"And you wonder why I think it's hopeless," Emmett sneered, pacing the floor.

Shay shook her head and bit her tongue.

"How many Deceptors are in each crater? How long will they hibernate?" Reilly asked.

"At least one. Some likely keep many of the demons hidden, until the next Eruption, which could be any second … or not for who-knows-how-long," said Alex. "Maybe centuries. None of us has been through an Eruption."

"But we survived being deposited!" Mila interjected. "Now, to prepare for the Eruption, we use what we learned about the Deceptors when we were still imprinted."

"I know what their plan is," Emmett said. "Human annihilation!"

Shay, who stood next to Emmett, put a hand on his shoulder. "The memories from our imprinting don't leave us," Shay said. "We can use that to our advantage."

"It's not that any of us looks forward to an Eruption," Alex continued. "On the other hand, the only chance we have of get-ting out of here is if there is an Eruption before we die … *and* we survive it!"

Reilly noticed Wyatt's eyes widening, and he wondered if this was the first time the younger boy had heard about Eruptions.

"You haven't told us much about yourself, Reilly," Tessa said, anxious to change the subject. "If you weren't imprinted and de-posited, how did you get here?"

"As I told Alex, I came through a vortex. I was at Stonehenge for the Summer Solstice and a portal opened in the crack of one of the sarsens when the sun rose over the horizon. Just before it happened, I recognized a person who I'd seen before … a long time ago … in a different life. I'm certain it was someone who had been imprinted."

Reilly didn't think it was wise to give the Watchers too much information. He tried to give them a truthful answer that would make some sense.

"What happens when a person is deposited?" Reilly asked the group.

"You probably know that Deceptors imprint people when they're most vulnerable," Thad said, eager to be part of the conversation. Reilly nodded. "Reversing an imprinting by depositing leaves that person physically vulnerable. When a Deceptor comes to the Bleak, it finds a spot to dig a crater, and as it dives in to hibernate, the imprinted body is separated from it, and the demon spits it out onto the bitter ground. Most people don't make it into the city because they freeze to death."

Reilly shivered. He wondered why he hadn't passed any dead bodies on his way to the Tower. He was certain that he wasn't the only one telling just part of their story.

"How far does the Bleak extend?" Reilly asked.

"We aren't sure," Alex replied, trying not to sound negative. "Emmett is right in saying the Deceptors intend to annihilate all of humanity. We have guessed that there are other remote cities like this one that function on some level, likely with other people who have been imprinted."

"Though I haven't been imprinted myself, I *have* had some experience with Deceptors," said Reilly. "But I …"

"If you haven't been imprinted, you don't know what it's like! It's Hell to be completely controlled by a Deceptor," Emmett interrupted. "The memories are madness."

"You're probably right," said Reilly, seeing Emmett's eyes filled with fear.

"Let's continue the tour," Tessa said, jumping in next to Reilly. She linked her arm through Reilly's before he had a chance to object and led the group to the center of the observation deck. "Here we have the dorms. Boys to the left. Girls to the right. The bathroom is in the small closet in the far corner. It's basic, to say the least, but Mila rigged up a water system that makes it bearable. No shower, just a toilet."

"Not exactly the Marriott," Reilly said, trying to keep the conversation light.

"This way is the kitchen," Tessa continued, pointing to a swinging door further to the left. "Most of the time we eat raw seafood, plankton, seaweed … whatever we can scrounge through a small hole we've managed to dig in the frozen Puget Sound."

The Puget Sound! It was music to Reilly's ears.

He walked to the east window and looked out at the frozen inlet towards where Bainbridge Island would be. Though it was daytime, it was too dark to see across the water, or any further than what should have been the Seattle ferry dock. There was no sign of any docks, ferries, or waterfront stores—just fallen buildings and piles of rubble along the shoreline. And countless craters.

"What's out that way?" he asked, pointing towards Bainbridge but still thinking it was too early to tell them he lived there—or that he *had* some time ago.

The Watchers looked at each other as if the topic was taboo.

Ending the awkward silence, Alex spoke up. "We call it the Crossing."

Looking out across the frozen water and into the dark sky, Reilly asked, "Why?"

"It's where the dead are finally laid to rest," Alex said. "We just hope they cross to a place where they will never suffer again."

Chapter Twenty-Two

A Flicker

With people being deposited and dying every day, the time for discussion was over. As far as the Watchers were concerned, the tour of the Tower had ended.

"We've got work to do," Thad said. "The buckets still need to be brought up."

"He's right," said Shay, turning towards the kitchen. "Dinner will be late as it is."

Emmett groaned and Zeke sighed. Everyone dispersed except Alex.

"No one has ever arrived before without being deposited," he said. "I hope I didn't mess up your schedule too much."

"Naw, we need the help." Alex motioned for Reilly to follow him, and they made their way around the inside perimeter of the Tower.

"Every other day is a Warming Day like today. Each night, after we prepare and serve dinner to the Dwellers, eighteen of them stay and sleep at the Tower for the night. If they eat one meal a day and warm up, even just a little, they survive much longer."

Abigail walked in holding something in her hand. "I thought you'd take about a size ten," she said, handing Reilly a pair of shoes made of strange leather. "They're ugly but warm."

Reilly took the moccasins and slipped them on. "My toes are toasty already," he said, looking down at his feet.

"We aim to please at the Tower," she said with a laugh.

Alex laughed, too, and said, "Abigail is our concierge. One of her jobs is to keep up the morale."

"For your further enjoyment, here's a bucket of water to freshen up," she added playfully.

"Thank you. So sorry I can't tip you," Reilly said with a grin.

"That's okay. There's nothing left in the gift shop that I want to buy anyway." She laughed again and excused herself to prepare for the Warming Day.

Reilly carried the bucket to the kitchen, following Alex's lead. When they walked through the swinging door, a rancid smell assaulted them.

"How are your cooking skills?" Shay asked as the boys entered the room.

"I've done some baking," said Reilly as flashes of Blackberry Bakers and Dante's medieval kitchen ran through his mind.

"Tonight it's seaweed soup with a few crabmeat flakes. We haven't had biscuits or bread in years," she said.

"Soup sounds good," Reilly said, wrinkling his nose, "but smells … terrible!" He scrunched his forehead and blinked hard, as if a mound of freshly chopped onions were stinging his eyes.

"I'll take that as an honest critique," said Shay with a smile. "That's the second quality you have that I admire, Reilly. The first was hope, and now, honesty."

Reilly scanned the room. "This is a real culinary setup," he said. "Practically a fully-stocked kitchen!"

"Soon after we arrived, we salvaged whatever was left in the Tower's closets, cupboards, and storage rooms," said Alex.

"The gift shop had lots of treasures, too," Mila chimed in, holding a blue plastic back-scratcher in her hand. "This gadget has several uses. For instance, it makes a perfect slotted spoon."

"Mila is incredibly resourceful." Shay added. "Don't let her modesty fool you. She's truly a genius."

"We made the nonperishable food last almost a year," Mila said. "There wasn't much meat. A few dozen cats and dogs stayed frozen outside until we needed them."

Reilly tried not to grimace. He'd never eaten a domesticated animal, not even in Black Castle. "Survival is rough," he said, hoping it didn't sound ambivalent.

"We've managed," Shay replied. "Mila also rigged up an efficient cooking system. However, to conserve fuel, we eat mostly raw fish and seafood."

Alex joined the conversation. "I had no idea I loved ice-fishing," he said, joking. "It's hauling the daily catch up here that's so exhausting! The Dwellers help when it's their turn to stay overnight. They're probably on their way up now. C'mon, Reilly, let's check on their e.t.a."

On the way to the stairwell, they passed the boys' dorm, and Reilly set his bucket of water just inside the door. "I'll clean up later," he said. "I'd rather help."

"See if you can pass some of your positive energy to Emmett," said Alex.

They waited at the top of the stairwell and saw Thad leading the way, with Zeke and eighteen Dwellers behind him, each carrying buckets. When they reached the top, Wyatt took a bucket from Thad and Alex grabbed one from Zeke.

"Fewer than last night," Zeke said, eyeing the crabs as he handed the bucket to Reilly.

"Got a few small salmon, too," said Thad, flashing a smile. "We're having dessert tonight!"

"Awesome!" Wyatt replied.

Alex introduced each Dweller to Reilly as they passed.

"Do you know the names of *all* the Dwellers?" Reilly asked.

"Most of them. Not all the new arrivals."

Reilly wanted to learn as much as he could. He stared out the window, trying to get his bearings but barely able to see beyond the rubble. "Are you sure there aren't other survivors out there, besides the Watchers and Dwellers?" he asked.

"We can't be sure. It takes all day to retrieve those who don't survive their deposit and to help those who do to get situated, catch seafood, and prepare dinner. There's rarely time to do anything else." Alex leaned forward, resting the weight of his body on his arms, braced on the window railing.

"It's strange that the Dwellers won't help more, especially when you're working so much to keep them alive."

Reilly noticed Alex grip the railing tightly. He trusted Alex, but he wondered if the Watchers had purposely withheld details about the Dwellers. He was hopeful, even confident, that the Watchers had the best interest of the others in mind. But something didn't make sense.

"Sometimes some of them help catch the seafood, but there's only one hole in the ice, so only a few people can fish at a time. Besides, Dwellers don't like the way we handle things at the Tower." His voice cracked slightly. "They'd rather have the benefits without the responsibility of what has to be done."

"You mentioned that earlier." Reilly leaned forward, trying to get Alex to look at him directly. "What other responsibilities? What else do Watchers do?"

Alex nodded at one of the telescopes, about twenty feet away, where Tessa perched. "Each day two of us monitor the telescopes, checking for anything unexpected. New arrivals almost always show up in the evening. If they don't survive the deposit, we have to retrieve them as soon as possible."

"Before they're frozen solid and too heavy to take to the Crossing?" Reilly asked.

"Not exactly."

"Alex, level with me," Reilly said, louder than he intended. Tessa waved at him to lower his voice. He nodded and spoke more softly. "I know a lot about Deceptors. Why do you think I'm the only person who arrived without being deposited? I'm here to help. But I need to know the truth about what goes on here."

Alex relaxed his grip. "Before I was imprinted, sometimes I judged people who did despicable things," he said, still avoiding eye contact with Reilly. "I didn't understand that the part of them that I saw wasn't who they were. One day, my own life took a turn. I didn't see it coming." His eyes met Reilly's. "Do you know what I'm saying?"

Reilly nodded. Alex stared out the window.

"Everything changed. *I* changed! I got into bad stuff and ended up on the streets. After two years, I couldn't take it anymore. I tried to end my life. Three times. But I failed miserably. I felt so pathetically alone! But I had no idea that I'd already been imprinted. Does anyone know when or how it really happens? One day, we just wake up in that Hell and we're cast into the fire for the imprinting. I was just a kid!" He smacked his fist on the thick window, and gripped the railing again. "Anyway, I had no one to turn to. So ... I turned to myself. I looked in the mirror and asked the person staring back at me what the hell I was doing there. Do you know what I saw in that mirror?"

Reilly shook his head.

"The shell of a person who had done despicable things."

Alex paused, waiting for Reilly to say something. Reilly just listened.

"I didn't have a chance to do anything about it," Alex said, his voice cracking as if he might cry. "The next thing I knew, I was here in this godforsaken place! When I was imprinted, I'd hardly ever thought about my life before. Now, after being deposited, I think about it all the time. They stole my life, Reilly! I wish they'd killed me instead. Now I live for *this*?" He jerked his hand towards the window.

Reilly looked out at the dreary sky. As always, he still had questions. This time his mind wasn't racing. There was a strange contentedness, as if a warm light had engulfed him.

"The point is, you *are* alive," Reilly said quietly. "What you do with your life, even here, is what counts in the end."

"What end?" Alex shouted. He faced Reilly directly, half expecting him to have an answer.

"The end that begins where you left off."

"I thought the Festival of Fire would be the end, but it was just the beginning of being imprinted. Then I thought being deposited would end it. Yet, like you said, I'm still alive. And now? Now ... I've seen hundreds of people's lives end in this bitter place. Every time I take one to the Crossing, I wonder if they become a Deceptor that haunts me."

"Why would you think that?"

"Because of the despicable things I do ... *now*."

Reilly was glad they were finally getting to the bottom of what the other responsibilities of a Watcher were. "What things?"

"After dinner tonight, you'll come with Thad, Zeke and me, and then you'll see. It's part of your debriefing. Anyone who wants to be considered for a spot as a Watcher has to be debriefed." Alex waved at Tess down the curved corridor. "Let's see what the count is today."

Alex and Reilly walked towards Tessa, who fiddled with the eye-piece of the telescope.

"Nothing to the north," she said. "There are three to the far south, two just past City Center, and three due east. Oh, and one not far from the largest crater at the edge of the water."

"The numbers are dropping," Alex said, with a hint of sullen-ness. "Not sure how everyone will handle that."

Reilly caught Tessa raising her brow at Alex. Could it mean the boy hadn't informed him about everything that it was his respon-sibility to tell?

Tessa released the telescope. "No need to spoil this gentleman's appetite by overwhelming him with *everything* about the Tower on his first day here," she said, slipping her arm through Reilly's. "I think I'll steal him from you and find a table for two with a view." She laughed and dragged Reilly away.

A stream of Dwellers had lined up along the west wall, each holding a large bowl with an unusual shape and a spoon. At the front, Alex and Abigail scooped the seaweed soup from two large pots and poured it into the bowls, one by one. Tessa escorted Reilly to the soup pots.

"The Dwellers know we eat first." Tessa sneered. "Work does have its rewards."

"I don't mind waiting. They were here first."

He wanted to be polite and he secretly hoped they'd run out of soup. He didn't know if he could stomach eating it with the over-whelming rancid smell penetrating the entire dining area.

"You're new here," said a Dweller in a strong Australian accent. He surveyed Reilly and fixed his eyes on his moccasins. "Me, too."

The boy was familiar. He wore loose-fitting brown pants and a muslin shirt with long, billowy sleeves.

"I barely made it to the city," the boy said. "You're a Watcher?"

"Excuse me!" Tessa bellowed. "Of course, he'll be a Watcher!" She snatched an empty bowl from Alex's hand and held it out.

"I haven't decided yet, myself," the boy continued, ignoring Tessa. "Shay started my debriefing yesterday but I'm still weighing the pros and cons."

"Great. Take your time deciding," Tessa snarled. "Until then, this Watcher eats before you do."

"Tessa!" Abigail chided. "Try to be nice! You're not making a good first impression." Abigail nodded at Reilly.

"Hmpf!" Tessa snorted. "Can you *please* give our new guests—*both* of them—some soup?"

"That's better," Abigail said. She handed Reilly and the boy full bowls of soup with extra lumps of crabmeat on top.

The boy, who Reilly guessed was older than the Watchers and the other Dwellers, veered off to the left to join his peers. Reilly reluctantly followed Tessa to a table on the north side of the Tower.

They'd barely sat down when Emmett joined them, saying, "Is it edible?" He gaped at the chunks of crabmeat in Reilly's bowl. "Hey, you're getting the royal treatment. I just got seaweed *broth*—no seaweed. It gets old." He frowned and let his spoon drop into the bowl.

"Mine's barely warm," Tessa said, as if she thought complaining qualified her to be Emmett's friend.

Reilly took a deep breath, trying not to gag before he tasted the soup. He liked seafood but the stuff in his bowl smelled atrocious.

"I'll take your crab if you don't want it," Emmett said.

Reilly picked up his spoon and tried a small bite. It tasted as bad as it smelled, but he didn't want to add to the whining.

"Go ahead," he said, pushing his bowl across the table. "I'm not hungry."

Emmett laughed hard. "Ha! You will be!" He dumped the crabmeat into his bowl and stirred it in. "It doesn't take long to notice that one meager meal a day isn't much." He swallowed a chunk of crab and then took another mouthful. "On the other hand, when there's a good catch, we get some real delicacies that the Dwellers don't."

"One of the perks," Tessa added between slurps.

"I think I'll wander around. Maybe I'll see if there's anything new through the telescopes." Reilly pushed his chair from the table. "Thanks."

Emmett picked up his bowl and chugged some green liquid without saying another word. Tessa frowned. "I'll catch you later," she said.

Reilly left the dining area, drawn to the north-facing window.

The entire sky was overcast in a thick, cloudless grey. It wasn't any darker outside than it had been when he'd arrived. There was no sun to set. No moon or stars appeared as the night wore on. Everything was the same dismal grey.

As he stepped up to a telescope, he felt as though his life was a series of continuous déjà vu moments in timeless parallel worlds. The scopes at the Vantage Post—where he'd become an expert aurologist—provided an interesting view with diverse colors. In contrast, the shades of grey across the Bleak were monotonous, almost boring. For a moment, he pretended that being a Watcher might be boring.

Checking again, unidentifiable hues of light filtered in from somewhere to the north, beckoning him. He could hear something with his heart, the way he did when he just *knew* something.

Tilting the telescope slightly upward, he blinked to focus. He scanned far to the right, then to the left, and back to the center, due north. A flicker of light caught his eye. Holding the scope steady, he waited … and kept waiting.

There was no doubt in his mind—he had seen something!

Gradually and ever so slightly, he fine-tuned the focus. The light flickered again! Far in the distance, barely poking through the blackness, a distinct light beckoned him.

It had been difficult to get his bearings from the top of the Tower. The windows looked like painted grey walls. None of the rubble in the city was visible unless he stood right up to a glass. Beyond that there was just a black fog—until now!

He was certain that the Watchers and Dwellers had not seen the flicker, though he didn't know why. He decided not to say anything about it. Not yet.

As he watched the quivering light, he knew where it originated—north of what was once Seattle, beyond Capitol Hill, where entertainment and culture had been alive and thriving, past the multi-lane bridge that had served countless vehicles in stop-and-go traffic across Lake Washington.

The light defied time zones, portals, and parallel worlds!

Reilly's gift of knowing rang inside him as clear as a bell chiming from a church steeple. It reverberated from a library he'd been to before. But he couldn't determine whether it came from the Suzzallo Library in Seattle—or The Library in Black Castle.

Chapter Twenty-Three

The Crossing

eilly wanted to run down the ten flights of stairs to the ground and head towards the flickering light, but restraint had been his friend before, and he knew it was a virtue he needed to rely on now. Moreover, he keenly remembered the gifts the Guardians had promised to bestow upon him: strength, clarity, and tranquility. He was content to wait.

Before the Dwellers finished eating, Alex, Thad, and Zeke found Reilly. Alex and Zeke each carried a bucket filled with utensils and gadgets. Thad had a large brown leather tarp under his arm.

"There you are," said Alex, no longer sullen. "Are you ready to go to the Crossing?"

"Yes, of course," said Reilly. "Can I carry anything?"

"Tessa spotted nine who didn't make it today," said Thad. "You can help us haul the bodies on the tarps. C'mon, you'll see."

The boys headed down the stairwell. A few minutes later, they heard someone racing down behind them.

"Hey, guys! Wait up!" A boy's voice echoed from a full flight up. When he reached the group, Reilly saw that it was the fellow he'd talked with in the line at dinner. "Shay said to catch up with you so I can finish my debriefing."

"Most newcomers don't want to stick around for the hard work. You must be considering a position as a Watcher," Thad said, handing the boy a tarp. "You can start by helping with this."

The boy awkwardly tucked the tarp under his chubby arm. Reilly noticed an unusual pin on his shirt, which he hadn't seen earlier, and peered at it. It was a small badge in the shape of a dagger, with a gargoyle on it! Exactly like the one on Thomas Jamieson's leather cap!

Alex took charge of the formalities. "I'm Alex. This is Thad, Zeke, and Reilly. He's new, too."

Reilly's eyes met the boy's, but he didn't get any indication that the boy recognized him from any meeting in the past. He stared at the pin. "Where did you get that?" he practically demanded.

"Nice to meet you, too." The boy laughed, still fumbling with the tarp. He touched the pin with his free hand. "I saw it lying on the ground right after I was deposited. I thought it looked cool, so I picked it up and put it on. I'm Tyrone, by the way."

The boys leaned in to inspect the pin.

"I bet Mila could put that gadget to good use," said Alex.

"Never seen anything like it," said Thad.

"I want one!" Zeke reached out to touch the pin.

Piecing together the facts, Reilly realized that he'd now seen the symbol of the gargoyle on three different people. He needed to know one thing.

"What's your last name?"

"Jarvis," said the boy. "Why?"

It was no coincidence! The three people connected to the image of a gargoyle were **Tyrone Jarvis**, **Thomas Jamieson**, and **Travis Jackson**!

"No reason." Reilly lied, now even more certain that he couldn't tell them anything else.

"C'mon," said Thad, taking the lead. "We're way behind schedule tonight." When they reached the ground level, he conducted the others around the base of the Tower and then behind it to a small roofless building fashioned out of rubble, the size of a large shed. Reilly hadn't noticed it before.

Once inside, Alex and Thad went directly to two bizarre carts and wheeled them out of the shed. The carts were made of eerie webbing—bones lashed tightly together with hair. To Reilly, they looked similar to the Pucatrows' ladder that he'd used to climb up the cliffs to Black Castle. The webbing hung from poles, which served as frames for the carts. He couldn't determine what the wheels were made from. The shed was full of buckets and large containers filled with odd frozen items that Reilly couldn't identify.

"If they're not too large, we can get all nine bodies to the Crossing in one trip," Alex said, handing each boy a pair of leather mittens. "That will save a lot of time."

"That would be nice," Zeke said, putting on his mittens. "I hate the all-nighters."

"Sheesh! Don't start whining already," Thad said. "I'm glad Emmett's not here tonight to bellyache with you."

"We've got Reilly and Tyrone to help tonight," Alex added. "Cross your fingers that we're back in time to get a couple hours' sleep."

Reilly and Tyrone put on their mittens. The boys put their buckets and tarps in the carts and followed behind Thad and Alex, who took the lead, pushing the carts. A few of the others carried unusual lanterns, which emitted a nasty brown smoke that smelled worse than it looked. The wheels made a scraping noise on the rugged, frozen ground.

The edge of the city wasn't far. Reilly guessed about half a mile from the shed. With the Dwellers still at the Tower for dinner, the city showed no signs of life of any kind. The stench of the Tower dissipated as they moved further away.

"Shay said there were two just past City Center," Alex said matter-of-factly, his cold breath mingling with the grey fog, "just up ahead."

They advanced the distance of a couple blocks and Tyrone spotted something first. "There's one!" he said, pointing at a body sprawled on the ground.

"Good eye!" Alex cheered, as they sped up to reach the spot.

"She's tiny," said Thad, lifting the girl into his arms. The other boys emptied the carts and Thad gently lowered the girl. "Still warm, though."

Nothing else was said and they wandered east, searching for the other person who had died near City Center that day. They'd almost passed it when Zeke tripped over its legs, protruding from the doorway of a dilapidated building. He swore as he stumbled to catch himself.

"Let's put him in this cart," said Alex. "He's heavy and it will give better traction until we find the others."

Alex, Thad, Tyrone, and Reilly each took an arm or a leg and heaved the man into the empty cart.

"Two down, seven to go," Thad declared, as if he was keeping track of innings at a baseball game. "The older ones never make it."

Though life at the Bleak was anything but a game, there were certain rules that had to be followed. Reilly needed to know all of them.

"I noticed you're all teenagers or younger," said Reilly. "Why?"

"Thad's right about the old ones," said Alex. "Depositing is too brutal. Their bodies just can't take it."

"The freezing temperature kills most of the others, especially the little ones," said Thad. He looked into his cart at the girl. "She can't be more than ten."

"Wyatt is the youngest survivor," said Zeke. "He's nine."

Reilly's experiences at Black Castle had given him a broader understanding of Deceptors than the Watchers had gained. "Deceptors don't usually bother imprinting young children," Reilly said. "But they influence younger and younger ones these days."

"*These days?*" Zeke blared. "How would you know? You said you haven't even been imprinted!" He spit into the foggy air.

"Shut up, Zeke," said Thad. "Reilly doesn't have to tell us anything about himself until the end of the debriefing. You know that." He steered his cart to the right and added, "We've got seven more to find. C'mon."

Moving slowly east, the drumming noise grew louder as they neared the city border. Through the thick fog, Reilly could see vapors from the geysers up ahead.

"This is where it gets tricky," Alex warned. "Watch your step. The craters are sometimes difficult to see, and the carts don't always fit between them."

They maneuvered the carts around several craters until the space between them became too narrow to risk pushing the carts further.

"This is as far as they go," said Thad. He stopped and reached into his cart for a tarp. "We'll drag the other bodies back to the carts on the tarps. Sometimes it's a couple of miles." Tyrone reached in to grab the second tarp.

"I still think losing a few in a crater wouldn't be so bad," Zeke whined.

"You say that all the time," Thad retorted. "You know it could trigger an Eruption! Why do we have to go over and over this concept?"

Zeke shrugged and veered off a short way to the left, weaving between craters.

Reilly maneuvered around the sinister bubbling holes. The geysers rumbled like distant thunder as they spewed into the night air.

His feet and hands were cold, but the moccasins and mittens kept them from turning numb. Occasionally, he held a hand to his mouth to breathe in some of his own warmth. He was grateful that there was no wind.

They walked for almost an hour over the haunting minefield.

Reilly hadn't taken time to wash the dried blood that looked like shrapnel wounds all over his body. Streaks of red had crusted into icy scabs, some frozen to the strips of his torn clothes.

The boys stayed within hearing distance of each other, ready to holler if they found a body. Passing two craters that were especially close to each other, Reilly's foot bumped against the next victim.

"Over here!" he blurted out. "Be careful. There's not much room."

The others made their way to Reilly. Thad spread a tarp a short distance from the body, where there was enough room to lay it flat.

"We'll have to carry it a ways," he hollered. "This is as close as I can get."

"Good. Tyrone and Reilly can get this one," said Alex, surveying the body. "He's tall and skinny. Tyrone, you take the arms. Reilly, get the legs."

Tyrone positioned himself near the man's head and prepared to grab near the elbows. Reilly gathered the legs at the knees, ready to lift. "On the count of three," Reilly said. "One! Two! Three!"

As they heaved it up in one swoop, Reilly caught another glimpse of the gargoyle pin on Tyrone's shirt. He shivered with vivid memories of Ukobach, the Prince of Hell—of facing that devil and watching him imprint Travis Jackson. The infernal fire in Black Castle had seared Reilly's body and tried to singe his soul.

Even as an Echtra, and now a Stelladaur Ambassador in training, he still felt the sting.

Reilly gripped the legs of the body, determined to do whatever it took to bring justice to the poor man—a man who'd been deceived, imprinted, deposited, and finally destroyed by a Deceptor.

As that thought passed through his mind, something whispered deep in his soul: *Justice is a wasteland in a heart with no mercy.* Then, as if his soul refused to acknowledge the message, he had a clear recollection of what Afismat told him: No Echtra had survived the Bleak!

Reilly moved forward, warning himself that his training had just begun.

"Watch your step behind you," Alex warned. "There are six craters in a row. Take your time."

The body was heavier than Reilly expected and it was awkward to skirt the craters. It took them several minutes to make their way to the tarp, where they let the body down.

"Nice job," said Thad. "That was the easy part. When we find the other two that fell out this way, the tarp will be too heavy to carry and we'll have to drag it back to the cart."

Fifteen minutes later, Alex and Zeke found two bodies in close proximity to each other. With three bodies heaped on the tarp, the boys dragged it painstakingly around dozens of craters, back to the carts. With the heavy loads, they weaved south for a few miles beyond the city. Alex, Zeke, and Reilly pushed one cart, and Tyrone helped Thad with the other.

Reilly guessed that it was near midnight, and they still hadn't found the three bodies Tessa had seen earlier in the evening. His back ached and his calf muscles cramped up, but he persevered.

"How do you do this when there are just three of you?" Reilly asked, though not as a complaint.

"It depends on where they're deposited and how close they manage to get to the city," Thad replied. "It usually takes a lot longer."

"Fewer are deposited these days than there used to be," said Alex.

"Usually Emmett comes, too," Thad continued. "With you two helping, I was happy to leave him behind. I'd rather work harder than listen to him whine and moan."

Wanting to understand protocol better, Reilly proceeded. "Does Wyatt come, too?"

"No!" Thad almost shouted. "He's too young!"

"Watchers vote on all important decisions," Alex explained calmly. "We decided before Wyatt arrived that Watchers had to be thirteen years old before they would be assigned to duties at the Crossing."

"Oh," said Reilly, wondering what all those duties were but knowing he'd find out soon enough. "How many Watchers can there be?"

"Ten maximum," said Alex, diverting a cart that had veered too close to a crater. "Shay and Mila made that rule before any of us arrived. I guess you could say they run a tight ship … in a good way."

"Mila can be demanding," Zeke added.

"We wouldn't be able to find any of the bodies if she hadn't rigged the telescopes," Thad continued, trying to show patience with Zeke's ignorance. "We'd all be dead if it weren't for her brilliant inventions. As far as I'm concerned, she can be demanding if she wants to be."

"Shay is practical," Zeke continued.

"Which is why she can distribute things fairly and evenly," said Thad.

After stabilizing the cart, Alex picked up where he'd left off. "The Tower can sustain ten core people over the long term. All newcomers are eligible for an open Watcher's position, but most never make it through the debriefing without choosing to live in the city as a Dweller instead. For those who want the job, the existing Watchers must vote in their favor unanimously when the debriefing is done.

And then, even if the position is offered, few newcomers decide to accept it."

"Emmett passed the voting?" Reilly asked, half joking.

"With the number of Dwellers dwindling, we agreed to let him join us," Alex said. "He complains a lot, but he's strong."

Winding further south around the craters, Reilly wondered if there was a better way to find the bodies. *More light would help*, he thought.

A few minutes later, Thad found two more, a young man and a young woman, huddled together.

"Seeing their arms wrapped around each other makes me wonder if they were deposited at the same time," said Thad, touching the girl's cheek first and then the boy's. "Maybe they were friends … or lovers."

The boys stepped in to get a closer look.

"They're smiling," said Zeke. "That's creepy."

Thad rolled his eyes. "Let's load them in the same cart," he said softly.

Reilly watched as Thad tenderly wrapped the arms of the bodies around each other after they were placed in the cart. He made a mental note that Thad might have left a girl behind when he was deposited, perhaps someone he thought about all the time.

With four bodies in one cart and three in the other, they chugged on. A short while later, they found the third body that Tessa had located. After shifting the buckets to make room for it, they headed north towards the Tower.

"We need to veer left and head west," Alex said, as soon as the Tower was in view.

Reilly helped to scoot his cart around another large, rumbling crater. He'd grown accustomed to the noises they spewed, but this one bellowed fiercely. He was glad that as they moved ahead fewer craters lay in their path.

"The Crossing is this way, about a mile on," said Alex, leading the group around the edge of the city. "The last body we have to find is near a crater by the water, and we'll be ready."

The boys picked up their pace. Reilly and Tyrone were eager to see the Crossing, and the rest were eager to be done with the duties of the day so that they could get back to the Tower and sleep. When they found the body, Reilly and Zeke piled it on top of the others in their cart.

They passed heaps of rubble that lay along the shoreline, and Reilly noticed that the water had frozen into solid ice. He kept his eyes to the ground and pushed hard past the strain in his shoulders.

Alex stopped the convoy in front of a wide ramp that disappeared across the ice into the fog. "We need to lift the carts onto the plank so the wheels don't get caught," he explained. "Everyone, we'll shift this cart first."

Reilly and Tyrone followed Alex's lead and helped hoist the carts onto the plank, positioning the wheels in two thick grooves in the wood. Once in place, the boys pushed the carts forward at a slight incline. Alex stopped fifty feet ahead, where the ramp leveled out.

Reilly heard the sound of rippling water. He peered over the side of the ramp, which was suspended like a bridge barely six feet above a large water hole in the ice, about twenty feet in diameter. Around the edge, and streaking outwards into the fog, the ice was red—a nauseating blood red.

Alex looked down and said, "The Crossing."

Chapter Twenty-Four

Buckets and Bins

"A moment of silence, please," Alex said, bowing his head. The others followed in unison. Reilly and Tyrone waited for instructions.

A breeze blew from the other side of the hole, and the same loathsome stench assaulted Reilly again. He covered his nose and mouth with his mitten hand, hoping the vile odor would pass in the wind.

"May the Crossing keep them free forever," said Alex.

"Free forever," said Thad and Zeke.

"Amen," said the Watchers in one voice.

Reilly and Tryone looked at each other. "Amen," they whispered. The ritual was over.

Then, as if the prayer was nothing but a mockery, Thad said, "Nine bodies tonight. Let's do it fast."

Tyrone gazed down into the water. "Are we dumping them in *there*?"

"If only that was all we had to do," Zeke said in a dreary tone.

"We disassemble the bodies," Thad explained without apology. "We salvage as much as we can. Almost every part is used."

Disassemble? Reilly thought. *Salvage? Used?*

He released his hand from his mouth. Turning his hands over, he looked closely at the mittens that kept his hands warm, and then at his strange moccasins.

Leather?

"Thad and Zeke will show Tyrone how it's done. I'll work with Reilly," Alex said flatly, as he began to push his cart across the ramp to the opposite side of the hole. The others followed.

The fog was lighter there, and Reilly had a better view of the landscape. He stood on rock-solid ice. The Tower poked above dark clouds in the distance. He calculated that Bainbridge Island lay behind them—at least, he hoped the island was still there—and that it should be seven miles to the west. He stomped his foot hard. Peering through the fog as far as he could see, he wondered if the ice was solid all the way across the Puget Sound.

Directly in front of him, two empty tables stood like butcher blocks begging for a knife to come down on them with a *thwack*. Alex, Thad, and Zeke unloaded the carts, placing several buckets beside each table. They removed various tools, knives, and other apparatus from the buckets and methodically laid them at one end of each table.

Not far away, Reilly counted sixteen large bins neatly aligned in two parallel rows. He couldn't tell from where he stood if they were empty or not. A dozen other buckets circled halfway around the hole in the ice, evenly spaced.

Alex interrupted Reilly's observations. "I'll take the legs, you get the arms," he said, grabbing at the calves of the body on top of the pile in his cart.

Reilly and Alex lifted the body and dropped it face up on the table. It fell with a thud.

"We remove all the clothes with precision," Alex took a knife from the table. "The bigger pieces of fabric are used to make new clothes, blankets, towels, and lots of useful things. We save the smaller pieces to salvage the threads." He cut the shirt and pulled it out from under the body. "Buttons are a real bonus."

Reilly picked up a knife and cut an opening in one of the pant legs.

When the body was naked, Alex pointed to the first large bin and told Reilly to put the fabric inside.

"Now we drain the blood." He picked up another knife. "We try to go in through the aorta. Grab an empty bucket and that piece of tubing," he instructed.

Reilly watched the blood drain into the bucket. He flinched with unexpected flashbacks of Black Castle ... Norah laying on Ukobach's table ... her blood dripping from her body ... the pool of blood he'd fallen into near the dungeon ... the cuts he'd sustained on his head.

Two minutes later, Alex was ready for the next job. "Okay, that's done. Put the bucket over by the fishing hole for now. Tomorrow we'll use some of it to help catch dinner."

Reilly did as he was told. When he returned, Alex had already begun cutting out the eyes. Reilly was nonplussed.

"I know ... this part is still gruesome to me, too," Alex said. "But it's the best bait! They freeze nicely and the salmon think it's a treat. Hold out your hands."

Alex laid the eyeballs carefully in Reilly's hand. "Put them in the large bucket near the hole in the ice, but be gentle," he said. "You'll see which one. It's almost full."

Reilly followed the instructions. Now he understood why most people were content to survive in the city as Dwellers, without *responsibilities*.

When he returned to the table, Alex had already cut the hair from the skull and put it in another bucket. Reilly ran his hand over his own head, trying to forget being shaved in Black Castle. He scowled at the mutilated cadaver, justifying that what he was doing now was for the survival of the Watchers and Dwellers … and himself.

But he wondered if it was true. Was there no better way to survive in the Bleak?

"You okay, Reilly?" Alex asked.

"Uh … I … sure."

"After a while, you just pretend to get used to it."

Reilly shook his head. "Maybe."

Alex noticed that the other boys were almost finished with their first body and told Reilly that if they hurried they could reach the Tower in time to get some sleep that night. Taking a hammer in his hand, he continued.

"We use the teeth to make cutting tools and some of our weapons. We haven't had to use weapons yet, but we need to be prepared for an Eruption."

"When the Deceptors come out of hibernation?"

"Yeah."

Reilly found another hammer and started to help Alex. Still not wanting to divulge everything he knew about the Deceptors, he said, "You know I've never been imprinted, so I might not understand everything. But why would the Deceptors rather hibernate than keep possession of the body they imprinted? I thought they wanted to live in a body more than anything else … except more power."

"Exactly. Hibernating in the craters recharges them somehow. It makes them more powerful than if they remained with a body they imprinted." He tapped away at the cadaver's jawline. "Some Deceptors would rather give up the pleasure of staying in a body to be a part of the Great Eruption."

"The final annihilation?"

"That's what we were told when we were imprinted. It's the worst thing you can imagine—being taken over by something that evil—you lose control of your own thoughts. You do crazy things. You have no idea who you are." Alex said, as he finished with the teeth. He grabbed a knife to begin on the skin. "Believe me, Reilly, living in the Bleak isn't so bad."

The irony of Alex's words weighed heavily on Reilly's mind.

"We scrape out the fat tissue. It's used for fuel," Alex explained. "The skin is tanned like other animal leather. We preserve it with salt and lay it flat to dry. Grab a knife."

Reilly watched how it was done for a few minutes and then asked for clarification. "If a handful of cities remain on the planet, and the hibernating Deceptors no longer want to imprint any of those bodies—nor can they, unless it's done at a Festival of Fire— what power are they so desperate to gain here?"

Alex stopped working and leaned towards Reilly. "The power of the Gods of Ifreann—the greatest power in Hell!"

Reilly nodded, recalling what he'd learned in Black Castle. "That's right!" he whispered. "Even Prince Ukobach doesn't have as much power as *those* gods."

"During an Eruption, the Deceptors battle each other to win the position of a Master Deceptor, like Ukobach. Master Deceptors have control over other Deceptors and eventually earn their place with the Gods of Ifreann."

Reilly remained quiet as he started to slice away some of the cadaver's skin. "So the Deceptors won't actually be fighting the Watchers and Dwellers. They'll battle each other."

"The Eruption itself will likely kill us. If by some miracle any of us survives, they won't last long," Alex said, carving out tissue. "It's probably hopeless. We just pretend it's not."

Reilly's mind raced. The juxtaposition of hope and madness was palpable.

"You must have *some* hope, for *something*, or you wouldn't do this," Reilly said.

"Death is the easy way out." Alex laughed. "That's what the Dwellers pretend to hope for. They hope to freeze—or starve—to death. Some end it themselves."

"And the Watchers?"

"We're different, I guess. We pretend *something*—or some*one*—will change all of it. We watch for it, whatever *it* is."

Reilly caught Alex looking at him as if he knew that they both had more knowledge than either of them had said.

"We hold on to dim beliefs that we had before we were imprinted."

"What belief?" Reilly stopped cutting, eager to hear if the answer would be what he expected.

Alex lowered his voice. "That even after all we've been through, and all we've done, maybe there's some good left inside of us. Something worth living for." Then he made another deep cut in the cadaver's skin.

"There is!" Reilly shouted. His eyes widened. "More than you might imagine!"

The other boys jerked their heads towards him.

"Imagine what?" Thad asked.

"Nothing!" Alex lied, dropping a chunk of flesh into a bucket. "Just imagining how fast we can get this done tonight."

"Not fast enough," Zeke whined.

"Right. So stop talking and keep working," Thad ordered.

Reilly was surprised by the efficiency of the process. They filled several buckets with fatty tissues and put them in the carts to take back to the Tower. The skin was spread out on the far side of the large crates to dry. Each organ was placed in a specific bucket beside the fishing hole: stomach, lungs, kidney, liver, appendix, and heart. The intestines were dumped in their own bin. The bones were divided according to size and placed in other bins.

Alex tossed the skull from the first cadaver he and Reilly had worked on into a bin filled with other skulls.

The dinner bowls? Reilly thought. He wondered whose job it was to carve the bowls, and what knives would be strong enough to do such a job.

They finished dissembling four bodies in the same amount of time that the other boys took to do five. The group finished by washing the knives, apparatus, and tools, scrubbing the tables with salt water, and filling buckets with the clean implements and coagulated chunks of fat for use in the kitchen. Then they began the trek back to the Tower.

Reilly stopped at the top of the plank to look out over the bizarre morgue. "Free forever," he muttered.

The boys returned to the Tower in time to catch a few hours' sleep before waking up to another dark day in the Bleak.

Sleep didn't come easily to Reilly. He lay awake calculating how many craters lay between the Tower and the flashing lights he'd seen through the telescopes to the north—and how long it would take to cross the ice to Bainbridge Island.

He realized that if, as Afismat had said, no Echtra had ever survived the Bleak, it meant that other Echtras had been there! If that was the case, then the Watchers must always be watching—even hoping—another one would come.

Chapter Twenty-Five

Ice Fishing

Reilly was breathing out into the cold air of the dorm when he awoke, as if he exhaled merely to melt the icy air. He was warm under the patchwork leather blanket. Sitting up, he saw Wyatt and Tyrone still asleep on their cots on either side of him. The other boys were not in the room. He spotted the bucket of water he'd left inside the door the day before. He put on his moccasins, retrieved the bucket, and brought it back to his cot.

After breaking the layer of ice that had formed on the surface, he reached for the cloth that had sunk down in the water. He caught his breath as he laid it over his face and scrubbed off the dried blood that was still there. He cleaned the other wounds on his chest, arms, and legs. A warm shower was a distant fond memory.

Tyrone rolled over, still asleep. Reilly could see the pin on his shirt and leaned closer to get a better view. No doubt about it, the pin was exactly like the one he'd seen attached to Thomas Jamieson's hat, and the emblem of the Gargoyle was identical to Travis Jackson's business logo.

Tyrone snorted and sat up with a start. "Get back!" he hollered.

Reilly jumped away.

"I don't want anymore of it!" Tyrone continued—but he was still asleep. He woke up in a sweat.

"Are you okay?" Reilly asked.

Wiping his forehead with his arm, Tyrone gained his composure. "Was I talking in my sleep?"

"Yeah," said Reilly.

"I do that sometimes." He took a few deep breaths. "I don't mean to."

"Nightmares?"

"Yeah. The same one over and over."

"I know what that's like."

"They started after I was imprinted," Tyrone continued. "I guess being deposited didn't get rid of them."

Wyatt squirmed in his bed. Not wanting to wake him, Reilly and Tyrone left the dorm quietly. They found Abigail in the hallway.

"I was on my way to wake you," she said cheerfully. "I hope you slept well. Today you'll continue the debriefing. The others have already gone to the shed to prepare the supplies for today's work at the Crossing. Are you ready?"

"Yes," Reilly said, ignoring his growling stomach and knowing there wouldn't be anything to eat unless they caught it in the fishing hole.

"Me, too!" Tyrone stretched and yawned.

"Do you know your way out?" she asked. Not waiting for an

answer, she continued. "I need to wake Wyatt. I just hate to do it. He's such a sleepyhead … poor little guy. Still, the telescopes *must* be manned." She sighed as she pulled a loose thread from her shirt and closed a fist around it.

Reilly thought it peculiar that the Tower was like the Embassy near Black Castle in several ways. In brief moments like this, he wondered if his life as an Echtra would just be a series of similar experiences—in one parallel world after another—until he succeeded in becoming a Stelladaur Ambassador in one of those worlds. Yet, he remained unsure of what the title truly meant.

"I'll be here with him today," Abigail said. "I'll get things ready for tonight's meal, and I'll prepare for the voting."

Tyrone jumped in. "Is there something we should know that might improve our odds of being selected as the Tenth Watcher?" he asked. "I don't think either of us is too keen on living as a Dweller."

"Not really," Abigail admitted. "We'd be impressed if you caught a lot of fish, but that's not the determining factor."

"*Is* there a determining factor?" Tryone asked.

"The vote must be unanimous," she said. "Of course, it isn't just how well you perform the task of collecting bodies around the city and the craters, or the work at the Crossing, that counts. It's what you brought here."

Tyrone was perplexed. "I didn't bring anything! Who has time to think about what to pack before they're deposited?"

"Funny!" Abigail laughed. "I'm not talking about *stuff*. We need to know what experience you've had—to check out your resume, so to speak."

"Of course. My resume!" Tryone joked. "Now *that* I remembered to pack!"

"Don't worry about it," Abigail said. "We do our best to ensure that the Dwellers are as comfortable as possible. We need them as much as they need us."

Reilly wasn't sure exactly why the Watchers needed the Dwellers. Feeding almost three hundred people every day and keeping them from freezing to death was no small task in the best of circumstances, but the Bleak was bleaker than even Reilly could have imagined.

Tyrone was stuck on figuring out what he might include in his resume when it was his turn to tell the Watchers about himself later in the day.

"Everything we do at the Tower must be a team effort," Abigail concluded. "Right now, the team needs you at the shed." She opened the door to the boys' dorm and went in to awaken Wyatt.

Reilly and Tyrone left the rancid stench of the Tower for the vile smell of death below, which wafted in on the breeze all the way from the Crossing to the shed. Each Watcher had a cart filled with everything that would be needed. They were lining up to start the morning trek.

Tessa spotted the boys first.

"My day just got better," she said, winking at Reilly. "Want to help with my cart?"

"Sure," Tyrone answered, thinking Tessa had winked at him. He moved to the cart and tried to interest her in the pin on his shirt.

She scowled but couldn't help gawking at the prize. Shay chuckled as she piled another bucket onto her cart.

Thad was in the lead, waiting for the others to get organized. "Morning," he said to Reilly and Tyrone.

Reilly nodded and stepped beside Alex, who handed him a pair of mittens. "Next time, bring the mittens we gave you yesterday. We only have a few extra pairs."

"Right," said Reilly, recognizing Alex's anxiety about making sure there were enough supplies. "I left mine on my cot. I can run back to get them."

"No need," said Alex. "It's not a big deal."

Reilly pulled the mittens over his hands.

Mila exited the shed with a loaded cart. "That's it," she said, closing the door behind her. Acknowledging the new arrivals, she added, "Hello. Glad you made it."

"That's a big load," said Reilly, looking into Mila's cart. "I'll help you push it."

Emmett and Zeke were stationed at the second cart in the line, arguing over where to put a large knife that didn't fit well in their already full buckets.

"Give it to me," Thad insisted. He grabbed the knife out of Emmett's hand and wedged it between two buckets on the bottom shelf of his cart. "Someone, please tell me these two won't need a babysitter today."

"C'mon, guys," said Shay. "It's too early to start getting on each other's nerves."

"She's right," said Alex. "Let's go."

The carts rumbled along the frozen ground making a discordant sound that mingled with the muted drumming of the geysers in the distance. The Watchers pushed their loads without talking, as if they all dreaded the day but had resigned themselves to the monotony and gloom of their responsibilities for survival.

Reilly figured he'd easily catch on to how the jobs were done. He'd fished with his dad on his sailboat, and had even gone ice fishing a few times. He already had a sense that the body organs in the buckets around the fishing hole would be used as bait. The bones would need to be cleaned up to make webbing, tools, and weapons, though he wondered what kind and where they were stored. Hair would be used for tying and fastening things. *It's just what the Pucatrows did,* he thought. Fabric scraps would be cleaned and made into useful clothing and other items. Tanned skin was made into leather. Everything would be repurposed.

It made Reilly think back to a time when he and Eilam sat on the dock at the Kayak Hut, watching crabs crawl on the pilings.

Eilam said each one was important and had purpose. Reilly shuddered as he considered how much had changed.

Sadness washed over him as he pushed the cart along, realizing there was nothing he could do to help those who hadn't survived being deposited. They had suffered being imprinted. Now they were dead. Their bodies had been mutilated into pieces, soon to be fed to fish, so that he and the others could eat.

There was no possible way to calculate how long it had been since Reilly had visited Eilam at the Kayak Hut. And he wondered if anything at all remained of Bainbridge Island.

Snapping out of his melancholy thoughts, he resolved to hold firm to his responsibilities as an Echtra. He vividly remembered facing Prince Ukobach. The demon had told him that an Echtra could sometimes save bodies that had been imprinted by a Deceptor other than Ukobach, though it rarely happened. He wondered if it was true.

He had, after all, rescued Norah from Black Castle. He'd prevented some of the prisoners from being imprinted at the Festival of Fire, though others were still held captive at the castle. What about the countless people who were currently imprinted by Deceptors, living their lives without anyone knowing they were possessed? Or not caring. What about those who had been deposited at the Bleak? Was there hope for them? Could he truly save any of them?

Reilly listened to the distant drumming as he pushed the cart with Mila. He longed to be in the Rotunda, where he would be safe with the Guardians and Keepers, or with Dante or Darwin in the worlds where he'd been somewhat sheltered from Deceptors during his long years of being Spliced.

In the present moment of the cold and desolate Bleak, Reilly longed for Norah. There were days when he could barely remember the warmth of holding her in his arms—it was nearly an incomprehensibly long time ago. He shivered, trying to shake off the doubts that threatened to rob him of his resolve and belief that a day would come when he could have what he desired most.

When Reilly and the Watchers arrived at the top of the ramp that led to the Crossing, they didn't stop to offer a brief prayer for the deceased. They didn't stop at all. Daytime was for fishing, and the Watchers were eager to get started.

Thad, Shay, and Alex positioned themselves around the hole, leaving several buckets between them. Reilly followed Mila to buckets in the center. He stood beside one with Tessa, while Mila stood beside another with Tyrone. Zeke and Emmett weren't fast enough to choose good fishing spots, so they took what was left. Zeke was at the far end near Shay, and Emmett reluctantly settled between Alex and Tessa.

Reilly and Tyrone watched as the others threw chunks of partially frozen human organs into crab pots made of tanned leather strips, which were tied to bones and woven into netting. The pots were fastened to nearby carts with long fabric ropes, and tossed into the water, breaking the fine layer of ice on the surface.

"Do you need help?" Tessa asked Reilly, as she secured her pot.

"Looks easy enough," he replied, grabbing the empty pot next to him. "Thanks, though."

He reached into a bucket of liver and tossed a piece into the groove in the pot designed to hold bait. He lowered the pot into the deep water and watched it disappear. Another eerie déjà vu swept over him.

"You can leave the pots to do their thing," Mila said, tying a piece of bait onto a fishing hook made of teeth. "We catch the fish with poles."

"And try to collect seaweed and kelp with the smaller nets," Tessa suggested.

Ignoring the girls, Reilly gazed ahead into the distance towards Bainbridge Island. The thick fog still clouded his view. Then he picked up a makeshift fishing pole that lay at the water's edge. After baiting the hook with a small piece of an organ he couldn't identify, he tossed it as far as the line would reach.

"Nice cast," said Tessa. "You're a pro already."

He held the pole, bobbing it slightly. "What do you catch?"

"Whatever bites," Tessa flirted.

"Dogfish sharks, wolf eels, rock cod, greenlings," said Mila. "Salmon ... when we're lucky."

"Sometimes squid," said Tessa. "That's a real treat!"

"Once we even caught an octopus with a large net, but it broke the net and got away," said Mila, as she pulled in a fish on her pole. She held it up and said, "A ling cod. Nice!"

They fished for several hours and pulled up their crab pots frequently to add fresh bait. Reilly tried to focus on fishing but often found himself staring into the foggy distance. He couldn't shake the feeling that something on the far side of the Crossing was calling him.

When Alex announced that it was time to wrap up the fishing so they could finish other chores, he shouted out his catch for the day. "Two crabs and one eel."

"One dogfish and one small salmon," Emmett said proudly.

"Three cod," said Tessa, beaming at Reilly.

"One big salmon and two dogfish," said Shay.

Zeke pulled up a crab pot and sighed. "Three crab. That's all I got."

"One cod and four crab," Thad added.

Tyrone surveyed the contents of his bucket. "I caught one crab and a spiny-looking fish."

"Three cod," said Mila. She leaned over to check inside Reilly's buckets. "How did you do, Reilly?"

"Five cod, two dogfish, an eel, and six crabs."

"*What?*" Tyrone blurted out. "We're all using the same bait. How did *you* catch so much?"

"Luck, I guess," said Reilly, calculating in his head the total number of fish and crabs that had been caught.

Tessa smiled at Reilly, as if she had brought him the good luck by fishing beside him. Mila laughed out loud.

"No one will have seconds tonight," Mila announced, loading her buckets onto her cart.

"There's less every day," Emmett whined, passing her with his cart.

"There are fewer Dwellers to feed than before, so it evens out," said Zeke, meaning to be optimistic.

"Not really," Thad corrected. "If there's no bait, we don't have anything to add variety to the seaweed."

"That's dwindling, too," Alex stated.

Following the others' example, Reilly cleaned up his fishing area, loaded a cart with his buckets of fish, and sorted tools for the next task. He and Tryone were assigned to scrape bits of remaining human flesh from the bones heaped in a large bin. Fortunately, the stench was masked by his inability to smell much of anything through his nearly frozen nostrils, and he'd never been so grateful for mittens.

It was a tedious job. Holding the knife at a sharp angle, he whittled the flesh away until the bones were as bare as his own naked body and as smooth as his shaven head once was, yet strong enough to bear the weight of the loaded carts that rolled through the Bleak in search of more bodies.

"Looks like you've done this before," Tyrone said, watching Reilly closely. "I thought you just arrived here yesterday."

Reilly squinted in the direction of Bainbridge Island. The fog was thinning slightly, and he could see further across the ice than before.

"In a way, I've been here longer than any of the Watchers and Dwellers," he said, watching his breath in the bitter air. "My home used to be seven miles in that direction—just past the fog."

"What's past the fog?" Emmett said, overhearing Reilly, his curiosity piqued. "I heard there's nothin' out that way." He and Zeke approached the two boys.

Tyrone frowned, visibly disappointed that his conversation with Reilly had been interrupted.

"You might be right," Reilly said, wanting to find common ground with Emmett.

"Ha! No one has said that to me since I've been here. Come to think of it, no one has *ever* considered that I might be right about *anything*. Sounds kinda nice." Emmett picked up a knife and eyed a fibula bone on top of the pile. "Fact is, as I understand it, those who attempt to go to the far side of the Crossing never return. The ice is unstable there, and somethin' worse than a hibernating Deceptor lurks underwater."

Tyrone raised a brow. Reilly whittled as he stared out into the fog.

"It's true," said Zeke. "He was lyin' when he said nothin' was out that way."

"A sea monster?" Tyrone asked.

"I doubt it's your run-of-the-mill Loch Ness creature, if that's what you mean," Emmett replied. "Of course, I haven't seen it." He picked up the fibula and started scraping. "But we all hear it—that's the truth!"

"Every six days, for an hour before midnight," said Zeke, sitting on the ground and not bothering to choose a bone to work on. "The most horrific noise you can imagine!"

"Sometimes I almost wish that I was still imprinted, just so I wouldn't have to listen to it," said Emmett, scraping the same part of the fibula over and over, even though there was no flesh left on the bone.

"It's driven some of the Dwellers to madness," Zeke continued. "One of the perks of being a Watcher is that the noise doesn't sound as shrill at the Tower. We're always glad when it's our turn to stay in from pickin' up new bodies on the sixth night."

"When is the next sixth night?" Tryone asked.

"Tomorrow," said Zeke. "But now we've got work to do." He finally picked up a small bone. "Mila needs a bunch of these for another invention."

"Beats sorting through intestines," said Emmett, dropping the fibula as he changed the subject. "We find some awfully bizarre things inside peoples' guts."

"Mila puts it all to good use," said Zeke.

Reilly noticed something he hadn't before. "There are no flies or insects. No maggots," he said.

"That would be another charming fact about the Bleak," Emmett snorted. "Besides the Dwellers and the Watchers at the Tower, the only life that exists in this hell hole is in the water under the ice."

Reilly stood up and looked into the Bleak.

"You might be right again," he said.

Chapter Twenty-Six

Debriefing

*L*ater that evening, after the day's catch had been prepared and served, and the Dwellers had gone back to the Bleak with their stomachs half-filled and their bodies warm enough to get them through another night, Reilly and Tyrone awaited their final debriefing instructions. The Watchers, with Shay in the middle, sat in a semi-circle on stools with jagged leather seats supported by three crisscrossed femur bones. A rope made of kelp divided them from the newcomers, who stood in silence.

Shay stood up to begin the meeting.

"Tonight marks an unprecedented event," she said with excitement in her voice. "This will be the first time two applicants hope to fill the tenth Watcher position. You both did exceptionally well collecting the new arrivals and learning the various duties required for the efficient use of the cadavers. Reilly, you're a hard worker and a natural fisherman. Tyrone, you're eager and careful. These are commendable qualities."

Tryone held his hands behind his back, twirling his thumbs. Reilly remained centered. He'd been interrogated several times before, and although his current surroundings were, in some ways, grimmer than other places he'd been, he felt completely calm in front of the nine Watchers. Even with Emmett's whining and Zeke's sometimes aloof attitude, he was impressed with the Watchers' ingenuity, commitment to teamwork, determination to help others, and remarkable stamina.

"It's apparent that neither of you wants to join the Dwellers," Shay continued. "Unfortunately, we can only choose one of you. Therefore, we'll continue the debriefing until it's clear what the choice must be."

She paused as if she expected a certain response from Reilly or Tyrone. Reilly nodded slightly. Tryone nervously touched the pin at his shirt collar.

"All right, then. Let's begin with Tyrone. Please tell us about your life before you were imprinted, followed by relevant information regarding the time when you were taken. We'd also like to know of anything you believe might be important about your deposit to the Bleak. Finally, what would you contribute to our team at the Tower? The Watchers may interject, but we're only here to help determine what's best for all Watchers and Dwellers, including you. Take your time." She smiled and sat down.

Tyrone clasped his hands in front of him and stepped forward. "Well … I'm not exactly sure where to start. I … uh … I'm eighteen. I grew up in Melbourne, Australia. My mother is an opera singer who travels around the world. She's never been home for any of my birthdays. My dad is a developer who builds high-rises, stadiums, and museums in Australia and Europe. I had a brother who died of a rare disease when he was four years old. I was eleven at the time. Our nanny quit after my brother died and my parents decided it was time for me to go to boarding school. I started mid-semester at a co-ed school in Zurich. It was a long way from home."

He shifted, waiting to see if the Watchers responded. They were silent, so he continued. "It was difficult to make friends. I kept to myself a lot. Later, I started to play a guitar my parents sent for Christmas—their token acknowledgement of my becoming a teenager in their absence. I found my niche and started a band. By the time I was fifteen, we were playing gigs in the city on weekends. School became irrelevant—an annoyance, really. All we wanted to do was play music. My grades dropped, but I didn't care. I left school with four of the band members. We found our way to London with high hopes of making it big."

"Had you already been imprinted by then?" Alex interjected.

"No. It happened at a studio when we were in the middle of recording our first demo album." Tyrone wrung his hands. "You know how it is. I mean … does anyone see it coming? It just happens. One minute, you think you've got the world at your fingertips. The next minute, you wake up and realize you've lost all control—your life is a mess—you have nowhere to turn. I had too much pride to go back home. I wanted to do it on my own … you know? Besides, I doubted my parents would let me come home anyway."

"How long had you been imprinted before you were deposited?" Thad asked.

"Two or three years."

"What did you learn about the Deceptors that could help all of us now?" Alex asked, trying to sound encouraging.

Tyrone put his hands behind his back and squared his shoulders. "They thrive on the type of music our band played—loud, with a strong beat and little melody. They go wild with lyrics about stuff that tortures their victims, like drugs, violence, pornography, war, sex- and hate crimes. Stuff like that."

"None of that is new information to us," said Emmett impatiently. "What else?"

"Well, it might seem trivial, but they cower when they hear beautiful music."

"That's it? That's the most you have to contribute?"

"Emmett!" Shay glared at him. "He hasn't finished explaining!" She nodded at Tyrone to continue.

"It happened by accident," Tyrone said. "I could never relate to opera, but one day I came across a recording of my mother singing an aria. The melody haunted me. She sounded like an angel! As I listened, something came to me. When I was young, an infant, my mother sang that song to me as she rocked me in her arms. The most remarkable thing was how different I felt when I listened to her sing on that recording from the music I played with my band. It was weird ... I knew then that she actually *loved* me." His voice cracked. He took a deep breath and continued. "Deceptors are uncomfortable around beautiful and inspiring music, because they know it can open a person's heart, even when nothing else can."

Reilly watched Tyrone intently, taken by the boy's vulnerability and admiring his courage.

Tyrone waited for a Watcher to direct the interview.

"I see," Shay said, nodding her head. "Why do you believe you were deposited?"

"I know exactly why! The Deceptor that imprinted me wanted to invade the body of someone who didn't know much about love. It made a mistake with me, because I *did* know. So, either it had to wait for a Festival of Fire to make an exchange or deposit me. It had already imprinted two people before. The first one got old and died. When it exchanged the second fellow for me, it left him to be imprinted by another Deceptor. When it decided to get rid of me, the quickest way to do so and ensure that its power would increase was to deposit me.

"Of course, when I was younger, I had no idea that my own choices would be the cause of my demise. I wish I'd heard the aria sooner."

Reilly listened to Tyrone's tragic story. He was troubled that Tyrone had never found his own Stelladaur. It hardly seemed fair.

"What can you tell us about that pin on your collar?" Mila asked. "You said you found it on the ground after you were deposited. Right?"

"Yes," said Tyrone, glancing at the pin. "Like I said, it was lying on the ground, so I picked it up. You're welcome to have it for one of your inventions." He took off the pin and held it up.

"May I see it more closely?" Mila motioned for Tyrone to bring her the pin. She examined it, running her finger over the strange emblem. "Do you have any idea of what this gargoyle might represent?"

"No. But ..." he raised his hand "... it just occurred to me ... Could it be the sea creature?"

She held the pin away, trying to get a different perspective of the gargoyle. "Maybe, but this monster isn't that formidable." She pinned the artifact to her own shirt and looked up grinning. "I'm sure I can find a good use for it. Thank you."

Shay asked the Watchers if they had any final questions for Tyrone.

"I do," said Alex, leaning forward on his stool. "Do you know anything about the two people the Deceptor imprinted before you?"

"The first was a man named Thomas Jamieson. When Thomas died, it imprinted another man named Travis Jackson. As you know, Deceptors have a fetish for victims with certain similarities, even if it's something trivial like their initials. Later, it exchanged

Travis for me and left him for another Deceptor to imprint. As I understand it, Deceptors can get bored with a person they've imprinted, which is one of the reasons they make an exchange. Truthfully, I think it got bored with me, too, but having imprinted two other people already, it decided it would rather deposit its third victim—me."

Reilly hurriedly pieced things together. Up until now, he hadn't understood that Fractions occurred in every direction and all dimensions—they weren't merely events that allowed access to portals leading to and from the Rotunda.

He'd been right about Thomas Jamieson! The Thomas on the train and at Stonehenge was the same man. Thomas had been imprinted by a Deceptor, whose plan was that Reilly should notice the unusual pin. Also, the first Deceptor that had imprinted Travis Jackson must have figured out that he knew something about love; otherwise, it never would have exchanged him for Tyrone.

Most startling to Reilly was the fact that Prince Ukobach had not chosen Travis randomly to imprint at the Festival of Fire at Black Castle. Could it be that when Ukobach was mesmerized by the love emanating between Reilly and Norah—which ultimately freed both of them from that Hell—he decided that he wanted something more than just bodies? What if the Prince chose Travis because of his potential for evil as vile as his own—but also because he still had a spark of love somewhere in his soul?

What if! Reilly's mind raced.

Before Tyrone or the Watchers spoke again, he considered another staggering possibility. Did his responsibility to rearrange history extend into the Bleak and include finding the Fraction in Time that would transcend even the coldest of hearts? Could such a Fraction give even Travis Jackson a chance to find his own Stelladaur?

Is that why I'm here? Reilly almost muttered aloud.

"Thank you, Tryone," said Shay, standing up to signify that this part of Tryone's debriefing had ended. "We won't hold your name against you. You did well."

The Watchers clapped enthusiastically. Tyrone stepped back, and Reilly stepped closer to the kelp rope in front of him, ready to say what had to be said.

When the clapping stopped, Shay cleared her voice and faced him.

"Mila and I have been here the longest. Then Alex. Wyatt was deposited soon after. We've insisted that Watchers be thoroughly debriefed, screened, and qualified, so that every person who is deposited is given an equal chance of survival. Each person comes with something to contribute, usually a bit of information about Deceptors, which helps us better understand this place and how to prepare for an Eruption. However, some people come with something besides just information. Mila came with a genius mind. Abigail is incredibly organized and has a unique ability to encourage others, even in dire circumstances. Wyatt's big smile can brighten any day. Alex came with intuitive powers, unlike any we've seen. Tyrone brought us the pin."

She motioned for Alex to stand up.

"Alex will continue this portion of the debriefing," she said, tossing her braid behind her back. "As Watchers, we depend on each person utilizing their own strengths, and we fill in for each other's weaknesses. With that said, we rely heavily on Alex's instincts." She nodded to Alex and took her seat.

"Thank you, Shay," said Alex. "Reilly, you're different from the rest of us. As I told you earlier, no one has ever arrived at the Bleak who hadn't been imprinted and deposited. But I've always believed that someday someone else would come. When I was a little boy, before I was imprinted, I found a treasure—a brilliant rock! The rock was magical, and it helped me get through some really awful stuff. It was like my guide, and it became the only friend I had.

Later, things in my life got even worse, and I lost my rock. I couldn't find it anywhere. Not long after that, I was imprinted."

Reilly felt all eyes on him. His heart beat hard, as if it had the power to silence the distant drumming from the geysers. But he remained silent, waiting for Alex to continue.

"When I watched you try to find a door into the Tower, I knew you had come to help us! I could *feel* it!" Alex thumped his right fist to his chest and let it rest there. "The way I knew things when I still had my rock." The muscles of his thick forearm tensed and bulged slightly. "Am I crazy, Reilly? Am I mad? Please … tell us you can help us!"

Simultaneously, the other Watchers drew in a breath and leaned forward on their awkward stools. Tyrone took a step backwards, as if Reilly was a magician who might need extra room to perform a trick.

In an instant, thoughts about Stelladaurs and portals, Deceptors, Guardians, and other worlds flooded Reilly's mind. Then he answered directly. "You're not crazy, Alex. Yes, I'm here to help."

Alex's arm dropped to his side. The Watchers waited anxiously to see what Reilly would do next. Wyatt, who sat next to Alex, looked at his brother.

"All right!" Alex said with visible enthusiasm. "Let's get on with it! Give us your story, Reilly."

Reilly decided to lay it all on the line. It didn't matter to him if the Watchers chose Tyrone to fill the vacancy. Reilly was there to fulfil his duties as an Ambassador in training, come what may.

"I'm not that different from any of you," Reilly began. "I'm just a guy whose life took twists and turns that I didn't expect and didn't see coming. It started when my dad died in a sailing accident. Even now, I blame myself for that." His throat tightened and he took a moment to steady himself. "Like Alex, I found a jewel. They're called Stelladaurs. Mine guided me through portals to strange places—parallel worlds—as I tried to find my dad. Like each one of you, I discovered my strengths and how I could help others. One day, my Stelladaur was missing. Just gone. I panicked! At first, I didn't know if I could continue without it.

"I grew up with an ageless sage who was my best friend. He disappeared from my life without warning or explanation. I discovered that my dog was my fourth great-grandmother! I've been given more responsibility than I could ever have thought I could handle. I've zipped through galaxies beyond my imagination, been transported through more vortexes than I can remember and confronted more demons than I knew existed. Each of these experiences left me with more questions than answers. I apprenticed with some of the greatest minds of all time under the ruins of Stonehenge. From there, I was Spliced, which means I lived in another person's body for a very long time with a portentous assignment to rearrange history. I have no idea how old I am. I met Thomas Jamieson and I know Travis Jackson better than I care to say. The last thing I want to say is that I faced and overcame one of the vilest Deceptors of all in Black Castle—Prince Ukobach. Although my resume sounds impressive, maybe even noble to some, the truth of the matter is there's a part of me that has no idea what I'm doing. I keep going because I'm selfish. I believe if I do what I was sent here to do, I can find and have my greatest desire—the thing I want more than anything else. It's the promise of the Stelladaur and I hold on to that promise. If I don't find it, my life ends in the Bleak." He hoped he hadn't said too much. "That's the short version," he added.

The Watchers' jaws dropped halfway through Reilly's monologue, and no one said anything when it ended. Even Emmett was dumbstruck and wide-eyed.

Reilly relaxed, giving them time to wrap their heads around what he'd just said, which he figured would make any person's brain hurt.

Alex, who was still standing, spoke first. "What is your greatest desire?"

"It started as a wish. I wished my dad hadn't died and I thought I'd be satisfied if I could see him again. Later, after I found my Stelladaur, something changed. I realized I also want to help people find their own Stelladaur. I wanted to stop evil people like Travis Jackson and demons like Ukobach from destroying Stelladaurs and people who had one. I still want all those things … but now …" Reilly paused, imagining that the bracelet was still tied on his wrist. "Now I want to go home and be with the people I love."

"*Home*," Alex whispered, staring at nothing.

Wyatt reached up and tugged at his brother's elbow, pulling him down to sit.

"Let's open it up," said Mila, finally finding her voice. "Where was your home?"

"It's seven miles past the Crossing, on Bainbridge Island."

"Island?" said Mila, scowling. "There are no islands out there. It's just frozen tundra. No life remained after the last Eruption."

"Do you know that for sure?" Reilly asked.

"We know that anyone who has gone too far beyond the Crossing never returned," said Shay. "We all heard their screams for help, as they were devoured by the monster under the ice. Everyone heard their death cries."

"Who went out there?" Reilly asked.

"Several Watchers. All the ones who filled the tenth slot. We haven't been able to keep that position filled." She attempted to smile.

Tyrone gasped and then bit his lip.

"Other questions?" Shay glanced around at everyone.

"When you were Spliced and lived in other people's bodies, did you imprint them?" Thad asked cautiously, but not accusingly.

"No. I didn't take over a body and hold anyone captive the way Deceptors do. I didn't steal anyone's mind or identity or dreams.

Splicing is done to help people and guide them to make different choices in their life—so that their destiny becomes the reality they hoped for."

"I wish I'd been Spliced," Thad muttered.

"No doubt," said Reilly.

"Why are you and Alex the only ones here who claim to have found a rare jewel?" Emmett asked. "A *stella*-something? Why didn't I find one?"

"Stelladaur. It means *Star Door*," Reilly replied. "One is created for every person ever born. The Deceptors have become so powerful, so deceitful, and so cunning that many people are imprinted before they have a chance to discover their own Stelladaur. Unfortunately, Stelladaurs are forgotten and discarded all the time."

"You talk as if there are people who still live in a world where Stelladaurs exist!" Emmett scowled and jumped up from his stool. "Have you looked around? Do you understand where you are?" He flailed his arms towards the dark windows. "The Bleak is the end! There's no going back!"

Everyone remained silent. Emmett slunk back onto his stool, realizing that no one faulted him for his outburst.

"Who is this *Travis Jackson* person?" Zeke asked.

"He lives—lived—on Bainbridge Island. We were practically neighbors when I was growing up. He was a world-renowned scientist, a genius—kind of like Mila, but unlike her, he used his intelligence to gain power and control over other people. He became a truly evil man. I witnessed Prince Ukobach imprint him at a Festival of Fire."

"How did you escape without being imprinted yourself?" Zeke asked.

"I held on to what I'd learned from my Stelladaur."

"What was that?" Abigail said, sitting on the edge of her stool.

Reilly took a deep breath, hoping the Watchers would believe him. "Love conquers all fear," he said. "Love overcomes all evil."

There was another minute of silence as the Watchers watched him, spellbound.

Reading between the lines, Tessa asked what she'd been dreading to ask since Reilly first mentioned a Stelladaur. "Who is she, Reilly? Who is the girl you love so much that you'd go to Hell and beyond for her?"

Reilly sighed at the thought of Norah, knowing she was his only reason for … everything!

"Her name is Norah."

Thad lowered his head and put his face in his hands. Abigail reached over and put her hand on his back. Shay squared her shoulders and addressed Reilly and Tryone together, in her business tone of voice.

"You've both done an excellent job presenting your stories," she began. "The night is getting away from us and we still have our usual jobs to finish. Wyatt spotted six deposits today. Two fell quite some distance from the city so it could be a long night. We need to make our decision and move on."

Before Shay could give any further instructions to Reilly and Tryone, Wyatt spoke up.

"Excuse me," he said, raising his hand as if he were in a classroom. "I didn't get a chance to ask anything."

Shay turned to the boy and nodded. "Of course, Wyatt! I apologize."

"What does a Stelladaur look like?" Wyatt asked Reilly.

"Like a diamond, but even brighter," Reilly said. "They are shaped like stars."

"Can they shine from as far away as stars do? Can they shine through darkness?"

A hush, filled with hope and anticipation, came over the Tower.

"Yes, they can," said Reilly. "Why do you ask that?"

"I've seen some … through the north telescopes … twinkling in the distance."

Chapter Twenty-Seven

Fireflies

The Watchers agreed that the decision about who would fill the tenth slot would have to wait.

"Tell us what you saw, Wyatt!" said Shay.

"I've seen them lots of times," he replied. "I didn't say anything before because I figured one of you had probably seen them, too. But no one else ever said anything, so I decided I was just imagining it—like I used to do when I wished on a shooting star."

Not waiting for permission to speak, Reilly said, "You weren't imagining it. Yesterday I saw the lights, too, through the telescopes. I didn't say anything either, because I'd just arrived and it wasn't the right time to mention it."

"Why didn't I ever notice them?" Alex blurted out, as he stood up.

"Yeah, wouldn't Alex have seen them?" Thad asked.

"I don't know," said Reilly. "I wish I could say that once a person finds a Stelladaur they always connect with the light of another one, but it's just not the case. You likely missed it because your attention was on something else that was important."

"What could be more important?" Alex sounded frustrated by Reilly's answer.

"Not *more* important. Equally important." Reilly hoped he didn't sound patronizing. "Sometimes a person's responsibility is to keep going even when they don't see the light ahead."

"What do you think we've been doing here?" Emmett blared, jumping to his feet, as if Reilly had started an argument that Emmett wanted to join. "Sometimes the fog is so thick we can barely see one foot in front of the other. But we keep going! I ask myself *why* all the time."

"Me, too," said Zeke, holding the edge of the stool, trying to stay grounded. "What are we surviving *for* anyway?"

"Sit down, Emmett!" said Shay, glaring at him in an attempt to regain control of the meeting. "We need to stay focused." She took a deep breath. "Wyatt is particularly skilled in watching through the telescopes. Although he should have informed us of this discovery sooner, we now have a second witness to confirm that something out of the ordinary exists to the north. Wyatt, how far north were the lights twinkling?"

"Further than any of you have gone to pick up bodies," Wyatt said. "Somewhere past the frozen channel."

Reilly pictured in his mind the geography north of Seattle and determined that the channel must be the passage of water that connected Lake Washington and Lake Union, or that did so in his past.

"Is that consistent with where you saw the lights, Reilly?" Shay asked.

"Yes."

"All right, then. I propose that Reilly stays here with Wyatt to watch through the telescopes. Hopefully they will have another chance to see where the lights are coming from. The rest of us will carry out tonight's chores. We can't let the Dwellers down, and we all need to eat tomorrow. It's Mila's turn to take care of the other jobs here at the Tower. All in agreement, raise your hand."

The girls' arms shot up in the air, as did Thad's. Reilly and Tyrone were still standing behind the kelp rope. Reilly wondered what would have happened if the Watchers had unanimously voted right then. Who would have become the esteemed tenth Watcher? Emmett frowned and reluctantly raised his hand. Zeke followed. Only Alex didn't raise a hand. All eyes were on him.

"Alex?" said Shay, surprised.

"I want to stay." He spoke firmly and looked across the room at Reilly, and then at Mila. "Please ... I ... uh ... Mila, would you trade with me tonight?"

"Why?" Mila asked, raising an eyebrow. "Is your instinct telling you something?"

"Yeah ... I think so."

Reilly could see anxiety ... even fear ... in Alex's eyes. He could tell that Mila saw it, too.

"Sure. No problem. But ... you owe me!" she said, winking at the boy.

"Thanks," said Alex.

"Okay. It's settled," Shay declared. "Let's head to the shed and get started."

Alex, Reilly, and Wyatt made their way to the north telescopes while the others descended the stairwell.

Wyatt stepped up to the telescope and adjusted the position. "This is the angle it was at when I saw the lights. At first, it happened just once in a while. Now, it's almost every night."

"At any particular time?" Reilly asked. It occurred to him that the reason he was Spliced and transported back in time wasn't just that he'd been chosen to rearrange history in other people's lives. He'd been Spliced to change events in his own life!

He had tried to alter the hands of time for himself before, but it didn't work. At that time, he hadn't yet been inside the Rotunda, where Stelladaur Ambassadors in training learn how to do it!

Just then, the *how* became clear to him! During his years of training and of living with Dante and Darwin, he'd become fully committed to and focused on helping them get what they wanted—so much so that he'd put what *he* wanted on hold. That was one of the secrets of becoming a Stelladaur Ambassador! Afismat told him he could have whatever he wanted, but only if he first helped others get what they wanted.

Reilly hadn't realized that the plan was intended for him, too, all along! Now his greatest desire—to be with Norah—felt closer to being fulfilled than it had since he left her at the Suzzallo Library, what seemed like eons of Spliced-time ago.

If it was true that he could actually have what he wanted most—and he held to the belief that it was—then he had to figure out what each of the Watchers and Dwellers wanted. He must help them believe it wasn't too late, as he'd done for some of the prisoners at Black Castle. Reilly didn't know exactly what would happen at the final Eruption—only that if it occurred, it might be too late for all of them.

"I usually see the lights go on and off for about an hour before midnight," Wyatt said. "It shouldn't be too much longer."

"Let me see," said Alex.

Wyatt stepped aside for Alex, who peered through the lens, holding it steady with both hands. He blinked several times trying to get a better focus.

"It's darker than usual tonight," he said. "It's difficult to see." He moved the telescope slightly. "Something is out there." Then he swiveled the telescope, scanning the entire northern area, stopping to refocus it at several points.

Though the air was as cold as usual, Reilly could see beads of sweat on Alex's forehead.

"Alex, let me have a try," he said.

"Sure." Alex wiped his brow with the back of his hand and stood aside.

Reilly aimed the telescope towards the spot where he estimated the University of Washington would be in relation to the Space Needle. He held the device steady for several minutes.

"Anything?" Alex probed.

Reilly said nothing but continued to watch. A few more minutes passed.

"There!" He gasped, stepping back and pointing. "There they are!"

Alex bounded to the telescope.

"I can see them!" Wyatt said, looking out the window. "You don't even need the telescope!"

"There are lots of them!" Alex shouted.

"Look at them all!" said Wyatt. "They're like fireflies! How could fireflies survive?"

"How could *anything* survive that far out?" Alex exclaimed.

"People are holding those Stelladaurs!" said Reilly. "That's what's keeping them alive."

"The people?" Wyatt asked. "Or the Stelladaurs?"

"Both."

"Are you sure?" Alex was practically singing.

Reilly chuckled. "I'm absolutely certain!"

"Why are you laughing?" Alex asked.

"Because once we rescue those people, we'll have a much better chance of defeating the Deceptors."

"*Rescue* them?" said Wyatt.

"*Defeat* the Deceptors?" said Alex. "What are you talking about? The Deceptors can't be defeated ... *Can* they?"

"Yes!" Reilly declared. "Let me explain. Before Deceptors decide to go into hibernation, they gather at Black Castle on Hallow's Eve. There they exchange bodies for imprinting, but when I was there, I saw about a dozen prisoners escape to the woods. Each one of them carried a light from an unclaimed Stelladaur."

"Unclaimed?" Alex asked.

"They were never found by their rightful owners," Reilly said, looking from Alex to Wyatt to the twinkling lights in the distance. "Those Stelladaurs had been changed to small rubies from the juice of Rowanberries, as if by magic. The rubies, which I offered to some of the prisoners, could save them from being imprinted. Some people were skeptical and didn't take one."

"What were they supposed to do with them?" Alex asked, as he peered through the telescope.

"Each person had to place the jewel in the center of their branding mark, which was seared over their heart."

Wyatt stared at Reilly's chest. Reilly pulled his shirt off his shoulder to reveal his own mark. A subtle red glow was still visible.

"No prisoner escaped the torture of being branded. The demons stole truth from the minds and souls of their prisoners." He released his shirt and continued. "If they melded a ruby into their mark they were saved from imprinting and the powerful jewel opened their heart to truth."

"Truth set them free!" said Alex, spellbound.

Reilly nodded. "After Prince Ukobach disappeared into Travis Jackson's body, several other prisoners who had taken a ruby but hadn't put it into their branding mark ran back to Black Castle. I hoped then, and still do, that the power of the Stelladaur hidden within the rubies would help them find another way to escape."

Alex stepped close to the window and squinted at the twinkling lights. "So they escaped from Black Castle."

"I'm not sure," Reilly said.

"Coming to the Bleak can't be any better. It's probably worse," Alex concluded.

"They're not actually here at the Bleak," Reilly explained. "The light from their Stelladaurs is shining through a Fraction in Time to reach us. It's sort of like the way the speed of light travels from a star to earth, but it's infinitely faster."

"A time warp," Wyatt said, his eyes twinkling.

"Exactly!" said Reilly, taking one last look at the lights through the telescopes. "We need to find the Fraction! And we need to go tonight!"

"We have to wait for the others," said Alex. "They should know all this, too. Besides, Wyatt can't stay here alone."

"I'm going with you!" Wyatt declared. "I saw the lights first!"

Alex stepped beside Wyatt and put his arm around his shoulders. "My brother and I go together!"

"Of course," said Reilly.

They spent the next couple of hours keeping an eye on the lights and gathering a few supplies. Wyatt admitted that the lights were shining brighter and flashing more frequently than he'd seen before.

When the Watchers returned, everyone gathered in the debriefing room. Reilly wasted no time explaining what Wyatt, Alex, and he had discovered. Dumbfounded, no one interrupted. He finished with a suggestion that surprised them all. "I vote that Tyrone be given the position of Tenth Watcher."

Mila was the first to speak. "Well … I suppose … since you've already rescued someone from Ukobach, and watched that despicable demon imprint a wretched soul, and helped several prisoners escape from Black Castle … I suppose you ought to have a vote." She laughed nervously, raised her hand, and added, "I second the vote."

"I agree," said Alex, raising his hand. "We'd be fools not to listen to Reilly."

"I'm no fool," said Abigail, lifting her hand high. "Count my vote in."

"Me, too!" Shay squealed and shot her hand in the air. "It makes sense to me. What about the rest of you?"

Tessa, Zeke, and Thad raised their arms simultaneously.

"He did quite a decent job tonight," Emmett said, trying to be funny. "I have no objections."

"It's unanimous, then! Tyrone, you are hereby the official Tenth Watcher of the Tower," said Mila, reaching out to shake Tyrone's hand.

"I won't let you down," said Tyrone, gripping her hand tightly. "You can count on me to stay because I don't take chances when it involves sea monsters. I won't go beyond the Crossing!"

Mila released his hand. "I further propose that we instate Reilly as the Eleventh Watcher."

"There's never been an Eleventh Watcher," Emmett protested before anyone else could comment. "We can't support another person in the long term."

"Thank you, Mila," Reilly said. "But I'm leaving—tonight—with anyone who wants to join me. Alex and Wyatt are coming. I can't guarantee that we'll be back. But if we find the Fraction, we'll come for you."

"The Dwellers, too?" Abigail asked.

"Anyone who wants to come," Reilly answered.

"You mean anyone who's still alive!" Emmett blared. "If we all leave the Tower tonight, who will pick up the bodies and do the fishing for the others? It could take days! We might all starve to death, especially with fewer and fewer being deposited each night."

"It's not an easy choice," said Reilly.

"We're wasting time!" Thad eyed the small pile of supplies. "This is our chance to get out of here!"

"I'm staying." Emmett lowered his head. "It's what I know."

Zeke stepped beside Emmett. "Me, too."

Tessa, Shay, and Abigail agreed to go with Reilly and the two brothers.

Mila removed the gargoyle pin from her tunic as she walked over to Reilly. "You have it," she said, pinning it on Reilly's shirt. "You'll probably put it to better use than I could."

"You're not going?" Shay asked Mila, confused.

"Those boys will need me here. Besides, someone needs to keep the home fires burning." Mila bit her lip as she attempted to smile.

"I'll stay, too," Tyrone said, without offering an explanation.

It was decided. Seven were leaving to find the twinkling lights that looked like fireflies in the distance. Four were staying at the Tower.

With lanterns in mitten-covered hands and leather bags filled with supplies slung over their shoulders, the seven Watchers left the Tower and headed north.

A few minutes later, Reilly thought he heard a piercing cry in the far distance and glanced back towards the Crossing. No one else noticed.

As he lifted his lantern, he wondered if he'd return to the spot where Bainbridge Island once peacefully lay in the Puget Sound and his kayak glided effortlessly across Eagle Harbor.

Chapter Twenty-Eight

The Passage

As the group weaved their way around dozens of drumming, bubbling craters, the Tower disappeared in the fog behind them, and the further north they went, the colder the air grew. The twinkling lights ahead guided their way like magical constellations against a black sky. Morning was marked by the Watchers' exhaustion—not streams of sunlight like what Reilly had seen around the sarsens at Stonehenge. Sunlight did not shine at the Bleak. They kept walking in single file.

Another hour passed. The fuel in the lanterns had almost burned away, and the lights ahead twinkled only occasionally.

"The lights aren't any closer than they were when we started," said Tessa. "How much further?"

"I'm not sure," Reilly answered. "We have to keep moving forward."

"I'm tired," Wyatt said softly. "Can we rest for a minute?"

Reilly put his hand on the boy's shoulder. "When we get to the passage. I think we're almost there."

"Here, Wyatt," said Abigail, offering her hand. "Stick with me." He took her hand and they continued on, trailing slightly behind the rest of the group.

Suddenly, a geyser burst into the air with a tremendous screeching sound—right in front of Abigail. Startled, she slipped on a patch of ice and fell, pulling Wyatt to the ground with her.

Reilly bolted back and tried to skirt the spewing geyser, but before he could reach them, Abigail tumbled into the crater, desperately trying to push Wyatt up at the same time.

Tessa, who had been walking near the end of the line, arrived first and grabbed Wyatt's hand, even as the hellish crater sucked him in. With most of his body already over the edge, she yanked hard and somehow managed to jerk him back onto the ground, out of immediate danger. But she lost her balance and plunged into the seething geyser near Abigail, who was suffocating in the acidic froth.

"Abigail! Tessa!" Thad screamed, running back to the hole.

Reaching the edge, Reilly dropped his shoulder bag, grabbed a rope from inside, and tossed it into the crater. Both girls flailed at the rope.

Another piercing noise wailed from deep below, and the terrible drumming raced and throbbed in a mad, uncontrollable frenzy.

Helpless and horrified, Reilly and the others watched as the geyser licked away Abigail and Tessa's flesh, and the girls dissolved into the deep.

Like a frozen statue, Thad stared blankly at the frothing black geyser.

The ground rumbled fiercely under their feet, as if the intrusion had annoyed the hibernating demon.

Wyatt gasped for air and began to convulse. Shay ran to him and flung herself over the boy's small body, trying to shelter him.

"We've got to keep moving!" Alex screamed at Shay, pulling her off his brother. "This might have triggered an Eruption! Get up!"

Reilly grabbed a blanket from his bag, threw it over Wyatt, and hoisted him up.

Alex grabbed Thad's elbow. "There's nothing we can do! Come on!"

Reilly took the lead, carrying Wyatt in his arms. Alex walked close behind with one arm around Shay's waist and the other around Thad to keep them moving. They'd abandoned the burnt-out lanterns near the crater.

The wind picked up and whipped their faces as they inched their way towards the passage, carefully dodging the craters.

The group huddled together, stumbling along and relying on the occasionally twinkling lights in the distance to guide them forward. Wyatt's body relaxed in the warmth of the blanket, but he needed something more to stay alive.

Reilly ignored the incessant drumming and focused on the beating of his own heart, trusting that listening to it was a constant he could depend on.

Then, as if a faint morning light was waking on the horizon, the fog parted.

"There it is!" Reilly said, spotting something ahead. He picked up his pace.

The sound of water gave Shay a burst of hope. "Is it another fishing hole?" she asked. She jumped ahead of Alex and Thad to walk beside Reilly. "That's not a *hole*!" she said, squinting. "It's an *ocean*!"

Sure enough, what Reilly had thought would be a narrow passage of land between two bodies of water that used to be Lake

Union and Lake Washington was now a single mass of water that spread out as wide as an ocean.

The group found themselves standing at the edge of a cliff with a twenty-foot sheer drop to the sea in high tide. Reilly looked out to see huge, thunderous waves rolling in and crashing against the rocky cliff below. He held Wyatt tightly to his chest. Alex dropped his jaw. Thad stood, mesmerized.

The twinkling lights beckoned them from a distant shore that was still too far away to see. Reilly cradled Wyatt's limp body, wrapping the blanket snugly around him.

"Now what?" Thad yelled. "There's no way in Hell we're getting across *that*! He should have stayed at the Tower! He's just a kid!"

"I'm taking him back!" Alex hollered in a sudden panic, pulling his brother away from Reilly.

"No!" Reilly said, grasping Alex's arm. "You'll never make it without the lanterns. We need to stay together and keep moving towards those lights."

"How?" Thad cried out above the roar of the waves. "The lights seem farther away than they did before we left the Tower."

Reilly searched the shoreline in both directions and peered out across the water. Something Thad said had struck Reilly. "You're right. They *seem* farther away, but things are rarely what they seem."

In a split second, he remembered a time when he and Norah accessed the portal to Bozka—the place where the strange creature, Aka-ula, greeted them and told them Bozka meant Divine Gift. There, they dived into water that *appeared* shallow but was really very deep. When they emerged from it onto a velvet mass of red sea moss, they were perfectly dry, and the water had receded to reveal a sandy beach covered in rubies. On several occasions, Reilly experienced the phenomenon of remaining dry while passing through portals under the sea.

An angry wave rolled in and crashed against the rocks, shooting water in every direction and spraying him and the four Watchers.

"Reilly's right," Shay shouted, shivering.

"I agree with Reilly, too" Alex said, regaining his composure and confidence as he held his little brother to his chest. "We need to keep moving, stay together, and find a way to reach those lights."

Frustrated, Thad shrugged and shook his head at Alex. The wind blew hard off the sea, sending another spray of water in their direction. Thad coughed and spewed salty water to the ground. "Well, we shouldn't just stand here!"

"This way!" Reilly was certain the tremendous waves in front of them were not as big as they seemed, nor were the lights so distant.

The others followed him along the cliff's edge. He watched Alex clutch Wyatt and knew the boy needed to get warm soon or he wouldn't survive.

Replays of events he'd experienced and secrets he'd been told began to flood his mind.

Looking across the waves, he remembered how Sequoran, the giant talking tree, had communicated with the waves on the far coast. If he could communicate with the sea now, he imagined that they would be able to unveil a passage through a safe portal for Wyatt to transport through, to a revitalizing place that was warm and dry.

He pushed aside memories of the time when all he wanted was for his dad to stay dry—not to drown in the sea or be laid to rest in the soggy ground at Blakely Harbor Cemetery, once his body was recovered. It happened a lifetime ago, but was something he could never forget.

He shifted his thoughts and replayed what Aka-ula had said, as if she'd spoken with him just moments ago. *Until your Earth feels true compassion from and towards those inhabiting it, it too will suffer. And it will die. All living things on your Earth will cease to exist.*

As far as Reilly could determine, little evidence of life remained on Earth—if that's what the Bleak once was. There were only Watchers, Dwellers, and whatever survived in the sea.

Aka-ula also said, *Every time a person extends love and forgiveness to another—no matter how insignificant they suppose it may be—the collective consciousness of the Earth is increased. A bit of the darkness is dispelled by the illuminated light of love. At that moment, life on Earth is extended. But the evil Spell of Darkness will only be permanently broken when the Divine Gift is realized by all.*

Aka-ula explained to Norah and him that the phenomenon of good and evil offered humans the power to choose their own paths. She ended with a final warning. *The choice of your heart determines which will prevail.* He and Norah held rubies to their hearts and repeated her mantra, *Divine Gift overcomes all*—and a moment later, they went through another portal together.

Reilly had put that knowledge to the test several times, both in Black Castle and while carrying out the responsibilities he'd inherited by being Spliced. The truth was, without all the knowledge he'd been given, he wouldn't have made it to the Bleak at all.

Remembering Sequoran's description of how the waves gather and organize themselves, Reilly found himself similarly arranging his thoughts … and the twinkling lights started to make sense.

Pointing to the lights as they walked along, he said, "The people who hold those Stelladaurs are shining their lights for us—because they love us!"

"What did you say, Reilly?" Shay shouted. "We can't hear you from back here."

Reilly stopped and turned around, bracing himself against the force of the wind at his back.

"They're signaling us!" he shouted.

"Who?" said Thad.

"The people are shining those Stelladaurs for us."

"You're crazy!" Thad yelled. "You don't even know for sure the lights are coming from Stelladaurs, let alone that *people* are out there!"

"Yes, I *do* know!" said Reilly, standing still as the wind raged past him.

Ignoring Reilly, Thad snatched Wyatt from Alex's arms. "You're insane! We should have stayed at the Tower! Abigail and Tessa are dead! What about Wyatt?" He held the boy out, and then cradled him like a ragdoll.

Shay jumped beside him and grabbed his arm. "Thad! Get a hold of yourself! Reilly is here to help us."

"Well, he sucks at it! I'm taking Wyatt back to the Tower!" Thad jerked his arm free from Shay and swung around in the opposite direction.

"Give him back to me!" Alex yelled, clawing at Thad.

Reilly instinctively held back, the way Eilam or the Guardians had done when he needed to figure something out on his own. Again, he peered across the waves at the twinkling lights. They were growing brighter.

Alex stood directly in front of Thad, holding him firmly with one hand and supporting his brother's body with the other, stopping the angry boy from walking away.

"Think about it for a minute," Alex pleaded. "No one has ever come to the Bleak without being deposited. Why would Reilly be here if he wasn't sent to help us? He's told us his whole story, Thad. We have to trust him!"

"That's the whole point!" Thad retorted. "I *don't* trust him! What if it's all a trick of the Deceptors? What about *that*?"

Reilly stared at the lights, mesmerized the way he was when he first held his own Stelladaur. The wind howled and blew his long blond hair in wild strands across his face. He heard Shay's muffled voice, as though he were far away or under water.

"It's not a trick." Shay placed her hand on Thad's back in a desperate effort to reason with him. "Ukobach could have released the Deceptors from hibernation a long time ago, but that wouldn't satisfy him. He wants those who once had or still have a Stelladaur, which neither you nor I ever did."

Thad stared at Wyatt, as if he expected the young boy to respond. The panic subsided, his shoulders relaxed, and he rocked back and forth, cradling the boy like a baby.

"Wyatt saw the lights before any of us," said Alex, prying open Thad's fingers to release his brother from the tight grip. "He must have known what they were. He must have remembered."

"Remembered what?" Thad muttered, in a daze.

"That light shines through darkness," said Alex, his eyes wide.

"You know this?" Thad asked, releasing Wyatt and allowing Alex to take him.

"We all do," Alex replied, rewrapping the blanket around his brother. "Just because we were deposited—or because you and Shay don't have a Stelladaur—doesn't mean we never knew. It's easy to forget."

As the waves crashed against the rocky cliff below, Reilly became aware that he was no longer part of the conversation and that the others hadn't noticed this.

A stream of memories flashed through his mind in an instant. He had a keen recollection of what he'd learned from Afismat, Olektor, and Radmund. Empowered by the gifts they bestowed on him in the Rotunda, he was infused with strength, clarity, and tranquility.

Then it occurred to him that he had to visit the third Keeper before he could finish his training. This time, he would have to find the way to that Keeper's past on his own—without going back to the Rotunda or through the Shield of Forgotten Memories. The portal to Moses' time, which he needed to access, was right in front of him—an ocean!

Alex's voice sounded muffled to Reilly as he continued to reason with Thad. "We know an Eruption will happen, but are we prepared? The Dwellers aren't going to be much help. We don't know for sure if our weapons will work. Who knows what the Deceptors will be like after hibernating? Can *anything* protect us? We need something to give us real hope. Isn't that what we, as Watchers, have been *watching* for all along?"

"Isn't hope what the light from our own Stelladaurs would have given us?" said Shay. "Before we gave up!"

Listening to the Watchers, Reilly knew what he must do. If he hoped to save them, the Dwellers, and those who were still under the Deceptors' torturous grasp, and if he hoped to reach the Stelladaur lights in the distance, he needed to use more than vivid imagination and noble affirmation. He needed to do something specific—to act as if the waves in front of them were merely a mirage—as if they didn't exist at all!

Reilly had chosen Moses as his third tutor because he presumed the ancient prophet to be wisest of all Keepers, but the real reason was now clear. This was the man who could show him how to part the sea!

Reilly began to understand that he needed to completely trust the supernatural power that lived within him, and which he believed had come from the great Star King! Watching the Stelladaur light dance off the water, he resolutely committed to his destiny.

Reilly dove off the cliff, leaving the Bleak behind.

Chapter Twenty-Nine

Nesori

*I*t was the shortest, smoothest portal Reilly had ever been through. There was no tunnel, no vortex, no kaleidoscope of colors, and no intergalactic symphony playing melodies that danced in magnificent energy forms. He simply dove off the cliff, and in the split second that he touched the water, warped back four thousand years in time.

Sweat trickled down his back and he licked his parched lips. Relieved that he was still mortal and had not been Blinked in the transport, he released the stopper of a large leather water jug that hung on a long strap over his shoulder, and took a drink of warm water.

Walking forward in the desert, surrounded by throngs of people, he moved to the edge of the crowd to get a better look. Men, women, and children stretched back as far as he could see, interspersed with herds of goats and sheep bleating noisily. Scores of people walked ahead; some struggled to keep camels from running off. Grateful that he'd arrived looking like one of the Israelites, whom the Egyptian Pharaoh had just freed from captivity, Reilly moved along in the great Exodus.

Half a mile ahead, the path inclined slightly, and Reilly spotted Moses, staff in hand, leading the multitude. Not wasting any time, he gathered up his linen cloak and advanced through the crowd. Nearing the head of the long train of people, he slowed to catch his breath and prepare himself. Then he wove through the remaining nomads in front of him and spotted a man who he was compelled to approach, just a short distance behind Moses. Reilly stepped beside him.

"Nesori!" the man exclaimed. "Where have you been? Moses has not had a drink in a long while."

"Forgive me," Reilly said, bowing and taking the crescent-shaped water jug off his shoulder. "I was detained by a small group arguing among themselves about how we will cross the Red Sea, assuming that Moses is leading us to the water's edge. They pestered me, as if I might know. Yet, I do not."

The man frowned as he took the water jug and picked up his pace to reach Moses. Reilly followed but held back a step behind both men.

"You must be thirsty, brother." The man handed Moses the jug, keeping his arms outstretched to take it back. "Nesori fell behind."

"Thank you, Aaron," said Moses. "I have suffered no inconvenience. Surely the young boy must grow weary, as well."

"Indeed," Aaron agreed, letting the container hang at his side.

"Fetch him for me," said Moses. "The journey ahead is long, and his company is refreshing."

Aaron motioned for Reilly to join them and handed the jug back to him.

"Come, walk with me, Nesori," said Moses, reaching out to Reilly. "Your task is not easy. Thank you for your diligence and commitment. These are fine qualities."

Reilly felt Moses' gnarly hand around his own, which strangely reminded him of Eilam.

"As I have told you in the past, your father also was a diligent man."

For a split second, Reilly thought Moses was referring to his dad, but realizing the patriarch meant Nesori's father, he said, "I am fond of that story—the one about my father helping to build the pyramid for Pharaoh. Will you tell me again?"

"Certainly," said Moses. "It began when I was an infant. Pharaoh feared that the Hebrews would become too powerful and someday take over Egypt, so he decreed that all male Jewish babies must be killed.

"My mother was a woman of great faith. She trusted that God would protect me. Following the inspiration of her heart, she placed me in a basket and released it to float along the River Nile, hoping I would reach the palace. My sister, Miriam, watched the basket, running along the bulrushes to ensure I would be safe.

"Pharaoh's daughter was bathing in the courtyard near the palace, where her servants found the basket. Seeing the innocent baby, she felt compassion and declared that she would raise me as her own son.

"Miriam approached the princess from the river reeds and offered to find a Hebrew woman to nurse and help care for me. Pharaoh's daughter agreed, and Miriam brought my mother to the palace. My mother had prayed that God would save her son for his holy purpose, and now her hope was fulfilled."

Reilly kicked the dust from his sandals. He tried to understand words like *faith*, *prayer*, and *God*. In the Rotunda, Moses had tutored him about his life and beliefs, but listening to the ancient prophet now, Reilly questioned his own beliefs. *What is real? Who am I? What is my destiny?* He didn't just wonder about these fundamental questions—he wanted to know the answers.

Reilly felt different from how he'd felt when he was Spliced as Raimondo and Truman. Something had changed. Perhaps it was because this time he'd conjured the portal himself. He'd plunged forward *expecting* it to be there—without waiting to be Spliced.

In an attempt to create what he believed truly existed, had he dared to see further than his eyes possibly could? Was that *faith*? Dante and Darwin had both spoken of faith as if their survival depended on it.

"As you know, Nesori, I was raised as Pharaoh's son—as Prince of Egypt. As a young child, my Hebrew mother taught me the ways of God, and because of her, I learned to follow him, trust him, and obey him. However, when I was about your age, Egyptian teachers educated me, and they taught me to adopt secular beliefs. Later, I participated in pagan cults. I lived for years with a traumatic sense of conflict in my heart. It was especially difficult for me when I saw the cruelty that Pharaoh inflicted on his slaves, who were Jewish and who loved God."

Moses gripped his staff and methodically placed it on the ground as they made their way further up the gentle hill.

"Is that when you met my father?" Reilly asked.

"Many slaves died due to lack of food or water. Some were beaten to death. God was not pleased with Pharaoh. Most important, God expected me to stand up for the truth—his truth. Even when I was a child on my mother's knee, I knew God had a plan for me. I did not know what it was, but I believed if I did my best to honor him, he would reveal it to me. So, when I witnessed an Egyptian guard beating your father, I intervened to defend him. I killed the Egyptian, though it was not my intent to cause his death, and I hid the guard's body in the sand. Then I carried your father to his home, praying that he would recover from his injuries."

"I was not there," said Reilly. "Mother and I were in the mud pit, making bricks for Pharaoh."

"Yes. As you know, your father died in my arms." Moses paused for a moment. "I have not told you what he said to me before he died."

"Why not? You never told me that he said anything at all."

Moses scanned the horizon and dug his staff into the ground. "There is a time for all things, Nesori. Now is the time. Your mother and father had waited a long while for you to arrive. They were not young. Do you know why they named you Nesori?"

"Yes," said Reilly. "*Nes* is for my mother. It means 'miracle.' *Ori* is for my father. It means 'my light.'"

"That is true," said Moses. "However, your parents were not able to explain the full meaning to you. Later that day, when it was discovered that I had killed the Egyptian who beat your father, Pharaoh's guards also killed your mother and your older brother. You became an orphan, and Aaron's kinsfolk took you in their care. Surely, you were spared for God's purpose. For some time, I've waited to tell you what your father said to me on the day of his passing."

Reilly held his breath, sensing that he was on the verge of understanding more about himself than ever before.

"The night before you were born, God sent your father a dream. In the dream, you walked with me along a dusty road and became my student. I taught you about faith and miracles that would spare the lives of believers. Your father spoke of a light that shines within each soul, even in people like Pharaoh. After learning what you had come for, your time arrived and the dream was over. Your father awoke, but he never understood all that the dream meant. Nevertheless, he trusted that your life had divine purpose. He believed your destiny was to let your light shine for others, to guide them to their own inner light."

Transfixed, Reilly felt his heart swell and fill with light—as if it was itself a Stelladaur! For the first time since he lost his treasure, he was certain that it had been transformed directly into his heart!

"I think I've known this for a long time," he said. Eilam had told him the same thing, but until Moses explained it, he hadn't truly understood.

"You are young," said Moses. "There are years of training ahead, from wise tutors. Perhaps they will come to you in forms you do not recognize. God's ways are perfectly timed, with every detail under his watchful care. This I did not fully comprehend when I was your age. For forty years I believed I was being trained to become the Prince of Egypt, but God was allowing me to develop skills that I would need to set my people free from bondage. Do you understand, Nesori?"

Before meeting Moses in the Rotunda, the sage was foreign to Reilly. Walking beside him now, as they escaped from Pharaoh, understanding dawned.

"Yes," said Reilly, confirming to himself that he was truly training with the wisest of all the Keepers.

Moses continued. "After killing the Egyptian, I fled to Midian where I worked for another forty years as a shepherd for Jethro, the father of my bride, Zipporah."

Hearing Moses mention his bride made Reilly think of Norah, and his vow to ask her to marry him when he saw her next. But what if he'd been gone for forty years? Where would she be? Would she recognize him?

"God tests his servants to see if they have sufficient patience and trust to do that which is impossible without his help. Developing this much patience and trust requires abiding faith, Nesori."

There was that word again! *Faith*! "How will I know if I have that much faith?" Reilly asked.

"Not *if*, but rather, *when*," Moses corrected. "Faith comes in the quiet moments when you wonder if God knows you at all, and then sends a sky full of twinkling stars that whisper to your soul that he knows every one of them."

"How can he know every star?"

"He made each one."

Reilly thought hard for a few minutes … piecing things together … things he'd learned in the past. Or had he learned them in a future that hadn't yet occurred?

"Is God the king of the stars? Is he the great Star King?"

"God is called many different things," said Moses. "Yet he is the same for all because he is all. He created all the stars, yet they are nothing compared to his greatest masterpiece."

"What is his greatest masterpiece?"

"His children," said Moses. "He loves each one, whether a Hebrew slave, a Roman centurion, the daughter of a shepherd, or an Egyptian prince."

"How can he have that much love? How can he love even those who do wicked and evil things, and who hurt his other children?"

"Because he created them in his own image."

"God has evil inside himself?" Reilly asked.

"No. God is perfect light. This pure light radiates in the heart of every child. Inside the light is where his children feel his love for them."

It finally made sense to Reilly. "If their light is hidden in darkness, it's harder for them to feel his love."

"Light can always shine through darkness," said Moses. "Just as night surrenders to the dawn, darkness flees when the light shines."

Reilly's mind was filled with flashbacks of the Summer Solstice, and his thoughts swirled in a kaleidoscope of time periods, and time elements.

They walked in silence for several miles. Reilly kicked a small stone along the dirt road in front of him with his sandaled foot. He appreciated that the man who would be known throughout Judeo-Christianity as a prophet of God was simply giving him space to think. It was a different kind of tutoring than anything he experienced at the Rotunda.

As he connected the dots between the Rotunda and Stonehenge, the Deceptors and the Bleak, and the Stelladaur light and Star Doors, Reilly's desire to learn more from Moses was ignited with a blazing force.

"What about the Star Queen?"

Moses smiled broadly as if he was about to share a secret. "All that is lovely, virtuous, and compassionate comes from her. Her perfect love is reflected as divine light in the heart of every child. This love is the greatest power."

This light twinkles! Reilly thought. He knew that a person who was Twinkled had *exalted capacity through an immediate infusion of Stelladaur light.* Each of the three Guardians had been Twinkled!

A flood of knowledge coursed through Reilly's veins. As questions streamed through his mind, the answers came simultaneously.

This was the moment when he started to just *know* things! It happened in his distant past and merged into his future present. It happened without his being Spliced.

Carried away in the euphoria of his accelerated epiphany, Reilly watched the landscape ahead of them change.

In a couple of days, Moses would lead the Israelites across the Red Sea on dry ground. And Reilly would understand how it was done.

Chapter Thirty

Miracles

For two days, Reilly carried the water jug for Moses, watching the host of believers—men, women, and children, of all ages—follow behind with their animals, belongings, and supplies. After living as slaves to the Egyptians for centuries, the Israelites' time for freedom had finally arrived!

Slate-brown clouds of dust swirled beneath their feet while Reilly listened to Moses retell the events that had led to his people's release from captivity.

"I did not want to leave Midian, my home of forty years, and return to Egypt to inform Pharaoh that he must free the Israelites or God would curse him. Nevertheless, this is God's work, not mine. His divine wisdom reigns over all things. I know this land as I know the back of my hand," he said, lifting his staff, pointing it ahead, and sweeping it across the landscape. "As we journey towards the sea in this mountainous desert, we have been blessed with pastures to rest in and water to drink."

Hour after hour, Reilly kept pace with Moses—left, right, left, right. With every step, his mind and soul were infused with knowledge.

"That which appears as adversity is the very thing that changes a boy into a man—if he will allow it," Moses said. "Even after God sent ten plagues to Egypt, giving Pharaoh opportunities to acknowledge the mighty God of Israel, the king refused."

A gust of warm wind blew past Reilly and he caught a mouthful of sand. He coughed and spit it out. Recovering, he said, "Tell me about the three days of darkness. And the final plague."

Moses shifted his staff to his other hand, as he did often while walking great distances. "For three long days, pitch blackness covered all of Egypt. The Egyptians could not see anything, unable to light even a candle, due to the curse. The Israelites, however, including the family you lived with, could see as usual inside their homes. When this act of God did not persuade Pharaoh, I implored him one last time to release the Israelites from bondage. But he refused. The final plague was a plague of death that took the life of each firstborn male on the last night of darkness, even Pharaoh's son."

"The noise that night was surely dreadful," said Reilly.

"The cries were heard throughout the land of Egypt," Moses said. "The king lamented—yet he would not believe in a power greater than his own. However, he did relent and set us free to return to the Promised Land."

They continued due east.

"I see water ahead!" Reilly said, raising his hand to shield his eyes from the glare of the late afternoon sun. "It's an ocean!"

"Ah! That is the Gulf of Aqaba," Moses explained, "on the northern end of the Red Sea—a narrow strip of water between the wilderness on one side and Midian on the other. It will take us three or four hours to reach the shore if we move quickly." His penetrating dark eyes looked straight into Reilly's soul. "Nothing is impossible for God, Nesori."

"You are leading all the Israelites to the water?" Reilly said, as he processed each step of the next miracle he knew Moses was going to perform. "And God will provide the way?"

Moses smiled. "Yes, Reilly. God *is* the Way."

Did Moses just call me by my own name? Reilly's eyes widened as more pieces of the puzzle simultaneously fell into place. Though Reilly was living as Nesori back in the time of Moses—to rearrange history—Moses had already seen Reilly's future life. It had happened without anyone else in *that* present time noticing. It had happened in a Fraction before Moses was even born! Reilly didn't understand how this could be true—but he knew it was!

Reading his mind, Moses added, "You will need additional knowledge and experience to face demons yet to come. Be on guard, lest you witness a mighty miracle and still do not believe. If this should be, it would be better that you never witnessed it."

As an Echtra, Reilly had learned that it was just as important to follow a great leader as to be one, so he knew not to disregard the ancient man's wisdom.

"Are all miracles mighty?" he asked.

"Miracles occur every day in everyone's life, but most are never recognized. People rarely acknowledge the divine source of miracles and dismiss them as coincidences. Some miracles are devalued by reason or intellect; others are mocked by blasphemy. Miracles are often designed as expressions of God's love for an individual, a family, or groups of people. All manifest by equal power: it takes no more power to paint a sunset across an evening sky or build mountains that rise out of the ground than to make wings for a bird to fly, or arms to hold a weeping child. Those who see the brilliance in a sunset, and those who give comfort to the frightened or downtrodden, are part of his endless miracles. All life is a reflection of his power and love."

Moses increased his pace as the wind picked up and blew at their faces. Pushing forward, people behind them pointed at the sea ahead and talked about what might happen to them.

"God uses mighty miracles in such a way that a single word, name, or expression allows his children to know his greatness in eternity—names like Abraham, Virgin Mary and Jesus. Yet, there are, and will be, other men and women who will serve and shape humanity—sages, prophets and prophetesses, saints, and noble philosophers from many nations."

Reilly had never read the Bible, and he'd only attended church a few times in his life. As a matter of fact, he wasn't sure if he was a Christian or not, or what the word meant to him. When his dad died, he doubted that God existed at all.

Each time he trained with a tutor—Dante, Darwin, and now Moses—his perspectives and perceptions changed dramatically. He had changed! He wondered how Moses would explain a word that had always implied universality.

"What is truth?" he asked.

"Are you asking for the meaning of the word?" Moses said, sounding a great deal like Eilam. "Or are you asking what it is?"

"Both."

"Truth is much greater than any imagined meaning of the word. Truth is knowledge in its purest form. All that we see and experience is in limited form because bodies and minds are also limited, whereas the spirit of man is limitless. We are here to find our own path. Truth comes when our heart is humble and pure."

"How does that happen?"

"It happens gradually, as we follow the light inside our own soul."

Many of Reilly's answers to questions about himself, Stelladaur light, and his role came full circle, over and over again.

The wind echoed off the mountains behind them as the weary but hopeful Israelites walked together. Moses, Aaron, and Reilly pressed forward steadfastly.

Reilly had the feeling that Moses harbored no concerns about what would happen when they reached the Red Sea. The prophet seemed to know what was going to happen—and how to do it! *He, too, must have been tutored and prepared for his destiny*, Reilly thought.

Arriving at the water's edge, Moses and Aaron climbed up a rocky hill, to higher ground, so that the multitude could see them. Reilly followed Moses to observe what he would do next.

Moses stood high above the crowd, steadying himself on his staff to withstand the strong wind. There he waited while thousands of Israelites pressed in to hear him, but the people were not at peace. Reilly listened to their frantic cries.

"Pharaoh's armies are coming behind us!" a man shouted, scrambling to get closer to Moses.

"We have nowhere to go!" an old woman cried.

"If we had stayed in Egypt we would have lived," another man hollered. "We are all going to die!"

"Save us, Moses!" the people chanted, raising their fists. "Save us!"

Horrified parents clutched their children, as if they feared the billowing waves would leap from sea to shore and swallow them. Cattle bellowed in fright. Sheep, horses, and other livestock began to scatter. Hundreds of people scrambled to climb the hill. The crippled and elderly sat hopeless on the ground, as others passed them by, unable to help them in the gales.

All the while, Reilly watched Moses gaze out across the water. The very waves seemed to be waiting for the command. Again,

Reilly thought of Sequoran, who could communicate with waves on the far coast. The tree had said they were organizing themselves in preparation for a big event, as if waves were alive and could do such things.

Reilly decided that if a talking tree comprehended truths about water and waves and oceans, then Moses could certainly know even more.

In the distance, Pharaoh's army and chariots swept into the valley from the mountains like a million tiny ants bursting from an anthill, marching and scurrying to accomplish their task, given by Pharaoh, to destroy the freed prisoners.

The freed Israelites feared that the lightning stroke of death would cast them down at any moment.

Through it all, Moses remained calm and steadfast, his cloak billowing about him and his long hair streaming back in the wind.

Then, when the throngs of Israelites had gathered in as close to the shore as they could without trampling each other or pushing those in front into the water to drown, Moses glanced at Reilly, and raised his arms to the sky.

Lifting his staff high above his head and grasping it firmly with both hands, he stretched his hands towards the stormy sea. A mighty gale swept out from the shore, across the water. The wind swirled the waves, gathering them together. And then—a miracle! The waves separated into two parts, folding away from each other! The sea rolled out like a scroll, pulling the water upward on both sides, until it transformed into two towering precipices against the dark sky.

"God calls the waters and the waters obey!" Moses shouted, lifting his staff up to the sky. "The storm is in his hands, and he shall hold its walls! Go forth! Make haste, my people!"

Panic-stricken, throngs of people flocked out across the ocean floor towards the far side of the sea. Others praised God as they moved quickly along the seabed, protected by the unfathomable shield of water, which stood contained as if in unearthly sheets of ice.

The barrier rose nearly a thousand feet on both sides and extended almost nine miles from where they had gathered to the far shore.

Reilly remained at his post, watching, profoundly amazed. As he observed the mighty miracle, an overwhelming and unprecedented power coursed through his body.

When evening crept in, Reilly still watched with Moses from the hill. Pharaoh's army, with six hundred chariots, thousands of mounted horsemen, and two hundred thousand foot soldiers approached, a mile away, to recapture the multitude.

"God will yet provide!" Moses cried. "Let there be a pillar of fire to light the way for his people, so that they might cross by night! Let the fire be a barrier in a cloud of darkness to halt the armies of Pharaoh!"

Moses spoke the words, and it was done. He climbed down the cliff's edge, and with Aaron and Reilly on either side of him, fled towards the safety of the Promised Land.

Inside the passageway created by the parted sea, the howling wind changed to a warm, whispering breeze that reminded Reilly of portals he'd traveled through before. Moses' people, making their way between the high walls of the sea, remained dry.

For several hours, late into the night, Reilly, Moses, and Aaron helped those who stumbled, who could not carry their belongings, or who were injured, and when necessary, they helped the people herd their animals. It struck Reilly that these two men, who Reilly guessed were both almost one hundred years old, had as much energy and stamina as he and the younger travelers did.

As dawn appeared, Reilly could see the mainland come into view, now only a half-mile away. Crowds of people had already reached the shore but several who walked just in front of Reilly, Moses, and Aaron, turned around and ran ahead, screaming in fear.

"Pharaoh's army approaches in the distance!"

"The chariots will trample us!"

"How long can the walls remain frozen? We are going to drown!"

"Why did you bring us out of Egypt, where we could have died peacefully?"

Without glancing behind, Moses raised his staff higher in the air, until the multitude on the shore could see him approaching, and until he exited the passageway.

Reilly followed closely behind Moses as he made his way through the crowd, until they climbed another rocky hill on the shore.

As twilight turned to sunrise, Moses surveyed Pharaoh's army advancing behind them, across the ocean floor. He gripped his staff in both hands and held it out towards the sea. A thunderous crack pierced the air! The icy walls that had been holding back the sea like a dam shattered and burst! Mountainous waves rolled over the dry gound, which his people had just crossed. Awestruck, Reilly and the Israelites watched the sea swallow Pharaoh's army with unrelenting force. Thousands of men, horses, and chariots were hurled up and pulled down by the force of the roaring, deafening waves. The entire Egyptian army drowned in the depths of the writhing waters.

Then it was over. The sea was calm. A gentle hum hovered over the water. A hush fell over the believers.

Moses lowered his staff and called Reilly to him.

"Some journeys end where others begin," said Moses. "You will not go to this Promised Land."

"No," said Reilly, looking out across the sea. "I have a different assignment, in another land."

"You have been given all you need to complete your work— strength like that in the waves, clarity like that in my staff, and tranquility like that in the morning light. You will yet have reason to remember these gifts."

Reilly nodded, indicating he was ready to hear everything Moses still had to tell him.

"Though you have witnessed a mighty miracle, it is not the eyes that see miracles," Moses continued. "Do you know what I speak of?"

"God?" Reilly asked, uncertain of the answer.

"God is indeed the greatest. He may reveal himself to man if, how, and when he chooses to do so. However, his magnificent light, which lives within all his children, must be understood from within that light. As a person follows their inner light, it grows brighter and brighter until they discover the inherent power to create miracles."

"Even mighty miracles?"

"Even parting the sea."

Reilly watched the gentle azure waves. "The name Moses will be remembered forever," he said. "My name will be forgotten."

Moses put his arm around Reilly and looked deeply into his eyes. "You will be remembered by your ancestors because of what you have already done, and by your posterity because of what you will do in generations to come. Above all, it is for them that you must fulfill your destiny. No price is too great." He kissed Reilly's forehead.

It occurred to Reilly that his destiny—to become a Stelladaur Ambassador—had more to do with leaving a legacy by giving all he had, as the Guardians had told him he must do, than he'd realized.

"Climb with me high up on this rock," said Moses, positioning his staff to start the ascent.

Reilly gathered up his robes to climb the steep cliff.

Now, facing the Red Sea, with Mount Sinai at their backs, Moses and Reilly watched the people below. They were too preoccupied with the miracle they'd witnessed to notice where Moses stood.

"Today they marvel at God's power and mercy. Today they are happy," said Moses. "I fear that for some, who will fail to discover their own light within, this happiness will be fleeting."

"What can we do?" Reilly asked. "If they forget the miracle, their doubt will affect the lives of millions of people who aren't even born yet!"

"Some followers of light are given grave responsibilities; thus, we stand on this mighty rock, united in purpose."

Reilly took a deep breath and nodded. "I'm ready."

Without reply, Moses rested a hand on his shoulder.

"This rock shall stand forevermore in praise of the memory of this day!" Moses' voice rang out like a song, which only Reilly could hear. "It shall become as stardust beneath your feet to light your way!"

Reilly saw him raise his staff in slow motion above his head—and then plunge it down to the rock beneath their feet. As the staff struck the ground, the rock split open in a burst of blinding light. Reilly raised his arms to shield his eyes as glittering lightbeams encircled him like a cocoon.

When he lowered his arms, he was in the Bleak.

Chapter Thirty-One

Limits

*Y*ou're right, Shay," Reilly said, rejoining the Watchers' conversation. "Stelladaurs *do* give hope. I knew you hadn't given up!"

Shay, Thad, and Alex, holding Wyatt, stood where he had left them on the cliff above the ocean. Not a moment had passed at all.

Shay smiled as she wrapped her ragged clothes around her body. "It's much colder this far from the Tower. We need to keep moving."

"Wyatt is turning blue," Alex said with desperation. "He's unconscious."

"Which way now?" Thad asked, looking to Reilly for the answer.

Reilly pointed across the channel, which looked like an ocean. "That way."

Not waiting for a response, he spread his arms wide and swept them in a circular motion several times in front of him, as if he was gathering the waves and absorbing them into his body. A gust of wind blew from the north, and he held his hands over his chest, one on top of the other. His eyes were closed as if he were in a trance.

The others stood astonished, watching the whitecaps settle into gentle ripples. Then astonishment turned to sheer awe as the current suddenly divided into two parts that flowed away from each other, in opposite directions, from one center point that extended in a straight line out from shore. The center point was Reilly.

Reilly opened his eyes and silently told the water to recede.

Rolling back like an ominous scroll, the water withdrew in a deafening long *whoosh*. The Watchers' jaws dropped as the ocean divided before their eyes and the fog lifted. The channel of seawater gaped to reveal dry ground, as black as coal, stretching to the far shore.

Stunned and wide-eyed, Shay whispered, "What happened?"

Alex held Wyatt tightly in his arms. "Who *are* you?" he asked, his eyes bulging.

"I'm just a kid … like you," Reilly tried to explain. "A kid who found his Stelladaur … a long time ago. That's all."

Looking down at his little brother and back at Reilly, Alex stepped closer. "We're staying with Reilly," he said.

Flabbergasted, Shay moved closer to Reilly and Alex. "I'm in," she said.

Thad gawked at the strange landscape that had appeared a moment earlier, as if by magic. "Me, too," he said.

Signaling to the others to follow him, Reilly led the group to a rocky pathway that wound back and forth down the side of the cliff. They stepped carefully along the path until they reached the ocean floor. As Reilly walked across the smooth black surface, he left footprints of glittering dust trailing behind him.

"What's *that*?" Alex asked, stepping around the sparkling footprints.

Lifting one foot at a time, Reilly surveyed the underside of his moccasins. "Stardust," he said, noting the magical footprints. "It's what Stelladaurs are made of." He kept walking.

Balancing Wyatt in his arms, Alex crouched down to look at the glittering dust. "It's a superfine powder," he said, reaching to touch it with his finger.

"Don't!" Shay cried, pulling him back.

"Yeah," Thad agreed. "There are lots of weird things happening here. We shouldn't touch it."

Several feet ahead, Reilly waited for the Watchers while they figured out what to do.

Dejected, Alex stood up and shifted his weight to regain a hold of Wyatt.

"This rock is strange, too," said Shay, stomping her foot to be sure the ground was solid. "I've never seen rock like this at the Bleak."

"Maybe it's lava," said Alex.

"Obsidian," said Reilly, beckoning them to keep walking. He tried to explain things in a way that would make sense. "It came from an Eruption that occurred long before any of us arrived in the Bleak or knew much about Stelladaurs. It was shortly after the vile Travis Jackson began to poison people, frustrated by his failure to find a portal to Tir Na Nog."

"Where is ... Tir Na Nog?" Shay repeated the name awkwardly, trying to pronounce it correctly.

"*What* is Tir Na Nog?" Alex asked.

"A place where no Deceptors have ever been," said Reilly, noting that they were watching him intently as if whatever he said was truth. "They never will."

"Does such a place exist?" said Alex. "Is it *real*?"

"Very real," said Reilly. "It's beautiful there … you get there through a portal … and it's closer than you might think."

Thad, Alex, and Shay watched the footprints appear as Reilly walked.

"Have you been there?" said Alex.

"Not yet," Reilly said. "But my dad is there, waiting for me."

Alex nodded as if he understood what Reilly meant.

The Watchers walked in silence, glancing from the sparkling footprints to the tremendous walls of frozen water on either side of their path.

When they reached the far shore, Reilly pointed at the twinkling lights ahead of them. "It's not much farther," he said.

Alex stopped. He gingerly lifted a corner of the blanket that covered his brother's face. "I think Wyatt decided to go to Tir Na Nog," he murmured.

"No!" Shay cried, grasping Alex's arm. "Not *Wyatt*!" She drew the blanket away. The boy's face was ghastly white. "No! No!"

"It's too late." Thad choked.

Shay flung herself into Thad's arms, sobbing. He clung to her, letting the tears run down his own cheeks.

Reilly moved to stand beside Alex and covered Wyatt's brow with his hand. The little boy stared blankly into the icy air, to a place no one else could see.

Reilly closed the boy's eyelids and laid the blanket over his face. "We'll bury him here," he whispered. "In the Stardust."

Alex and Thad watched Reilly walk in a circle, leaving a ring of footprints behind him. Shay pulled away from Thad, still crying softly.

Reilly waved his hand above the glittering ring. The dust gathered, swirled up, and floated back down to the black earth, where it formed a shallow mound. He took Wyatt from Alex and gingerly laid the boy on top of the sparkling mound.

Using his newfound power to do remarkable things—even create mighty miracles—he scooped a handful of Stardust from the mound and held it over Wyatt's frozen body. He took a deep breath and blew the dust away from his hand.

The remaining Watchers looked on in sublime amazement as the dust swirled over Wyatt in a beautiful slow-motion dance. When the first minuscule speck touched Wyatt's body, he vanished.

"Where did he go?" Shay whispered, wiping her tears.

"To a beautiful place," Reilly replied.

Alex crouched down beside the mound and reached out to touch what remained of the glittery pile. "Dust to dust," he said. Sifting through the powdery residue with his finger, he drew Wyatt's name.

As if by magic, the letters lit up like gentle, divine fire and cast a warm glow across the Watchers' faces. They each closed their eyes, as if to soak in sunshine after a rainstorm.

Alex opened his eyes first. "Look!" he said, pointing to something that had materialized where the name "Wyatt" glistened moments earlier.

The others opened their eyes. Thad and Shay gasped.

"Ha!" Reilly laughed, smiling broadly.

"Is it what I think it is?" Alex asked, restraining from touching it.

"Your very own!" said Reilly.

"A Stelladaur!" Alex said under his breath. He reached tentatively for the golden cord tied to the gem. He dangled it away from his body, mesmerized by its brilliance. Then he grasped the jewel tightly in his fist and held it to his chest.

Seeing the Stelladaur infused Reilly with hope, strength, and conviction. He silently reviewed the ancient promise, letting the truth of it wash over him once more. *The very dust beneath your feet responds more lovingly to our footsteps because it is the ashes of our ancestors.*

Speechless, Thad and Shay hovered over Alex in wonderment. Alex looped his Stelladaur over his head and let the stone rest against his chest. Neither Thad nor Shay doubted that it belonged to Alex.

Reilly thought he was in another strange Middle—a sliver of a place between *here* and *there*—but this time it lay between the walls of a frozen ocean, where he stood on black rock that now danced with light.

Reilly was getting the hang of creating mighty miracles! However, as often happened after an Echtra witnessed or executed a miracle, his growing resilience met with unexpected mayhem.

A shrill noise pierced the tranquil air!

Reilly and the others fell to their knees, covered their ears, and shut their eyes tightly. The sound was much more terrible than what they'd heard from the Tower every sixth night. It was worse than the Deceptors' horrific cries that Reilly had heard echoing through the halls of Black Castle. This was unbearably louder!

The high-decibel sound shrieked through the frigid air so intensely that Reilly wondered if it would shatter the ocean walls, causing the waves to crash down on them and snatch them up in their torrent. He held his throbbing head.

Raising his head slightly, he managed to open his eyes enough to see Alex's Stelladaur hang from his chest. The jewel shone a light on the wall in front of the Watchers.

Reilly stared in horror! A giant monster was trapped in the frozen wall, clawing to escape. The beast bared its razor-sharp teeth, like those of a killer shark, ready to swallow Reilly and his friends like specks of plankton.

"Run! NOW!" he screamed.

The Watchers couldn't hear him. Their eyes were still closed and their hands covered their ears. Shay lay on the frozen obsidian ground, curled in the fetal position. Reilly staggered towards Alex, grabbed his arms, and pulled them away from his ears.

"Help Thad!" he shouted. "Use your Stelladaur!" Reilly motioned how he should hold out the jewel in front of him. "I'll get Shay!"

Alex stumbled towards Thad, allowing the Stelladaur to flash light on the boy's closed eyes. Thad opened his eyes and stood up, but his hands still covered his ears.

"Move!" Alex yelled. "That way!" He shone his Stelladaur towards the shore. Then simultaneously, the boys noticed the gaping monster behind the wall of ice. They froze in sheer terror!

"Run!" Reilly screamed, bumping into the boys to push them forward. He was carrying Shay, draped over his shoulder like a life-size ragdoll. "Don't look at it! Just run!"

The three boys ran for their lives towards the shore. Adrenaline kicked in and Reilly managed to carry Shay without stumbling. The Stardust footprints no longer trailed behind him.

With about forty feet to go to reach the shore, the boys raced with all their might up the slope of the ocean floor towards the base of a cliff.

As suddenly as it had started, the shrill noise stopped. Shay awoke with a jolt! Wide-eyed, she leaped from Reilly's arms. She and the boys paused momentarily in the haunting silence. Then, in one motion, they jumped and ran harder and faster than ever before, giving everything they had to reach safety. Increasing the pace, Reilly and Shay took the lead. Alex and Thad sprinted at either side of them, forcing themselves to keep up.

Then, a tremendous cracking sound echoed behind them.

No one turned back.

With just twenty feet to the shore, they heard the oceanic walls of ice burst with a thunderous crash! They knew the monster had broken the frozen dam.

Reilly and the Watchers heard the ocean crashing towards them. They felt the tumultuous wind and spraying water as they fled up the black obsidian ground. They were six feet from the shore. Then, like a tornado, the fierce wind whipped against their backs and hurled them high in the air!

The savage monster leaped out of the water and snapped its gigantic jaws at Reilly. It thrashed angrily, flashing its flaming red eyes at him. Reilly spiraled upward, but managed to glance down to see icebergs colliding against the cliff below—and then the massive beast sinking into the sea like a submarine of war. In that instant, he saw Thad being pulled into the center of the raging storm. Flailing, Reilly reached out for him—but his friend was hurled out to sea, and was suddenly gone!

Moments later, Reilly, Alex, and Shay were flung out of the turbulence and deposited on the cliff above the shoreline. For a few moments, they lay still, stupefied. Then they pulled themselves up on the dry, rocky ground, and sat looking out over the torturous sea that had buried the entire basin of obsidian ground.

Reilly pushed his dripping hair away from his face and searched for any sign of Thad. He saw no one.

Suddenly, horrifically, the beast broke the water's surface and twisted its scaly body in grotesque contortions. Its fiery eyes glared at its targets, as it thrashed its tentacle legs out of the water and uncoiled its serpent tongue above the waves. Still unable to reach the boys and Shay, safely perched on top of the cliff, the monster spewed as its jaws gaped, displaying its gigantic sword-like teeth. The spray pushed Alex and Shay backwards on the ground. Reilly braced himself against the onslaught and remained upright. Wondering if he could create another miracle to bring Thad back, he stood up and searched the horizon.

With a final ghoulish hiss, the monster pulled back its tentacles, slunk down below the water's surface, and disappeared into the deep. As if in slow motion, the waves receded and the icebergs floated in the water. The howling gales gave way to a chilly breeze.

"I'm sorry," Reilly said softly. "I couldn't reach him." He shivered at the memory of his dad falling to his death at sea. "I tried."

Alex pulled himself up and limped to stand beside Reilly. "I know," he said, putting his arm around Reilly's shoulder. "It's not your fault."

Reilly allowed Alex's words to sink into soul. He knew that even though he was an Echtra and he could create some mighty miracles, a Stelladaur Ambassador in training had limits. When or how someone dies was not something he could decide.

Chapter Thirty-Two

Beacons

Reilly fumbled at the buttons that had loosened on his shirt, exposing his bare chest to the bitter air. He glanced quickly at his faded branding mark and pulled the ragged fabric tightly around him, trying to wrap himself up. Glancing from Shay to Alex, he cupped his hands to his mouth and blew hard.

"There!" he said between breaths. "The twinkling lights are just ahead."

Shay and Alex looked ahead and nodded. With the water calm behind them and the sea monster out of sight, they focused on Alex's Stelladaur beaming its light in front of them.

Alex drew in a deep breath. "You're right," he managed. "It's not far."

They pressed forward through the black night, with Alex in the middle.

"I can't feel my toes," said Shay, looking behind her at the trail of blood from her bleeding bare feet. "I never liked those moccasins anyway."

"Me neither!" said Reilly.

Until Shay mentioned it, he hadn't noticed that he, too, was barefoot. Alex stopped and pulled off his moccasins.

"Take mine," he said, handing the shoes to his friend. "You need them now. We'll trade off wearing them to protect our feet."

Shay didn't argue and flinched as she pulled on the strange shoes.

Reilly wiggled his toes and wished frostbite would be the worst thing they'd still have to deal with. Knowing wishes would do him no good in this insalubrious place, he determined to reach the lights as soon as possible.

"C'mon," he said, sprinting forward and waving his arms at the others to catch up. "The lights don't look like fireflies anymore. They're merging together like mini starbursts!"

"You're right!" said Alex. "Like real Stelladaur light!"

"If the lights are from Stelladaurs, why didn't anyone ever come to help us?" Shay asked, slightly breathless.

"My guess is we'll find out soon enough," said Alex, clutching his gem against his chest as they ran. "This thing is almost too hot to hold on to."

"That's weird," said Reilly. "There must be some sort of ionic charge radiating from the lights in the distance, attracting your Stelladaur."

"An invisible force?" Alex asked.

"Exactly," Reilly answered. "Light attracts light,"

After a good mile's run, they slowed down and walked for several hours. The landscape changed dramatically when a rocky hill came into their view in the distance.

"What's that?" said Shay, pointing. "That's where the light is coming from!"

The lights flickered intermittently around a steady white beam.

"The air is warmer here," said Reilly, noticing their puddled pathway. "Water is trickling out of that hill." He noticed something in the midst of the twinkling lights. "There's an entrance," he said.

"It's a cave," said Alex.

"Maybe," said Reilly, taking the lead.

The narrow entrance tunneled back at an angle so they couldn't see in. The beam of light was gone. Just a faint filtered light escaped from inside. It was obvious that only one person would be able to squeeze sideways through the opening at a time.

"I'll go first," said Reilly. "Then Shay. Alex, you come last. Keep your Stelladaur around your neck, but hold it up as you come through." Both Watchers nodded.

Reilly stepped into the darkness. Feeling the rough walls on either side, he wove his way through a turnstile in the passage. His eyes adjusted to the dim light, which glowed from somewhere inside. Shay was behind him.

As Alex moved through the cave, his Stelladaur cast crooked, tubular shadows on the walls as the light bounced off strange rock formations on the floor and ceiling. He scanned the area with his light. "Stalagmites," he whispered. Gazing up he added, "And stalactites. It's a cave, all right."

Shay cupped her hands around her mouth. "Hellooo!" she hollered into the darkness. "It echoes like a cave." She repeated the call, lowered her hands, and waited for a reply. There was none.

As they advanced, the cave widened and the glow from the lights ahead increased, seeming to target Alex's Stelladaur.

"Some things are different from what they appear to be," said Reilly, stroking a jutting rock formation beside him. "These aren't coming from drops of water the way stalagmites do. They're *melting.*"

"So, they're rocks that were frozen, but now are gradually melting?" Alex asked.

"I think they're statues." Reilly said. "Calcified prisoners."

"*People*?" Shay squealed, jumping away from one of the rocks. "*Prisoners*? ... Of *whom*?"

"We're in a burial chamber under Black Castle," said Reilly. "A dungeon."

"We didn't see a castle from the outside," said Alex, looking back towards the entrance.

"There wasn't one," said Reilly. "We stepped through a portal at the entrance. I know this place!" He took a deep breath and released it slowly as he stroked another stalactite. "We're far underneath that terrible Hell. This is where all evil of past, present, and future exists at once."

Shay and Alex walked around a few of the statues, observing closely but not touching them. "There are hundreds," Alex whispered.

"A faint red glow is coming from inside of them," said Reilly. "See?"

The Watchers nodded.

Alex held up his Stelladaur, shining it into the darkness. "Let's keep going," he said, leading the way further into the dungeon.

"We're right behind you," said Reilly.

As they maneuvered around the statues, the lights from ahead started to flicker, turning to rays that bounced around the calcified prisoners. The further they went, the wider the burial chamber became.

"We're almost there," said Reilly.

All three of them had to shield their eyes from the glare of the lights, which fused into one powerful beam.

Alex relaxed his grip on his Stelladaur and let it fall to his chest. He stopped to allow Reilly and Shay to move to either side of him.

As if on queue, the lights lowered to reveal eleven teenagers and a much younger girl standing just a few feet away from the boys. No one spoke. Each of the children had a Stelladaur on a golden cord around their neck. Threadbare tunics hung loosely over their thin bodies. They were gaunt and pale. But it wasn't the gossamer fabric or their haggard appearance that caught Reilly's attention. It was their brilliant eyes!

"Charlotte said you would come," said a blue-eyed girl at the end of the row. "She said we would wait many years but you *would* return."

Shay and Alex jerked their heads sharply towards Reilly, who took a step closer to the girl.

"I'm sorry it's been so long." It was all Reilly could think of to say. Once again, he wondered how long it had actually been.

"We shone our lights, hoping they would bring you here somehow," the girl said. "My name is Rachel."

"My little brother, Wyatt, saw you first," Alex said quietly. "He's gone now."

"Gone from your view perhaps," said a boy standing beside Rachel. "He's closer than you think. That's what we've believed all these years about our Echtra." The boy smiled at Reilly. "I'm Logan."

"Why would you think I am your Echtra when Alex carries a Stelladaur ... like each of you?" Reilly thought Alex and Shay would understand better why they were there if one of the teenagers explained.

"The castle echoes the name *Reilly*. The Deceptors seek revenge against you," said the next teenager in line. "Charlotte met us in the forest soon after we escaped from the Festival of Fire. She told us all about you."

"That's Aimee," said a boy beside the girl. "I'm Avery. We're twins but you wouldn't know it by looking at us." The boy had jet-black hair and the girl was blonde.

As if on queue, the remaining teens introduced themselves.

"I'm Elleah. You told my story at the auction." Reilly studied her and then nodded his recognition. "Apparently you didn't make my story sound enticing to the Deceptors because I was neither sold nor imprinted. I thank you for that."

"My name is Frederick. People here call me Freckles." The name suited the boy. He had carrot-red hair, freckles dotting his face and arms, and eyes the color of a harvest moon. "I know it sounds like a name for a dog, but I don't mind. It gives me something to smile about in this hellish place."

"I'm Clint and this is my brother, Cole." Both boys laughed heartily. "We're twins, too. Good luck telling us apart!" They snickered and playfully traded places.

"Forever the jokesters," said the next girl in line. Her deep brown eyes glittered from the light of her Stelladaur. "Good humor is a rare gift that I've learned to appreciate. I'm Maria. I tend to be more serious than necessary, but I'm as happy to see you as anyone here!" She tried to straighten her tangled caramel-colored hair with her fingers as she spoke.

"Me, too," chimed the next girl. Her eyes glistened like flecks of gold in sunlight. "I'm Kay. Spelled K-A-Y. My full name is Jacqueline Kay and people used to call me J.K. But I didn't want to just be two sequential letters in the alphabet, and my first name is too hard to spell. So my friends call me Kay. Or, if they really want my attention they call me Kay-Spelled-K-A-Y."

Reilly, Shay, and Alex chuckled.

"Moving right along," drawled the last teenager in the line. "Kay-Spelled-K-A-Y can be a bit long-winded. I'm Cutler. Nothing fancy. Just Cutler." He flashed a big grin at the last person in the row, as if to speed things up.

"Bailee." The child was clearly the youngest of the group. After stating her name, she ran up to Reilly and threw her arms tightly around his waist. "You finally came!" she squeaked.

Reilly drew his arms gently around Bailee and felt her Stelladaur between them. The combined light of all their Stelladaurs infused him with clarity. Glancing at the others, he gathered his thoughts. Bailee released her grip and gazed up at him with eyes that sparkled like amethysts.

"Yes, I've come to help you," said Reilly, hoping to reassure the child. "I *am* the Echtra you've waited for."

Bailee clapped her hands and took two skips back to her friends. The group cheered and hugged each other. Shay and Alex straightened their shoulders, proud to be the friends of an Echtra. When everyone had settled back in the line, Reilly stepped between Alex and Shay.

"This is Alex," he said, putting his arm around the boy's shoulder. "He recently discovered his Stelladaur." Reilly reached for Shay with his other arm. "This is Shay. Her Stelladaur isn't far away."

"Now that you've arrived, we must not waste time," said Rachel, glancing behind her towards the end of the chamber. "What do you need to know? What do you need us to do?" She spoke as if they were prepared to follow whatever the Echtra said.

Reilly released Shay and Alex and surveyed the surroundings. He walked a few feet in each direction, gazing up and down at the dark rock walls. The lights from the Stelladaurs followed his movements, dancing off the walls. Facing Rachel and the others, he took a deep breath, inwardly trusting that he would know what to do next.

"Where is Charlotte?" he asked.

Rachel stepped forward. "She is in her own time. A few days after you and the Pucatrows helped us escape from the Festival of Fire, Charlotte found us in the forest."

"Of course," said Reilly. "Sorcha, Charlotte's sister, who was also a prisoner of Black Castle, saw at least a dozen prisoners run into the woods that terrible night."

"We had placed a ruby in our branding mark," Rachel explained, "so we were protected from the Deceptors, at least for a while.

Charlotte told us that after we found our own Stelladaurs, we must return to Black Castle to help the prisoners escape. There were others who ran with us into the forest, but we are the only ones who went back. We call ourselves Beacons."

Hearing their title declared, the Beacons lifted their jewels and pointed them to the center of the room, casting light rays that merged into a single brilliant beam. Shay and Alex shielded their eyes. Reilly stared directly into the beam. When the Beacons released their gems, he spoke.

"Where did you obtain more rubies to take to the prisoners?" he asked. "Did you discover unclaimed jewels at the Sea of Stelladaurs, as I did?"

"Charlotte assured us that the dog, Tuma, would find us and bring the rubies. We all left through different portals, and Tuma came to each of us in our own time and place. She helped us find our Stelladaurs. Charlotte remained in Wicklow."

Reilly caught his breath at the mention of Tuma's name. Now he understood clearly what Sam, the giant whale that had guided him to the Sea of Stelladaurs, meant when he said, "Tuma will be nearby when you need her most. She will remain part of your story, as she always has been."

Deciding that it wasn't necessary to explain that Tuma was also Charlotte, his fourth great-grandmother, Reilly simply said, "She is a special dog."

Some of the Beacons nodded as if they were more deeply attached to the dog than Rachel had indicated.

Reilly shifted his attention to the group, rather than directing himself only to Rachel.

"I assume that when you returned to Black Castle, the Deceptors had little use for you, since the ruby in your branding mark protected you from imprinting," Reilly said. "They've kept you here under the castle, hoping to steal the power contained in the rubies. Right?"

"Exactly," said Elleah. "But as you know, they can't steal that power."

"Aimee and I returned together, after Rachel," said Avery. "The others came at different times."

"None of us knew what would happen," Aimee added. "We all hoped we could get the rubies to the others in time. We *did* manage to deliver them, but the Deceptors put a spell on the prisoners as soon as Rachel arrived with the first pile of gems."

"The spell was a curse," Maria interjected. "If a prisoner placed a ruby in their mark, their body was instantly changed into a stone statue and transported to this dungeon, where we've also remained since they captured us. We should never have let our guard down."

Reilly, Shay, and Alex surveyed the cave and spotted hundreds of stalactites and stalagmites.

"Didn't the prisoners find out about the curse?" Alex asked.

"Yes," said Rachel. "Even so, some preferred to be trapped in stone—possibly forever—than to live in despair in the castle, or to refuse the ruby and surely be imprinted." She clasped her hands in front of her and held them just under her Stelladaur. "They believed an Echtra would come to free them."

Alex and Shay didn't say anything. Reilly also remained silent as he walked around a nearby statue, studying it intently. The others waited anxiously. He pressed his hand on the statue.

"The rubies preserved them," he concluded. He walked towards Rachel, holding the gaze of her sapphire eyes. He stopped inches from her and continued. "Breaking the curse doesn't mean I can guarantee their protection."

"If you don't break it," she said, moving so close to him that he could feel her breath on his face, "you guarantee their eternal imprisonment—and our death."

Reilly frowned. He didn't understand.

"Our Stelladaurs gave us the power to withstand the Deceptors' advances when we delivered the rubies. However, the demons' power diminishes whenever they're near light, so they never enter this holding place. Doing so could permanently weaken them," Rachel gripped Reilly's arms. "But ... our Stelladaurs do not make us immortal," she whispered.

Reilly nodded, realizing the curse had deeply affected the Beacons. "How have you survived?" he asked.

Rachel released him and stepped back, as if to signal that the other Beacons could interject.

"A prisoner delivers food once a day, but not much," said Logan. "Sometimes they're able to sneak in other stuff to us, too."

"The Deceptors believe they'll find a way to dim our light—to steal it from us!" said Maria.

"Idiots!" Freckles blared. "When Hell freezes over!"

Reilly shot a glance at Alex and then Shay. Something Freckles had said caught their attention.

Reilly needed to know something else before he could implement the escape plan that had been percolating in his mind since they first entered the cave. He turned to Rachel.

"Can you see beyond the cave entrance?"

"We never knew there was one," she said, lowering her head. "We've tried to use our Stelladaurs to clear a passage through these walls, but the force of the curse is too great. There must be an invisible barrier that opened when you arrived." She lifted her eyes to meet Reilly's. "We discovered that our light beams melt the statues. It takes tremendous concentration and is excruciatingly painful, so our progress is slow." She pointed at the entombed prisoner Reilly had been studying minutes before. "You can see that our light has melted some of the stone ... enough to reveal a red glow deep inside. At this rate, we'll all die before we can possibly reverse the curse."

Reilly's eyes flashed from one Beacon to the next. He was exuberant. "Your efforts have done more good than you know! Do you see? The light you aimed at the statues to free them flickered through the invisible shield. We saw your lights and thought you were signaling us!" He looked at Alex and Shay, bursting with joy. "The twinkling lights we saw from the Tower came from their Stelladaurs!"

Relieved and amazed, the Beacons exploded into uproarious laughter, jumped up and down, and hugged each other.

"It worked!" Clint hollered, as he and Cole danced around each other and traded places in line.

Shay and Alex laughed, too, happy to have brought some hope to the Beacons.

As Reilly watched the others cheer, he grew serious. They had no time to celebrate a premature victory. If they didn't pass through the invisible opening in a matter of moments, Shay, Alex, and he would be trapped in the holding cave forever.

For Reilly, the situation was harrowing. Even if he could reverse the curse, he would need something far more powerful than hope to stay alive through the terror of what he must face next … beyond the Bleak … utterly alone.

Chapter Thirty-Three

The Curse

Even before the cheering subsided, Reilly decided on his next move.

He had swept the room, searching for something to help him break the curse—something he could gather, as he'd done before, to create another mighty miracle.

He had gleaned dust from the ground to escape through a narrow window portal back to the Rotunda when he was Spliced as Raimondo. He had gathered ocean waves and changed them into a frozen wall so that he and the Watchers could find the twinkling lights. And he had gathered Stardust to release Wyatt on his journey to Tir Na Nog.

He concluded that his ability to gather was a vital part of his training.

What in this dungeon can be gathered? he wondered.

There were no loose rocks or dirt. The thin film of water in small pockets on the cave's floor wasn't the right element for the mighty miracle he needed to perform. The moment he thought of borrowing the Stelladaurs, he heard a voice drift through the cheers, into his mind and heart.

"Each of them *must* keep their gem around their neck and hold it to their heart," the voice whispered. It was Radmund, Guardian of the Mind, who'd promised to bring Reilly clarity. Knowing only he had heard the instruction, he nodded, as if the Guardian were standing in front of him.

"Gems," Reilly murmured. Then he shouted, "The rubies!"

"What about the rubies?" Alex asked, as the others turned to face the Echtra.

The beautiful, piercing eyes of each Beacon settled on Reilly. The cave was silent.

"The rubies preserved them," he said, gazing around at the hundreds of statues that dotted the chamber, creating a strange maze formation. "The power in their gems will set them free."

He raised his arms. Alex and Shay stepped back, knowing they were about to witness an Echtra perform another remarkable feat. The Beacons stared at Reilly in anxious anticipation of whatever would happen next.

Reilly swirled his hands as he'd done before, concentrating on what he was envisioning. He called out instructions, raising his voice above a growing rumbling noise. "No matter what happens, keep your Stelladaur around your neck and hold it to your heart! Help the others!" A stream of red fog started to seep out of each statue. "Alex and Shay! Stay close together!"

Each of the Beacons grasped their Stelladaur to their chest, and the light began to diffuse. Shay grabbed Alex's shoulder and clutched his ragged clothes.

Still circling and sweeping with his arms, Reilly gathered the fog to him. "The curse will be broken, but their freedom will come with a price," he cried. His voice echoed through the cave, but the deep rumbling noise had become almost overpowering. "The moment the prisoners are released, the light from your Stelladaurs will dim. The Deceptors will come! The cave entrance will open until I lower my arms. You must run immediately!"

There was no time for anyone to respond or refuse. The miracle was in motion!

As the red fog oozed from the entombed prisoners and the stalagmite and stalactite formations melted away, an eerie wailing sound pierced through the walls of the cave.

Reilly's heart beat faster. He swirled his arms and hands more rapidly.

Alex and Shay darted towards the cave entrance. The Beacons clutched their Stelladaurs, running close behind. Bailee tripped and fell hard to the ground. Cutler scooped her into his arms and sprinted forward.

"Even the rocks thrill with memories of past events," Reilly chanted. *"The very dust beneath your feet responds more lovingly to our footsteps because it is the ashes of our ancestors."*

As he recited the chant, the stone around the entombed prisoners melted like wax, as if they were statue exhibits in a bizarre museum, now coming to life. Then …

The rumbling noise grew until it shook the cave, and—the prisoners were freed! Stunned, disoriented, they looked frantically in every direction. Some followed the Beacons, heading towards the cave entrance. Others moved towards Reilly near the back of the dungeon, still swirling and chanting, *"The soil is rich with the life of our kindred,"* lilting in a whisper. The red fog continued to gather around him.

Reilly knew he was, in some inexplicable way, connected to each prisoner through the whisper. His responsibility as an Echtra and Stelladaur Ambassador in training included changing the destiny of those whose lives had been shortened by a Deceptor. There was no doubt in his mind that gathering power from the rubies had reversed the curse and changed destiny. Fortunately, doing so had not diminished the power within the freed prisoners.

Standing in the protection of the cloud, he could see the faded light from the Stelladaurs showing the way for the crowds. They were almost at the entrance. It would remain open from both sides for only a few minutes.

"This way!" Logan hollered.

"Follow us!" Elleah cried, straining to juggle a satchel she had grabbed and thrown over her shoulder.

"Run!" Clint and Cole shouted.

"That's the wrong way!" Rachel screamed, looking over her shoulder and seeing dozens of people running the opposite direction. "Come back!" She lifted her Stelladaur as far as she dared, keeping its cord around her neck. "Come with us!"

Reilly held his arms up high and watched the desperate scene. Bewildered, some of the prisoners tried to reach into the fog that surrounded him, but they couldn't penetrate the mysterious protective shield. Dejected and confused, they retreated to a corner behind him.

Then —a wicked boom thundered through the cave! The chamber darkened. A horrible screech pierced the air. Reilly looked at the walls and saw dozens of Deceptors clawing their way in through the stone.

The prisoners in the corner contorted in pain, unable to cry out. Reilly watched in horror as breath and life were sucked from their helpless bodies, and they withered into a mangled, bloody heap. There was nothing he could do but hold up his arms until it was over.

The Deceptors' gaping jaws protruded from their hooded capes, dripping with blood like ravenous vampires' mouths. They swooped around Reilly with demon eyes spewing acid flames, their claw-like, red-stained hands grasping at the fog. Unable to penetrate the protective cloud, they wailed in rage and darted towards the cave entrance.

Reilly stood on his toes and stretched up, whirling his arms as high and fast as possible. He looked through the fog and, to his relief, saw that Alex and Shay had made it safely to the other side of the entrance. He didn't spot any of the Beacons in the dungeon.

The only light left in the cave shone from the rubies in the prisoners' branding marks. Their light had dimmed when Reilly gathered some of it to show the way to the entrance and keep it open.

He grimaced at the horrific scene he had to witness through the crimson cloud. A hundred freed prisoners clamoring to the exit dropped to the floor as if they had been caught in a firing squad. Blood splattered the walls as the demons engulfed them and spit out their remains in demonic aggravation.

Reilly had barely a moment to exit the cave to freedom—and just one chance!

Mustering every iota of strength he had, he infused his own soul with all the energy he'd borrowed from others, trusting that it would be enough. Then he plunged forward into the red fog, with his hands still swirling above his head.

"Light prevails!" he cried out, as he ran in a whirlwind through the furious swarm of Deceptors. "Light prevails!"

From somewhere outside the infernal walls of Black Castle, further than the desolate Tower and the Bleak, and beyond the Rotunda, where he'd been promised added strength, clarity, and tranquility, Reilly experienced a surge of powerful energy unlike any he'd known before. Whether it came from the collective light inside the red cloud or his own inner reservoir of strength, gained from years of training, he didn't know. From a Fraction in Time he hadn't yet seen, a burst of immortal power propelled him forward.

As he finished his proclamation, he had flown past most of the Deceptors and the carnage that filled the dungeon. As he blazed towards the portal door, the Deceptors in his path moved away from the mighty and mysterious fog. With a split second before the invisible entrance closed, locking him inside the dungeon of Hell forever, Reilly plunged through the narrow doorway, taking the dim red fog with him, and leaving the battleground of slaughtered bodies behind.

A mighty vacuum sucked in the air as Reilly squeezed through the turnstile walls. He emerged around the last corner with his arms still high above his head.

The whirling cloud dispersed and circulated in misty red paths back to the rubies inside the branding marks of the prisoners who had escaped. Stunned, they watched the miracle in silence.

Stelladaur light filled the place, shining from the jewels that hung from the Beacons' and Alex's golden cords. For the first time in the outskirts of the Bleak, it looked like a sunny day. Everyone embraced each other and smiled. Their faces were warm with hope.

Only when all the fog that Reilly had gathered was back in the rubies did he lower his arms. The crowd faced him, holding their hands over their branding marks, as if they were ready to recite a pledge in his honor for his heroic deeds. Alex and Shay pushed their way forward and took their places on either side of him.

Reilly wanted to acknowledge their collective victory, yet prepare them for what would come next without destroying their hope. He knew that greater challenges still awaited them all.

"We won that battle!" he declared. "You were strong and valiant!" His voice carried a new quality of command and resolve.

"Now, we must fight the war!" he shouted. "With the curse broken and the dungeon deserted, the full power of the Deceptors will soon be unleashed!"

The crowd simultaneously closed their eyes and lowered their hands from their branding marks, as if this was a ritual they'd rehearsed over and over for this occasion. As their hands dropped, their rubies faded into their bodies, and around each of their necks, a Stelladaur on a golden cord emerged.

A gasp of wonderment filled the chilly air.

Just then, Shay felt a bump under her right moccasin and lifted her foot. Under it was a Stelladaur. It had appeared as if by magic! She laughed with sheer delight, picked it up, and looped the golden cord over her head.

The Beacons formed a line behind Reilly and his two close friends, arranging themselves in their usual order.

Shay held up her Stelladaur. "Light prevails!" she said boldly.

Alex lifted his gem to his heart. "Light prevails!" he bellowed.

At once, everyone except Reilly raised their Stelladaur and shouted the declaration in unison. "Light prevails! Light prevails!"

Reilly breathed deeply before he spoke again. He was grateful for his new friends, but he knew he must warn them of what was to come.

"The Great Eruption will soon occur. When the Deceptors come out of hibernation in the craters, the darkness they bring with them will snuff out the light of your Stelladaur and strangle you with the cord." The truth came through the words as he spoke them. It was the kind of truth that made him shiver down to the marrow of his bones. "The demons will come from behind and devour your soul. They will leave your body to shrivel to death in excruciating pain. We must go now and reach the Tower before the Eruption begins!"

The crowd murmured, desperately clutching their Stelladaurs. The Beacons joined hands and stood tall to show their support. Alex and Shay did not flinch, showing complete loyalty.

"There are tens of thousands of hibernating Deceptors," Reilly continued. "We are perhaps five hundred."

A few in the crowd were disturbed and began to argue with the others. Then they turned towards Reilly and one of them shouted,

"Why did you bring us here? At least we were left alone in the dungeon at Black Castle. Now we face the horror again!"

Several people ripped their Stelladaur from its cord in anger and threw the jewels on the ground. They turned and started to run back into the shadows, heading towards the cave.

Reilly waited, and the others waited with him.

Finding no trace of the entrance, the resentful prisoners reluctantly returned and rejoined the crowd.

"If you keep your Stelladaur on its cord around your neck and hold it to your heart, its light can destroy more than a hundred demons at once," said Reilly.

"What's the point?" one of them demanded as she picked up her gem.

"We're outnumbered!" another hollered, shaking his Stelladaur in his fist.

"Where's *your* Stelladaur!" another person yelled. "You don't know what you're talking about!"

Reilly knew that he didn't have all the answers, and he never would. Nevertheless, he responded in the way that had become natural for him to speak.

"Your light within is more powerful than the light that you see with your eyes!" he shouted to the crowd. "Together, we are more powerful than the Deceptors. If you hope to succeed, you will each need to rely on your own light, yet be willing to share it with all. Our only chance is this way," he said, pointing towards the Bleak with determination.

The crowd parted for Reilly to lead the way. Shay and Alex kept their places at his side. The Beacons formed their line, creating a wall of light for the others to follow. Collectively, hundreds of Stelladaur lights lit the dark night, making it look like day.

The luminous white light from the jewels streamed in the sky like an aurora borealis. It encircled the crowd, moving with them as they advanced, leaving the thick darkness in their wake. Most people were wonderstruck by their newfound freedom. They walked in silence.

But the Beacons wanted answers.

Kay spoke first. "Will the Deceptors leave the castle … to hunt us down?"

"Not in the way you might think," said Reilly, keeping his attention focused straight ahead. "We stepped into another time when we escaped from the dungeon. We went *forward* in time! *Those* Deceptors will stay at the castle until they imprint or deposit someone."

"What do you mean *those* Deceptors?" Logan asked.

"We left the demons at the castle behind, yet we are also the ones they wait for ahead."

"Please explain," said Alex.

"The freed prisoners were imprinted just as you were, each in a different Fraction in Time," Reilly said calmly, expecting them to understand and believe whatever he told them. "All the Deceptors who at some point aborted a body, choosing to hibernate until the Great Eruption, wait for us now."

"I thought the Deceptors would never come near light," Logan protested. "You said our light will keep us alive."

"I said you'll need to rely on your own light *if you hope to succeed*," Reilly corrected. "The Deceptors in Black Castle resisted your light because they intended to steal it when your guard was down. Hibernation increases their power, and at the start of the Eruption, the demons in the craters will try to take your light. As I said earlier, when the Demons of Hell are unleashed, Stelladaur light itself can be extinguished as fast as a candle is snuffed out."

The Beacons glanced at each other. Cutler took Bailee's hand in his own. Rachel looked back to see whether anyone behind the line of Beacons could hear the conversation. Most were too enthralled with the halo above and relieved by their freedom from the curse to notice.

Rachel picked up her pace and squeezed between Reilly and Shay.

"Reilly," she said tentatively. "Who unleashes the demons from hibernation?" The light of her sapphire eyes reflected in Reilly's like glittering jewels.

He replied without hesitation. "We do."

Chapter Thirty-Four

Eruption

Rachel gasped and clutched her Stelladaur to her chest. Shay and Alex stared straight ahead, unshaken by the revelation.

"Never let them see fear in your eyes," Reilly whispered. "The Beacons rely on your strength."

Rachel bit her lip and raised her chin.

"You and the other Beacons have had a Stelladaur for a while," said Reilly, "so you're more skilled with them than the others. There's no time for training. You'll need to trust me."

From the corner of his eye, he caught a slight frown on Shay's face. He ignored it and increased his pace.

The icy ground beneath their feet melted in the warmth from the Stelladaur halo that encircled the crowd as they moved ahead.

Reilly let his ragged shirt hang loose, open to his waist, welcoming the warm air against his skin. He ignored his growling stomach.

Suddenly, a cool gust invaded the warmth around him and blew his long hair behind him. He felt the tartan pin on his shirt, which Mila had given to him, flutter against his chest. He'd forgotten about it.

The wind blew swiftly through him and exited the halo, without affecting the others. Reilly eyed the pin as they walked further along.

Soon Shay noticed a landmark ahead. "We're here already?" she said, pointing to the cliff by the water's edge, where Thad had vanished. "How did we get here so soon?"

Reilly squinted, trying to see the landscape clearly through the light. "Time is illusory, like a mirage," he said. "It appears only in the moment when we experience it."

"Something always happens when you say strange things like that!" Alex chuckled. "I can't wait to see this!"

Reilly narrowed his eyes and focused his thoughts. The crowd gathered in closely, and he listened to them talk about the eerie sea as they approached the cliff's edge. The water, black and thick like wet tar, rippled slightly. Rachel and the Beacons huddled close to Reilly, Shay and Alex. Everyone inched forward.

Without warning, Reilly spread his arms wide open. Everyone stopped and fixed their attention on him.

"If you want to go any further, you'll need to burn your boat with your Stelladaur," he said.

The people murmured, not comprehending.

"You won't need a boat to cross this water." Reilly started to move his arms. "*Burn your boat* means this is the point of no return!"

As he uttered the words, the ground beneath them began to vibrate. Inside the protection of the Stelladaur lights, no one resisted. No one retreated. No one doubted that something miraculous had begun. Euphoria filled them.

Reilly brought his arms together. He hoped the sea monster, hidden somewhere below the water's surface, would not appear.

Astonished, everyone watched the cliff they stood on break away from the mainland behind them! It moved them slowly across the murky sea towards the landmass on the other side. As they floated towards the shore, the thick water receded into the blackness behind them.

Reilly's hands became illuminated, as if he were holding a ball of pure light. When the divine boat was twenty feet from the shore, he interlaced his fingers, and the cliff nestled into the frozen landmass, fitting perfectly like a jigsaw puzzle piece taking its original position.

Reilly took a deep breath, released his hands, and called out to the crowd, "If we reach the Tower before the Eruption, it will be possible for us to defeat a great number of Deceptors with our collective light. We need everyone!"

Alex pulled his tunic around his body. "What if we don't make it to the Tower before the Eruption?" he asked.

Not wanting to give false hope, Reilly answered in the best way he could. "More of us will survive if we stay together along the way."

Instinctively, the Beacons tightened their line behind him.

"Light prevails!" Rachel cheered, raising her Stelladaur to her heart.

"Light prevails!" Reilly, Shay, and the Beacons shouted in unison.

Alex whispered the mantra along with them, unable to hear his own voice above theirs.

"This way!" Reilly yelled. "Hurry!"

He leaped ahead to lead the way, with Shay, Alex, and the Beacons at his heels. Keeping pace, the freed people charged forward inside the ball of light. A tangible energy circulated through the crowd, infusing them with courage, strength, and optimism.

"What are those?" Logan called out to Reilly a few minutes later. He had spotted the first bubbling geysers ahead.

"I'll explain in a minute." Reilly stopped and signaled to the crowd to gather in tightly. Everyone waited eagerly to hear what he would tell them.

"Those strange geysers are the hibernation chambers," he said. "At least one Deceptor waits inside each crater, but most geysers probably hold several demons. Our task is to navigate around the deadly geysers and reach the Tower before the full Eruption takes place. When we reach the top of the Tower, our light will reflect in every direction, far enough to protect us until the Eruption is over." He paused and scanned the crowd to do a quick calculation of their numbers. "There's no escape for anyone who falls into a geyser. The bubbling acid devours the body."

Shay and Alex shuddered, remembering the horror of losing Tessa and Abigail. The people gasped. Some reached for their neighbors, filled with dread.

"As I explained before, our strength lies in the unity of our collective light. However, not far ahead the craters are extremely close together on the ground," Reilly continued. "There's not enough room for us all to maneuver around them at once. We'll divide into smaller groups," he said.

"Can't you cover the geysers ... to stop the Eruption?" Shay asked. "You know—make another miracle!"

"The miracles will have to come from your own light," Reilly said, trying to connect with each person in the crowd. "Remember what I told you before—when the Eruption occurs, the Deceptors will awaken with even greater power than before. You absolutely *must* keep your Stelladaur at the level of your heart!"

Everyone grabbed their Stelladaur and steadied it at their heart without taking their eyes off of Reilly.

"We'll divide into fourteen troops," Reilly instructed. "Each Beacon will lead a troop except Bailee, who will go with Cutler." Cutler nodded and pulled Bailee to him. "Shay, Alex, and I will lead the other three troops. Beacons, as soon as I call out your name, count thirty-three people to join your troop. Gather your troops close to you so I can see how many people remain. First, Rachel!"

Rachel counted thirty-three people, and they moved away from the crowd. Logan was next and he did the same, followed by the twins, Aimee and Avery. Within minutes, each of the Beacons had stepped into the shrinking crowd to form their own small troop. Last, Shay and Alex established their troops.

"The rest of you will come with me," Reilly said firmly.

The last thirty-seven people joined Reilly. The apprehension on their faces indicated that they knew the troops were still too large to successfully maneuver every geyser.

For a moment, Reilly wished there was time to give in-depth training ... to tell them all about Stelladaur power ... or at least to send them to the Bleak knowing the Affirmations of the Stelladaur that he'd learned so long ago and which had helped him navigate the most dangerous pitfalls—including bypassing death's doorstep. Setting his futile wishes aside, he placed a hand over his heart and continued.

"My troop will go first, followed by Alex's to my right and Shay's to my left." Alex and Shay nodded and signaled to each other, determining to meet at the Tower. "The Beacons will also spread out with their troops." Reilly pointed left and right. "Do you see the break in the light between each group already? Stay as close together as possible and there will be enough to light your way to the Tower. No matter what, keep your Stelladaur—"

A sudden *boom!* assaulted the air in the distance. Another *boom!* blasted closer by. The geysers they could see spewed high into the air, and deadly acid fell to the ground like shrapnel.

The troops spread out and ran forward at full speed towards the Tower.

More *booms* echoed through the darkness. For a quarter of a mile, the troops successfully dodged bubbling hibernation craters.

Falling acid splattered a few of them. Their screams pierced the air, but they pressed forward.

Minutes later, the Tower came into view. But the spewing geysers were now perilously close together—and there were too many of them. The cry of death cut through the air from all directions. Startled, some dropped their Stelladaurs from their heart. Others slipped on the icy ground, unable to hold on to their jewels. Several lost their footing, and were swallowed alive. Darkness pressed in. The collective light diminished.

Reilly skirted the geysers, repeatedly calling out, "Light prevails!" It was difficult to hear his voice in the commotion. He couldn't determine who was still alive. Muffled screams begged for his attention.

The ground rumbled louder than all the other noise, and the Bleak shook violently. The Great Eruption had begun!

Dozens of people stumbled and fell into bubbling geysers before anyone could grab them away. The black acid rained down and burned others who couldn't hold on to their Stelladaur. The world was at the dark edge of twilight.

The Tower was now close enough for Reilly to see the silhouette of someone watching from the north window. "Light prevails!" he shouted again. It was the only thing he could do to help his remaining troops before another horrific *boom!* reverberated through the darkness that threatened the dimmed Stelladaur light.

Suddenly, the ground stopped shaking with a jolt that threw more people off balance and thrust them into geysers!

A haunting silence seeped through the thick darkness. Blaring through it, Reilly called out a final command to his troops. "Run! Keep your Stelladaur near your heart! Run for your life!"

It was their only hope! The Tower was fifty feet away, and Reilly's inner strength propelled him forward. He ran harder! Faster!

Thirty feet to go!

As the gap closed, Reilly caught a glimpse of Shay a few feet to his left and Rachel just behind her...

Twenty feet!

A second later, the moment the demons of that Hell had waited for arrived. The hibernation craters burst open and unleashed legions of Deceptors. It was a full Eruption!

The hellish devils spewed from their craters, shrieking insanely! The ground trembled violently and people tumbled over each other. Light diminished rapidly as the Deceptors swooped upon those whose Stelladaur fell below the level of their heart. Caught in the pelting acid rain, the victims writhed in pain. The demons laughed heinously.

As the survivors converged close to the Tower, Reilly saw the halo of Stelladaur light increase. The collective light thwarted dozens of demons that tried to attack.

Ten feet to go!

He glanced to the right. Alex wasn't there.

Rachel grabbed Reilly's arm with her free hand.

"Push now!" he yelled.

Together, Reilly and Rachel slammed hard into the Tower door.

"Go upstairs!" Reilly yelled, opening the door. "Hold your light high at the window."

"I will!" Rachel sprinted towards the stairs, breathing hard.

Reilly held the door wide open for Shay, Logan, and Freckles, who'd plowed to the Tower. They leaped passed him to safety. Just behind them were a handful of troops. Reilly shouted to them to get upstairs and direct their lights out across the Bleak.

A stream of Beacons and dozens of others came next, keeping the halo lit around the base of the Tower and repelling the Deceptors.

The pitiful cries of those who had fallen mingled with the shrill laughter of the Deceptors. The hellish cacophony sounded more horrific to Reilly than the cries of the prisoners being imprinted at the Black Castle Festival of Fire!

The halo in the darkness grew smaller as the remaining survivors arrived.

"We're the last ones!" Aimee hollered as she and Avery bounded through the door. As Reilly closed the Tower door behind them, he shot a final glance through the darkness.

In the distance, a light flickered inside a small halo! The flicker was too far away for him to leave the door open—the Deceptors would swoop in on him and enter the Tower—but he couldn't abandon someone who was still alive out there!

He waited, estimating the time it would take the survivor to arrive safely, while deafening shrieks penetrated the walls. When he thought the halo was wide enough for them to enter the Tower, protected from the lurking demons, he opened the door a crack.

Light poured in and he opened the door further. Cutler was running towards him with Bailee in his arms. She held her own Stelladaur to her heart with one hand and Cutler's jewel to his heart with the other.

Reilly flung the door open. Then the last two dungeon survivors leapt through the door. He slammed it shut and bolted it. Cutler and Bailee were safe! They climbed to the top of the Tower, Reilly last of all, and joined the others, leaving the stairwell dark behind them.

Stelladaur light filled the round room and shone out through the windows, casting light beams in all directions.

"Reilly!" Mila cried, throwing her arms around him.

He hugged her tightly. "What about the others?" he asked, pulling away.

"After you left, the deposits stopped altogether," she said. "It wasn't long before there was no bait left to catch the fish. The seaweed is gone, too. The Dwellers either died in geysers, wandering around looking for food, or starved. Emmett and Zeke left a few days ago. I've seen no sign of them since."

Reilly nodded, wondering how long he'd been gone from the Tower. "And Tyrone?"

Mila shook her head. "He went mad. I found him in the shed." She took a deep breath. "I managed to get him into a cart and dropped his body in the water at the Crossing. As soon as I did, the water became thick like tar and froze over. I made it back here alone. It's just me now." She looked at Reilly's tattered shirt. "Where's the tartan pin? Did you use it?"

Reilly reached for the spot where Mila had pinned the strange ornament to his shirt. "No. It must have fallen off." A shiver coursed through him, and he rubbed his arms briskly to warm up. "Did you see Alex in the crowds?" he added.

"No. Only Shay."

"Tessa, Abigail, Wyatt … and now Alex—they're gone!" They hugged each other again, but he choked back his emotions. He pulled Mila's hand. "Come on. We have to stay focused. Let's see how the Stelladaurs are doing."

They walked around the perimeter of the room together.

"Count everyone. I'll check to see which of the Beacons made it," he said, glancing around to do his own assessment.

"Beacons?" Mila asked.

"The leaders," he explained. "They've had their Stelladaurs longer than the others."

"The stones are magnificent, Reilly! Exquisite!" Mila said. "You and I are the only ones who don't have one right now. Well, of course, you *do* have yours, but it's not visible like the others."

Reilly reached for her hand. "After the Eruption, I'm certain you'll find yours, too."

She smiled and left to do a headcount.

Searching for the Beacons, he made his way through the crowd, encouraging them to shine their jewels through the windows across the Bleak. "It's working," he told them. "You're doing great!"

"How long will the Eruption last?" someone asked, holding his Stelladaur against the window.

Reilly went near him. "Clint! It's you!"

"I made it, too!" said Cole, standing beside Clint. "Maria and Kay are over there." He pointed towards the girls, further along the window.

Reilly noted that every Beacon had made it to the Tower except Elleah.

"Stay at your post, people. Every light must shine until the Eruption ends."

"How long until it's over?" Clint repeated.

"I don't know."

It was true. Reilly did not know. In all his years training in the Rotunda, and living with Dante, Darwin, and even Moses, he hadn't been privy to much information about an Eruption. He was told that there would be a final test before he qualified to be a Stelladaur Ambassador and that it would be worse than anything he'd ever experienced. In some ways, what he witnessed at the Bleak had been even more gruesome and harrowing than the horrors of Black Castle and the Festival of Fire. However, he was sure that the Great Eruption was not his final test.

He walked across the room and looked out the window towards the Crossing. With the distant scene lit by the Stelladaurs, he could see more details than before. Far beyond the edge of the light, something was summoning him.

Mila stepped beside him. "What is it?" she asked.

"I need to leave," he said, holding the handrail. "It's *me* they're fighting over. The Eruption will end only if I face Ukobach."

"Face him *where?*"

"Past the Crossing," he said. "Near my home."

"I don't understand. Surely your home isn't out *there!*"

As if in a trance, he replied, "It once was."

"You mean all the demons are after *you*?"

Reilly answered in a monotone voice. "Only Echtras can become as powerful as Ukobach. He needs an Echtra to take his place so that he can become one of the Gods of Ifreann—the *most* powerful Deceptors. Every Deceptor wants to be the one to take me to Ukobach, and that's why so many chose to hibernate in the Bleak." Reilly shook his head to bring himself back. He took a deep breath and declared, "They knew I would be here! Don't you see? The Eruption would never have occurred if I hadn't come!"

Mila's eyes widened. She put her hand on Reilly's arm. "I thought you said Stelladaur light is stronger than *any* evil?"

"Collectively, yes." Reilly reached for his own invisible Stelladaur, which he had not held for an inestimable amount of time. "Everyone here will soon die without food. Their light will go with them. It can't stay in this place. The Deceptors' demonic laughter shrieks in mockery of everyone, because no matter what you do, no one will survive." He lowered his hand from his chest and stepped closer to Mila. "Not unless an Echtra—specifically, one who is training to become a Stelladaur Ambassador—rearranges history so that none of you actually came here at all."

Mila studied Reilly's face. Her understanding dawned. "I see," she said with conviction. "All the lights need to project out through the windows on the west side of the Tower so they can collectively shine as far as possible past the Crossing."

Reilly nodded.

"I counted seventy-one people, including me," she whispered.

"It will have to be enough."

Chapter Thirty-Five

Stelladaur Scrolls

When everyone had gathered at the west window, the collective Stelladaurs lit a magnificent path from the top of the Tower across the frozen Bleak and past the Crossing, towards the island where Reilly once lived.

The Deceptors' heinous laughter permeated the walls.

Reilly looked into the distance once more. "Home," he muttered almost inaudibly.

He told the crowd to keep their light shining out the window for as long as possible. "A few of you stay on guard at the other windows. The Deceptors may try to find a way to come in from behind."

He had spotted Bailee pushing through the crowd. When she reached him, she said, "If I hold my light up really high, can I go home when the Eruption is over?"

"Yes, Bailee," Reilly said quietly. He knelt and hugged her. "When it's over, we'll all go home."

He didn't want to explain to her or the others that if he hadn't come to the Bleak at all, none of them would be there in the first place. He trusted that Mila wouldn't tell them either. Some things were better left unsaid. She stepped to meet him as he stood up.

"Here," she said, handing him a new pair of moccasins. "It's the last pair."

He thanked her, put the strange leather shoes on his feet, and left the room.

When he opened the door at the top of the stairwell, he saw a Stelladaur light coming from the bottom. As he neared the ground, the person holding the light shifted the beam slightly and Reilly saw a girl's face. Her eyes glistened in the light.

"Elleah!" Reilly cheered.

"You were helping some of the others and didn't see me slip through the door," she said. "I was too exhausted to go on and collapsed under the dark stairwell past the tunnel. I heard the door open just now and it woke me."

"You made it!" Reilly said, giving her a quick hug.

Elleah lifted the satchel from her shoulder. "I managed to avoid the geysers, even while carrying *this*."

She handed him the bag and he opened it. "Bricks?" he said, looking inside. He reached in and pulled out three strangely familiar bricks.

"They're from Cormack."

"You know Cormack?"

"He was in the forest with Charlotte after the Festival of Fire. When it was all over and everyone had either escaped or gone back into captivity at Black Castle, Cormack retrieved them from the ashes of the bonfire. When we met, he told me to keep them."

"You kept them ... for me? All this time?"

"You saved me at the auction," she said, squaring her shoulders. "Besides, I always hoped you would come back."

"Let me guess," he said, replacing the bricks in the satchel and looping the bag over his shoulder. "Cormack told you I'd know what to do with them."

"Right."

"Thank you, Elleah. These aren't ordinary bricks."

Reilly opened the door and walked outside into the beam of light, which shone for miles into the distance.

He ran hard, eager to reach the Crossing and find out how much further he could see from there. He ignored the Deceptors' wailing and the relentless rumbling noise coming from beyond the safety of the Stelladaur beam. Inside the light, the fog had dissipated and it was warm enough so that he no longer saw his breath. The ground beneath him had thawed, at least on the surface.

Soon he reached the bridge to the Crossing and walked across it gingerly, peering over the edge. He caught his breath as he watched the tarlike water ooze, melting from the light shining across it. Further on, he shuddered as he hurried past the dreadful burial ground, which had been the saving grace for every human survivor at the Bleak.

The steady light from the Tower behind him warmed his body. A thin film of water splashed over his moccasins. Knowing the urgency of the challenge that awaited him, he picked up his pace. His stamina did not wane with the weight of the bricks.

Two hours later, Reilly reached the end of the beam of light without any intrusions. He stopped and turned around to view the Tower. It rose above the bleak horizon like a steeple at the edge of a dire and desolate expanse. For a few moments, he watched the light flicker from the Tower window.

The air grew noticeably colder. Like smoke from a candlewick whose flame had just been extinguished, thick fog crept into the space around him. He hoisted the satchel over his head so the strap crossed his chest. Then he stepped into the darkness.

The Deceptors' haunting laugher rang in the distance, while an uncanny silence circled him. His eyes adjusted to the dark as he walked on. Trying to keep his bearings, he veered west into what he determined was—in another time—Eagle Harbor.

Then, a *crack!* pierced the eerie silence. Caught off guard, he slipped and fell forward onto his hands and knees. Another mighty *crack!* reverberated in the thick fog. The ice was breaking beneath his feet.

Suddenly, the frozen ground burst open! In a tumult of ice and heaving, viscid waters, the violent sea monster that had attacked him with the Watchers and devoured Thad emerged. The ground around Reilly broke apart and shattered into icebergs and a torrent of ice splinters like shards of glass pelting in every direction!

Reilly fell onto his back and slid twenty feet on a chunk of ice that bobbed violently on the water. He reached out feverishly, trying to catch hold of something—anything! But there was nothing to grab, and the bag of bricks pulled him down each time he tried to get up.

The grotesque beast thrashed its tentacle legs and spewed black tar-like muck from its gaping mouth. Its tongue uncoiled and reached for Reilly like a giant lizard ready to snatch a pesky fly. Reilly rolled over, barely out of reach of the monster. The bricks rolled with him, pounding against his chest.

Plunging forward, the beast sprawled over the water, creating enormous swells of gooey black muck. It hissed fiercely and eyed Reilly with its flaming red eyes.

Reilly managed to stand up on the mass of ice and rip open the flap of the satchel. He grabbed a brick in each hand and braced himself in a wide stance.

The beast cackled malevolently, taunting Reilly and his puny bricks.

But to Reilly, they represented a former victory, and he fully intended that they would serve him now! They were no ordinary bricks, but weapons made of powerful Pucatrow hair.

With another growling hiss, the monster's mouth gaped open and it stretched two tentacle legs towards Reilly, angling to coil around him.

In an instant—and with the power of a highly skilled Echtra—Reilly hurled a brick into the right eye of the beast. A split second later, he targeted the other eye with a second brick. Bursts of fiery red liquid sprayed into the cold air, and the beast shrieked with rage. Blinded, it thrashed its tentacle legs chaotically, whipping Reilly's shoulder.

Reilly grabbed the final brick and lunged it into the monster's gaping mouth. Its jaws snapped uncontrolledly while it choked and sputtered.

Reilly removed the satchel from his shoulder and dropped it to his feet as he watched the sea monster sink back into the thick black muck.

The debris settled, the water became calm, and the air cleared enough for him to see ahead. In the distance, he saw a small gleaming light—and inexplicably, just twenty feet away, a boat floated past that looked remarkably like *The Ark*—his dad's sailboat, where Reilly had last seen him alive!

Silence engulfed him—thick, heavy, dark silence.

Reilly knew the legions of Deceptors and the sea monster were behind him now. They wouldn't return. However, if he intended to free those who remained at the Tower—and if he ever hoped to go home—he must still face the final demon!

He had dealt with Travis Jackson several times, and he'd faced Ukobach, the Prince of Hell. But he hadn't done so when they inhabited the same demonic form.

With his eyes fixed on the sailboat, Reilly breathed heavily and leaped from the chunk of ice, catching his footing on solid ground.

He walked towards the vessel as it bobbed in the water beside the barren ground just ahead.

Though the boat resembled *The Ark* in several ways, there were significant differences. It didn't bob on rippled water in a scenic harbor full of other boats. It stood alone—upright in the frozen wasteland with the mainsail wide open, towering over him in full display. Shadows danced on the sail in grotesque gyrations, accompanied by an eerie *whooshing* noise.

Reilly gripped the railing and stepped onto the boat. He'd done it countless times before. Now, as an Echtra on course to change his own history, he wondered if this time was before any of the other times he'd travelled to.

Before the Rotunda and the Keepers.

Before Tuma.

Before Norah.

Before his dad died.

Even before Eilam.

Had he finally gone back far enough in time to truly rearrange and change all of that?

As he painfully made his way around the upper deck, an evil force descended around him and started to eat away at him. With each breath, the bitter cold air cut to his lungs like knives. His eyes stung, but he was barely able to blink. His lips cracked in bloody grooves. With his exposed flesh burning as if it was on fire, he fumbled to open the door to the galley and stumbled down the stairs.

Thick icicles hung from the ceiling throughout the interior of the vessel. It was as if *The Ark* had been frozen—preserved in time for this moment.

It was all so familiar—yet so different!

Expecting Ukobach to be waiting for him somewhere on the boat, Reilly searched each room, ready to face him. Finding no demon below deck, he staggered up the stairs, past the ship's wheel, and across the deck to the side railing. He looked up high to the top of the mainsail and noticed that the violent shadows were gone. Then he peered over the side, down to the dark water below.

Just below the surface, Reilly saw the Devil of Hell appear. It was the demon who wanted his soul—his power, his light, and his knowledge of Tir Na Nog!

No longer hidden in the hood of Ukobach's cloak, his face emerged. It was the imprinted Travis Jackson!

Reilly stepped back as the demon swooped up out of the icy water and then plunged nefariously past him onto the deck, landing near the boom of the mainsail. Frozen, as if under a spell, Reilly watched him remove something from the front of his cloak and position it at the point where the bottom of the mainsail met the boom, fashioning a makeshift gooseneck for the boom to swivel on.

When he was done, he narrowed his eyes and glared at Reilly. "Your hatred and rage will free me at last!" he whispered. "Then you will take my place in Ukobach forever!"

With that, the demon soared to the top of the mainsail and disappeared into the darkness with his odious laughter echoing in Reilly's ears.

Bewildered, Reilly forced one foot in front of the other and stepped up to the boom. He stared at the strange tartan pin Travis had fastened there.

Stunned by the realization that the imprinted Travis Jackson had rigged the boom—that in doing so, *Travis* was responsible for the boom's malfunction when his dad last sailed the *Ark,* and ultimately for his untimely death—Reilly reached out to remove the pin and fix the gooseneck so history could be righted!

The instant his finger touched the gargoyle etched on the pin, he left the Bleak. He simultaneously hoped that he'd just rearranged history for his dad!

"Welcome back!" Afismat said, spreading her wings and hugging Reilly. "The Keepers, as well as Olektor and Radmund, have waited patiently for you."

When she released him, she pulled a strand of hair from his face and said, "Very good. You survived well after all!"

Reilly tugged at his tattered clothes and wiggled his toes, noticing that he was barefoot again. "I feel naked," he said.

"Certainly!" Afismat agreed, smiling at him. "And hungry, no doubt. Your room is just as you left it. Get cleaned up and eat something. We shall wait for you in the Rotunda." She escorted him to his room. "We're so proud of you, Reilly." She opened the door and Reilly walked in.

A plate of hot food was on the end table, just as it had been each day during his years of training at the Rotunda. Some of his clothes were folded neatly in the dresser and the rest hung clean and pressed in the closet. Reilly stripped off his filthy rags, threw them in a trash bin in the bathroom, and stepped into the shower.

Until then, he'd never considered the unusual fact that there was running water at the Rotunda. He closed his eyes and let the hot water soothe his weary body. The salty taste of his tears mingled with the fresh water, and he swallowed hard. The soap smelled like a blend of pine and sea breeze. For a moment, he thought he was home, and he remembered Norah.

After getting dressed, he ate ravenously, grateful for every bite.

He found Afismat and the others waiting for him in their usual places at the round table. When he entered the room, Olektor, Radmund, and the Keepers stood up and clapped felicitously for so long that Reilly grew uncomfortable. Afismat motioned for the applause to stop and everyone to be seated. She and Reilly remained standing.

"You've completed your responsibilities as an Echtra," she said, wasting no time to explain what would happen next. "You accomplished all you were meant to do—everything that was expected of you as a Stelladaur Ambassador in training."

Reilly leaned forward, bowing slightly. His heart was beating fast at the thought that he would soon have everything he'd ever wanted, as promised, even his *greatest desires*—if he succeeded in his assignments!

"We can offer you no further training to become an Ambassador for the Kingdom of Stelladaurs," Afismat continued. "The decision will be yours. We can only bestow gifts that you may take home."

"*Home?*" Reilly whispered, barely able to say the word.

"Soon," she replied. "First, the gifts."

Afismat reached into the folds of her robe and pulled out the Fireglass, which had remained at the Rotunda while Reilly fulfilled his mission to rearrange time. Holding it up, she said, "This holds a record of all your training at the Rotunda, which you input before you departed through the Shield of Forgotten Memories. Now, it also holds the secrets of the Stelladaur Scrolls—all the writings of every Guardian and Keeper here at the Rotunda."

Olektor, Radmund, and the Keepers clapped their hands and cheered. Afismat handed the Fireglass to Reilly. Awestruck at the device's extraordinary capacity to hold information, he held it with reverence and honor, as only an Echtra could do.

"Finally, the Fireglass stores a full audio-visual recording of your time with Dante, Darwin, and Moses, and with the Watchers, Beacons, and demons."

Reilly's eyes grew wide. He held the device at arm's length, watching the etched Stelladaur whirl around the outside of it.

"What should I do with it?" he asked.

"When you return, you will know," she said.

Reilly nodded, certain that what she said was true.

"Two scrolls are not recorded in the Fireglass," Afismat said with a clear hint of warning in her voice.

Olektor and Radmund each handed her a small scroll. She raised her wings as she took the treasures in her hands.

"You must vow not to read them until you return home," she said. "If you do, they will not go with you."

"I understand," Reilly agreed.

She gave Reilly the final gifts. "We will adjourn. You need rest."

Olektor, Radmund, and the Keepers stood in unison. They formed a line and saluted Reilly with his own mantra. "Light prevails! Light prevails!"

Afismat escorted Reilly to his room and bid him good night.

Reilly set the Fireglass and the scrolls on the nightstand. He gazed out the window at a night sky dotted endlessly with stars. He fell asleep feeling as if he were in his own room on Eagle Harbor Drive. And he dreamed of Norah.

In the morning, Reilly awoke to unusually bright sunlight streaming in through the window. He jumped out of bed, grabbed the Fireglass and the scrolls, and bounded to the door, eager to meet the Guardians and Keepers for the last time.

When he flung open the door, he stopped in his tracks! It didn't open to the usual hallway that led to the main room of the Rotunda. Instead, he stepped into the hallway in his home on Eagle Harbor Drive!

He was home at last!

Clutching the Fireglass and the scrolls, he raced through his house. Hoping he'd actually turned back the hands of time, he called for his mom, his dad, Tuma, Chantal, and Norah.

No one answered. Tuma was not there.

He ran from room to room, hollering for his family!

Everything looked just as he remembered. The kitchen smelled of bacon and hash brown potatoes. A note from his mother was stuck to the fridge door, saying she'd left early for the bakery. Pictures of Chantal and James were scattered on the coffee table beside a half-filled photo album. His dad's sweater was draped over a chair on the couch.

Then the Fireglass vibrated in his hand. He extended the device and looked through the crystal knob. He gasped, startled by its revelation.

He watched in horror as an image of Travis Jackson came into focus. Travis was on *The Ark*, fastening something to the gooseneck of the boom.

"This must be a recording of what happened at the Bleak!" Reilly reasoned aloud. "I took the pin out! I changed history! *Didn't* I?"

Frantic, he found the keys to the Jeep, laid the Fireglass and scrolls on the seat beside him, and raced towards the marina. When he arrived, he grabbed the treasures and ran along the empty dock to *The Ark*. He bounded onto the boat and stopped abruptly beside the very boom that had jerked out of position and knocked his dad overboard, burying him at sea. All the ropes were in their proper places. The gooseneck was positioned correctly and fastened securely.

Reilly walked to the rail and leaned over the edge. The water was calm and clear. He could see fish swimming, barnacles clinging to the hull of the boat, and tentacles of purple sea anemones floating back and forth in the undercurrent. The warm sun shone on his back, and seagulls called overhead. Everything seemed normal, as it should be.

His eye caught something on deck flutter in the sunlight. He moved slowly towards it, holding the Fireglass and the scrolls in one hand. His chest tightened. Bending down, he reached for the thing with his free hand. It was poking up from under one of the deck boards, and he pulled it out. It was the tartan pin!

"NO!" Reilly screamed. "NO!"

Travis had killed his father! He had tampered with the gooseneck and rigged the boom to malfunction!

Frantic to understand—and feeling like neither an Echtra nor an Ambassador—Reilly dropped the pin as if it were cursed. He fumbled, trying to unroll one of the scrolls. Grasping for breath, he read it silently:

IF TRAVIS HAD NOT BEEN IMPRINTED, HE WOULD NOT HAVE BECOME THE PERSON HE IS. YOUR FATHER WOULD STILL BE ALIVE. WHERE, THEN, IS JUSTICE? TRAVIS, THE DEMON, WILL REMAIN IMPRINTED IN PRINCE UKOBACH FOREVER UNLESS A STELLADAUR AMBASSADOR TAKES HIS LIFE. SUCH IS THE MIGHTY POWER THAT THE PRINCE OF HELL HUNGERS FOR MOST. TAKING TRAVIS'S LIFE WILL INDEED SAVE YOUR FATHER—BUT YOUR OWN WILL BE SACRIFICED. IS THAT MERCY? IF YOU BECOME THE DEMON, YOUR HATRED AND RAGE WILL FREE TRAVIS BUT IMPRISON YOU. ONLY YOU CAN DECIDE IF YOU WILL CHANGE THIS HISTORY. WE HAVE PLACED THE GUARDIAN STONE WITH THE SWORD OF JUSTICE, THE SWORD OF MERCY, AND THE SWORD OF TRUTH TO HELP YOU ON YOUR JOURNEY HOME. SEARCH FOR THOSE GIFTS.
　—AFISMAT, OLEKTOR, RADMUND
　　THIS STELLADAUR SCROLL IS BESTOWED
　　UPON REILLY MCNAMARA
　　AT THE ROTUNDA UNDER STONEHENGE

Panic-stricken, Reilly reread the message. "It isn't supposed to be this way!" he cried. "This is ALL WRONG!"

He fell hard to his knees. "Why *ME*?" he screamed, raising his fist to the sky. "I don't want to change any more history! NO MORE!"

He lay on the deck, sobbing angrily. A dark cloud rolled overhead. A moment later, it burst, and rain flooded the harbor like a monsoon downpour.

Reilly scrambled to gather the Fireglass and scrolls and rushed for cover under the awning above the wheel of the ship. As he watched the pelting rain, he was engulfed in deep sadness, as he was after his father's death.

It was unfair! It was unjust!

Setting the Fireglass and the unrolled scroll on the captain's chair, Reilly unfurled the other scroll and read the inscription on the parchment, searching for a final answer:

MY GREATEST WORK, "BETROTHAL OF MY HEART,"
IS ONE OF THE UNKNOWN SECRETS OF STONEHENGE.
YOU MUST REVEAL IT TO THE WORLD, ALONG WITH THE
KNOWLEDGE FROM THE STELLADAUR SCROLLS NOW
IN YOUR POSSESSION. YOU MAY BORROW MY POEM TO
BEATRICE TO WIN THE HEART OF THE ONE YOU LOVE.

When time weaves breath into the budding flower,
Painting fuchsia lips that speak to your sacred heart,
The seasons will pass with sparkling rain and starlit nights
Until they unite us in heavenly delights
And nature whispers, "You ne'er will be apart."
My love for thee cannot be written on devil's parchment,
Nor comprehended through mere drops from my quill,
Yet God will atone for each petal that drifts
To the depths of the Tyrrhenian Sea; then lifts
Us to dream of our divine love blooming, still—
Our love is but a winter rose—fresh, yet melts the ice
That binds unfeeling traditions of conformity

With attempts to plant seeds of doubt and fear;
But lo! Deliverance from such anguish is near—
Alas! Spring will yet come with promise of our eternal unity.
   Dante Alighieri, 1277
    "Betrothal of My Heart" for Beatrice

The rain ended as quickly as it had begun.
Reilly stepped off the sailboat to find Norah.

Book Four

Foverver Changed

After Reilly discovers the truth about his dad's death, he questions his ability to carry out his responsibilities as a Stelladaur Ambassador.

Safeguarding the secrets of Stonehenge—yet revealing to the world the priceless information held in the Fireglass—seems an insurmountable task in the emotional aftermath of surviving the Bleak. He searches for the one person who can give him the hope he desperately needs—but finds betrayal instead.

When revenge consumes him, a precocious young child takes him on a journey that keeps him closer to home than any place a portal has led him to before. Challenged to go far beyond the limits of his own fears, he faces a battle that makes him look at life—and death—in a new light.

But if Reilly fights the battle, will he win his greatest desire, as promised?

The Stelladaur Academy

Where Young People are the Difference

- ⌁ Educational Enrichment ⌁
- ⌁ Character Development ⌁
- ⌁ Self Discovery ⌁
- ⌁ Creative Renewal ⌁
- ⌁ Diverse Scholarship Opportunities ⌁

Visit our online campus at
www.stelladauracademy.org

About the Author

Author, educator, and Founder and President of The Stelladaur Academy, S. L. WHYTE was born in Minnesota and raised in Victoria, British Columbia. "I inherited my love of stories from my aunt, who was a professional storyteller on Mississippi steamboats. As a teenager, I wrote short stories, poetry, and song lyrics. Diagraming sentences became a strange obsession in tenth-grade English class. When I write, I see more clearly, feel more deeply, and share more truthfully. I hope The Stelladaur Series ignites the magic of your imagination as a means of self-discovery and creative renewal." S. L. Whyte lives in Puget Sound, Washington with her husband.